CROSSING THE LINE

Quinn stared into Amelia's dark eyes. The phrase "fall in and out of love" echoed in his head, and he felt strangely innervated.

With her encouraging words, she had freed him from the horrible despair that had choked him for the past several hours. His black mood was gone.

Poof.

But now there was something even more dangerous in its place: desire.

Her hand was still on his, and he swore he could feel the heat of her touch radiating throughout his entire body. He took a deep breath, battling the urge to move closer to her.

He pulled his eyes from hers, and his gaze dropped to the pale skin exposed by the V neck of her dress. She wore a silver necklace with translucent green and blue beads, and one of them had found its way into her creamy cleavage. As he stared at that lucky bead, his blood grew hotter, running thickly through his veins toward his cock.

His brain and his body disconnected, and he saw his hand move toward her, fingers spread.

Don't do it! Don't touch her!

His fingers stroked the warm skin of her throat, her pulse throbbing against his thumb. Her skin was so soft, so warm, he imagined she could heat all the cold places inside him.

Wrapping his hand around the back of her neck, he pulled her closer. She stumbled a little in her high-heeled boots, and he steadied her with a hand on her hip.

When he felt that beautiful curve within his grasp, the blood drained from his head, along with every bit of sense he possessed. With his intellect obliterated, his primal self was in control, and it wanted more.

Right now.

All the Right Places

JENNA SUTTON

BERKLEY SENSATION, NEW YORK

BERKLEY
SENSATION

An imprint of Penguin Random House LLC
375 Hudson Street, New York, New York 10014

ALL THE RIGHT PLACES

A Berkley Sensation Book / published by arrangement with the author

ISBN: 978-0-425-27995-3

PUBLISHING HISTORY
Berkley Sensation mass-market edition / June 2015

PRINTED IN THE UNITED STATES OF AMERICA

10 9 8 7 6 5 4 3 2 1

Cover photo of Couple © LJM Photo / Design Pics / Corbis;
Golden Gate Bridge © larryimage / iStock / Thinkstock.
Cover design by Sarah Oberrender.
Interior text design by Kristin del Rosario.

Penguin
Random
House

To Mike,
for thinking I'm the funniest, smartest,
and most interesting woman on the planet.
I hope you never realize that I'm not.

And to Steffanie,
for investing so much of yourself in this book.
Your suggestions made it (and me) a lot better.
I couldn't have done this without you.

Acknowledgments

There are so many women in my life whom I need to acknowledge . . . Special women who make me stronger, smarter, and more successful.

Mom—in case you didn't know this, I'm putting it here, in black and white: I think you're extraordinary.

Leis Pederson—I feel so blessed that you wanted me to be one of your authors. You took such care with *All the Right Places*, and I'm grateful that you're my editor.

Jenny Bent and Beth Phelan—thank you for taking a chance on me and finding the perfect home for the Riley O'Brien & Co. series. An extra special thanks to Beth for guiding me through this process and talking me off the ledge when necessary.

Jamie—if an award for Best Critique Partner existed, I would give it to you. But you're so much more . . . You're a wonderful friend, and I'm so lucky I met you.

Melinda—you really get me, my books, and my characters. I am so grateful to have you as a critique partner and a friend.

My sister-in-law Mandy—you never doubted that *All the Right Places* would be published, and your unwavering faith made it impossible for me to give up. Now you can say, "I told you so."

My best friends Alison and Kristen—thank you for providing more support than an underwire bra. Without you, I'd be sad and droopy.

Jennifer Irene—thank you for always being on my side, cheering me on, and giving great advice about writing and life in general.

Chapter 1

DERRIÈRE. ASS. BACK PORCH. BADONKADONK. RUMP. NO MATter what you called it, the butt was Quinn O'Brien's favorite part of the human body.

Yes, he had the typical male appreciation for the female form, but truly, most of his interest was professional. In fact, some would say it was part of his DNA. He was the fifth generation of O'Briens to be involved in the family business, Riley O'Brien & Co., proud designers and manufacturers of blue jeans since 1845.

"Pay attention to how our jeans conform to the wearer's body, especially the butt," his father had schooled him and his younger brother when they were kids. At the time, Quinn hadn't realized scoping out every backside within sight might cause problems, especially when he stared just a bit too long at a crooked seam on a stranger's rear.

And right now, that's exactly what he was doing—staring at a stranger's ass hard enough to make his eyes cross. Who could blame him, though, since it was right at eye level above him on the escalator? And oh, what an ass it was—high and tight, yet still nicely rounded.

He sighed. The woman in front of him might have a great

ass, but she wasn't wearing Rileys. That was a big mark against her in his book.

Shifting his gaze from her curvy backside, he reviewed the brown leather belt encircling her slender waist. Embellished with beads and intricate stitching, it was eye-catching, not gaudy at all.

But it wasn't nearly as eye-catching as the red corkscrews of hair that fell down her back almost to her waist. They glinted with gold and amber from the early morning sun shining through the skyscraper's windows. Her hair was so curly it kinked in some places, creating sharp angles that made him want to pull on a strand just to see how quickly it would recoil.

The woman stepped off the escalator into the reception area of Riley O'Brien & Co.'s global headquarters, cutting his perusal short. Unlike most high-rises in downtown San Francisco, Riley Plaza's first floor was filled with retail space, including the requisite Starbucks and a small shop that sold Riley merchandise. From the first floor, an escalator brought visitors and employees to the mezzanine level, where they checked in with reception or headed to their offices.

He pulled his gaze from the woman in just enough time to avoid tripping over the escalator lip and crashing onto the floor. Yeah, ogling asses could be hazardous.

As the redhead made her way to the reception desk, Quinn held up a hand and called out a greeting to the security guard posted by the double doors that led to the executive offices.

"Hey, Frank, did you see the new commercial last night?"

Riley O'Brien & Co. had recently launched a new advertising campaign featuring several well-known male athletes. The first commercial highlighting Quinn's best friend, Nick Priest, had debuted last night during Sunday night football.

Priest and Quinn had played football together at the University of Southern California. While Quinn's football career had ended when he graduated from USC, Priest had gone pro. He was one of the best wide receivers in the NFL, and his talent transformed every team he joined.

"Yeah, I saw it," Frank answered. "If you wanted to make women all over America lust after Priest even more than they do now, you succeeded."

Quinn laughed. "So, you thought Priest looked hot?"

"Hell, no," Frank barked. "But the wife couldn't take her eyes off the TV while he was on-screen."

"Who can blame her? She's had to look at your ugly face for more than thirty years. She needs a break."

Frank grinned and shot him the bird. "Get to work, son."

Quinn pulled open one of the heavy wood doors to the executive wing, and as he did every morning, he took some time to enjoy the walk along the polished concrete floors to his office. A timeline highlighting the major milestones in Riley O'Brien & Co.'s history stretched from one end of the hallway to the other. It started with the founding of the company prior to the California Gold Rush, and old sepia images, black-and-white pictures, and a handful of color photos brought it to life.

He could see glimmers of himself in some of the images on the wall. All the men in his family had hair so dark it was almost black. And like his grandfather's, Quinn's hair was slightly wavy.

It was hard to tell from the early pictures what color his ancestor's eyes were, but legend had it that Riley O'Brien's eyes were so cold a glare from him could stop even the roughest of gold prospectors in their tracks. No doubt, he must have been one mean son of a bitch to build a successful business at a time when California was nothing but a territory full of wild and avaricious men.

Quinn turned his attention from the timeline and entered his office. Before he could sit down, a sharp knock sounded on his door, and his sister's dark head poked around it.

"Do you have a minute?" Teagan asked, slightly breathless. Her blue eyes were wide behind the black-framed glasses she wore.

"Sure. What's up, T?"

She slipped inside his office, shutting the door behind her. Her black dress crossed over the front of her body and tied on the side. Dotted with big red cherries, it was a perfectly nice piece of clothing, but he was immediately pissed off she wore it.

"Why are you always wearing a damn dress?" he growled.

"You don't like it?" she asked, feigning confusion.

"Our family fortune was built on jeans," he reminded her. "Can't you put on a pair once in a while?"

It was a discussion they'd had many times, and her answer was always the same. He could have repeated it verbatim, and now he got to hear it again.

"Rileys look good on you. They look good on most men. But they do not look good on most women. They especially don't look good on short women. Or women with big butts, big thighs, or big anythings. Ergo, they don't look good on me."

Quinn held up his hands, sorry he'd brought up the subject. "I don't want to get into another argument about the women's division," he backtracked hastily. "Your dress is fine. You look very pretty."

Ignoring Teagan's rude snort, he settled in his chair and propped his feet on his desk. "What did you need?" he prompted her as he inspected his new boots.

She eyed him for a few moments before answering. "Amelia Winger has agreed to design our new line of accessories."

He dropped his feet to the floor and sat up. The accessories were all Teagan's idea, and the little sneak had gone behind his back to make them happen.

She had wanted to revamp the entire women's division, and when Quinn refused, she had persuaded their dad to give his stamp of approval for the line of accessories. Now Quinn had to suck it up and play nice with the new designer until their dad officially resigned and handed the reins over to him.

"So she's definitely going to do it?" he asked.

"I think so. She requested a meeting with you, since you're going to head up the project, but as long as you don't blow it, I think she's on board."

He huffed out a breath in annoyance. "Why would *I* blow it?"

"Quinn, you can be really intense about Rileys. It's . . . well, it's a turnoff to some people."

He nodded, agreeing with Teagan's assessment. He *was* intense. He was devoted to protecting the Riley O'Brien brand, and he never forgot every single pair of Rileys ever produced was branded with his last name.

He realized Teagan was still talking. ". . . knew you were going to be in the office today, so I told her it would be okay."

"Wait, what did you say?"

Looking down, she tapped her fingers against her bottom lip. He tensed. She was a terrible liar and an even worse poker player because she always tapped her lips when she was nervous or unsure.

He stood. "Tell me," he demanded when she stayed silent a beat too long.

"I told Amelia Winger you would be available to meet her this morning."

"Shit, Teagan! You know I hate it when you ambush me with things like this. . . ."

She stopped tapping her lips and started tapping her toe, never a good sign for innocent or not-so-innocent males nearby. "This is a priority, Quinn," she shot back. "I've already worked out all the legal details with Amelia. All she wants is a meeting with you. So it's not on your calendar. Deal with it."

"When will she be here?"

"She's already here."

"Of course she is," he said dryly. He ran a hand through his hair before smoothing the mess he had made. "Let's go get her."

With Teagan click-clacking alongside him, he made the trek down the hall. He wasn't looking forward to this meeting, and not just because his sister had sprung it on him. The women's division limped along like a three-legged dog, and he doubted some new belts and purses would make a difference.

"Are you sure Amelia Winger is the right person to design our accessories?" Quinn asked.

He'd reviewed the information Teagan had provided about the designer, but he still had his doubts, especially since Amelia Winger had no formal design training, and she'd never done any work for a company like Riley O'Brien.

"I'd never heard of her before you mentioned her," he continued. "Just because her best friend is a country music star and wears her designs doesn't mean Amelia has any real talent. It just means she's smart enough to capitalize on Ava Grace Landy's success."

"Ava Grace doesn't wear Amelia's designs just because she's her best friend. She wears them because they're incredible."

Pushing open the door to the reception area, he ushered his sister through it before following. Frank turned at the sound, winking at Teagan.

The security guard tilted his head toward the only person

sitting in the reception area. "There's your girl," he said with a smile.

Teagan hurried toward the woman with her arms outstretched. "Amelia, it's so nice to see you again!" she exclaimed.

The woman dropped the magazine she'd been reading and quickly rose from her orange chair. It clashed horribly with her long red hair, and his heart kicked in his chest as Teagan gestured toward him.

"Amelia Winger, this is my brother, Quinn O'Brien. Quinn, this is the fabulous designer we talked about."

Amelia released Teagan's hands and stepped forward to greet him. "It's nice to meet you," she said, offering her hand to him. Her voice had a slight twang to it, betraying her Texas roots.

Clasping her hand, he gazed down at her. She couldn't have been more than an inch or two above five feet tall because the top of her curly head didn't even reach his shoulders. Her brown eyes crinkled as she smiled, and he noticed a slight gap between her top front teeth.

Her smile wobbled a bit as he stood there silently, staring into a face sprinkled with freckles that reminded him of brown sugar. Finally, he spoke, but when he did, it wasn't exactly what he had intended.

"Nice ass," he said.

Damn. Did I really say that out loud?

Chapter 2

AMELIA'S MOUTH DROPPED OPEN. HAD QUINN O'BRIEN JUST said "nice ass"? Maybe her anxiety about this meeting had affected her auditory nerve, and it had sent the wrong signals to her brain.

As she stood there staring at him, he squeezed her hand. His fingers were warm and slightly callused.

"Nice to meet you," he said, one side of his mouth lifting in a hint of a smile.

She'd obviously misunderstood the "nice ass" comment. There was no way a guy as hot as Quinn O'Brien would meet her for the first time by telling her she had a nice ass.

She took a deep breath, pulling in a lungful of Quinn's cologne. Oh, God, he smelled delicious.

Had anything ever smelled so good? Yes, Ava Grace's red velvet cupcakes smelled that good. And they tasted good, too, with their decadent cream cheese frosting. Ava Grace was always generous with the frosting.

As her mind wandered, she wondered how Quinn would taste. Better than cupcakes, she'd bet.

Teagan cleared her throat, startling Amelia from a fantasy involving Quinn and baked goods. What was she doing? She was blowing the biggest opportunity of her short career!

She shook her head, and that small movement was like a jump-start to her brain. She withdrew her hand from his clasp.

"I'm really excited to work with a company as iconic as Riley O'Brien," she said, and to her surprise, she actually sounded normal. She had expected to sound like a tween girl at a boy band concert. "I can't wait to get started."

"I'll let you two talk," Teagan broke in. "Call me when you're finished."

She scowled at Quinn before stalking to the elevators. He turned his dark blue eyes back to Amelia, and for just a second she actually forgot where she was and why she was there.

"I wasn't expecting to meet with you this morning, and unfortunately, I don't have time to give you a tour," he said apologetically.

She had been so nervous about meeting Quinn she hadn't paid any attention to the office. She glanced around, taking in the décor, which was an unexpected mix of rustic and industrial.

Metal sheeting covered the sections of the wall that weren't glass, and the concrete floors were stained a dark bluish gray. Exposed wood beams stretched overhead, studded with huge metal rivets.

Noticing the direction of her gaze, Quinn said, "The interior designer thought it would be fun to use rivets in the office design. Sort of a way to pay homage to the jean rivets that were patented by Riley O'Brien in the late 1800s."

"That's clever. I really like the colors, too," she added, pointing to the bold pops of orange and dreamy shades of blue and green that teased her visual senses.

The office gave off a trendy, hip vibe—a kind of energy she'd never experienced before. Of course, she spent more of her time in her workshop than in a high-rise office.

The elevator dinged, and a large group of employees streamed out, laughing and chatting. She noticed they all wore Rileys. With their distinctive button flies, seamed pockets, and black pocket tags, the jeans were not only recognizable; they also had a certain element of cool—for guys, at least.

"Everybody's wearing Rileys," Amelia noted. "Is it some kind of dress code?"

Quinn grinned. "Let's just say it's implied. It's not like we'd tar and feather someone for wearing something else, but we might get out the whip for wearing another brand of jeans." He shot her a teasing glance. "I noticed you aren't wearing Rileys."

She battled the urge to reach behind her and cover up the pockets of her jeans, which were clearly labeled as non-Rileys. Why, oh why, hadn't she thought about that earlier?

A quick look at his long legs confirmed he also wore jeans. She couldn't tell what kind because he'd left his shirt untucked and it covered his rear—more's the pity—but she had no doubt they were Rileys.

Along with his dark-wash jeans, he wore a black western-style shirt with pearly snaps down the front and on the pocket flaps. Although it wasn't tight, the shirt highlighted the width of his shoulders and chest along with his well-muscled arms and flat stomach.

She had a momentary fantasy of undoing a couple of those snaps and running her hands across his abdomen and down to the waistband of his jeans. She wondered if his Rileys had a traditional button fly or if he preferred the newer zipper design. She clenched her hands at her sides, worried for a moment her fingers might reach out and grab him.

"My office is this way," he said, gesturing toward the double doors.

They entered the executive wing, the heavy door banging shut behind them. Her steps slowed as she took in the living history displayed on the walls of the hallway. The lighting cast a glow over the images and glinted off objects in shadow boxes.

The display was breathtaking, and it spurred a pang of wistfulness deep inside her. She wondered what it would be like to have such deep roots, to have a birthright that was beloved throughout history and a name that was recognizable in nearly every household over several generations.

One of the oldest pictures caught her attention, and she leaned closer to get a better view. The shaggy-haired man in the sepia photo towered over the other people in it. He looked as if he could break a grown man in two with his bare hands.

Realizing she no longer followed him, Quinn turned. His eyes lit up when he saw what had captured her attention.

"You're looking at the original Riley O'Brien, my great-great-grandfather."

"He's huge."

"Yeah, he was a giant," he agreed, pride tingeing his voice. "Most of our memorabilia was destroyed by the earthquake and fires in 1906, but a pair of his jeans survived. And based on the size of them, we know he was almost seven feet tall and had a fifty-inch waist."

She was stunned. "Whoa!" she breathed. "You're so much smaller."

She squeezed her eyes shut in embarrassment. She'd made it sound as if Quinn were a midget, when he was at least six three. But compared to his mountainous ancestor, he *was* small.

When she opened her eyes, his gaze held a wicked twinkle. "I've never had any complaints." His full lips quirked in amusement. "In fact, I've been told I'm bigger than"—he paused before finishing with a roguish grin—"average."

Amelia could feel her face turn red as she imagined all the places where Quinn might rival his great-great-grandfather. Flustered, she switched her attention to another photo on the wall.

Dated 1953, the black-and-white image showed a tall, dark-haired man with a small boy perched on his shoulders in front of the Golden Gate Bridge. The man had a big smile, and he was missing an arm.

"My grandfather, Patrick, and my father when he was two years old," Quinn said, his voice rumbling a rich baritone close to her right ear.

While she'd been preoccupied with his measurements, he'd moved behind her, close enough for her to feel his breath on her hair and the heat of his body. A small shiver of awareness chased over her. The back of her nape prickled, her nipples hardened, and her stomach tingled.

"My grandfather was just a few years older than me when this picture was taken," he continued. "He lost his arm in World War II, but at least he came home. His three brothers died in Europe."

She tried to concentrate on what he'd said. "Do you remember him?" she asked, shifting her big leather bag to her right shoulder to put some space between them.

"Yes. He and my grandmother both died when I was a teenager," he answered gruffly, obviously still affected by their deaths.

Since she didn't want to bring up painful memories for him or delve into her own regret that she had never known her grandparents, she redirected the conversation.

"You could be his twin," she noted, referring to his grandfather.

She had no doubt Patrick O'Brien in the flesh had been just as gorgeous as his grandson. She heard a huff of laughter from Quinn and turned to him.

He leaned against a nearby doorframe and crossed his arms over his chest. His sleeves were rolled up, showing off ropey forearms dusted with dark hair. A chunky silver watch encircled his left wrist.

"Did I say something funny?"

"Grandpa Patrick was a real ladies' man before he met my grandma Violet," he said, his blue eyes glinting in the shadows cast by the hall lights. "Legend has it he was so good-looking, women pretended to faint just to get his attention."

"That seems a little extreme. Was your grandmother one of those women?"

"No. She said she had other ways of getting his attention."

She laughed. "I can imagine."

He smiled slowly. "Since you think I look just like him, are you going to swoon at my feet?"

She knew she was in trouble when she saw that smile. Oh, yes, Quinn O'Brien was well aware of the effect he had on women. It was a wonder he didn't swagger.

Like his grandfather, he probably attracted women like flies to honey. In fact, she wouldn't be surprised if scientists eventually discovered men like him had a special strand of DNA that compelled women, regardless of their age, to lose their minds, discard their morals, and drop their panties.

Since she wanted to keep her panties exactly where they were, she moved the conversation back to business. "I don't need to pretend to faint. Because we're working together, I already have your attention."

His eyes roamed over her face. "Yes," he agreed in a low voice, straightening from his slouch against the door and moving closer to her. "You definitely have my attention."

His reply sounded like both a warning and a promise.

Chapter 3

AMELIA'S BIG BROWN EYES WIDENED. SURROUNDED BY LONG lashes several shades darker than her hair, they reminded Quinn of dark chocolate. The expensive kind, not the cheap crap.

Glittery gold eye shadow covered her lids, which should have made her look like a stripper or a showgirl. Instead, it just made her skin glow and shimmer.

He couldn't remember if Teagan's report had mentioned Amelia's age, but he figured she was in her mid-twenties. Her face was unlined, and her skin was clear and smooth.

She licked her lips, leaving them shiny and wet. He wanted to put his thumb right in the center of that lush lower lip, opening her mouth just enough for him to lean in and taste her.

Everything about Amelia, from her cinnamon-colored hair and dark-chocolate eyes to her brown-sugar freckles and creamy skin, made him think of dessert. And he wanted to take a big bite.

As he and Amelia had made the trip to his office, he had been preoccupied with the way her jeans shaped her ass, which had made the fit of his own pants a bit tight behind his button fly. He'd had no idea he had checked out Amelia

Winger while he'd been on the escalator, and he wanted another look at that shapely behind.

Truthfully, he wanted to do more than look. He'd like to pull her into his body, wrap his hands around those plump curves, and give them a hard squeeze.

His mouth had clearly been on the same wavelength when Teagan introduced him to Amelia, and it had malfunctioned. It was the first time he'd ever greeted a woman by telling her she had a nice ass. He could only pray it also was the last time.

Teagan would have plenty to say about his blunder when she got him alone. He winced at the thought. Even though she was three years younger, her rebukes always left him feeling like a preschooler relegated to time-out. The thought of Teagan's displeasure was enough to remind him that Amelia was here to do a job, not serve as his dessert.

He turned and strode to his office. Pushing open the door with the heel of his hand, he waited for Amelia to step inside before closing it behind him.

"I just realized I haven't offered you a drink. Would you like a cup of coffee before we get started?" he asked.

"No thanks, I don't drink coffee."

"No coffee in the morning?" He shuddered at the thought of that kind of deprivation. "How can you function?"

"I drink juice."

"Juice," he repeated incredulously.

She laughed. "Yes. Juice. About a year ago, I read an article about juicing and its health benefits, and now I'm addicted. I splurged on an outrageously expensive juicer, and I drink my own concoctions every morning, or at least I do when I'm at home."

He imagined drinking liquefied spinach, and his stomach lurched. *Yuck.*

But maybe juice was responsible for her shiny hair and gorgeous skin. If so, he wholeheartedly supported her addiction.

"So what's your favorite?" he asked, trying to make some small talk so she'd feel comfortable and relaxed. He wanted them to have a productive discussion about what he expected from her.

"Definitely my tropical fruit juice, which has mango, pineapple, kiwi, and a splash of coconut water."

"That sounds good, but not nearly as good as a mug of dark roast," he said before inviting her to take a seat.

She moved forward, her gaze slowly roaming his office. Her mouth curved when she saw the sofa against the far wall. It never failed to catch the attention of whoever visited his office.

Upholstered with hundreds of Rileys jean pockets, the sofa was a piece of art and history rolled into one oversized piece of furniture. Adorned with large, puffy pillows, it was a patchwork of different shades of denim, from powder blue to deep indigo. He loved that sofa like a mother loved her first-born child.

"How do you like my sofa?"

"It's definitely unusual."

"You know how jeans feel once you've broken them in and the denim is all soft and worn? My sofa feels exactly like that."

She looked longingly at the sofa. He could tell she wanted to see if he told the truth.

"Go ahead, try it," he urged.

Amelia walked over to the sofa, but instead of sitting, she ran her nails along the fabric before smoothing it with a caress. The action made him think about her fingers on his skin, and he swiped a hand across his damp forehead.

He couldn't remember the last time he'd felt this kind of overwhelming attraction, and he was slightly resentful she'd managed to distract him so completely and with no effort. He was acting like a horny teenager instead of an adult male who received more than his fair share of female attention.

He'd been propositioned by women twenty years his senior, cornered by aggressive co-eds, and used by hard-as-nails businesswomen. He knew when a woman wanted him, and Amelia hadn't given off any "do me" vibes.

"I bet you've spent a lot of afternoons on this sofa," she teased.

Did she think he was a lazy bum? Well, she was right, at least about the time he spent on the sofa. He worked hard, but he also stretched out on it every time he needed to work through a problem, personal or business.

"It comes in handy."

She gave the sofa a final stroke before taking a seat in one of the distressed leather chairs facing his desk. She leaned over to put her bag on the floor, the movement straining the buttons on her aqua-colored shirt.

He fervently wished at least one would give up the fight so he could get a peek at what was under her shirt. Did she prefer the sensuality of lace or the sportiness of cotton?

When he realized what he was doing—staring at Amelia's chest and daydreaming about her bra—he gave himself a mental kick in the ass. What the hell was wrong with him? Hundreds of women had sat in his office for business meetings, and he hadn't imagined any of them topless. He shouldn't be thinking about Amelia that way, either.

He dragged his eyes back to her face just as she sat up and crossed her legs. It was then he noticed her cowboy boots, which were so spectacular he momentarily forgot all about her breasts and what might or might not cover them. They were made of pale blond leather, a creamy color like freshly churned butter, and featured a pointy tip and a three-inch heel embellished with studs.

Elaborate stitching in contrasting dark-chocolate thread covered the vamp and toe area. The expertise of the craftsmanship was obvious, as was the quality of the materials.

"Did you design those?" he asked, pointing to her boots.

"Yes, I did, along with the belt I'm wearing and my bag," she answered with no small amount of pride. "I wore them today because I thought it would be a good idea to show you the goods, so to speak."

Quinn had an obscene thought that involved her showing him *her* goods, but pressed his lips together to make sure none of his stray musings escaped him like they had earlier this morning. He rose, rounding the desk to stand in front of her.

"Do you mind if I take a closer look?" he asked, kneeling at her feet to get a better view of the boots.

When he put a hand near her ankle to push up the leg of her pants, she jerked. "I'll just take them off."

"Let me help," he offered, and she reluctantly placed her foot in his hands.

After a couple of tugs, the boot came loose, uncovering

her pink camouflage-print sock. He leaned back on his heels to study her boot more closely but was distracted when she stood.

Her new position put his face almost nose-deep in her cleavage, and when she realized it, she stumbled backward, barely saving herself from a fall by grabbing the back of the chair. Before he could say anything, her hands went to her waist, and she began to unbuckle her belt.

What the hell is she doing?

Just like that, all his efforts to keep his thoughts firmly in PG territory drained away in a wave of lust so powerful he had trouble catching his breath.

AMELIA WAS MORE FLUSTERED THAN SHE'D EVER BEEN IN HER life. She could only think of one other occasion when she'd been so rattled, and that was the night Ava Grace had sung her heart out to win the *American Star* title.

She was off balance because she wore only one boot, and her fingers felt numb, which was not only alarming but inconvenient, too. She needed to take off her belt so Quinn could study it without getting any closer. He had already been too close. Her body flushed when she thought about the graceless move that had forced her girls into his face.

He still knelt on the concrete floor, and the office was so silent she could hear his breathing. His chest moved in a deep, fast rhythm.

She leaned against the chair. After a moment, her fingers worked again, and she resumed unbuckling her belt.

"So what do you think?" she asked, referring to the boot he still held in his hands.

Her voice sounded just like Marilyn Monroe's when she'd sung "Happy Birthday" to JFK, and she cringed in embarrassment. When he didn't reply, she glanced up from her belt.

His head was bowed, his knuckles white where they clenched her boot. Finally, he responded.

"I think you should stop fiddling with your belt," he said roughly.

She froze, torn between running and staying exactly where

she was. If the air had been heavy with sexual tension before, it now crackled with it. She had never felt anything like it, and she definitely didn't want to feel it with this man.

She waited a beat before speaking. "May I have my boot back?"

He relinquished his hold on her footwear, and she moved to the sofa to pull it on. Out of the corner of her eyes, she saw him get to his feet and make his way toward the windows.

He stared down at the street below, one hand propped on the window and the other rubbing the back of his neck. "Teagan thinks you're the right person for this job," he said without turning.

His voice was hoarse, and he cleared his throat. "I'm inclined to agree with her. I like what I saw here today." He stopped abruptly, muttering something under his breath. "I like your designs," he clarified.

He turned from the window, his face blank. "You asked for this meeting. Is there anything in particular you wanted to discuss?"

"Yes. I'm curious how much supervision you plan to give to this project."

He smiled, a quick quirk of his lips. "Haven't you heard? I'm a terrible micromanager."

She tensed, shuddering inwardly at the thought of him hanging over her shoulder, watching her every move. Her dread must have been visible because he chuckled.

"Relax, Amelia. I'm far from a micromanager. I trust people to do their jobs, at least until they give me a reason not to trust them. And you've not given me any reason not to trust you."

"So you aren't going to provide a lot of supervision. What kind of involvement do you expect to have with the design process?"

"What would you say if I told you I didn't want to be involved?"

At first, his answer delighted her because it meant he wouldn't bother her while she worked. But then she was a little disappointed. This was his family business. Where was his sense of responsibility?

"I'd say it's very unwise to not be involved."

"Really?" he asked, his dark eyebrows winging up his forehead. "Why would you say that? I'm not the expert in women's fashion. *You* are."

"I get the sense the women's division is suffering from benign neglect."

"You're probably right. It has been largely ignored, almost since it was first created. But partnering with you for this line of accessories is the most attention I can give it."

"Don't you want the women's division to be successful?"

He sighed loudly. "If you think about Riley O'Brien & Co. as a big oak tree with deep roots and long, thick branches, the women's division is nothing but a short, skinny branch." He grimaced. "It's rotting, and it might be time to take a chainsaw to it."

She digested his comments. Now she had a much better understanding of why Teagan had felt compelled to take matters into her own hands, or rather, put matters into Amelia's hands.

And it also explained why Teagan refused to supervise the project. She believed Quinn's involvement in the accessories would make him more connected to the women's division.

Amelia addressed the next item on her mental list. "I estimate the design process will take three to six months because each piece will need to be tweaked and approved," she said, looking for confirmation because she wasn't sure how the process worked at Riley O'Brien & Co.

"That's about right," he said, leaning against the window. "You'll also need to work with our purchasing department to make sure each piece is constructed of materials that can be sourced easily and inexpensively. And you'll need to work with our manufacturing folks to make sure your pieces can be made on our existing equipment."

Teagan had neglected to share those specific details. Amelia was a little intimidated at how extensively he expected her to be involved in the process once her designs were completed and approved.

"That would mean my involvement would last well beyond six months."

"Is that a problem?"

Yes, it was a problem, a huge one. If she got this worked up simply by being in the same room with Quinn, she needed to make sure she did most of her design work far away from him. Several states away, preferably.

Rising from the sofa, she returned to the chair she had vacated so abruptly. "I'm not willing to be away from Nashville for that long."

"Why? Do you have a man who wants you by his side day and night?" he asked, a hint of sarcasm in his deep voice.

She stiffened. This was not the way she wanted the meeting to go. She wanted them to be allies, not enemies, so she did her best to lighten the mood.

"Not just one man. The entire defensive line of the Tennessee Titans is at my beck and call," she quipped.

When he scowled at her, she held out her hands, palms up. "If you want me to produce samples, I need to have access to my workshop."

"Believe it or not, we actually have workshops here," he replied dryly.

Realizing she wasn't getting anywhere with her argument, she clenched her fists in her lap. "Do you have a problem with me doing the majority of the design work in Nashville?"

"Is it a deal breaker if I do have a problem with it?"

Her mouth went dry. Was it a deal breaker?

She knew she'd do her best work in an environment where she felt comfortable and confident, but she could work anywhere. Was she going to lose the biggest opportunity of her career because she was afraid she couldn't control her hormones?

She struggled to find an answer, ashamed she even had to think about it. Her lustful thoughts about Quinn shouldn't factor into her decision. Her career was more important than sexual attraction.

After several seconds of silence, he sighed. "Fine. You can do the majority of the design work in Nashville. But I expect you to be here to get the project off on the right foot."

She went limp with relief. He had given in. "How long did you have in mind?"

After a brief pause, he said, "Four weeks."

A month on-site wasn't ideal, but she didn't think he was being unreasonable with his request.

"You also need to make time to tour one of our manufacturing facilities. And I want you to present the samples in person."

When she didn't answer immediately, he asked sharply, "Is that acceptable to you?"

"Yes, that's acceptable to me, as long as you pay for my airfare, lodging, and food while I'm here."

She couldn't afford the expense of flying back and forth from Nashville to San Francisco along with the high hotel rates in the Bay Area.

Quinn's eyebrows shot up. "Of course. That's a given."

She knew she had exposed her lack of previous business experience. Covering her gaffe with a big smile, she said, "I have to finish up another project before I start on yours, but it shouldn't take long, only a couple of weeks."

His broad shoulders lifted in a shrug. "That's fine."

She stood and offered her hand to seal the deal. He looked at it for a moment, and when it was obvious he had no plans to take it, she tucked it into her pocket.

"Are we finished?" he asked, pulling out his mobile.

He had already dismissed her, and instead of being offended by his rudeness, she was relieved. She turned to grab her bag, but his words drew her attention.

"Teagan, hey . . . Amelia and I are finished," he said into the phone. "Come and get her and then treat her to an early lunch." He paused for a second before answering, "Okay. See you in a second."

Disconnecting the call, he placed the phone on his desk. "Teagan's on her way."

Amelia nodded before bending down to pick up her bag. As she turned to face him, she noticed his eyes were focused on her lower half. She was almost certain he'd been checking out her butt.

"Quinn."

His eyes jerked to her face. "I'm sorry," he said, a tide of red sweeping over his face. "I missed what you said."

Oh, yes, he definitely had been checking out her butt. She

should be insulted, but surprisingly she wasn't. Instead, she was flattered a hot guy appreciated her anatomy.

But not just any hot guy. *This* hot guy.

"Can you repeat what you said?"

"I just wanted to thank you for the opportunity," she said sincerely. "I think it's going to work out great."

Quinn smiled, but it looked more like a grimace. "Yeah, I'm sure it will."

Chapter 4

"SO, HOW DID IT GO?" TEAGAN ASKED AS SHE AND AMELIA MADE their way along Market Street.

Teagan had promised to take her to one of the best lunch spots in the city, and they were heading to a place called Zuni Café. Although they had walked silently for a few minutes, Amelia had yet to figure out the best way to describe her meeting with Quinn, so she deflected Teagan's question with one of her own.

"Is the weather always this gorgeous in September?"

This business trip was Amelia's first visit to San Francisco, and she was surprised by the warm, sunny weather. Like most tourists, her knowledge of the city was gleaned primarily from movies. As a result, she had expected fog, the Golden Gate Bridge, and Alcatraz.

"Yes. Most people don't know it, but we have Indian summers here. October is even nicer." Teagan gave her a sidelong glance. "Are you going to tell me how your meeting with Quinn went or are we going to keep talking about the weather?"

Amelia smiled wryly. She liked Teagan, but she wouldn't say they were friends. They had only known each other a few months, and their discussions had been limited to business with a bit of Teagan's family history mixed in.

Ava Grace had introduced them at a concert to raise money for the nation's largest hunger relief organization. Teagan had been there because Riley O'Brien & Co.'s charitable foundation was one of the event sponsors, while Ava Grace had performed at the concert along with several other country and rock musicians.

"The meeting wasn't bad," Amelia said finally. "Quinn was pleasant. Nice, even."

Teagan snorted. "First of all, if that were true, you'd be damning him with faint praise," she retorted. "Second, my brother is a lot of things, but 'nice' is not an adjective most women use to describe him."

"How do most women describe him?" Amelia asked, eager to gain some insight into Quinn from such a reliable source.

Teagan made a sound of disgust. "Hot." Her red lips twisted. "But I think 'hardheaded' is a better adjective. Although 'clueless' also works."

Amelia laughed. "Maybe you're right. He's still blissfully unaware of our real plans."

"So he still has no idea you're going to reimagine our women's jeans, in addition to creating some new styles and expanding the product line?"

"No, we only talked about accessories," Amelia confirmed. "He noticed my boots right away, and I think they convinced him that I was up to the challenge."

"I knew they would. He likes shoes even more than I do, and I'm a shoe whore."

She looked down at Teagan's heels. "Yes, you are," she agreed with a laugh.

The red suede peep-toes were a perfect complement to Teagan's wrap dress, which clung to her considerable curves. "That's a fabulous dress, by the way. You remind me of a 1940s pinup."

Teagan smoothed a hand over her dark, wavy hair. "I always wear dresses or skirts to work." She sighed wistfully. "I would love to wear jeans, but I can't wear the competition to the office. Can you imagine? It would be like cursing during Mass. And I refuse to wear Rileys. I hate the way they fit."

Amelia nodded. "Me, too. They're too long for me, and I have to go up a couple of sizes for them to fit my butt, which makes the waist too loose. Even Ava Grace looks bad in them."

"And they're so uncomfortable in the crotch."

Amelia snickered. "The dreaded camel toe."

"Ugh," Teagan groaned. "If you can find a way to design a pair of jeans that prevent camel toe, you'll be doing the whole world a great service."

Teagan shifted her red Gucci bag to her other shoulder and stopped in front of a storefront topped with a bright yellow awning. "This is it," she announced, ushering Amelia through the door.

Soon after the hostess seated them in a booth near the window, their server came by to take their drink order. Amelia was surprised when Teagan ordered a dirty martini.

"I know it's early, but talking with Quinn about the women's division always drives me to drink," Teagan noted with a scowl. "The men in my family are so stubborn. I really thought things would change once Quinn stepped in to run the company when my dad got sick, but he hasn't done anything to help the women's division. It's infuriating."

The server delivered the drinks to their table, and Teagan took a moment to reduce him to a quivering mass of hormones with some over-the-top flirting. When she finished with him and the poor guy had stumbled away, she raised her martini.

"To a successful redesign," she toasted.

When Amelia didn't raise her glass, Teagan frowned. Sighing loudly, she returned her cocktail to the table with a sharp click.

"I know you feel guilty about going behind Quinn's back," Teagan acknowledged. "But he needs to realize how important the women's division really is."

"I do feel guilty. I'm not a naturally deceitful person."

"You just need a little practice."

Amelia shook her head in exasperation. While Teagan didn't seem to have any hesitation about working behind her older brother's back, Amelia continued to struggle with her decision.

Initially, Teagan and Amelia had only talked about accessories. When Teagan had broached the subject of working on a comprehensive redesign, Amelia hadn't been interested because of the secrecy required.

But Teagan had been very persuasive, agreeing to fund Amelia's longtime dream of owning a chain of boutiques where she could sell her designs exclusively. Teagan's investment was contingent upon Amelia's success. Quinn had to agree to put her designs into production or she didn't get anything for her efforts.

Amelia met Teagan's eyes. "Are you sure you want to do this? I only spent a short amount of time with Quinn this morning, but I have no doubt he'll be furious when he finds out what we're doing."

Going behind Quinn's back made Amelia feel as if she was compromising an important part of herself in her quest for success. She had the unpleasant notion this was exactly how executives devolved into criminals. Little by little, they put money and success ahead of character and integrity.

"My dad ignored the women's division, and Quinn doesn't think it can be successful, no matter what," Teagan grumbled, her frustration evident. "He refuses to listen to me, and I have to do something big to make him see the potential."

After taking a sip of her martini, Teagan said, "I've been thinking about the best way to tell Quinn about the redesign. I know we've only talked about sketches, but maybe you should create samples, too. Then we could have a mini fashion show."

Amelia considered Teagan's suggestion. "I think that's a good idea. But I'll need extra time to create the samples."

"How much time?"

"At least twelve weeks . . . maybe more," she replied, knowing her answer would disappoint Teagan. "And that doesn't include the initial design process."

Sure enough, the other woman's mouth turned down in a disappointed frown. "So January at the earliest?"

Amelia nodded apologetically. "I know it will be hard to keep the project a secret from Quinn for that long."

"We don't have any choice. We have a much better chance of gaining his support if he can see your designs on real bodies. You know what they say: seeing is believing."

"There's still a good chance he won't put them into production," Amelia warned.

Teagan nodded. "You're right, he might not. And if he refuses to see it my way, I'll take it to the board."

Amelia pondered Teagan's statement. It sounded as if she was willing to push Quinn out of the CEO suite if he didn't go along with her ideas.

"Just to be clear, do you want to take over the company?"

Teagan frowned. "I doubt it would come to that."

"And if it did?"

"I don't want to take Quinn's job from him. Let's just hope he eventually sees the light."

QUINN STABBED THE DOWN BUTTON ON THE ELEVATORS LEADing to the parking garage below Riley Plaza. Since it was nearly seven in the evening, no one else waited for the elevator. He impatiently slapped his leather messenger bag against his hip, eager to be on his way home.

This morning's unscheduled meeting with Amelia Winger had messed up his routine. After handing Amelia off to Teagan, he'd immediately rushed into a meeting with the head of real estate, Sam Sullivan.

During the meeting, he and Sam had discussed the possibility of opening more Riley O'Brien retail locations. Currently, the company employed a multichannel distribution model, selling its products in bricks-and-mortar locations, online, and through print catalogs.

Customers could purchase Rileys from big-name department stores, regional clothing chains, and smaller boutiques, along with Riley O'Brien–branded shops. While online sales were growing, most people still bought their jeans from a retail location.

In general, neither men nor women liked to buy a pair of jeans without trying them on. In fact, market research showed most people considered several different brands and tried on multiple styles before buying even one pair of jeans.

The elevator arrived with a ding, its doors swishing open. Stepping inside, he pushed the button to take him down to the third level. While most companies reserved prime parking spaces for executives, Riley O'Brien & Co.'s coveted spaces were awarded monthly by lottery. The process served as a constant reminder that all employees were valued equally.

Arriving at the designated floor, he made his way to his Audi Q7 and clicked the remote to unlock the doors. He'd bought the luxury SUV on a whim one rainy Saturday afternoon a few months ago.

Since he hadn't been seeing anyone romantically, and his brother, Cal, had been out of town, he'd been bored out of his mind. He had been watching ESPN when an Audi commercial had come on, and he had decided to visit the local dealership.

When Cal had seen his new toy, he'd pointed out that most people went for a run or to the movies when they were bored. His brother had concluded Quinn needed a hobby, or even better, a honey, and then he'd begged to drive it.

Teagan, meanwhile, had said he had too much time on his hands and too much money in his bank account, something he didn't bother to dispute. "You should try volunteering," she'd suggested snidely before demanding that he take her for a spin.

Opening the door, he tossed his bag in the passenger seat and jumped in. The smell of expensive leather enveloped him, and he clicked his seat belt in place.

After connecting his iPhone to the car radio, he turned it on. He'd been edgy and agitated all day, and loud, angry music always helped him decompress.

As he drove home, he tapped his fingers against the steering wheel to the thumping beat of Godsmack's "I Stand Alone." The music was suddenly silenced as the car's console lit up to let him know he had a call. He pressed a button to connect it, and Teagan was immediately there with him, in voice if not in body.

"Quinn, where are you?" Her voice came through the speakers loud and clear, much to his displeasure.

"I'm heading home."

"You avoided me all afternoon," she accused.

"You think so?" he replied, knowing his answer would irritate her.

"I know so, you jerk."

He grinned. Annoying his little sister was so much fun, and he did it as often as he could.

"And here's more proof you don't know everything," he mocked. "I had meetings all afternoon, and it was just a happy coincidence I was able to avoid you at the same time."

Teagan's rude snort echoed throughout the car. "I wanted to talk to you about your meeting with Amelia."

Quinn sobered. He'd been trying *not* to think about that meeting all day.

"What about it?" he asked cautiously.

Her questions flew at him with the rapid staccato of a machine gun. "How did it go? Did you like her? What did you talk about? Were you satisfied?"

Thinking about Amelia made his gut tighten with renewed arousal. No, he definitely hadn't been satisfied.

"It was fine."

Teagan sighed loudly. "You're just as bad as Amelia. She barely said two words to me about the meeting."

Quinn's curiosity was piqued. "What did she say?"

"She said you were nice."

Nice? Now he felt like ramming his head into a brick wall.

"What did you think of her?"

That was a good question. What *did* he think of Amelia? She hadn't been anything like he'd expected, and he found her interesting, smart, and sexy.

In the short time they'd spent together, she had shown interest in his family's history and an appreciation for the company's traditions. She had a sense of humor, and she was a hard negotiator, not giving up on her desire to work from Nashville despite the pressure he'd put on her.

He had definitely been impressed with her design skills. He had underestimated her talent by assuming she had achieved her success solely because of Ava Grace Landy. Her boots had been works of art, and he was sure she would be able to come up with some kick-ass accessories for the company.

But he was less sure he'd be able to keep his hands to himself, especially when he thought about her round ass, shiny hair, and pink lips. His extreme reaction to her was worrisome since he shied away from any personal relationships that might jeopardize Riley O'Brien & Co.

"When will Amelia be back?" Teagan asked.

"Didn't you two discuss that during lunch?"

"No."

Apparently, Amelia had left it to him to explain their agreement to his sister. She wasn't going to like what he had to say, and Amelia owed him for taking fire for this. He had a vision of her showing her appreciation on her knees with his hand fisted in her fiery red hair and her plump lips wrapped around his cock.

"When will she be back?" Teagan repeated, rudely interrupting his fantasy.

"In two weeks. But she's only going to be here for a month. She's going to do most of the design work in Nashville."

He expected a verbal explosion from Teagan, and he didn't have to wait long.

"Are you serious, Quinn?" she burst out furiously. "She needs to be here!"

He cut her off. "Look, Amelia was ready to call off the deal if I didn't agree," he explained, wondering why he bothered to defend himself when he hadn't done anything wrong. "Since the accessories are your bright idea, I thought you'd be happy I saved them. Instead, you're bitching at me."

Reaching his driveway, he pushed the button to open the garage doors situated below his trilevel Victorian and drove in. Teagan had been silent for so long he wondered if the call had dropped.

"Are you still there, T?"

"Yes, I was just thinking. Maybe we should throw a party to announce the partnership with Amelia. It would generate some buzz for the new accessories."

"Why don't you talk to Cal and see what he thinks?"

"I will."

He shifted the Audi into park. "Are we done?"

"We should offer the penthouse to Amelia. That might entice her to do more of the design work here."

Quinn sighed. He doubted anything would convince Amelia to spend more time in San Francisco than she had to. He was pretty sure she wanted to avoid him.

Despite his efforts to hide it, his desire for her had been obvious. He was just glad his jeans had concealed his erection. He had no doubt she would have ended the meeting if she had seen it. Riley O'Brien & Co. would have been forced to find another designer, and now that he'd met her, he definitely wanted Amelia.

In more ways than one, a little voice inside him whispered.

He scowled, annoyed by his surprising and inconvenient attraction to Amelia. He needed to get his shit together and focus on what she could do for Riley O'Brien & Co. She was an extremely talented designer. He needed to give her the same level of respect he would give any other professional.

With that in mind, he said, "I don't see a problem letting Amelia use the penthouse as long as it's not booked for someone else."

"I'll double-check, and if it's open, I'll go ahead and reserve it for the next few weeks." She cleared her throat. "Quinn, is there something I should know? Did something happen during the meeting?"

Leaning his head against the headrest, he closed his eyes and squeezed the bridge of his nose. He wasn't in the habit of lying, especially to his sister, and he wasn't going to start now.

"Working with Amelia is going to be interesting," he finally said. "I'm home. I'll see you tomorrow."

He disconnected the call before she could say anything else.

Chapter 5

THE BUZZ OF QUINN'S ALARM CLOCK PULLED HIM FROM A DEEP sleep the next morning. Covering his eyes with his forearm, he debated whether to lounge in bed an extra hour or get up and go for his regular morning run.

He'd gone to bed way too late after spending several hours online searching for information on Amelia Winger. He was intensely curious about her, but he hadn't wanted to quiz Teagan because his sister was smart enough to smell smoke where there was a little fire.

Unfortunately, his research had uncovered very little about Amelia, although she showed up briefly in a number of articles where Ava Grace Landy was the main subject. He'd discovered she and Ava Grace were from a town in Texas called Electra, population 2,772. The pair had been friends since kindergarten, and they were both twenty-six years old.

When Ava Grace had won *American Star* three years ago, she moved to Nashville, and Amelia came with her. They now shared a house outside the city, although he wasn't exactly sure where.

With so many pictures of Ava Grace on the web, Amelia's designs were everywhere, and he had reviewed them with interest. In Ava Grace, Amelia had found the perfect canvas to showcase her designs. With her long, lean body, the country music star was a living mannequin, and no matter what she wore, she looked stunning.

Sighing tiredly, Quinn threw back his down comforter and sat up. He knew he would feel better after he got some exercise, so he swung his legs over the side of the bed and stumbled to the bathroom.

After taking care of business and brushing his teeth, he grabbed a long-sleeve maroon T-shirt, gray running shorts, and athletic socks from his dresser and pulled them on. Stepping over the pile of dirty clothes on the floor, he headed downstairs to find his shoes.

As he made his way into the living room, his feet slid a little on the shiny hardwood floors. He had bought his Victorian three years ago, and prior to purchasing the four-bedroom home in Laurel Heights, he and Cal had shared a condo in Cow Hollow, a trendy neighborhood bordering the Marina District.

He quickly slipped on his running shoes and strapped his iPhone to his bicep. He jogged down the steep front steps, and with his earbuds in place, he headed west toward the park at a slow, easy pace.

Running always gave him the opportunity to prepare for the day ahead and mull over anything that bothered him. He picked up his speed, his feet pounding the pavement to the funky rhythm of Daft Punk's "Get Lucky." Meeting Amelia had upset his equilibrium, but he was much calmer this morning than he'd been yesterday during his drive home, and his music choice reflected his mindset.

His most recent girlfriend, Luna, had told him that she could judge his mood simply by the music he chose. His taste was eclectic, and he listened to everything, from classical to country, heavy metal to hip-hop.

He had met Luna in California Pacific Medical Center's cafeteria. He'd spent a lot of time there while his dad received his cancer treatment. With her cap of shiny, dark hair and olive skin, she'd caught his eye, and he had been intrigued when she jumped into a heated conversation with one of the food servers, Spanish flooding from her lips and her hands gesturing wildly.

Luna had been intense, probably because her job as a pediatric oncologist had been life-and-death stressful. When he had been with her, he listened to a lot of moody and dark classical composers, particularly Wagner and Berlioz. Maybe the music should have been the first clue Luna hadn't been the one for him.

Looking back, he admitted their relationship had lasted longer than it should have. He had been going through a difficult time. His dad had been sick, and Quinn had been forced to take on more responsibility at work sooner than he had expected. To make matters worse, he'd just moved into his new house and had been living alone for the first time in his life.

Luna had been the perfect distraction. Although their jobs had made it difficult to get together often, he had enjoyed the time he spent with her. She was intelligent, kind, and passionate about her job and her patients. And the infrequent sex had been pretty good, if not brain-melting.

He'd had plenty of brain-melting sex in college. Wild, athletic, anonymous sex.

But that wasn't his priority anymore. His family was his priority, followed closely by Riley O'Brien & Co.

Unfortunately, Cal and Teagan hadn't connected with Luna. It had bothered him that his favorite people in the world didn't like his girlfriend, and when Quinn had confronted Cal about it, his brother was quick to set him straight.

"I do like her. The problem is that you like her, too, and that's all you feel for her," Cal said bluntly. "Don't you get it? You're not in love with her."

But when things had gotten rough with his dad, Luna stepped up in a big way. And although Cal had been right when he said Quinn wasn't in love with Luna, he had been damn grateful for her.

He had happily settled into what he thought was a mutually satisfying relationship. That's why he had been blindsided when, after being together for more than a year, Luna had admitted she was in love with the father of one of the little girls she'd been treating.

Luna had assured him she hadn't cheated on him, and he believed her. Nonetheless, he had felt betrayed because he thought she was happy with him.

She hadn't even apologized. "Deep inside, you're okay with this," she said. "Your heart isn't broken, Quinn."

He hooked a left at the intersection, shaking off the memory of Luna. Thinking about her wasn't painful, but it sure as hell didn't make him feel good, either. As he crossed the street, one of the songs he had recently added to his playlist came on.

Ava Grace Landy's distinct, raspy voice flowed sweetly into his ears. As she sang the first few lines of her hit "Lost & Found," thoughts of her best friend Amelia Winger filled his head. An image of her deliciously round ass flashed across his vision, and he stumbled.

So much for calm.

Chapter 6

AMELIA LEANED A HIP AGAINST THE HEAVY WOOD TABLE IN HER workshop and rubbed her forehead. Thanks to the time difference between the West Coast and Tennessee, she hadn't arrived home until almost two in the morning, and she was exhausted. Even her special "oomph" juice hadn't helped.

Twirling one of her curls around her index finger, she studied her sketchbook and cast a critical eye over the minidress she'd drawn. She planned to construct the dress out of supple red leather.

It was the first piece of clothing she had ever designed for someone other than herself or Ava Grace, and she had serious anxiety. Most of her unease stemmed from the person who would wear it, a pop princess known simply as Cherry whose star power eclipsed Ava Grace's considerable fame.

The teen sensation was known for being a diva, and Amelia was nervous about working with her. But, according to Cherry's manager, Gary Garson, she adored Amelia's creations.

Picking up a fat pencil, Amelia flipped to a blank page in the sketchbook and started to draft the next piece for Cherry, a formfitting catsuit that would highlight the young woman's perky breasts, flat stomach, and well-toned legs. She strongly believed that in the right circumstances, showing less skin was even sexier than near nakedness.

Amelia snorted. Her mother had definitely not agreed. Janna Winger had pranced around their small town in tight cutoff shorts and midriff-baring shirts, even when the weather had demanded layers.

Janna's clothing had communicated her ambitions more loudly than a bullhorn. She had constantly been on the lookout for a new man, her standards low enough that she'd rarely been without companionship. As long as he'd had the money to buy booze and could get it up, her mother had been satisfied, at least until she found her next victim.

Amelia's fingers tightened on the pencil. Describing her mother as trailer park trash was being generous, although the two of them had never actually lived in the aluminum ghetto. Janna had been promiscuous, crass, and lazy. While Amelia's mother hadn't been a prostitute, she had used her body instead of her brain to survive, and she had paid for that decision.

Amelia's phone chirped again, this time notifying her that she'd received a text message. With a sigh, she tossed down the pencil and picked up the phone. Only a handful of people had her mobile number, and she didn't want to ignore an important message.

The two-line text was from Ava Grace. "Home soon. Be ready to talk."

Amelia grinned at the screen. Ava Grace's bossiness was a big part of her charm.

She checked the time on her phone before returning it to the table. It was a little after one p.m., so she'd been working for nearly four hours. She picked up the pencil again and resumed sketching.

When she had woken this morning, bleary-eyed and cranky, she'd been relieved to see Ava Grace had already left the house. She had needed time to decide how much of her trip to San Francisco she planned to share with her best friend.

Without a doubt, she knew Ava Grace would have compelled her to spill every humiliating and disturbing detail of her meeting with Quinn within minutes, if not seconds. If Ava Grace hadn't found fame as a country music singer, she could have been a huge success in law enforcement.

She was persistent, observant, and downright relentless when it came to ferreting information from even the most recalcitrant sources. Amelia had been on the receiving end of Ava Grace's interrogations many times.

The two of them had grown up together in a little burg that didn't even have a Walmart. Ava Grace's family situation had been better than her own, although not by much. Her mother had died when she was a toddler, and shortly thereafter, her father, Chuck, had dumped his only child with his mother. June had been a cold woman who'd been less than thrilled to raise another child, especially one as precocious as Ava Grace.

Now that she was an adult, Amelia had a better understanding of Chuck's decision. He'd been a roughneck, and his work on offshore oil wells had taken him away from home for months at a time.

As little girls, Amelia and Ava Grace had been linked by poverty and neglect. Hungry for love and attention, they'd become each other's family. They had tackled life as if it were the two of them against the world, and they'd lived together since Ava Grace's grandmother had died just days after Ava Grace's fifteenth birthday.

By God's grace, June had owned the house she and Ava Grace shared, so Ava Grace hadn't been homeless. Knowing the horror of Amelia's own living situation, her best friend had demanded that she move in with her. They'd managed to stay in school and had kept themselves afloat by working nights, Amelia serving greasy food at a twenty-four-hour diner and Ava Grace pressing clothes for the local dry cleaner.

Amelia heard the crunch of gravel as a car drove into the driveway, and she quickly tidied up her worktable. She met Ava Grace as the tall blonde stepped out of her car, a flashy red Camaro she'd splurged on when her song "I'm Not Your Anything" had hit number one.

Ava Grace's short black dress showed off her long, tan legs, and her hot pink cropped jacket matched her cowboy boots. Her platinum-colored hair was in a long braid down her back, and long silver earrings dangled from her lobes. If Amelia didn't love her so much, she would have hated her for being so beautiful.

"Hey, girl," Ava Grace said, pushing the door to her Camaro shut with her hip since her hands were filled with her big purse and a white paper sack. "I figured you hadn't had lunch yet, so I brought us some soup and sandwiches from Main Street Deli."

"Yum," she replied, just now realizing how hungry she was.

Ava Grace hummed her agreement. "And I had Beth toss in a couple of caramel brownies," she added, chuckling as Amelia licked her lips hungrily. "They're a bribe for you to tell me *all* about your trip."

"Why would you think I'd need a bribe to talk about it?" she prevaricated.

"Because Teagan left me a voicemail that you planned to do all your design work here, and that Quinn acted weird when she asked him about it. She also told me they want you to stay in the company-owned penthouse while you're there."

Amelia ground her teeth together. "Why didn't she just pass you a note during homeroom?"

Ava Grace ignored her, and they made their way toward the big front porch that wrapped around the farmhouse. She placed the sack of food on the metal bistro table near the front door before heading inside.

Reaching into the bag, Amelia pulled out two sandwiches wrapped in deli paper, along with two cups of soup. She dug around the bottom and uncovered some plastic spoons and napkins, but no brownies.

The screen door slammed shut, signaling Ava Grace's return to the porch. She carried two glasses of iced tea, and she'd taken off her jackets and boots.

Frowning, Amelia put her hands on her hips. "Where are the brownies?"

"I hid them inside the house. You can have one after you've answered my questions."

Amelia growled. "You're such a brat sometimes. No one would buy your music if they knew."

Ava Grace rolled her eyes before placing the glasses on the table and taking her seat. "I got chicken salad for you," she said, reaching for her own sandwich.

Amelia dropped into her chair. It was hard to be mad at Ava Grace when she'd been thoughtful enough to get her favorite sandwich, a creamy mixture of diced chicken, pecans, and red grapes on a buttery croissant.

After they'd enjoyed several mouthfuls, Ava Grace turned her hazel eyes to Amelia. "I Googled Quinn O'Brien before you went to San Francisco. I trust Teagan, but I wanted to know more about him and what you were getting into."

She wasn't surprised by Ava Grace's admission. Her best friend was fiercely protective of her, despite the fact that Amelia had been taking care of herself for most of her life.

Ava Grace leaned back in her chair and crossed her legs, the glittery blue polish on her toenails sparkling in the afternoon sunlight. "From what I read, he's pretty impressive. But you and I both know very few people live up to the hype," she said cynically. "All hat and no cattle."

Amelia nodded, agreeing with Ava Grace's assessment. They had realized that truth soon after Ava Grace had won *American Star.* Suddenly the two of them had socialized with famous people they'd only read about, and more often than not, they'd been disappointed by the reality.

"So what was he like in the flesh?"

At the thought of Quinn's flesh, Amelia choked on the iced tea she'd swallowed. Ava Grace thumped her on the back before tossing her a knowing look.

"What's got you all choked up?" When Amelia didn't answer, Ava Grace sighed and picked up her spoon. "Are you going to take them up on the offer to stay in the penthouse?"

"Yes. I think it's nice of them to let me use it."

"Very nice." She pointed her spoon at Amelia. "And since you'll have a comfy, safe place to lay your head, I want you to tell me why you're not going to stay in California until the project is complete."

She sighed. This was a situation in which Ava Grace's bossy nature was decidedly *not* charming.

"Because I'm worried Quinn will distract me, and I won't be able to do what needs to be done."

As much as she hated to admit it, she had serious concerns about the sparks that flew when she and Quinn were in the same room. She didn't want to be unprofessional, and she definitely did *not* want to mix business and pleasure.

Even if Teagan's redesign project wasn't successful, this

partnership for the accessories line was important. It was a crucial step in achieving her career goals.

"I'm not sure I understand," Ava Grace replied after a moment. "You think he's going to be all up in your business, asking questions and pushing his opinion on you?"

She shook her head. "No. He told me he doesn't micromanage his people."

Ava Grace's eyebrows rose. "Then what do you mean when you say 'distract'?"

"Distract as in I can't think about anything else but stripping him naked and pulling him down on top of me," she admitted.

After a beat of shocked silence, Ava Grace hooted with laughter. "Oh, really?" she teased. "Is he that hot?"

She considered Ava Grace's question. "Yes, he's that hot. But it's more than that . . ." She struggled to find the right words. When she couldn't, she shrugged her shoulders. "He appeals to me," she explained lamely.

Without question, Quinn was physically tempting. But she liked him, too. She had enjoyed their meeting more than she had anticipated, and she admired his obvious dedication to Riley O'Brien & Co., even if he had a blind spot when it came to the women's division.

"Did he give you any idea he might be interested in you, too?"

"I don't want him to be interested in me," she replied emphatically.

Heaven help her if Quinn actually turned the full strength of his hotness her way. She'd never be able to resist the temptation.

At that alarming yet enticing thought, she broke down and told Ava Grace about the face-in-the-cleavage debacle, causing the gorgeous blonde to almost fall off the chair in hysterics. When Ava Grace's laughter subsided, Amelia kicked her best friend's shin with the tip of her worn ballet-style flats.

"Give me my brownie."

Ava Grace grinned slyly. "I'll give you both brownies if you tell me how you felt when his face was *this close* to your ta-tas."

Chapter 7

AMELIA EVALUATED HERSELF IN THE FULL-BODY MIRROR IN THE penthouse's bathroom. She'd chosen a chocolate-brown shirtdress for her first official day at Riley O'Brien & Co.

It was one of her favorites and never failed to give her a boost of confidence. She definitely needed that boost today.

Smoothing her hands down the front of the dress, she fiddled with the buttons that ran from collar to hem. She couldn't decide if she was more excited or nervous. Either way, she decided some positive self-talk might be in order.

You can do this. You will do this. You're going to kick butt and take names, and the whole world will want to buy your designs.

She wanted to show off some of her best pieces while she was here, but doing so would be a challenge since most of them looked best with jeans. She knew she couldn't walk around in a pair made by the competition without inciting Quinn's displeasure, but she refused to wear Rileys in public, at least until she'd redesigned them.

As a result, dresses and skirts made up the bulk of the clothes she'd brought to San Francisco. She'd made sure they would look good with her designs, and the shirtdress was the best of the bunch.

Made of crisp yet soft cotton piqué, the dress had a subtle texture and a dressy sheen. It conformed to her petite figure so the skirt wasn't too full and the bodice wasn't too tight. As Goldilocks had said in *The Three Bears*, it was just right.

She'd replaced the matching brown belt with one of her own designs. Constructed from caramel-colored leather and accented with dark brown leather stitching, the three-inch-wide belt was held together in the front by a narrower strip of the same leather and a delicate gold buckle.

Turning sideways in the mirror, she debated which shoes to wear. She definitely didn't want to go overboard and wear boots every day, so she eventually decided on a pair of nude peep-toes.

The light color made her legs look longer, which was important because she was kind of stubby, and the four-inch stacked heel gave her some much-needed height. By the end of the day, her feet would ache, but the pain might be worth the gain, for today at least.

As she dug through her bag of jewelry to find the right necklace and earrings, she went over her agenda for the day. When she had arrived at Riley Plaza late last night, the security guard on duty had given her a thick packet of information that included a map of the headquarters, her schedule for the next several days, the name and location of her assigned work area, and the key code to the penthouse.

This morning she would meet her liaison and receive an orientation of sorts to review the company's history and corporate structure. After lunch with Teagan, she would be introduced to the CFO and the head of the women's division.

She finally found the pieces she wanted—a long, chunky gold chain with a big amber pendant and matching drop earrings. She put them on before heading to the kitchen to grab her bag. She didn't want to be late and make a bad impression.

As she made her way to the elevators to head downstairs, she wondered if Quinn would participate in today's meetings. Since he had indicated he had little or no interest in this project, she doubted she would see much of him. That suited her just fine. The more time she spent with him, the greater the likelihood she'd end up doing something stupid.

The elevator dinged to let her know she had arrived on

the second floor. Stepping out, she ran headlong into a hard male body, one that stood way too close to the entrance. She scowled, annoyed by rude people who crowded elevators and refused to let other passengers disgorge before they pushed their way in.

She teetered on her heels, and one of them got stuck in the crack between the elevator and the floor. Strong hands grabbed her upper arms to keep her from windmilling backward.

"Whoa, careful."

The deep voice sounded so much like Quinn's rich baritone she knew immediately she'd just run into Callum O'Brien. She righted herself, and he dropped his hands and stepped back so she could move away from the elevator.

"You must be Amelia."

She looked up, way up. She was surprised to see Callum was even taller than Quinn, although not by much. He was also leaner than his older brother, although he was by no means skinny.

"You must be Callum."

He nodded. "You can call me Cal."

She noticed he and Quinn looked enough alike it would be obvious to strangers they were brothers. But Cal's jaw wasn't quite as defined as Quinn's, and his lips weren't nearly as full.

The biggest difference between the two men was their eyes. While Quinn's eyes were a dark, deep blue, almost navy, Cal's eyes were light blue, like fresh water under a layer of ice, with a darker ring of blue around the edge of the irises.

The combination of his dark hair and icy blue eyes was arresting, and she caught herself staring. The O'Brien siblings were definitely blessed when it came to looks.

"I've heard a lot about you," they said in union and then laughed awkwardly.

"Let's try that again," Cal said, tossing her a smile that would give most women heatstroke. She had the fleeting thought that Quinn's smile was much more attractive.

"Teagan has raved about you for months now."

Amelia knew Teagan was a fan of her work because she was vocal with her praise. "She thinks I can shake things up," she teased since Teagan had advised her that Cal was far more enthusiastic than Quinn regarding the new line of accessories.

He laughed. "I hope we can handle it," he said. "Do you need any help with directions? I can walk with you."

"I'm waiting to meet my liaison," she replied, and a second later she heard the sound of her name from behind her.

"Amelia Winger. I've been waiting ages to meet you."

She turned to greet the body attached to such a strong drawl and was taken aback to see a black man about her age with a head full of dreadlocks. Based on the accent, which she had identified as Deep South elite, she had expected an older white man.

"Aldridge Davis?"

He held out his hand for a quick handshake. "Yes, ma'am, although everybody calls me Deda," he said, pronouncing his nickname as "Deed-uh."

He smiled, the contrast between his smooth, dark skin and white teeth striking. "I'll be your liaison while you're here."

Deda turned to Cal, and they bumped fists like teenage boys. "Yo, Cal, thanks for keeping Miz Winger company while she waited for me."

Cal smiled. "It was definitely my pleasure." He pointed toward Deda. "This guy will take good care of you," he said, winking at her. "I'll see you later."

Amelia turned back toward Deda. Someone clearly thought she needed a babysitter, and poor Deda had drawn the short straw.

"I'm sorry I'm taking you away from your daily responsibilities," she began, but Deda cut her off.

"Honey, I am abso-freakin-lutely delighted to hang with you," he said, patting her shoulder. "Don't worry about it."

Stepping back, he ran his eyes up and down her body, his gaze assessing rather than lecherous. "Oh, I just adore your style. I was so excited when I heard about the new line of accessories. Finally, we're going to have something new to talk about."

He pushed back the paisley-patterned cuff of his lavender dress shirt to peer at his watch. "We should probably get started so we can finish in time for lunch with Teagan." He held out his arm to her as if they were a bridesmaid and groomsman. "Shall we go?"

As they made the short trip from the reception area to the third-floor collaboration area, she questioned him about what his liaison duties entailed. "Basically, I'm here to make sure you meet everyone you need to know and that you have everything you need including all the background information on the company."

They reached their destination before she could quiz him about what he did when he wasn't babysitting her. "Collaboration area," she realized, was just a fancy phrase for "conference room."

Regardless of what it was called, it was empty. Deda explained they'd have the room to themselves until this afternoon when the CFO and division vice president joined them.

"Both of them have been with the company for more than twenty years. Between you and me, I think they're having a hard time adjusting to Quinn being in charge."

If Deda meant to arouse her curiosity with his statement, he definitely succeeded. But before she delved into the discord that existed between Quinn and two key employees, she was eager to learn more about Deda.

"What do you do when you're not hanging out with me?"

"I have a very impressive title." He winked at her. "Executive vice president of business development."

"That is a very impressive title," she said gravely, but her smile gave her away. "And what does an executive vice president of business development do?"

He took a few moments to outline his main responsibilities. He and his team were in charge of building new relationships for Riley O'Brien & Co., and those relationships included a wide range of potential business partners, from investors and suppliers to distributors and vendors.

"On a typical day, I talk with new retailers about carrying our products, track down companies that can supply our raw materials like denim and zippers, and vet trucking companies to join our logistics network, among other things."

The complexity of his job awed her. "Aren't you a little young to have so much responsibility?"

He stared at her. "Just how old do you think I am?"

"Maybe I'm not a good judge, but I thought you were my age," she admitted.

He guffawed, slapping his palms on the conference table. "Oh, honey, you just made my day! I can't wait to tell Harris."

"Who's Harris?"

"My partner."

He looked closely at her as he disclosed this information, as if he weren't sure how she'd respond to the knowledge of his homosexuality. She knew a lot of people weren't okay with it, but she didn't care one way or the other.

"Well, you can tell Harris that I think you look much younger than your . . . You never told me how old you are," she reminded him.

"Forty-two."

"Wow. Now I don't feel like such a loser because I've got some time to ascend to your level," she joked.

Some of her self-doubt and insecurity must have bled through her levity because Deda gave her an appraising glance. Before he could say anything, she posed a question to him.

"How many people do you manage?"

"Right now, we have fifteen people in the biz-dev group. Under normal circumstances, you would have worked with my team to get the ball rolling with Riley O'Brien, but Teagan spied you first." He smiled broadly. "That girl is something else. She doesn't let anything stand in the way of what she wants."

She laughed. "I'm torn between fearing her and admiring her."

Deda nodded in agreement. "She runs circles around her brothers, that's a fact. And if she wanted to run this company, she would. But she doesn't, and neither does Cal." He paused. "This company is in their blood, and they want to see it thrive, but it's not in their hearts."

Amelia was intrigued by his comments. "And what about Quinn?" She longed to gain a deeper understanding of what motivated him, and Deda seemed like a veritable font of information.

He considered her question for a moment. "A lot of people wondered why Quinn was the heir apparent, but I was never one of them," he said, putting his hand to his chest as if he were swearing on a Bible. "Quinn's heart and soul is tangled up in this company so tightly it's hard to tell where he ends and it begins. I can guarantee that for every decision he makes, and for every move he makes, he's thought about the impact on this company."

"So you've never seen him put his own desires above the well-being of Riley O'Brien & Co.?"

Deda drummed his fingers against the table. "No," he said emphatically. "And frankly, I can't imagine any circumstance where he would."

After a moment, he stood up and headed toward the audio-visual controls at the front of the room. "If it's okay with you, I want to show you the presentation my team gives to all potential partners."

He put the presentation on the projector screen and turned off the light so she could see it better. It started out with the history of Riley O'Brien & Co., and she was familiar with the major milestones.

During the hardscrabble years of settling and building the nation, Americans had worked in Rileys. The men had fought wars in them when they were shipped to Europe and Japan, and the women had worn them to build bombs and airplanes at home.

When the men had come home, they donned Rileys to do yard work, and the women had made them an essential part of their children's school wardrobe. Eventually, the jeans had become a staple in every closet, appropriate for all occasions, from first dates to job interviews.

The next section provided an overview of the company's products. She was shocked to find out there were only four styles for men and two for women.

He moved on to more interesting topics including a flowchart that explained Riley O'Brien & Co.'s executive leadership and the company's organizational structure. She hadn't been clear on how Quinn and his siblings worked together, and the charts were very enlightening.

This version of the presentation still had James O'Brien listed as the president and CEO. As chief operating officer, Quinn was listed just below his dad, and Teagan and Cal reported to him. She wondered when Quinn would officially take over his dad's title since it seemed that he'd already assumed most of his dad's responsibilities.

She interrupted Deda. "How long has Quinn been leading the company?"

"Since Mr. O'Brien got sick, which was more than three years ago." She couldn't see Deda's face very well in the dark, but he sounded sad.

Teagan had told Amelia that her dad had been very sick, but she hadn't offered any specifics, and none of the articles Amelia had read as part of her research had alluded to any particular type of illness.

"Has he recovered?"

Deda was silent for a long time. "I don't really know anything beyond what Quinn has told us at company-wide meetings. At our last meeting in July, he said Mr. O'Brien's health had improved significantly and the cancer treatment was working. But he didn't indicate when or if his dad was coming back. That's made the environment here a little tense because no one likes uncertainty."

As a rule, Amelia tried not to be nosy (Ava Grace was nosy enough for both of them), but she really wanted to know what kind of cancer, so she posed the question to Deda.

"I don't know," he answered. "They've kept that information private. But it was bad, and we could tell all the kids were torn up by it. Especially Quinn."

Chapter 8

QUINN GAVE A SHARP KNOCK BEFORE OPENING THE CONFERENCE room door and stepping in. The room was dark, but he could see Deda's outline against the glow of the projector screen.

"We just finished," Deda said. "You can turn on the light."

Flipping the switch, he got his first look at the woman he'd thought about way too much over the past two weeks. On his way to the conference room, he had wondered if he had exaggerated her sex appeal in his mind, but now that he was in the same room with her again, he knew he'd underestimated it.

"Hey there," he said, encompassing both Deda and Amelia in his greeting.

Deda came around the table. "I was expecting Teagan, not your troublemaking self," he said in his Tupelo honey drawl.

Quinn chuckled. "Troublemaking? I had no idea you thought so highly of me, Deda."

Grinning, he slapped the older man on the back. Deda was one of his favorite employees. Hell, he was one of his favorite people outside of his family. That's why he'd asked

Deda to shadow Amelia while she was here. He wanted her to feel comfortable, and he knew Deda would take good care of her.

He focused his attention on Amelia, who had remained seated at the table. She smiled tentatively.

"Hi, Quinn."

"Amelia, I know this is going to disappoint you, but Teagan can't go to lunch with you today. She got held up with some type of contract negotiation with one of our vendors, and she asked me to take her place." He spread his arms out to his sides, palms up. "So here I am."

Her smile faltered. "Oh, you don't have to do that. I can have lunch on my own. Or maybe Deda can keep me company?" She shot a beseeching look toward Deda, who looked toward Quinn for direction.

Quinn clenched his jaw. She obviously didn't want to spend time with him, and that pissed him off. They were business partners, after all, and she could be a professional and damn well eat a simple meal with him.

He shot Deda a look that said, "She's coming with me." He didn't want to think about why he was so determined to have lunch with her when she acted like it would be torture. Deda, smart man that he was, gave him a salute and started toward the door.

"Deda's got some things to take care of here, so I guess you're just going to have to suffer my company."

Amelia's cheeks pinked at his response, and he flashed a smile, perversely pleased by her unease.

"It's very nice of you to take time out of your day to take me to lunch," she said finally.

"I know. I'm a busy and important guy who has much better things to do." When she stared at him with an appalled expression, he burst out laughing. "I'm kidding, Amelia. I really want to take you to lunch, so grab your bag and let's go."

As she rose from the table, his laughter died in his throat, and he barely suppressed a groan. Jesus, the woman had curves that just wouldn't quit, and her brown dress accentuated every single one of them.

Maybe going to lunch with Amelia wasn't such a good idea. The best way to resist temptation was to avoid it. If he were a compulsive gambler, he wouldn't hang out at the track, would he? No, he wouldn't.

Amelia met him near the door, and he almost swallowed his tongue when he got a look at her sexy shoes. They showed off her shapely legs and gave him a peek of her raspberry-painted toenails. He reached up and casually rubbed a hand across his mouth, afraid he might be drooling.

There was no maybe about it. Going to lunch with Amelia *definitely* wasn't a good idea . . . especially since he wanted to nibble on her instead of a club sandwich.

She stopped beside him, and he was reminded of how short she was. Even in those sky-high heels, he still had more than half a foot on her.

"Where are we going?"

"If you like seafood, I'd like to take you to the restaurant that Cal's girlfriend owns. It's right on the bay, and the views are stunning this time of year."

"That sounds great. I haven't really had the chance to see it up close."

He pointed to her shoes. "Looks like we might need to drive."

Smiling apologetically, she nodded. "They look good, but they aren't good for walking."

He stared down into her big brown eyes. She was right. Her shoes looked good.

Too good.

AS QUINN DROVE UP TO THE RESTAURANT, THE LONE VALET attendant sprinted around the SUV to open his door. He glanced at Amelia.

"Wait a second, and I'll get your door."

His mother had instilled good manners in all her children, even if he and Cal forgot to use them when they were together. Opening the door for a woman was one he adhered to at all times.

Pulling open the passenger door, he extended his hand to help Amelia out of the vehicle. It was a little high off the ground for her, even with those heels.

As she grabbed hold of his fingers and turned in the seat

to step down, her dress inched up. The small slit near the hem widened, giving him a glimpse of her upper thigh. Like her face, it was dotted with freckles, and he couldn't find the strength to look away.

His mouth watered at the thought of tasting that smooth white skin and those tiny brown-sugar dots. He wanted to trace them with his tongue before moving higher. . . .

The valet's voice pulled him from his fantasy, and he made sure Amelia was safely on the ground before he took the ticket. Placing his hand on the small of her back, he ushered her into the restaurant.

Inside, Cal's girlfriend, Saika, chatted with the hostess. When she saw him, she smiled and greeted him with a hug.

"Quinn! Why didn't you tell me you were coming by today? I would have set aside a table for you so you didn't have to wait." She turned toward Amelia, and her smile widened. "You're the new designer, right? Cal mentioned you would be here this week."

Quinn quickly introduced the two women, and as he did so, he noted that Saika and Amelia were a study in contrasts. Saika was nearly six feet tall with a willowy figure like a runway model.

She was half Japanese, and her shiny black hair was cut close to her head, drawing attention to her dark, almond-shaped eyes and her high cheekbones. Her smooth skin was a light olive color, her lips pale pink.

Quinn had always considered Saika a beautiful woman. He never missed a chance to tell Cal that she was way too good-looking to be with him. But with Amelia standing next to her, Saika was a black-and-white drawing compared to Amelia's saturated color photo.

"Amelia, do you want to eat inside or outside?" he asked.

"Oh, I'd love to sit outside."

She looked thrilled at the prospect, and he asked Saika if she could arrange a table on the waterfront deck. Within just a few minutes, they had been seated and had already placed their lunch orders.

"I'm starving," she admitted. "I didn't have anything for breakfast."

"If I recall correctly, you usually have liquefied spinach

for breakfast." It was something he really didn't want to remember because it made him want to gag.

"I don't have a juicer here."

He felt like slapping his forehead. Of course the penthouse didn't have a juicer. He wasn't even sure it had a coffeemaker.

"I guess a carton of OJ just isn't the same," he joked.

Amelia laughed before gazing across the bay. Her eyes sparkled in the sunlight, and the light breeze tossed a couple of coppery corkscrews over one eye. He wondered if they were as springy and soft as they looked.

"So what do you think? Is the view worth putting up with my company for an hour or so?"

"It's a great view, but who knows how I'll feel when lunch is over."

He smiled at her tart rejoinder. He could see why she and Teagan got along so well.

"How did your morning go?"

During the short ride to the restaurant, he had made sure she liked the penthouse and that she was settled in. They hadn't had an opportunity to discuss her first few hours in the office.

"Well, I ran into your brother as I came out of the elevator. Literally ran into him."

He chuckled, understanding exactly what she meant. "It's one of his more annoying habits. He never thinks about the people who need to get off the elevator."

Her answering laugh was almost a giggle. The light, happy noise filled his chest, making him feel as if he had bubbles inside him.

"Did you and Cal have a chance to talk?"

She shook her head. "We introduced ourselves, but I was waiting on Deda, and I think Cal had somewhere to be."

"How do you like Deda?"

Amelia took a sip of her iced tea before answering, almost like she was stalling. Concerned, he cocked his head toward her.

"Most people really like him. That's why I asked him to be your liaison."

Looking down, she traced the rim of her glass with her fingertip. "He's great."

He could hear a "but" in there, and it wasn't long in coming.

"But I don't understand why you assigned me a liaison. Did you think I'd need a babysitter? Someone to keep me on task?"

He was shocked by her assumption. "No." She looked at him skeptically, and he repeated his answer more emphatically. "*No.* Of course not. I know you're a professional."

"Then why did you ask Deda to ignore his job, which sounds very important, by the way, to babysit me?"

He ran a hand through his hair. He had been trying to help her, and he'd ended up offending her instead.

Shit.

"Deda's not a babysitter, Amelia. He's one of the most important people in this company, and one of the most knowledgeable. You should think of him as your guide through a foreign and dangerous country."

She stared at him for several seconds before her shoulders very obviously relaxed. He realized she had been quite upset about the idea of having a "babysitter." She smiled, a teasing tilt of her tempting lips.

"Are you comparing Riley O'Brien & Co. to Somalia? Or maybe Libya?" She raised her eyebrows, and he felt a little foolish at his description. "I wish someone would have told me that I was risking life and limb by taking on this project. Should I arm myself?"

He gazed at her across the table. She had plenty of weapons at her disposal, starting with her sweet face and luscious body. But her most powerful weapon was her smart mouth, and she wielded it with skill.

"I'd say you're already well-armed."

She shot him a suspicious glance, clearly not sure if she should be offended by his comment. "It's a compliment," he clarified.

"Should I feel compelled to give you one in return?"

He feigned hurt feelings. "You can't think of one nice thing to say about me?"

She tapped her lip with her fingers, pretending to think hard. "Hmmm. Not really." The sparkle in her eyes told him she was joking.

"Now that's a real shame because I can think of plenty of nice things to say about you."

AMELIA EVALUATED HER ALMOST EMPTY PLATE. SHE HAD WORried she might be too nervous to eat, but sharing lunch with Quinn had been thought-provoking rather than nerve-wracking. She had relaxed once he had made it clear that having Deda as a liaison was an honor.

They'd discussed business for a while, but when Quinn found out Amelia knew almost nothing about San Francisco's history, he had shared his firsthand knowledge of his hometown. The O'Brien family had lived in the Bay Area for more than 170 years, maybe longer, and Quinn had been full of fun facts and interesting trivia.

They had finished their meals, and she expected Quinn to immediately ask for the check. Instead, he leaned back in his chair and propped his leg on his knee as if he were settling in for a long chat. His blue plaid shirt stretched across his chest, outlining his pectoral muscles, and she wondered what he did to maintain his impressive physique.

Anyone with eyes could see O'Brien men, past to present, were blessed with studly DNA. But even with such lucky genetics, surely it wasn't possible for him to look so good without having to work at it.

She shuddered to think how she would look if she didn't put some effort into keeping in shape. Like her mother, she had a pear-shaped body, and she had to work hard to keep her bottom half under control.

Before she could start to obsess about the size of her butt, he asked if she had any questions about the presentation Deda had given earlier this morning. Since the older man's comments about the O'Briens had really stirred her interest, she decided to take this opportunity to talk with Quinn about taking on the president and CEO job.

"Deda told me that you took over the company when your dad got sick. That must have been hard, dealing with a new job and his illness all at the same time."

Exhaling loudly, he rubbed the back of his neck with his hand. "Yeah, it was not an easy time for any of us."

She didn't comment, hoping he would continue. After a long pause, he spoke again.

"I wasn't one of those sons eager for his dad to vacate his position. And even though I'm the oldest, I didn't assume I would be his successor. Teagan and Cal have just as much of a right to this job as I do. But they didn't want the responsibility, which worked out because I did."

She considered what he'd said. She definitely had the impression that Teagan would take Quinn's job if she thought her older brother wasn't performing.

Teagan had a ruthless streak that Amelia found both unexpected and unnerving. She wondered if the redesign might be the catalyst to bring the other woman's ruthlessness to the forefront.

She brought her attention back to the subject at hand. "Is your dad better now? And if you don't mind me asking, what kind of cancer does he have?"

"Colon cancer. Stage III." He looked at her, his dark blue gaze so bleak she expected to hear bad news. "Yes, he's better. His cancer is in remission."

If that was the case, why did he look so troubled? Did he dread the day his dad came back and he had to step down?

"I'm so glad to hear that. It must be a big relief."

"Being in remission does not mean he's cured. Not even close."

He rolled his shoulders, and she could tell he no longer wanted to talk about his dad's cancer. "Do your parents live close by?"

"Pretty close. They live in an area called St. Francis Wood. They're still in the same house where I grew up, but Mom has been talking about buying a condo in one of the high-rises downtown. I keep telling her that she won't like it, but she's convinced it will be better for Dad. She doesn't want him climbing up a ladder to change a lightbulb or crawling under the sink to fix a leak anymore. If they lived in a condo, the condo association would take care of that stuff."

She wondered what St. Francis Wood was like. She was curious what kind of home Quinn had been raised in. He and his siblings were heirs to a significant fortune, and they had probably grown up surrounded by luxury.

She had no doubt his childhood home and the place where she had grown up had only one thing in common: they were both located on the planet Earth. Beyond that fact, she couldn't imagine any other similarities.

Before Amelia had moved in with Ava Grace, she and her mother had shared a one-bedroom apartment in a rundown duplex. She'd slept on the sofa with one eye always open in case one of her mother's boyfriends ventured from the bedroom to "explore."

"What about your parents?" he asked. "Do they still live in Texas?"

Nausea churned in her stomach. Her background embarrassed her, and she didn't want to share it with someone of Quinn's privileged existence. He was everything she wasn't—wealthy, educated, successful, good-looking, and from a good family.

"No," she answered curtly, hoping he would get a clue that she didn't want to talk about her family.

He tilted his head. "Where do they live?"

"My mother is dead, and I don't know where my father is."

Her voice was hard, unfriendly. She didn't want to invite more questions because if she were honest, she'd have to admit she didn't know *who* her father was.

"I'm sorry to hear about your mom," Quinn replied quietly, his eyes dark despite the sun reflecting off the bay.

She shrugged off his condolences. Her mother had caused Amelia more pain in life than she had in death. Maybe it made her unfeeling, maybe it made her a monster, but when she'd received the call that her mother was dead, she had been relieved.

When she had moved in with Ava Grace, she had tried so hard to distance herself from her mother. When Janna had died, she had finally obtained the distance she needed.

At the time, she and Ava Grace had saved every penny so they could move to Nashville, and Amelia had been angry, so very angry that she'd been forced to use that money to bury her mother. When she thought about it now, her earlier anger caused her such shame she could barely stand to look in the mirror.

She realized she had a lot of unresolved emotional issues

stemming from her childhood. She knew this because she watched Dr. Phil occasionally and she read a lot of self-help books. Together, they were a cheap therapist.

Quinn cleared his throat, and she realized she'd been staring into space, who knew for how long. She focused on his handsome face, and not for the first time, she wished she could be proud of the person she was today.

Proud enough to share the details with someone like Quinn.

Chapter 9

AMELIA MADE IT BACK FROM LUNCH WITH QUINN JUST MOments before Deda walked into the conference room with two other people, a woman and a man, both in their fifties.

"Diana, Vandy, this is Amelia."

Deda provided a little bit of background on both of them, and she did her best to commit the details to memory because she didn't want to offend them. Diana Stanton was the chief financial officer, and Karl Vandenberg, known to everyone as Vandy, headed up the women's division.

Diana had worked for Riley O'Brien & Co. since the mid-eighties, starting out as a secretary for Mr. O'Brien. She reported directly to the president and CEO, and since Quinn currently filled that position, she answered to him. Vandy, meanwhile, had been childhood pals with Mr. O'Brien and joined the company in 1989. He also reported directly to Quinn.

As soon as Deda finished the introductions, Diana took control of the meeting. Amelia found her demeanor very abrasive, and she wondered if it was because Diana was part of the generation responsible for advancing women in the workplace and breaking the glass ceiling.

"Quinn directed me to share some very specific financial information with you." Diana sniffed, as if the very idea offended her sensibilities. "I can't imagine why he'd want to do so since you won't be fronting any of the costs related to your project nor will you be sharing in any of the profits."

Since Amelia didn't like the woman's attitude, she was quick to correct her. "That's not entirely accurate, Diana. Teagan and I worked together to come up with a compensation plan that is based on performance. If and when my designs reach a certain sales threshold, I'll start to get a percentage of each sale."

Diana flushed at her rebuttal, a defiant expression on her face. The tension in the room was palpable, and she wondered if the older woman was equally combative with Quinn.

Is that what Deda had meant when he'd said some people were having a hard time with the transition from Mr. O'Brien to Quinn? If so, she had an entirely new level of respect for Quinn. She also felt strangely protective of him, and it made her angry that his employees might not fully support him.

Vandy cleared his throat. "Quinn thought it was important for you to know how much the women's division contributes to the company's overall revenue. In other words, how important the division is in the whole scheme of things."

Vandy passed a thick report to her. "This shows the total dollar revenues for the company for the past twenty years broken down by division and product."

She flipped through the pages, taking note of some of the more important charts, while Vandy continued his explanation. "It also includes several pie charts that show what percentage of the revenue is attributable to each division. Last year, for example, revenue generated by the women's division accounted for eleven percent of the company's total income."

Diana scoffed. "She doesn't understand what you're saying, Vandy. She's interested in fashion, not finance."

Amelia was not only shocked by the other woman's verbal assault; she also was angered by it. "Since we've known each other for less than an hour, I find it strange you think you know what I am and am not interested in."

Deda choked, but she didn't take her eyes off Diana. The other woman glared at Amelia, crossing her arms over her chest.

Although Amelia didn't want to start her project on a bad note, she wasn't about to let this woman insult her. She had taken care of herself and stood up to bullies before she'd been able to ride a bike.

"I understand Riley O'Brien & Co. needs to be more competitive so it can survive for five more generations. The women's division needs to pull its own weight. It should generate a lot more money and account for a larger percentage of the overall revenue." She tapped her pen against the report. "The only thing that is debatable is how to make more money."

With that statement, she took control of the meeting, not really caring she lacked experience in the corporate world. She tucked her insecurities away, for the moment, and tackled the problem.

"Vandy, since Riley O'Brien only produces two styles of women's jeans and those styles have been around for thirty years or so, it doesn't sound like you spend a lot of time on product development."

The older man nodded. "You're right. We don't have a single person dedicated to product development for our division. My group is focused on manufacturing and distribution."

"How do you feel about adding a line of accessories to your division?"

Vandy had the guts to answer her question honestly. "I don't know. Although I'm sure you're very talented, I doubt accessories will make much of an impact on our numbers."

"And how would you feel about a complete redesign of the existing products and possibly expanding the product line to include jackets, shirts, skirts, and maybe even dresses?"

She knew she took a huge risk by asking the question since it could give away her true objective. But she really needed to understand the level of resistance she faced.

"James didn't like the idea of diluting the Riley brand," Vandy said with a frown. "He didn't want to turn it into something it wasn't. We're a jeans company, that's all."

"That's where you're wrong," Amelia countered. "Rileys are an American icon, and icons remake themselves so they never lose their place in society, no matter what."

Judging by their frowns, neither Vandy nor Diana liked

what she'd said. Amelia glanced toward Deda, curious to see what he thought. He winked and gave her a thumbs-up.

QUINN HAD TO DEAL WITH A MINOR EMERGENCY AFTER HE AND Amelia returned from lunch. He was on the phone when his brother stuck his head into his office, and he beckoned Cal inside with a wave.

"Three days," he said into his headset. "That's it."

As Quinn ended the call and clicked off the headset, Cal shot him a curious glance. "What was that about?"

He filled Cal in on the crisis. Several of their manufacturing facilities were experiencing production delays due to a denim shortage. There were a lot of things that caused shortages, and in this particular instance, the recent flooding in the Northeast had interrupted operations for several textile producers.

Fortunately, they were well past the back-to-school shopping season or they'd really be screwed. They had some time to fix the problem and get things back on track before the holidays.

"I gave our procurement department three days to find a new source of denim. Deda's group has already vetted several potential vendors."

Cal frowned. "I'm glad you're the one who has to deal with that bullshit and not me."

Usually, Quinn loved solving problems like a production delay or a denim shortage. But he was a little distracted by thoughts of Amelia and their lunch conversation. He had enjoyed talking with her more than he'd enjoyed getting naked with other women.

He snorted. It had been so long since he'd had sex, his memory of the pleasure was surely dulled. Otherwise he'd never compare a simple conversation to an energetic romp in the sheets. He hadn't been with anyone since Luna, and they'd broken up just after Valentine's Day last year.

Although he'd always had a strong sex drive, his dad's illness and his own expanded job responsibilities had devoured all his physical and emotional energy. But his sex drive had returned with a vengeance. In fact, it had revved up right about the time he met Amelia. Whenever he was around her, he felt electrified, like the air right before a bad thunderstorm.

Cal moved across the room toward the sofa, drawing Quinn's attention. "Did you have a reason for stopping by? Something important to tell me?"

Cal dropped onto the sofa, stretching out his long body and letting his feet dangle off the armrest. Quinn's blood pressure rose as he took in his brother's position.

He didn't mind when other people sat on his sofa, but he hated for anyone else to lie on it. Cal knew how much he hated it, which was why his brother lounged on it every chance he got.

He scowled. "Get off my sofa."

The jackass ignored him. "I met Amelia this morning," it said, braying loudly.

"That's what I heard. Get off my sofa."

"Who told you?"

"Amelia. I took her to lunch because Teagan got stuck in a meeting with Boaz." He paused. "Get off my sofa."

Cal chuckled. "Amelia reminds me of that Disney heroine . . . the Scottish one with the curly red hair."

"I have no idea what you're talking about. Get off my sofa."

Cal sighed. "Right. Of course you don't, because you don't have kids."

"You don't, either." Saika had a five-year-old daughter, though, so that might explain Cal's extensive knowledge of Disney characters. "Is that what you wanted to talk about? The fact that Amelia looks like a fairy-tale princess?"

"You think she looks like a fairy-tale princess?" Cal asked with a big grin.

He growled. "Cal, I'm going to punch you in the face if you don't *get off my sofa* and get to the point in five seconds or less. Five, four, three . . ."

"Okay, okay." Cal swung his legs to the floor and rose to his full six four. "I just got the preliminary report from the firm we hired to conduct market research for the women's division. The research team is going to be here next Wednesday to present the findings. You might want to think about attending the presentation." He exhaled loudly. "The findings are going to upset you, Quinn. They made me sick to my stomach."

His stomach soured just from the look on Cal's face. "Why?"

"Because the research proves what we've suspected. We're so far behind our competition that we're not even in the race. We've lost more market share than I expected. Frankly, I'm not even sure it's possible to reverse the trend."

Cal was sharp. Very little slipped by him, and he had the education to back up his instincts. His brother was finishing up the final quarter of his MBA at the University of Pennsylvania's Wharton School of Business, the number one business program in the nation.

The school had an extension program in San Francisco that competed directly against Stanford, where Quinn had received his graduate degree. Undoubtedly, he and Cal would argue over which one of them had the best education, and he had plans to deface one of Cal's Wharton sweatshirts with a big red S.

Taking a seat in front of Quinn's desk, Cal speared him with his icy blue gaze. "You know the saying 'Using a Band-Aid to stop a hemorrhage'? That's where we are."

Scrubbing his hands over his face, Quinn exhaled roughly. "Do you have anything good to tell me?"

Cal considered his question. "Demand for apparel, and jeans in particular, is still strong."

"That's good since we make jeans," he said sarcastically.

Cal continued as if Quinn hadn't said anything. "Sales of accessories continue to grow across all categories, including handbags, belts, and shoes."

"That sounds like opportunity to me, especially since we're doing this line with Amelia."

Cal nodded. "The most encouraging research finding is that none of our competitors are pairing jeans and accessories and selling them as a package, and none of them are doing a good job capturing demand for boho-chic items, which basically describes Amelia's style."

"So we made a good choice?"

"Teagan made a good choice," Cal reminded him. "Amelia has more name recognition with younger adults than we expected, and more than any other designers who might have partnered with us. So, we just need to make sure we keep her happy, at least until she finishes the project."

Quinn nodded, thinking it shouldn't be too hard to keep her happy, as long as he kept his hands to himself. But then his amoral alter ego chimed in.

Maybe you could make her even happier if you didn't keep your hands to yourself.

Chapter 10

CAL HAD BEEN RIGHT. THE MARKET RESEARCH FINDINGS ABOUT the women's division were depressing as hell.

After Quinn talked with his brother last week, he'd taken Cal's suggestion and cleared his schedule for this afternoon so he could attend the official presentation.

Because of an unexpected phone call from one of the banks that provided financing for Riley O'Brien & Co., he'd been late getting to the collaboration area and all the seats were occupied. Although he stood in the back of the room, he was still able to see and hear the presentation clearly.

The presenter, a woman named Shelby Carruthers, headed up one of the best market research firms in the nation. The firm focused exclusively on apparel and apparel retailers, and Shelby knew her stuff better than anyone else in the business.

This wasn't the first time Riley O'Brien & Co. had worked with the firm, but it had been several years since the company had conducted a comprehensive market research study. And it was the first time any research had been done specifically to find out how consumers felt about Rileys for women, further proof the women's division had been neglected for far too long.

Using a blue laser pointer, Shelby referred to a slide with

a colorful pie chart. "As you can see here, Riley O'Brien & Co. owned the biggest market share of all jean manufacturers throughout the 1980s and 1990s. The company dominated the industry."

The slide animated to highlight different slices of the pie chart. "Even the collective market share of your two main competitors fell short. For decades, Riley O'Brien & Co. had a jeans monopoly. Rileys are synonymous with jeans just as Coca-Cola is synonymous with soda."

Quinn had always thought his dad had done a great job leading Riley O'Brien & Co. The company had flourished during his tenure, with revenue and profit increasing every year. Quinn knew that kind of success couldn't have been luck alone. At the same time, however, he realized the company had not faced as much competition when his dad had been at the helm.

Shelby advanced to the next slide, which delved into the numbers. "It's important to point out here that Rileys dominated the market for men's jeans by a huge margin, but they've never dominated the market for women's jeans."

Quinn's gaze fell on Amelia, who sat toward the front of the room. Her curly head was bent over a notebook as she took notes studiously.

She was such an intriguing combination of sass and serious, playful and professional. Her comments were in turn insightful and irreverent, and he wondered what she thought of the information Shelby had shared so far.

Did she regret her decision to partner with Riley O'Brien & Co.? He gave her one last glance before turning his attention back to the presentation.

Shelby faced the audience. "I have two words for you: 'designer denim.'"

The words flashed on the screen, the individual letters designed to look like denim. They were studded with rhinestones that twinkled at the audience. Shelby had bedazzled her presentation, and if the topic at hand wasn't so damn disheartening, Quinn would have laughed.

"Designer denim has *completely* changed the jeans industry," Shelby announced. "Twenty years ago, no one would have dreamed that the average woman would pay more than fifty bucks for a pair of jeans. Today, it's commonplace for her to spend double that amount, even triple. Upscale department stores and trendy boutiques now carry a variety of designer denim brands."

Another slide flashed on the screen dotted with hundreds of different logos. "This is just a small sample of the upscale brands that want to steal your customers."

Amelia waved her pen to get Shelby's attention. She said something, but Quinn was too far away to hear it. Whatever it was, Shelby must have agreed because she nodded emphatically, her strawberry blond bob swinging around her jaw.

"Amelia just pointed out that the impact of designer denim is not just limited to women's jeans, and she's right, especially when it comes to Riley O'Brien & Co.," Shelby said. "Over the past three years, designer denim has pulled male customers away from Rileys. They've abandoned their old favorite."

That statement clearly didn't sit well with the audience because several people began to mutter. Shelby held up her hands in supplication. "Look, I'm not saying that men don't like Rileys anymore."

Shelby eyed the people grouped around the table. "You," she said, pointing at Mateo Morales, the guy in charge of store operations.

Mateo touched his thumb to his chest and asked, "Are you talking to me?"

"Yes. You don't have a girlfriend or a wife," she stated confidently.

Mateo's dark eyebrows crawled up his forehead. "What makes you so sure of that?"

Shelby smiled sweetly. "If you had a woman in your life, she wouldn't have let you out of the house in such a hideous sweater."

Her snarky comment made the whole room crack up. Mateo grinned, completely unoffended by her insult.

"What if I told you that I wear ugly sweaters to get the attention of pretty women?" he asked.

Shelby rolled her eyes before pointing at Leo Damashek. He always looked as if he had just completed a photo shoot for *GQ*.

"You look really good," Shelby complimented Leo. "Who picked out your shirt and blazer?"

Leo grinned. "My fiancée. She picks out all my clothes, and every morning she tells me what to wear."

"You should be ashamed to admit that," Mateo told Leo with a smirk.

Shelby pointed at Mateo again. "You should be ashamed for wearing that sweater. You need to burn it."

Before Mateo could reply, Shelby turned her attention back to the presentation, clicking to the next slide. It showed the total dollar amount of apparel purchases in the U.S. and drilled down into the buyers.

"Women account for the majority of apparel purchases in the nation, and when they buy designer denim for themselves, they also buy it for their husbands, lovers, fathers, and brothers." She raised her hand. "Okay, ladies. Raise your hand if you've ever bought clothing for a man, even a pair of socks."

Every woman in the room held up her hand, everyone but Amelia. Before Quinn could think too much about that mystery, Shelby clicked to the next slide and pointed out a significant shift between Riley O'Brien & Co. and its competitors.

Even though he'd grown up in the business, Quinn was still surprised to see how much Rileys' overall market share had eroded since 2000. Every year it got smaller and smaller.

"Rileys have a midrange price point, and consumers seeking a more upscale look are choosing other brands," Shelby noted. "As a result, Riley O'Brien & Co. is no longer on top."

As Quinn stared at the pie chart on the screen, his head began to pound, the heavy beat drowning out Shelby's voice. His ears rang with the fear he'd suffered since his dad had gotten sick and temporarily turned the company over to him.

Am I the right person for this job? Am I going to wreck something that took four generations of O'Briens to build?

Am I going to destroy my legacy, ruining the chance for my children and grandchildren to be proud of their heritage? Am I going to fail?

Unable to bear the noise in his head, he turned away from the presentation illustrating the slow decline of Riley O'Brien & Co. in colorful pie charts and graphs and walked out of the room.

Chapter 11

TOSSING BACK HIS SECOND GLASS OF WHISKEY, QUINN plunked the barware down on the linen-covered high-top table near his elbow. He wasn't drunk, and he wasn't planning on getting drunk, at least until he got home.

A party to formally announce the partnership between Amelia Winger and Riley O'Brien & Co. definitely was not the right time or the right place for him to get shit-faced. And he had enough self-control not to over-imbibe no matter how much he might want to after that god-awful presentation this afternoon.

He had managed to find a fairly secluded area within Riley Plaza's rooftop garden. He was close enough to hear the mellow rhythm of the jazz band and the muted buzz of conversation, but he hoped he wouldn't attract anyone else looking for conversation.

Exhaling roughly, he leaned his forearms on the table and turned to look out on the city of San Francisco. Even the breathtaking view couldn't pull him from his misery.

Tonight, Riley O'Brien's legacy felt like a burden, the history and tradition making Quinn feel trapped rather than rooted. It wasn't a feeling he was used to, but it was one that had gotten worse over the past few months.

A cool breeze blew across his face, ruffling his hair and

bringing a whiff of the garden. The deep tones of Cal's laughter floated to him, and he turned to look for his brother. His height made him easy to spot, and Quinn experienced an irrational rush of anger when he saw Cal and Amelia together. They were alone, and they stood close to each other.

Way too close.

In one glance, he took in the temptation that was Amelia. Her luscious curves were encased in a close-fitting black sweaterdress that hit well above her knees. The color made her hair look even more vibrant, like a match burning in the dark.

A kelly-green leather belt hung low on her hips, its unique cut-out design drawing attention to her waist, and her feet and legs were covered in a pair of black leather stiletto boots that screamed, "Bend me over and fuck me hard."

If only I could.

Amelia smiled up at Cal, and Quinn clenched his fists when his brother tugged on one of the fiery curls falling across her eye. He had a sudden and intense urge to break his brother's hand, maybe his entire arm, and his blue mood abruptly turned black.

He told himself he wasn't jealous. He had no right to be. But if Amelia was off-limits to him, if he couldn't touch her because it would be unprofessional and jeopardize their working relationship, then his goddamn brother sure as hell couldn't put his hands on her, either.

Quinn stalked down the path toward them, his cowboy boots making a hollow noise against the pavers. At the sound, they both looked in his direction. When Amelia saw his face, she took a step back, but Cal merely raised his eyebrows.

"Hey, brother."

Before Quinn could ask what the hell they were doing, Cal's phone vibrated. His brother held up a finger and grabbed the phone from his pocket.

"I need to take this," he said, reviewing the screen. "Excuse me, Amelia."

Cal turned on his heel and headed back along the path, leaving Quinn alone with Amelia. He looked down at her.

She obviously wanted to follow Cal because she was edging away from him. Reaching out, he wrapped his hand around her forearm, not hard, but tight enough to keep her from going anywhere. The sleeve of her dress was soft, maybe cashmere, and he clenched his fingers in it.

"Why don't you stay here and talk to me for a while."

He'd phrased it as a demand rather than a request. She glanced down at his hand before bringing her dark eyes back to him. Her cheeks were pink like the asters bordering the walking path.

"Okay."

Her voice was soft, softer than he'd ever heard it, and it raised the fine hairs on the back of his neck. He led her to the table where he'd stood before. He would have preferred more privacy, but it was the best he was going to get.

"Thank you for the party, Quinn. It's incredible."

He ignored her words of gratitude. "What were you and Cal doing?"

His question came out in a low growl, fiercer than it should be. He might not like or understand the aggression coursing through him, but it was there nonetheless.

She frowned at his tone. "Talking and walking." Then she smiled suddenly, winsomely, her lips plump and rosy. "I can do both at the same time."

Her response startled him so much he let out a sharp bark of laughter. "That requires real talent." He rested his arm on the table. "What were you talking about?"

"Shelby's presentation."

He slanted a narrow-eyed look toward her. "And what did you think? Are you sorry now that you took on this project?" he asked, his voice much harsher than he had intended.

She looked at him intently. "No," she said slowly. "Not at all."

"We must not have been at the same presentation."

He could hear the defeat in his own voice, and he was suddenly, horribly ashamed. She moved closer to him, and he caught a whiff of something sweet that reminded him of Christmas cookies. She placed her hand on top of his on the table, and he studied it, small and white with a smattering of freckles. Her nails were short and painted a pale pink, and she had calluses on a couple of her fingers.

"I can understand why it upset you," she said, gazing at him sympathetically.

He grimaced. Upset didn't really describe how shitty he felt.

She squeezed his hand. "That research told us how things are today. But things can change. *You* can change them." She paused to let her words sink in. "What people think about Rileys today doesn't have to be what they think about them tomorrow or five years from now."

Quinn was shocked by her absolute confidence in him and his ability to change the course of Riley O'Brien & Co.'s future. Everything had always come easily to him: grades, sports, women, success, money. With minimal effort, he had obtained things most people wanted desperately but never actually received.

Hard work didn't scare him, and he didn't mind getting down in the trenches with his employees, but was that enough? His life-long confidence had deserted him, and he wasn't sure he had what it would take to change the direction Riley O'Brien & Co. was heading.

When he didn't respond, she sighed softly. "You should think about the connection between consumers and Rileys as a long-term relationship," she suggested. "People who've been married for fifty years don't feel the same about their spouses every day of their lives together. They go through ups and downs, periods of intense attraction and extreme irritation. They fall in and out of love."

He thought about Amelia's analogy. Could American consumers, especially women, fall in love with Rileys again? Was it really that simple?

He stared into Amelia's dark eyes. The phrase "fall in and out of love" echoed in his head, and he felt strangely innervated.

With her encouraging words, she had freed him from the horrible despair that had choked him for the past several hours. His black mood was gone.

Poof.

But now there was something even more dangerous in its place: desire.

Her hand was still on his, and he swore he could feel the heat of her touch radiating throughout his entire body. He took a deep breath, battling the urge to move closer to her.

He pulled his eyes from hers, and his gaze dropped to the pale skin exposed by the V neck of her dress. She wore a silver necklace with translucent green and blue beads, and one of them had found its way into her creamy cleavage. As he stared at that lucky bead, his blood grew hotter, running thickly through his veins toward his cock.

His brain and his body disconnected, and he saw his hand move toward her, fingers spread.

Don't do it! Don't touch her!

His fingers stroked the warm skin of her throat, her pulse throbbing against his thumb. Her skin was so soft, so warm, he imagined she could heat all the cold places inside him.

Wrapping his hand around the back of her neck, he pulled her closer. She stumbled a little in her high-heeled boots, and he steadied her with a hand on her hip.

When he felt that beautiful curve within his grasp, the blood drained from his head, along with every bit of sense he possessed. With his intellect obliterated, his primal self was in control, and it wanted more.

Right now.

AMELIA QUIVERED WHEN QUINN GRABBED HER HIP WITH HIS big hand. The heat of it sent a trail of sparks directly to her center, where she had turned damp and hot. Off-balance, she reached out, and he was close enough for her to clutch his lean waist, the tips of her fingers grazing his leather belt.

He moved closer, crowding her against the round high-top table. The pressure of his hand on her throat forced her to lean her head back, and she stared into his face, twilight shadowing the sharp angles of his cheekbones and his full lips. Dark stubble covered his jaw, and she fought the urge to cup his cheek so she could feel the sharp prickles against her palm.

Quinn wasn't the most handsome man she'd ever met, but he fired up her senses in ways she had never experienced. She could smell him all around her, a mix of his cologne, somehow woodsy and citrusy at the same time, and his own unique scent.

She was drowning in Quinn, and she wanted to push her nose into the hollow of his neck and breathe in until her lungs were full of him. She wanted to find the place where his scent was strongest and place her tongue against it, licking until she could taste his essence.

She felt Quinn's gaze on her chest, which rose and fell rapidly from her shallow breaths. She shivered when his fingers trailed down her throat, tracing her necklace until he reached the large bead hanging between her breasts. Gently, he touched it, rolling it across the delicate skin of her cleavage. As his fingers grazed her skin, he blew out a rough breath.

His fingers clenched her hip, and he lowered his head, nuzzling the underside of her jaw before moving up. She gasped when he gave a small lick to the corner of her mouth and turned her head so she could taste him, no longer caring about all the reasons it was a stupid idea.

"Amelia? Are you back here?"

At the sound of Teagan's voice, Amelia jerked away from Quinn, and he slowly released her hip. He glanced over her head, and she cast a frantic look over her shoulder, worried Teagan had seen them together. She was relieved she couldn't see the other woman yet. But she could hear her footsteps.

Quinn moved to the other side of the table, its long linen drape blocking his lower body from anyone who might come down the walking path. She knew it was a deliberate move since she'd felt his erection against her stomach.

Casually leaning his elbow against the table, he picked up his empty glass as if he hadn't had his hands all over her just seconds ago. He looked completely calm and collected, distressingly gorgeous in his charcoal-colored suede blazer and gray-striped dress shirt.

Amelia resented how easily he had put the past few minutes behind him. In comparison, she was an emotional and physical mess. Her ears rang, and she could feel the heat in her cheeks and across her upper chest.

She knew her skin was an ugly, mottled pink, the curse of being a fair-skinned, freckled redhead. And maybe it was her imagination, but she smelled him on her skin, and she still felt the imprint of his tongue where it had laved the corner of her mouth.

She glared at him, and in response, he raised an eyebrow as if he had no idea why she was upset. *The jerk!*

She turned away from her tormenter with the intention of meeting Teagan, but the other woman was already within sight and heading toward them with brisk steps. She pasted a fake smile on her face, hoping Teagan either couldn't tell the difference or at least wouldn't notice.

Teagan grinned when she saw them. "Cal said he'd left you two back here a while ago."

Reaching the table, she pointed at Amelia, her fingernails a bold and aggressive red. "This is your party, Amelia. You can run, but you can't hide," she teased.

Despite the lingering tension from her interaction with Quinn, Amelia laughed. "I wasn't running or hiding," she denied.

She eyed Quinn. Night had fallen over the city, and despite the festive lightbulbs strung around the garden and the glow from nearby buildings, she couldn't see the expression on his face.

He straightened abruptly, acknowledging his sister with a brief, unfriendly nod. "I'm going to get another drink," he bit out, quickly making his way from the table with a long-legged, masculine stride that made her mouth go dry.

Teagan stared after Quinn, a small crease between her brows. "What's his problem?"

Amelia hesitated before answering. Her first instinct was to keep her discussion with Quinn private, but then she realized his distress over Shelby's presentation could present an opportunity. Now that he realized the seriousness of the situation, he might be willing to embrace Teagan's plan to revamp the women's division, and they wouldn't have to go behind his back.

"He's upset by the information Shelby presented today."

"He should be."

Amelia frowned at Teagan's tone. It was not only devoid of any sympathy but downright frosty. She felt compelled to defend Quinn, although she had no idea why.

"I think he was truly surprised by the results of the research. I don't think he realized how much the competition had eroded the company's market share, and not just for the women's division."

"He shouldn't have been surprised. I've been telling him

the same thing since he took over when my dad got sick. He just chose to ignore me because he's an arrogant ass."

She bristled at Teagan's description of Quinn. "Well, he realizes it now, and I think we should look at this as an opportunity to share your plan—"

"No," she said sharply. "Absolutely not."

"But I think he'd be willing to listen now."

Teagan stared at Amelia, her eyes cool behind her black-framed glasses. "There's no discussion, Amelia. I hired you to redesign our women's jeans, and you agreed to do it. You knew Quinn wasn't on board, and I'm not sure why you suddenly have a problem with our agreement." She paused meaningfully. "Of course you still have the option of not being involved with Riley O'Brien & Co. in any way."

Teagan's warning was clear, and Amelia tensed, unsure how to respond. Everything Teagan had said was true.

"I know my brother, and his feelings on the subject haven't changed, regardless of that presentation. Trust me. We need to stick to the plan, and when the designs are complete and you have samples, we can present them to him as a done deal."

A cool breeze swept across the rooftop, and Amelia shivered. She didn't have a good feeling about this project any longer. But she knew she couldn't walk away from this opportunity, not when it would give her everything she'd ever wanted.

She decided it was well past time to return to the party. "We should head back," she suggested, and Teagan nodded her agreement.

As they made their way back to the party, Amelia thought about what Teagan had interrupted. She was appalled she had just stood there and let Quinn touch her.

She growled beneath her breath, and Teagan glanced sharply at her. She summoned a smile and a plausible lie.

"My feet hurt."

"Yeah, those boots rock, but you're going to be in some serious pain later tonight."

Amelia was glad to hear Teagan's voice had lost some of its edge. She didn't want their relationship to be tense. They had reached the area where the bar and band were situated, and Teagan touched Amelia's elbow to get her attention.

"Are we on the same page?"

Amelia nodded but was unable to speak because several people had made their way over to the two of them, eager to meet her. With a smile on her face, she answered their questions and participated in casual chitchat, but the whole time she talked, her eyes scanned the garden for Quinn.

She finally spied him leaning with his back against the living wall, his booted feet crossed at the ankles and his arms over his chest. He was more tempting than the most decadent caramel brownies, and even though she tried to resist their chocolaty goodness, she always gave in.

And that wasn't the worst of it. When she finally gave in, she was never satisfied with just a little taste. She always had to have the whole thing.

Yum.

Chapter 12

QUINN TOSSED THE BASEBALL UP AND GRABBED IT OUT OF THE air as it came back down toward his face. He was stretched out on his beloved denim sofa, his feet propped on the armrest and crossed at the ankles.

It was his favorite thinking position and, God knew, he had plenty to think about. He threw the ball over and over, hoping the monotonous movement would calm him, physically and mentally.

Yesterday had not been one of his best days, and he cringed when he thought about the time he'd spent with Amelia in the garden. She had done her best to make him feel better during the party, and he'd repaid her efforts by grabbing her and squeezing her and licking her . . .

Damn. He had to stop thinking about Amelia and all the dirty things he wanted to do to her, or do with her since he'd really prefer her participation.

On the way to work this morning, he'd had a long talk with himself. He explained that Amelia was a crucial element of Riley O'Brien & Co.'s future success, and that scaring her off with his Neanderthal behavior was a big no-no.

Recalling Cal's suggestion about keeping her happy, he

had decided to buy her a gift. He had taken a long lunch and made the trip to nearby Union Center to visit the Williams-Sonoma there. He spent almost forty minutes reviewing the juicing machines on display and quizzing the customer service rep about the difference between a slow juicer and a regular one before making his purchase.

He'd walked out of the store with the best juicer on the market, or so the rep had assured him. Supposedly this model worked equally well on crisp fruits and vegetables without mangling softer produce.

He grunted. Who knew juicing was so complicated?

Quinn placed the baseball in the crook of his elbow and pulled back his cuff to look at his watch. Six thirty p.m. She should be back in the penthouse by now.

Rising from the sofa, he placed the baseball back in its holder and hefted the cardboard box that held the juicer. He had three bags of organic produce in his Audi, but he hadn't been able to carry in everything when he'd returned from lunch. He would have to go back down and get those later.

The trip to the thirty-second floor took less than a minute. Bracing the box against the penthouse's door to free one of his hands, he knocked loudly. He didn't hear any movement from inside, so he repeated the motion, this time with more force.

Nothing.

He dropped his head against the maple door. He'd thought about Amelia all day, almost to the point of obsession, which wasn't like him at all. And now he felt like a kid who had waited in line *forever* for an ice cream cone only to drop it the minute he had it in his hands.

He stood there for a moment, wondering if he should take the juicer back downstairs or let himself into the penthouse and drop it off. If he waited to give it to her, he'd be able to witness her excitement when she saw it. If he let himself in, he could unpack the juicer, and she would have a nice surprise when she finally arrived.

He smiled at the thought of surprising her and quickly keyed in the code to open the door. The penthouse was designed in a large, open floor plan. The kitchen, dining, and living areas flowed together, flanked on both sides by a bedroom and en suite bathroom.

Once inside, he made his way to the kitchen, which was separated from the dining area by a long granite bar. A matching island split the kitchen, and that's where he unloaded the box.

Pulling a Swiss Army knife from the front pocket of his jeans, he sliced open the box and got to work unpacking the juicer. He'd just placed it on the island when he heard a high-pitched scream from behind him.

Startled, he spun around to see Amelia standing in the dining area wearing a fuzzy, pink robe. Her long hair was in soggy spirals around her face, her mouth was open in a big O, and her eyes were bugged out with surprise.

Shit. She was here, and he'd obviously just scared her to death.

"It's just me," he said and then wanted to roll his eyes at the stupidity of that statement.

When she didn't respond, he held up his arms like she was a police officer who'd just shouted, "hands up." He rushed to explain. "I'm sorry. I knocked. Loudly. When you didn't answer, I thought you weren't here. So I let myself in. I wanted to surprise you—"

She'd clearly found her voice because she interrupted him. "I'd say you were successful," she said dryly. "What are you doing here, Quinn?"

Dropping his arms back down to his sides, he leaned his butt against the island, trying to look as nonthreatening as possible. "I brought you a gift. But now I have a much greater appreciation for the wise person who first realized that no good deed goes unpunished."

AMELIA COULDN'T HELP BUT LAUGH AT THE MIX OF CHAGRIN and embarrassment on Quinn's face. She turned back toward the bedroom.

"Give me a second to get dressed, and you can show me the gift," she tossed over her shoulder. "Then I'll decide if you need to be punished."

Once inside the bedroom, she leaned against the door and tried to calm her furiously beating heart. She hadn't heard his knocks, and the last thing she'd expected to see when she had walked out of the bathroom was a man in the kitchen.

That had been more than enough to get her heart racing. But her heart had nearly burst from her chest when she had realized she was naked under her robe, and the object of her X-rated fantasies stood less than ten feet away.

Pushing herself away from the door, she grabbed a pair of stretchy yoga pants from the dresser along with a T-shirt and hoodie. She started to pull on the pants before she realized she hadn't put on any underwear.

Geez, get a grip, Amelia!

Hopping on one leg, she extricated herself from the black pants before jerking open another drawer. She rummaged through it until she found a pair of panties and an underwire bra—her girls needed every bit of help they could get—and slipped on the pieces of stretchy lace before pulling on the rest of her clothes.

Whew!

Now she needed to do something with her hair. Left to dry naturally, it would end up a kinky, frizzy mess, and there was no way she was going to let Quinn O'Brien see that horror show. She contained her curls with a pair of enamel chopsticks and a quick twist.

Quinn had his back to her when she returned to the dining area. He wore a maroon waffle-knit Henley that hugged his broad shoulders and his requisite Rileys. The shirt ended just below his waist, and she was able to get a quick look at his butt before he turned around.

Oh, mama.

Why did he pay Nick Priest to model Rileys when he had the goods? She thought she might need to fan herself.

Deciding not to tempt herself by moving any closer, she leaned her elbows against the bar. "So, do you break into women's homes often?"

He smiled, showing his even, white teeth. Obviously, his parents had sprung for braces. "No. Usually they beg me to come in."

She snorted. She had no doubt his dates were more than happy to progress from good-night kisses to good-night gropes and beyond.

"I'm not sure this penthouse has enough room for you, me, and your ego."

He laughed before beckoning her toward him. "Come see what I brought you."

Edging around the bar, she came to stand next to him. "Oooh," she breathed. "You bought me a Breville Juice Fountain Duo."

She ran her hand across the juicer's stainless steel body. Quinn might be the star of her lusty daydreams, but the Breville was a supporting cast member. Her juicer at home wasn't nearly as nice, and she couldn't wait to get this one alone.

He moved closer until they touched from shoulder to hip. She looked up at him, and he stared into her eyes.

"Do you like it?"

"Yes, so much."

He let out a breath like he'd been afraid of her answer before smiling boyishly. "It's a combination welcome gift and an apology for last night."

She tensed. She didn't want to think about last night and how close she'd come to doing something very stupid.

"I also have some fruit and vegetables for you in my car."

She was stunned. He'd not only bought her an expensive juicer, but he had remembered to buy the ingredients she needed to use it?

She had to lock her knees to keep from jumping into his arms and wrapping her legs around his waist. Except for Ava Grace, no one had ever done anything this nice for her. In fact, she'd never received a gift from anyone other than her best friend.

When she just stood there silently, he said, "So, no punishment?"

She shook her head. "Hardly. You deserve a reward for being so thoughtful."

"A reward, huh?" he asked, his eyes gleaming with blue fire from the overhead can lights.

His look made warmth trickle through her. "I can see that you have something in mind. What?"

"Dinner. Tonight." He cleared his throat. "With me," he clarified as if he were worried she would misunderstand his invitation.

She knew she shouldn't go. This was exactly what she had worried about. She feared her fascination with Quinn and her desire to spend time with him would derail her career goals.

"I don't think that's a good idea. It's late and—"

He interrupted her. "It's only seven thirty." He looked closely at her. "Do you have other plans?"

At that moment, Amelia wished she had taken Teagan up on her offer for dinner. She thought about lying but then admitted she didn't have anything else to do.

"Then what were you planning to eat?"

She shrugged. "I hadn't really thought about it."

"Think about it now," Quinn urged. "We can go somewhere close by, somewhere casual. You don't even have to change."

She really wanted to spend more time with him, but she couldn't risk a repeat of what had happened at the party.

"I have dinner with business partners and colleagues all the time," he said. "It's not a big deal."

Finally, she nodded her acceptance. "Okay."

He smiled slowly, obviously pleased she'd given in. "Don't forget your shoes, Juice," he advised, christening her with a new nickname.

Chapter 13

QUINN TOOK AMELIA TO A SMALL PIZZERIA NEAR RILEY PLAZA. He'd promised casual and close by, and he had delivered.

When he had made his way to the penthouse earlier, he'd had no intention of inviting Amelia to dinner. He was a big boy, and he knew better than to play with fire. And after last night, he had no doubt she would burn him alive.

But once he'd seen her again, he had been eager to spend more time with her. He had dreaded the thought of going back downstairs and heading home to his empty house, and he'd felt an overwhelming sense of relief when she had agreed to dinner.

She sat across from him in the wood-backed booth, studying the leather-encased menu. Her dusky purple T-shirt and matching hooded jacket made her red hair look darker. It was finally drying from her earlier shower, and ringlets were springing out around her face.

Her head was tilted down, and he evaluated the two black things anchoring her topknot. Damned if they didn't look like pieces from the game pick-up sticks. He'd seen Teagan wear similar hair ornamentation, and the vagaries of women's fashion baffled the hell out of him.

With Amelia fully occupied with the menu, he took

advantage of the opportunity to study her. He'd told her to take her time getting ready, but he could tell by the constellation of freckles on her face she hadn't put on any makeup. They were more obvious than usual, and his fingers itched with the need to trace them, especially the ones on the crests of her cheeks.

She must have put some kind of gloss on her lips, though, because they were shiny and wet-looking. Clenching his fist against his thigh, he turned his attention from her pink lips because he was getting hard.

This woman had reduced him to a horny teenager, and he didn't know whether he should laugh or get drunk. He decided a couple of glasses of wine wouldn't be amiss.

"Do you want some wine? We could share a bottle," he suggested.

She looked up, pursing her luscious lips. "I don't drink alcohol. But I don't mind if you want to get something."

He stared at her in disbelief. "But you had a drink last night at the party. I saw you," he said, somewhat accusingly.

She shook her head. "Still water and a lime. Fools people into thinking I'm drinking."

He was surprised. Stunned, really. She didn't drink coffee, and she didn't drink alcohol. Was she a member of a church that forbade tasty beverages?

She noticed the expression on his face. "It's not a religious thing," she said, clearly reading his mind. "It's just a personal choice."

He was interested in hearing more about her personal choices, especially when they involved giving up two of life's greatest pleasures. "So what else don't you do?"

He hadn't meant for the question to come out with any sexual overtones, but he wasn't surprised it had. He'd been thinking about sex since he had seen her wrapped in a robe and looking like a Hostess Sno Ball snack cake.

Her russet eyebrows rose. "I have a whole list."

"Tell me." When she looked at him doubtfully, he added, "Please, I really want to know."

And he did. It went beyond mere curiosity. He had an overwhelming urge to understand her, to know what made her tick.

"You already know about the coffee and the alcohol."

He nodded for her to continue. Her sigh indicated she didn't want to pursue this conversation.

"Fine, I'll tell you." She paused, obviously gathering her thoughts. "I don't drink out of straws. I don't swear. I don't open my mail on the day I get it. I don't go to church. And I don't wear orange or any color in the orange family, ever."

He silently considered her list for a moment. "I can see why wearing orange is a don't," he said finally, nodding toward her coppery hair. "But if you don't swear, what do you say when you're angry?"

She shrugged, and he could tell she was embarrassed. "United States presidents."

He was confused. "You say, 'United States presidents,'" he repeated.

"No, I say their names, like John Fitzgerald Kennedy or Franklin Delano Roosevelt."

The thought of Amelia screaming out a president's name in anger put him into hysterics. Who knew why it set him off, but he let out a deep belly laugh like he hadn't enjoyed in months, maybe even years. Since his dad's cancer diagnosis, there hadn't been a lot of laughter in his family, although they all had tried to maintain a positive attitude.

He laughed so hard his eyes watered, and other people in the restaurant stared. The harder he laughed, the pinker Amelia's face became.

"So, let's say you stub your toe, and instead of saying 'damn' or 'shit,' you take our presidents' names in vain," he clarified.

She nodded. "You should try it. It's a good history lesson," she said prissily, which got him going again.

When he had finally stopped chortling and caught his breath, he moved on to another don't that had caught his attention. "Why don't you open your mail on the day it arrives?"

She frowned. "I never agreed to tell you why I don't do certain things."

"Maybe one day you will."

He really hoped she would, although he didn't know why it mattered so much to him that she would trust him with something so personal. "Is that all that's on your list?"

She leaned forward, crossing her arms on the table. The movement drew his attention to the V neck of her shirt where the upper curves of her breasts were visible, and he started to sweat.

"No, that's not all, but it's all I'm going to tell you right now."

Now he was really intrigued. He raised a brow, indicating that he wanted her to continue. She shook her head.

"Why don't you tell me about some of the things *you* don't do?"

"A better question is what haven't I done yet?"

She smiled at his quip but didn't speak. She looked at him expectantly, and he took a few moments before answering her question as honestly as he could.

"I don't eat avocadoes. I don't fly coach. I don't lie to people I love. I don't wear pajamas to bed. I don't have one-night stands." She gave him a skeptical look, compelling him to add "anymore" to his last statement.

She was silent for a moment. "We have some don'ts in common."

"Which ones?"

She sent him an arch look. "What do you think?"

Before Quinn could blink, his mind had conjured up an image of Amelia in *his* bed, sans pajamas. Talk about wishful thinking.

"I'm not going to guess."

She smirked at his cowardice. "I'll give you one. I don't lie to people I love, either."

He nodded his approval. It was a good rule to live by.

"Why no avocadoes?"

"I'm allergic to them. I break out in hives."

It was really too bad since he loved guacamole, but if he didn't resist the temptation, he ended up in the ER. There had been a couple of times when he'd actually thought it was worth it. Of course, he'd been a stupid kid at the time. He was smarter now and had more self-control.

Just keep telling yourself that, chief.

She nodded. "Then that's definitely a good don't."

He realized the whole exercise, which had seemed silly at first, made him feel strangely exposed.

It felt like Amelia knew more about him than anyone he'd

ever dated, and that intimacy sent conflicting emotions of delight and dismay swirling through him. He looked at her and instinctively knew she felt the same way. Fortunately, the server stopped by to take their order, and Quinn was able to direct the conversation to a safer topic.

"I read that you moved to Nashville with Ava Grace after she won *American Star*. Do you like living there?"

She nodded. "Yes, I love it."

"I've only been to Nashville a couple of times, but I really liked it."

"Why did you visit? Business or pleasure?"

"Pleasure. I was visiting Nick Priest. Do you know him?"

"Yes, I know Nick." She smiled, her brown eyes dreamy. "His picture must be in the dictionary beside the words 'eye candy.' "

He felt a surge of irritation at her statement. Did every female on the planet think Nick Priest was God's gift to women?

He groaned. "Not you, too."

She shrugged. "I appreciate a good-looking guy as much as the next girl."

"Do you also appreciate silence?" he joked because Priest rarely spoke. Apparently his lack of verbal skills didn't hurt his standing with the ladies.

She laughed, the husky sound rippling across Quinn's senses. He shifted, trying to lessen the pressure in his jeans. He couldn't believe he was getting a goddamn hard-on while Amelia sat across from him talking about another man.

He took a big swig of his beer, hoping it would cool him down. He desperately tried to concentrate on Amelia's words instead of imagining her propped on the edge of the table with his head between her legs and his tongue against her clit. He caught the end of her sentence—something to do with Ava Grace—and picked up the thread of conversation.

"You and Ava Grace seem to have a unique relationship."

By all accounts, the pair was devoted to one another, and he found their relationship very interesting, what little he knew about it, anyway.

Amelia nodded. "We're each other's biggest fan."

He wondered where her family fit into things. His parents and siblings were his biggest fans. He also had a handful of buddies. Priest was one of those guys, although he didn't talk to Quinn much more than he talked to anyone else.

"When Ava Grace gets compliments on the stuff I've designed for her, she sees it as an invitation to tell everyone how fabulous I am. She's been doing that for most of our lives."

Her comments were heavy with self-deprecation, and that surprised him. He was under the impression her designs were hot commodities, and most fashion designers he knew were well aware of their status.

Before he could delve into that conundrum, their food arrived. They'd decided to share a pepperoni pizza, and the decadent smell wafting from the gooey pie made his mouth water.

He quickly served up a piece to Amelia before placing two slices on his plate. He took a big bite, moaning around a mouthful of cheesy deliciousness. Cheese, any kind of cheese, was his favorite food, hands down.

He looked up to find Amelia staring at him, her own slice of pizza frozen at her lips. He couldn't decipher the look on her face, but he figured she was appalled by his lack of manners. When it came to food (and sex), he tended to be more caveman than gentleman.

AMELIA COULDN'T TAKE HER EYES OFF QUINN'S FACE. HIS REACTION to the pizza gave new meaning to the phrase "making love to your food," and when he'd let out that sexy sound, her panties got damp.

Realizing she had pizza hanging from her mouth, she took a quick bite. It was good, but it wasn't as fantastic as his moans had led her to believe.

They ate in silence for a while, and with her mind left to wander, she had a brief fantasy of what could have happened if Quinn had arrived at the penthouse just a few minutes earlier while she'd been in the shower. She imagined him joining her under the hot water, turning her toward the tile wall, and pressing his tall body against her back before pushing her legs apart and thrusting his hardness inside her.

"Amelia." She glanced up to find Quinn waving his hand in front of her face. "Hey, there you are."

William Jefferson Clinton!

How long had she sat here fantasizing about getting down and dirty with Quinn? She'd known going to dinner with him was a bad idea.

She cleared her throat. "Sorry. I was just lost in how great this pizza tastes."

He smiled. "I'm glad you like it. This is one of my favorite places."

She let her gaze wander around the restaurant. She and Quinn definitely had different ideas of casual.

Although small, the pizzeria was well designed and sported high-end finishes. Metal sconces highlighted the exposed brick walls and gleaming hardwood floors. Pendant lights hung over the booths, which were upholstered in buttery-soft leather.

"It's not as casual as the restaurants I'm used to. Nashville isn't a fancy place."

When she and Ava Grace had been poor teenagers stuck in a dinky, dirty town, they'd had dreams just like all the other people who hated their lives. Amelia had dreamed of studying fashion and eventually moving to New York, and Ava Grace had dreamed of nabbing a record deal and touring with country music stars like Carrie Underwood and Miranda Lambert.

Their dreams had seemed as far away as the moon, especially for girls who bought their clothes at the thrift store and ate peanut butter and jelly sandwiches for most of their meals.

But Amelia and Ava Grace were pragmatists at heart, and while dreams were nice, the two of them had possessed something even better. They'd had plans.

In Amelia's mind, dreams rarely came true, but plans . . . Well, they were a different animal altogether. A smart woman with a good plan and the gumption to stick to it could change her life.

So Amelia and Ava Grace had plotted, devising a plan to move to Nashville. They had considered Austin, but both of them had wanted to get away from Texas and any reminders of the way they'd grown up.

"I stayed with Priest when I visited," Quinn said, "and it seemed pretty fancy to me. Do you live near him?"

She laughed at the thought. Nick's huge house was located in one of the most expensive enclaves in suburban Nashville, a far cry from the home she and Ava Grace shared.

"No. We live way out of the city in an old farmhouse."

Quinn's dark eyebrows rose. "That seems like an odd choice for a country music star and an up-and-coming fashion designer."

"I'd agree, but Ava Grace is not the typical country music star, and I needed room for my workshop."

When she and Ava Grace had first arrived in Nashville, everyone had recommended they rent an apartment downtown or lease a bungalow in one of the trendy neighborhoods where a lot of other musicians lived. But Ava Grace had been insistent that they choose a place with a workshop for Amelia.

"Speaking of workshops, what do you think of the ones at Riley Plaza?" Quinn asked.

"They're fine." She wrinkled her nose. "I'm not a diva, you know."

His oh-so-kissable lips quirked at her statement. "Correct me if I'm wrong, Juice, but during our first meeting you were ready to tell me to fu—kiss off if I didn't agree to let you work in your own workshop."

She smiled when Quinn quickly changed his word choice, obviously respecting her "no swearing." She didn't really mind if other people used bad language; she just wasn't going to.

Her mother had been unable to say a single sentence without dropping the F-bomb, and Amelia had vowed she would do everything she could to *not* be like her mother. That was also the reason why she didn't drink.

"You're a smart guy. You know I can work anywhere. I just thought I'd do my best work in familiar surroundings."

Liar. You were afraid this would happen.

He snapped his fingers. "Finally, you've found something nice to say about me."

Although she laughed at his quip, she was disturbed to realize she could find plenty of nice things to say about him. The more time she spent with him, the more she liked him. And liking him was dangerous.

Spending time with Quinn was like walking along the

edge of a ravine. Sooner or later, she'd stumble and fall, crossing the line from colleagues to . . . something more.

And that would be a disaster. A catastrophe of gigantic proportions.

She didn't want people to think she slept her way to success, but that wasn't the worst of it. The secret deal with Teagan made it impossible for them to be anything more than colleagues, not even friends.

Friends didn't go behind each other's back . . . except for Brutus, of course. He stabbed Julius Caesar in the back—literally. She didn't want to be a Brutus, so she had to keep her distance from Quinn.

He gestured toward their empty plates and the pizza pan. They were bare except for a couple of crumbs.

"I'm kind of disappointed there aren't any leftovers. Now I have to find something else for breakfast."

She chuckled, shaking her head in disbelief. Was he serious? Only college kids ate pizza for breakfast. Adults ate yogurt and egg-white omelets.

"Unbelievable. You eat pizza for breakfast, and you still look like that."

She clamped her mouth shut before she blurted out a truly regrettable comment about what her butt would look like if she made such poor dietary choices. He gazed at her intently.

"Look like what?"

Tall, dark, and handsome, that's what. And he totally knew it.

Their interactions had given her plenty of evidence his self-esteem was healthy. In fact, it was so healthy it probably participated in marathons.

"Please," she scoffed. "You don't need me to stroke your ego."

At the word "stroke," his gaze heated and fell to her lips. When he brought his eyes back to hers, the dark blue irises were nearly obliterated by the pupils. The proof of his arousal made her lightheaded.

"You're right," he said huskily. "My ego's just fine."

Chapter 14

AMELIA TAPPED HER BALLET FLAT AGAINST THE POLISHED CONcrete floor as she waited for Quinn in Riley Plaza's second-floor reception area. After they'd finished dinner at the pizzeria and walked back to the high-rise, he left her at the elevator bank while he detoured to the parking garage to get her fruits and veggies.

She wondered if he had bought any leafy greens like spinach and kale. If not, she might have to make a trip to the store. She would probably need to pick up some coconut water, too, since it was unlikely he'd thought to buy that. If he had, she'd have no choice but to rip off his clothes and have her way with him.

The elevator dinged, and the doors opened to reveal Quinn. His muscular arms held two large canvas bags, and another bag sat on the floor near his feet. All three overflowed with a variety of produce, filling the elevator with the tangy scent of citrus and the sweet aroma of mangoes, peaches, and strawberries.

He beckoned her into the elevator with a tilt of his head. "Get in," he ordered tersely.

She wondered what had happened to make him so cranky. He'd seemed fine at the restaurant.

Once they arrived at the penthouse, she placed her canvas bag on the floor to key in the code. He must have made a serious dent in the produce section, and her bag was so heavy she had to carry it with both arms.

She held the door open for Quinn, and as he passed through it, his forearm brushed against her breasts. She sucked in a breath at the brief contact, and he turned his head sharply toward her. She was sure her desire was obvious on her face, and she averted it, hoping he wouldn't see how much she wanted him.

After returning to the hall to grab her bag of produce, she had just stepped inside when she ran into him. Without a word, he took the bag from her and headed back to the kitchen to deposit it on the island.

She followed behind him, appreciating the way his Rileys hugged his rear. She was a little overheated, so she shrugged out of her purple hoodie and hung it on the back of one of the tall, wooden chairs situated near the bar.

"Thank you so much for the juicer, Quinn. And for the produce. And for dinner."

He didn't respond to her words of gratitude. Instead, he unpacked the bags, disgorging a kaleidoscope of colorful produce onto the granite island. The bright hues of bananas, lemons, oranges, and carrots contrasted sharply with the intense red of strawberries and apples, the deep indigo of blueberries, and the dark green of spinach.

He remembered to buy leafy vegetables!

She moved to the island to help him unload the rest of the goodies, and he stiffened slightly when her arm brushed against his. She looked up, and they stared at each other, barely breathing, until he leaned down. His nose brushed the top of her hair, and he took a deep breath.

"You smell good. What is it?"

The vibrations of his deep voice near her ear made her whole body break out in goose bumps. She was so affected by his nearness she had a hard time pulling in a deep breath.

"Almond oil," she gasped. "I use it on my hair to keep it from getting frizzy."

Shifting closer, he bracketed her body against the island with his arms, enveloping her in his heat. He nuzzled his nose behind her ear before flicking his tongue against the sensitive skin of her nape where several curls nestled. She shivered at the rough wetness, imagining it on other parts of her body.

She sensed his hands near her head moments before he pulled the chopsticks out of her hair. He made a low noise in his throat as it fell in a tangle of curls down her back—a deep growl that made her nipples harden and her knees tremble.

"*Damn,*" he said hoarsely.

Swiftly, he turned her in his arms. Grabbing her around the waist, he hoisted her easily onto the island, making all her lovely fruit and vegetables roll to the floor.

Ignoring the produce carnage, he immediately wrapped his big hands around her rear and pulled her roughly toward him until his erection was wedged between her legs. He was long and hard, and she wanted to press against him.

Cupping her face in his hands, he looked into her eyes. "I tried," he said mysteriously.

She opened her mouth to ask what he was talking about, but before she could get the words out, he slid his hands into her hair and brought his lips to hers.

HE'D TRIED TO KEEP HIS HANDS OFF AMELIA. IN FACT, QUINN had silently lectured himself the entire walk back to Riley Plaza.

She works for you. Do you really want to be one of those bosses? But then his wicked alter ego had whispered in his ear, *She's not officially your employee. She's a business partner. As a business partner, you can touch her as much as you want and anywhere you want.*

Since a very specific part of him had agreed with his clever alter ego, he'd switched gears. *She's a key part of Riley O'Brien's future success. You don't want to endanger the company.* That had done the trick because he would never do anything to jeopardize the legacy his ancestors had entrusted him with.

He'd been ready to say good-bye to Amelia and her produce, no harm done. But then she had stepped on the escalator in front of him, just like the day they'd met. Only this time, it had been so much worse because her stretchy black pants clung to her ass so tightly he could see the cleft between her sweet cheeks.

He'd had to shove his hands in his pockets to keep from reaching out and running his fingers along that enticing crevice, from top to bottom. He was desperate to trace it . . . desperate to cup her mound and feel her heat.

The short trip to his car had allowed him to gain a small measure of control, but then she had brushed up against him in the kitchen. He'd gotten a waft of her scent, so deliciously sweet that his lust made his vision hazy. When he had realized she wanted him, too, his control crumbled like a cookie in the hands of a toddler.

Now that he had his mouth on hers, he was torn between devouring and savoring. He ran his tongue against her bottom lip before sucking gently. She gasped, and he darted his tongue into her mouth. The taste of her was better than he'd imagined, and he couldn't get enough of it.

He slanted his head to delve deeper into her sweetness, holding her captive by weaving his hands into her fragrant hair and tilting her head back. When her tongue met his, he sucked on it lightly. It felt so good he increased the suction, and she moaned loudly.

Lust slammed through him as she wrapped her legs around his hips. Pushing up his shirt, she grasped his back just above the waistband of his Rileys. Her fingernails dug into his skin, the dual pain and pleasure of her touch sending a tingle up and down his spine.

Bright lights exploded behind his eyelids, and blood rushed through his veins, heading straight to his cock. He was sure he'd never been so hard, the buttons on his fly pressing painfully into his length.

He fed her several deep, wet kisses before pulling back and trailing his lips down her neck. He gently bit the tendon where her neck and shoulder met. She whimpered, and he soothed the small bite with his tongue.

"I've been thinking about this since I first saw you," he breathed against her skin.

He leaned back to look at her, his balls tightening at the

sight of her obvious arousal. Her eyes were shut, her cheeks were flushed cherry red, and she was breathing in short pants.

The low neckline of her purple T-shirt contrasted beautifully with her opalescent skin, and the tops of her breasts were dusted with those delicious brown-sugar freckles. He could think of nothing else but putting his mouth on them to see if they were as sweet as they looked.

He dropped openmouthed kisses on her skin, licking and sucking in some places, before trailing his tongue down the valley between her breasts. He'd fantasized about getting his face in her cleavage since that first day in his office.

Grabbing the hem of her T-shirt, he pulled it over her head. He was so glad the lights were on because he wanted to see her. His breath caught in his throat at the first view of her firm breasts. They were encased in aqua-colored lace that played peekaboo with her nipples. He cupped the plump mounds through the stretchy lace before reaching between them to unclasp her bra.

Her breasts spilled out of the lace cups, the nipples puckered with arousal. They were pale pink, and he knew they'd taste just like cotton candy.

Dropping his head, he pulled one into his mouth while his hand played lightly with the other. As he rolled her pebbled nipple over and under his tongue, he realized he'd been right: they were sweet and feather-soft.

"Your nipples taste like sugar," he rasped.

She moaned again, palming his head and pressing his face against her breasts. Releasing her nipple with a soft pop, he brought his attention to the other one, sucking it into his mouth. After several delicious swirls of his tongue, he bit down gently on the tip, making her jerk and pull him even tighter against her.

He burned to be inside her, and as he moved his hand toward the waistband of her pants, he heard a loud thud. Looking down, he saw the coconut water he'd bought lying on its side on the floor, fluid leaking from a puncture on the side of the carton.

"*Shit.*"

His curse opened Amelia's eyes, and she turned her head

to see what he looked at. Glimpsing the mess on the floor, she whispered, “Coconut water, too?”

Since his brain was still in nuclear meltdown, and his cock was hard enough to drill through the Earth’s crust, it took him a moment to answer. “Yeah. The woman at Williams-Sonoma told me that most juice recipes call for it, so I put it on my list. . . .”

Amelia shifted on the hard countertop, and he forgot what he was saying. Her bra still hung off her shoulders, her breasts displayed delightfully to his gaze. When she saw where his eyes had settled, she blushed, and he watched in fascination as color swept across her chest, shading the pale curves of her breasts a dusky pink.

Grasping the edges of her bra, she deftly clasped it before lowering her gaze to the floor. He assumed she was embarrassed, so he focused on cleaning up the spilled coconut water. As he knelt down to pick up the carton, he heard something that made his heart skip a beat.

“I think you bruised them.”

He lurched to his feet. *Jesus, was I too rough with her?*

Moving in front of her, he gently grasped her shoulders so he could peer down into her face. “I hurt you?”

“What?”

“You just said they were bruised. How badly did I hurt you?”

The thought of injuring Amelia, even accidently, made him sick to his stomach, and nausea rose in the back of his throat. She stared at him blankly before bursting into nearly hysterical laughter.

“Oh, Quinn,” she choked out between her giggles. “I was talking about the fruit that fell to the floor.”

Chapter 15

AMELIA GRABBED THE REMOTE AND INCREASED THE VOLUME on the big-screen TV in the penthouse's living area. The weather segment was coming on next, and she wanted to see if it would be a good day to fly.

After Quinn had left the penthouse last night, she'd decided to go home for the weekend. Her schedule was fairly empty because she had wanted to spend some time today on the first draft of designs for the new line of accessories.

She had planned to stay in San Francisco through the weekend, but she really needed to get away from here. To be more accurate, she needed to get away from Quinn, a.k.a. her biggest almost-mistake.

She was running, and she wasn't ashamed to admit it. No, she was ashamed about something else—the fact that she'd been half-naked and moaning on the kitchen island.

If she hadn't been so appalled by her behavior, she might have been quite in awe of herself. She'd never had an adventurous sex life. In fact, calling her brief and meaningless carnal experiences a sex life was grossly inaccurate, and it was kind of nice to know she could lose herself to passion.

But losing herself to passion with *Quinn* was unacceptable. Not only did he have too much influence over her career; she lied to him every time she looked at him or spoke to him.

She knew a lot of people had sexual relationships with coworkers, colleagues, and other assorted business partners. She had never wanted to go down that path, and she didn't know if she admired or pitied the people who were willing to risk their professional lives for a little nookie, no matter how good it was.

She wanted her relationships to be free of conflict and lacking in drama. She'd had too much of that as a child, and the word "boring" didn't mean the same thing to her as it meant to other people.

More important, entering into a personal relationship with Quinn while she worked behind his back was abhorrent to her. It was something her mother would have done, and she didn't want to commit that kind of character suicide.

Plopping down on the leather sofa, she tucked her feet under her as she stared at the TV screen. Why was the news anchor talking about penguins? Who cared about penguins? Where was the weather?

She pulled one of the decorative pillows to her chest, her nipples peaking when its softness brushed against them. "Dwight David Eisenhower," she muttered.

Her body had yet to recover from the extreme arousal Quinn had ignited last night. Even though she knew it was stupid and selfish, she wished he'd finished the job before the coconut water had fallen to the ground.

She knew Quinn was just as shaken as she was by what had happened on the kitchen island. He'd said only one thing before he had skedaddled from the penthouse: "Coconut water is really sticky." To which she had replied: "It has more potassium than a banana."

She was *so* glad they'd tackled that awkward conversation. Uh-huh.

Finally the weather came on, distracting her from thoughts of Quinn. The forecast was clear so there was no reason to dillydally.

Rising from the sofa, she made her way to the kitchen to grab some juice. As usual, she had made it first thing when she'd woken up. She liked for it to chill in the fridge while she answered her emails, showered, and dressed for the day.

Today, however, she was still in her favorite pajamas, which were printed with bacon and eggs. Ava Grace had bought them for her, a gift of whimsy from one pragmatist to another.

She had just poured herself a glass of juice when she heard a hard knock on the door. It was still early, just a few minutes after eight o'clock, and she froze, worried it might be Quinn.

She had no intention of letting him inside this penthouse ever again. In fact, she preferred to limit their interactions to locales where it was unlikely she'd end up topless.

A quick look through the peephole revealed Teagan on the other side of the door. Relieved, she opened the door, greeting her with a smile.

"Want to come in? I was just about to have some juice, and I'm willing to share."

Teagan wrinkled her nose. "It depends on what kind of juice. Ava Grace told me that you drink beets, and if that's what you have on tap this morning, then, heck no, I don't want any. If you're talking about normal juice, then, yes, thank you, I'd love some."

She laughed. "No beets, I promise."

Teagan followed Amelia to the kitchen before hopping on one of the barstools. She looked expectantly toward Amelia.

"Hit me," she said, slapping the bar like she was in an Old West saloon.

Amelia poured another glass of juice and slid it along the countertop to Teagan. Her blue eyes, which were so much like Quinn's, widened as she took a tentative sip.

"This is really good," she praised before taking a larger swallow.

"You shouldn't have doubted me."

Teagan frowned. "You made this? How?"

She pointed to the juicer in answer. She had placed it next to the sink so she could admire its sleek lines.

Teagan stared at the stainless steel appliance. "Where did that come from?" Her eyebrows rose. "Did you bring that thing all the way from Nashville?"

"Of course not."

Amelia was hesitant to tell Teagan where the juicer had come from. Surely she would wonder why Quinn had given her a gift.

Left with no other choice, Amelia disclosed the source of her newfound joy. "Quinn gave it to me."

"My brother?"

She sighed in exasperation. "Yes, your brother. Is there another Quinn lurking nearby?"

Teagan frowned. "How did he know you're a juicing fanatic?"

"We talked about it."

Teagan's face cleared. "Oh, I get it. His assistant usually orders the welcome gifts for our guests, and Quinn probably told him to get you a juicer instead of the usual wine basket. Jeff always signs Quinn's name on the card."

Her pleasure in the juicer diminished. But her spirits rebounded when she remembered Quinn had mentioned talking with a woman at Williams-Sonoma.

"Quinn picked it out, not his assistant," she blurted without thinking. "And he gave the juicer to me in person."

She had a naughty image of what else he'd given to her *in person.*

Teagan's mouth fell open in shock. "He picked it out," she repeated. "I find that hard to believe. Quinn wouldn't know a juicer from a food processor. Cal's the chef in our family." Her eyes narrowed. "He gave it to you in person? When?"

Amelia wanted to kick herself for inviting more questions, but she had no choice but to answer. "Last night. He dropped by the penthouse."

Her face burned as she recalled what she and Quinn had done amid all the fruit and vegetables. She had no doubt a mediocre comedian could make all kind of jokes out of that scenario, starting with "What happens when you mix fruit and sex? A fruit cock-tail. Get it?"

Too bad she wasn't laughing.

"Did you have juice for dinner?"

"No, Quinn invited me out, and we went to a pizza place a couple of blocks away," Amelia admitted.

It wasn't a secret that she and Quinn had shared dinner. Plus, Teagan would have found out anyway.

Teagan studied her for a moment. "Why are you still wearing your pajamas? You've been at work every day this week before eight."

She looked down at the granite countertop. "I've decided to fly home for a few days."

When Teagan didn't reply, Amelia looked up. "I'm coming back," she reassured her. "I'll be back in the office on Tuesday. Wednesday at the latest."

Teagan had a speculative look on her face that she found slightly alarming. "I thought you planned to stay here with no breaks."

Amelia could feel her face turning red. Could she look any guiltier?

"Yes, but I changed my mind."

"Does Quinn know you're flying back to Nashville?"

"No. I didn't even think to ask him if it was okay."

"Oh, I'm sure he'll understand."

Amelia could have sworn she saw a tiny smile on Teagan's glossy lips before the brunette jumped down from the barstool.

"I need to run. Thanks for the juice."

And she was gone before Amelia could reply.

"YOU'RE HERE EARLY."

Quinn looked up from his monitor to see Teagan standing in his doorway. "So are you."

Entering his office, she took a seat in front of his desk. She crossed her legs, giving him a glimpse of her thigh through the slit on her dress.

He quickly averted his eyes. It was too early in the morning for an accidental flashing from his younger sister. He might go blind.

"How long have you been here?"

He checked the clock on his computer screen. "A couple of hours."

"Me, too. We must have come in about the same time."

Despite the early hour, she looked bright-eyed and bushy-tailed, as his dad liked to say. Her dress, which was the color of a ripe apricot, was the perfect foil for her dark hair. It brought to mind Amelia's claim that she didn't wear orange or any color in the orange family. He figured apricot fell into that category.

He knew he looked like shit. Or, to quote his dad again, he looked like bear shit after a long hibernation. Last night he'd stuck around the penthouse long enough to help Amelia clean up the mess before making a quick exit.

He couldn't even remember what he'd said to her. And if she stood in front of him right now, he didn't know if he would ask for forgiveness or demand a kiss.

He hadn't made it home until nearly midnight, and he'd been way too hyped up to sleep, so he had watched ESPN for an hour. When that hadn't worked, he had gone for a punishing run, finally stumbling up the stairs to his Victorian around two in the morning.

Unfortunately, the long run hadn't cleared his head. Nor had it exhausted him enough to prevent an erection as soon as he slid into bed and his mind drifted to Amelia. He'd finally given in, wrapping his hand around his cock and moaning her name when he came.

At the memory, he rubbed both his hands over his face. Propping his elbows on his desk, he rested his head in his hands.

Amelia had done something to him. He didn't know what, exactly, and he didn't know where to go from here.

Teagan stared at him, a speculative expression on her face. "Are you okay, Quinn?"

He sighed. "I only got three hours of sleep. I'm tired."

She made a sympathetic sound. "You have a big job. And it's going to get even bigger now that Daddy has decided not to come back to work."

"I know."

He wished his dad had made a different decision, but he understood why he hadn't. Even though his cancer was in remission, James still tired easily. More important, his dad no longer had the same passion for his work.

No one outside of the family knew James had decided to retire. Quinn wasn't sure when his dad would make the official announcement.

"Do you ever worry you devote so much time and energy to this company you'll never find someone special?" Her eyes were locked on his. "I think about it a lot. I don't want to be a party of one anymore."

An image of Amelia popped into his head, and he scowled. "What's with the introspection, T? Isn't it a little early in the day to talk about our life goals?"

"I heard you and Amelia went out to dinner."

It took him a moment to catch up with the new direction of the conversation. One of Teagan's best negotiating skills was her ability to change the subject abruptly, catching people off guard.

"Where did you hear that?"

"Amelia. I stopped by earlier this morning to check in with her before the day got too crazy." She smoothed the skirt of her dress. "She shared some of the freshly squeezed juice she made with the juicer you bought her."

He tried to think of something to say that wouldn't incriminate him. "That was nice of her."

"It was nice of *you* to give Amelia something she'd like instead of the generic welcome basket. In fact, it was a really thoughtful gift. It's something I would never have imagined you'd do."

Quinn was offended by her assessment of him. "I'm thoughtful," he countered, raising his hand and ticking off examples of his largesse. "I remember your birthday. I've never forgotten Mother's Day, and I always bring Cal truffles whenever I'm close to his favorite chocolatier."

"We're your family, and you love us. Plus, you know Daddy would beat you within an inch of your life if you forgot Mother's Day." She leaned forward, her manner changing. "Since when do you buy a juicer for a woman?" Her tone was both accusing and incredulous. "Isn't that in the bachelor rulebook—thou shalt not buy household appliances—for fear of sending the wrong message?"

His mood, which hadn't been all that great to start with, soured. He wasn't going to suffer through a lecture from his younger sister because he'd done something *nice*.

"You've got one more minute before I kick your ass out of here," he warned.

She held up her hands. "I just thought you might want to know Amelia's flying home to Nashville today."

Blood rushed from his head, and he heard a roaring sound in his ears. He thought it might be his pulse.

"What?"

He was obviously having trouble with comprehension. He could have sworn his sister had said Amelia was leaving.

"She's leaving," Teagan said, enunciating each word.

"No, you're wrong. She's supposed to be here for two more weeks."

"Well, she changed her mind."

When he realized what Teagan had actually said, he vaulted out of his seat. If he had to, he'd tie Amelia to a chair in the penthouse to keep her from leaving him.

Wait, what? She wasn't leaving *him.* She was just going back home, where she belonged.

"Amelia said she'd be back on Tuesday."

His pulse returned to normal when Teagan disclosed that important detail. He was so relieved he was a little light-headed, and he grabbed the back of his chair. He'd almost forgotten Teagan was still in his office until she spoke.

"Quinn, it's obvious something is going on between you and Amelia."

With an intent expression, she waited for him to respond. Unfortunately for her, he had nothing to say.

"Your minute was up a while ago," he said, pointing toward the door. "This conversation is over."

She must have known he meant business because she left his office without another word. He dropped into his chair, leaning his head back to look at the ceiling. He studied the exposed ductwork while his mind tried to make sense of the mess he'd made.

Should he go up to the penthouse and talk to Amelia? If he did, what would he say? "I'm sorry I ripped off your shirt" or "I'm sorry we were interrupted. Now let me take off your panties"?

He groaned, pressing his palms against his eyes. Maybe it was better if he just left her alone. He snorted. There was no maybe about it. It *was* better if he just left her alone.

He just wasn't sure he could.

Chapter 16

"HOW'S THE PRESSURE? WOULD YOU PREFER IT DEEPER? Harder?"

Moaning from the pleasure, Amelia closed her eyes in bliss. "*Ooh*. It's perfect now."

"As you wish, Miss Winger," the massage therapist replied, continuing to stroke and knead her shoulders and upper back with strong hands.

Amelia was ensconced in a treatment room in Beaubelle, one of the most exclusive spas in Nashville, and Ava Grace relaxed on a massage table less than a foot away.

"Thank you for arranging this," Amelia said.

"You needed it," Ava Grace murmured.

Amelia had texted Ava Grace before she'd boarded the plane yesterday to let her know she was returning to Nashville for a long weekend. When she'd woken up this morning, her best friend had announced she had booked them for a spa day. She couldn't think of a better way to spend her Saturday.

The soothing sound of chimes filtered from speakers cleverly hidden in the ceiling, and the air was perfumed with frangipani massage oil. Amelia and Ava Grace enjoyed the diligent ministrations of their therapists for several minutes before Ava Grace broke the restful silence.

"Why don't you tell me what's wrong, Millie."

Amelia hesitated, not sure where to begin. Should she start with Teagan's threat to fire her if she told Quinn about the redesign? Or should she go straight to Quinn's thoughtful gift and everything that had happened afterward? It was all related.

"I'm afraid I've made a big mistake," Amelia admitted, her voice cracking slightly.

Ava Grace already knew Amelia was involved in two projects for Riley O'Brien & Co., the official project designing the new line of accessories and Teagan's secret project to revamp the entire women's division. She had also already heard about Amelia's meetings with Deda, Diana, and Vandy during previous phone calls.

As the massage therapist worked on Amelia's legs and feet, which had been tortured this week by impractical shoes, she shared the disappointing news from Shelby's presentation and Quinn's resulting distress. She also described everything that had happened after she and Quinn had talked about the presentation but left out the charged moment when he'd almost kissed her.

"Quinn was hurting. *Badly.* I wanted to tell him about the redesign because I thought it would give him hope for the company's future, but Teagan was insistent we stick to our original plan and not tell him. She told me I still had the option of not working with the company if I didn't want to keep our project a secret."

"She threatened you?" Ava Grace asked fiercely.

"Not in so many words."

"That's bullshit. It was an implied threat, for sure. So what did you do?"

"I kept quiet because I didn't want to lose this opportunity. It's just too important to me. If I go against Teagan, it's over . . . both the accessories line and the full redesign. I won't have anything."

Her words tripped over themselves, and she paused to catch her breath. "You know I could work my entire life and never have another opportunity like this one. This partnership is a once-in-a-lifetime kind of deal. If Quinn likes the redesign, Teagan will fund my boutiques. Where else would I find that kind of money?"

"I know you see this partnership as your one chance to make it big. That's why you went along with Teagan's plan in the first place. What's different now?"

Amelia didn't have to consider Ava Grace's question for long. She knew exactly what was different: her feelings toward Quinn.

"When I agreed to work with Teagan and go behind Quinn's back, I didn't even know him," she reminded Ava Grace. "I hadn't even met him. The redesign was about what I wanted and what it would do for me. I didn't care how it would impact him. I know that sounds horrible and selfish, but it's true."

"Well, it's obvious you don't feel that way anymore."

"He's a good guy, Ava Grace, and I don't want to be the catalyst for him to lose everything he cares about. He's already struggling with taking over his dad's job. Some of the employees don't support him, and this redesign forces him into a corner. I wasn't sure before, but now I have no doubt Teagan would push Quinn out if he doesn't support the redesign."

"I thought the O'Brien siblings were really close. Would Teagan really do something like that to her brother? It's so . . ." Ava Grace paused, clearly trying to find the right word. "It's so mean."

"I agree. And I know it sounds stupid, but I'm disappointed in Teagan. I knew she was frustrated by Quinn's attitude, but I guess I thought she would at least give him the benefit of the doubt once I told her how upset he was."

The massage therapists finished their work, and after letting Amelia and Ava Grace know they could stay in the room as long as they wished, the two spa employees left the room. She and Ava Grace remained on the massage tables but turned their heads to look at each other.

"But there's a chance he would support the redesign, right?" Ava Grace asked. "You just said he was upset the company isn't as strong as it used to be. If you tell him, and he's okay with it, you don't have a problem."

Amelia sighed. "I'm not sure how he would react. Teagan was so sure the presentation didn't change his mind, and of course, she knows him better than I do."

"Do you have the option of testing the water with Quinn? You could casually bring up the idea of doing something entirely new with the women's division—maybe not be specific, but just the general idea—and see how he reacts. And if he reacts negatively, you could make it a priority to change his mind. Kind of like a Jedi mind trick."

She laughed at Ava Grace's suggestion. No one would ever have guessed, but Ava Grace was a *huge* sci-fi nerd. Huge as in she had a set of toy light sabers at home and routinely cajoled Amelia into dueling with her.

Ava Grace deepened her voice and waved her hand in front of her face to imitate a Jedi. "You want to revamp the women's division. You're eager to expand the product line. You can't wait to see my new designs."

Holding her sheet under her arms, Ava Grace sat up on the massage table and tucked her feet under her. Amelia did the same, and they faced each other.

Ava Grace studied her intently. "There's more, isn't there?"

She nodded. "Things got a little messy."

Ava Grace plucked an elastic band off her wrist and pulled her blond hair into a loose ponytail. As she gave it a final tug, she pinned Amelia with a knowing glance.

"Don't they always," she quipped cynically. "What happened?"

Amelia unloaded. She told Ava Grace about Quinn's surprise visit to the penthouse, dinner at the pizzeria, and getting busy among the produce. Surprisingly, Ava Grace remained silent the whole time, although her hazel eyes got bigger and bigger as the story spilled from Amelia's mouth.

Finally, she finished her story. She looked at Ava Grace, her best friend, her only family, the person who knew her better than anyone in the world and loved her anyway.

"Wow," Ava Grace whispered, her eyes unfocused. Then she very obviously came back to Earth because she added in a much louder and firmer voice, "I no longer think you're the smart one in this family. I'm the smart one."

It was the absolute last thing Amelia had expected her to say. She shook her head uncomprehendingly.

"What?"

"Millie, that's not messy, that's a freaking disaster. What were you thinking?"

Amelia's mouth dropped open in shock. Where were the love and understanding she needed from the person who was supposed to love her unconditionally and support her without question?

"Oh, my God, Ava Grace! Are you blaming me?"

"Well, you were the one who went all *Girls Gone Wild* on the kitchen island," Ava Grace shot back.

Anger washed over Amelia. It wasn't as if Ava Grace was perfect, after all.

"I thought you would understand—" she began hotly, but Ava Grace interrupted her.

"Amelia Deanne Winger, you know better! When you first told me about Quinn O'Brien, I never, *ever* thought you'd let things move past flirting. That's why I teased you about him. I didn't think you'd lose your mind and have sex with him!"

"We didn't have sex!" Amelia exclaimed loudly, uncaring that she might disturb the spa's other clients.

"Close enough," Ava Grace countered.

When Amelia opened her mouth to reply, Ava Grace held up her hand. "It's one thing to get involved with someone you work with. It's not smart, but a lot of people do it, and usually no one ends up dead, unemployed, or brokenhearted. But you can't expect anything but heartache if you start a relationship when you're keeping a huge secret and lying to the other person about something so important."

Leaning forward, she squeezed Amelia's knees. "I don't want my next hit song to be about you, and if you continue down this path, it will be. Count on it."

Amelia pulled away from Ava Grace and hopped off the table. Grabbing her fluffy white robe from the hook, she jerked it on.

"Since you're the smart one," she said sarcastically, "what do you suggest I do?"

Ava Grace stood up, the sheet wrapped around her like a toga. "You know what to do. Stay away from Quinn O'Brien or tell him the truth about what you're really doing. Better yet, demand that Teagan tell him."

Amelia leaned against the massage table. "I can't tell him the truth. If I do, I'll not only lose the accessories, but I'll lose the possibility of Teagan's funding. I can't give up this opportunity. And I can't force Teagan to do anything."

Ava Grace studied her grimly. "Then you have to stay away from him. You can't even be alone with him in the same room because you clearly can't control yourself."

Amelia sighed. She knew with every fiber of her being Ava Grace was right. But she wished things were different.

"I know. I *will* stay away from him."

Chapter 17

WHEN QUINN STUMBLED FROM HIS BEDROOM ON SATURDAY morning, he found Cal sitting at the bar in his kitchen. His brother's dark head was bent over a tablet computer resting on the soapstone countertop.

The smell of freshly brewed coffee was strong, and he noticed two large to-go cups sitting near Cal's elbow. Without bothering to say hello, he grabbed one and took a huge swallow.

He could literally feel the caffeine flood his veins, and he sighed with delight. How could Amelia intentionally forgo such pleasure?

With his requirement for coffee fulfilled, he addressed his next overwhelming need. "Food?"

Cal pointed to a covered pan on the Viking range, and Quinn punched him in the arm as he walked to the stove. He removed the lid, and fragrant steam drifted to his nostrils.

"Yes," he breathed, almost drooling. "Denver omelets."

Taking two plates from the white glass-fronted cabinets, he quickly transferred the omelets from the pan and slid one in front of his brother, along with a fork. He didn't even bother to sit down before taking a huge bite of his own, moaning as the smoky flavors of ham and cheddar burst in his mouth.

Cal was a kick-ass cook. In fact, his brother kicked ass at everything he did. It was unnatural.

Leaning against the counter, he pointed to Cal with his fork. "Why are you here so early?" he asked, his mouth full of omelet. His mother would have killed him if she'd witnessed his hideous lack of manners.

"I booked us for an eleven o'clock tee time at the club. You need to get your ass moving and change your clothes so we don't miss it."

Quinn thought a day of golf with his brother sounded awesome, but he was annoyed by Cal's assumption he was free. He should have at least checked to make sure he was available.

"How do you know I don't have plans for today? And you could have interrupted something by showing up here so early. I might have had company." He waggled his eyebrows.

Cal had the affront to laugh boisterously. "Yeah, right."

With a scowl, he cuffed his annoying brother on the head. "Asshole," he muttered before gobbling down the rest of his omelet.

Hurrying to his bedroom, he pulled a red golf shirt and khaki trousers off their wood hangers in his walk-in closet. As he donned his clothes, he assured himself that he could have had a woman in his bed if he wanted one there.

In fact, he had gone out for drinks last night with a woman he'd met at the neighborhood market. After a long day worrying about Amelia running back to Nashville because he couldn't keep his hands to himself, he'd stopped at the store to buy some beer.

He had been in the produce section to grab some oranges for his wheat ale, and the fruit had reminded him of Amelia and their intense make-out session on the island. As he stared into space with a semi hard-on, a tall, thin blonde approached him. Her gray suit jacket showed off a nice rack, and the matching skirt drew his eyes to her long, lean legs.

"You need to squeeze those oranges to see if they're ripe," she suggested, her eyes letting him know *she* was ripe.

She stuck out her hand. "Charlotte. But my friends call me Charlie."

Charlie had known exactly what she wanted, and she

wasn't shy about getting it. While she had fondled the fruit, she asked him out for a drink.

"Let's go right now," she suggested when he agreed, taking his arm and leading him out of the store.

They'd ended up at Murray's, a hole-in-the-wall bar located just a few blocks from his house. During their walk, they had chatted a bit about their jobs. She was an accountant for one of the big firms, and she had fished a business card out of her purse as soon as they found a table.

"In case you need someone good," she said, somehow making that innocuous statement sexual.

Two drinks later, Charlie's hand had been on his crotch, and her mouth had been sucking his earlobe. He had mentioned he lived nearby, and she must have tucked that information away for future use because she whispered, "Take me back to your place and fuck me. Right now."

Like any normal man, he'd had a hard-on, and he had been ready to end his dry spell with Charlie. He had already figured out the fastest way to get to his house and get his dick in her mouth. But then Amelia and her damn brown-sugar freckles popped into his head, and he lost all interest in the blonde sitting next to him.

So he'd removed himself from her talented hands and mouth, thrown a fifty-dollar bill on the table, and said good night. He had gone to bed alone, thinking of Amelia, and he'd woken up alone with a painfully hard erection after dreaming about her all night.

He finished dressing, buckled his belt, turned off his bedroom light, and returned to the kitchen. Cal looked up as he entered the room.

"You want to drive?" his brother asked.

"Hell, yes. I'm embarrassed to be seen in your car."

For reasons known only to himself and God, Cal drove a huge powder blue Cadillac their Grandma Violet used to own. It was old enough to be vintage, but it wasn't "cool" vintage; it was just ancient. Even worse, it was a gas-guzzler.

Cal shrugged, clearly unaffected by his scorn. "Belva gets the job done."

He smirked. "I've always wanted to know . . . since you named your car, did you also name your penis?"

"No, I didn't, but Saika did," Cal answered, grinning like the Cheshire cat. "She calls it 'Drill Sergeant.' "

With a laugh, he grabbed his keys off the counter. "Then you must be doing something right, little brother."

QUINN SHOVED HIS FOUR WOOD BACK INTO HIS GOLF BAG. HE and Cal were at the sixth hole at the Olympic Club's Lake course, and he'd just hooked his drive left, sending his ball into the deep rough next to a tree.

"Nice shot," Cal jeered.

He shrugged, resisting the impulse to ram his fist into his brother's face. With a handicap of zero, Cal was a scratch golfer. Playing with him always dinged Quinn's ego.

The Lake course was one of the top golf courses in the nation, and it had fantastic views of Golden Gate Park and the Golden Gate Bridge. As they zoomed down the cart path toward Quinn's poorly positioned ball, he enjoyed the amazing panorama.

The O'Briens had been members of the Olympic Club since it opened in the early 1900s. Quinn, Cal, and their dad had played the club's three courses regularly until James got sick. They didn't play as frequently as they used to, primarily because Quinn was busy with work and Cal spent most weekends with his girlfriend and her daughter.

"Why aren't you with Saika and Valerie today?" he asked as he swerved to avoid a squirrel that clearly had a death wish since it'd stopped right in the middle of the path.

Grabbing the dashboard, Cal shot him an evil glare. "They're visiting her sister in Los Angeles," he answered curtly.

Quinn took in the frown on his brother's face. "Are you annoyed because you almost fell out of the cart or are you having trouble with Saika?"

"Your driving sucks, no matter if we're in your Audi or in a golf cart." Cal crossed his arms over his chest. "And yes, Saika and I aren't doing so great right now."

Quinn was sorry to hear things weren't going well between the two of them. He really liked Saika, and her daughter had the sweetest giggle. You couldn't help but smile when you heard it.

He didn't want to turn their outing into some kind of pathetic therapy session, but he also didn't want Cal to think he didn't care. "Do you want to talk about it?"

"No."

He brought the cart to a stop and was about to hop out when Cal turned his head and gave him a penetrating look. "Do you want to talk about what's going on between you and Amelia?"

Quinn froze, jerking his eyes away from his brother's prying glance. He clenched the cart's steering wheel but didn't say anything.

"I thought you were acting strange at the party, and then Teagan told me that you bought Amelia an expensive gift and took her to dinner. Was it just coincidence she flew home the next morning when she'd told me that she planned to sightsee this weekend?"

He blew out a breath in frustration. "No, it wasn't coincidence. But I didn't interrogate you about Saika, and I expect you to return the favor."

"Too bad, because I'm not going to. I want to know what happened."

Stepping out of the cart, he began to search the rough for his golf ball. Cal came up beside him and, in less than a half a second, the bastard found the ball.

Quinn stalked back to the cart to grab his five iron and returned to his ball. After a few seconds of evaluation, he assumed his stance and was ready to take a swing when Cal spoke.

"Try not to shank it this time," he advised.

Quinn growled. "Shut up, or I'll hit you with this club."

He took his shot and watched helplessly as the ball soared directly toward the water hazard, falling into it with a loud *plop*.

"*Shit*."

Cal laughed as he scratched his head. "That was masterful. Way to go, Jack Nicklaus."

Leaning on his golf club, Quinn stared at the water hazard. Maybe it was a metaphor for his life. He'd tried to avoid doing something stupid with Amelia, but he hadn't been able to, and now he had to figure out how to move forward.

He turned to Cal. "You know how you said we needed to keep Amelia happy? Well, I'm pretty sure I did something that made her very *unhappy*."

"What did you do?"

"Well, let's see . . . I groped her at the party. I broke into the penthouse and scared her to death just as she got out of the shower. And after I took her out for pizza, I groped her some more."

Cal stared at him as if he'd just witnessed an alien emerging from his forehead. After a moment of stunned silence, he let out a roaring laugh that sent the birds flying from the trees.

When Cal's mirth had died down, he pointed at Quinn. "Sounds like you had a busy week." He slapped him on the back. "Honestly, I'm relieved to hear you've still got the urge. It's been so long since you've had sex I was worried you were planning to take vows and become a priest."

Quinn tried to smile at Cal's joke, but it must have looked like a grimace because his brother threw his arm around his shoulders and gave him a manly one-armed hug. "It could be worse, brother. At least it didn't go any further."

"But I wanted it to."

The truth slipped out before Quinn could swallow it. And now that he'd said it out loud, he decided he might as well go all in.

"I want Amelia," he admitted in a low voice. "It's like I'm obsessed with her or something." He ran a hand through his hair in agitation. "I thought it might be because I haven't gotten laid in a while, but a hot blonde begged me to fuck her last night, and I turned her down."

"Where did you meet a hot blonde?"

Trust Cal to get hung up on the one detail that didn't matter. Quinn told him about Charlie, and his brother's eyebrows crawled up his forehead almost to his hairline.

"Why did you turn her down, man?"

When he didn't respond, Cal laughed in disbelief. "You turned her down because of Amelia?"

Quinn turned to walk back to the golf cart, and Cal grabbed his arm. "Is that why?"

He threw off his brother's hold. "Yes. I'm not going to

have sex with one woman while I'm thinking about another one."

He had before, and he wasn't sure why he wasn't willing to now.

Cal snorted. "Why not? I'd bet most married men do that every single time they have sex with their wives."

He scowled. "If that's what you really think, no wonder you and Saika are having problems."

Cal's expression turned ugly. "Careful. My relationship with Saika is not up for discussion."

Quinn noticed another golf cart coming down the path and motioned for Cal to get into their cart.

"Fine. Let's stop talking."

Cal protested. "No, I want to continue our conversation about you and Amelia."

After releasing the cart's brake, Quinn headed toward the fairway. "There is no me and Amelia."

"But there could be."

He shook his head. "It's a bad idea even if it's not officially sexual harassment. It's unprofessional, and it makes us both look bad."

"I don't agree."

"Okay. How about the fact that she's an integral part of the company's future success? Do you really want me to mess around with her and ruin it for all of us?"

Cal sat silently for quite a while, and when Quinn looked over at him, his brother's eyes were closed. Had he fallen asleep?

"I'm not sleeping," Cal said, obviously sensing Quinn's gaze on him. "I'm thinking. And do you want to know what I think?"

His question was clearly rhetorical because he continued without pause. "I think you never put yourself above this company. I think you should find a way to get what you want, even if you want Amelia. I think you can maintain a professional relationship in public while privately screwing Amelia's brains out every chance you get. And I think you can handle any potential fallout. That's what I think."

Quinn had some serious doubts about that. At the same time, however, he also felt a thrill at the thought of screwing Amelia's brains out, as his brother had so colorfully put it.

"So you wouldn't let a professional relationship stop you from moving forward with a personal relationship? Is that what you're saying?"

Cal nodded. "That's exactly what I'm saying. The only thing that would stop me is if the woman didn't want me the way I wanted her."

Quinn's heart thudded heavily. That was the most important question of all.

Chapter 18

AMELIA FLIPPED THROUGH THE FABRIC SWATCHES RILEY O'BRIEN & Co.'s procurement department had provided. She wasn't happy with the selection, but she wasn't sure if the swatches were truly inferior or if she was just cranky from traveling. Even though it was Tuesday, it felt like Monday because she'd wasted an entire day flying back from Nashville.

Pulling a swatch from the rack, she studied the floral pattern. She might be a little cranky, but this fabric was a lot ugly.

Amelia approached design in two distinct ways: she either drew inspiration from a person or relied on a specific material to guide her. With the Riley O'Brien accessories, she wasn't sure if she should design her pieces with an eye toward the people who would wear them or if she should find materials she loved and then create designs to show off the materials.

She knew she approached the design process differently than other designers, and she blamed it on her lack of formal training. Without question, nearly every other designer she had ever known possessed more training and experience than she did.

It made her deeply insecure, and although she recognized

she had talent, she wished she had a degree or an apprenticeship to back it up. And though she knew it was pathetic, she always felt inferior to people with fancy degrees from expensive universities.

Earlier in the year, she'd applied to the Savannah College of Art and Design in Georgia to attend its fashion design program. She had thought the school was her best choice because Savannah was close enough to Nashville that she'd be able to visit Ava Grace regularly.

She hadn't told anyone about her application, so the disappointment had been hers alone when she had received notice she hadn't been accepted to the program. She hadn't really been surprised. Her academic background was unimpressive, according to the school's dean, and that was a kind description.

In truth, her high school grades had been atrocious. She liked to think they would have been better if she hadn't spent most nights fending off horny truck drivers while working as a waitress.

Despite her poor grades, she had learned the basics of her trade in high school. Because of the school's rural environment, the curriculum emphasized agricultural, vocational, and technical programs, and all students had been required to take courses that would help them find a job once they graduated.

At the time, she had been uninterested in all the courses. She hadn't wanted to be a nail technician, a mechanic, or a ranch hand, so she'd picked textile design and management by process of elimination.

Moving to the next clothes rack, she flipped through more leather swatches. She wasn't a fan of the grain, texture, or color.

Three strikes and you're out.

She stepped back from the racks and returned to her worktable. There were at least seven hundred fabric and leather samples in the workshop, and she'd found three swatches she liked. Maybe she hadn't been specific enough when she'd talked to the woman in charge of finding and buying materials and supplies.

Amelia wondered if it would be possible to visit some

textile suppliers and fabricators. She wanted to slap herself for not suggesting it sooner because touching and feeling was a much better way to approach the process.

At the thought of touching and feeling, her mind made a sudden detour from textiles to Quinn. She hadn't seen or heard from him since that night in the penthouse, and she was torn between relief and regret. She'd never met a man who appealed to her more, and that scared her since he was so tangled up in her career goals.

Ava Grace had been right when she'd said Amelia's behavior was out of character. Because her mother had been so promiscuous, Amelia had gone the opposite direction, determined to be very cautious and deliberate in her sexual relationships.

She hadn't even considered having sex until she and Ava Grace had shaken the Texas dust from their boots. Once she'd arrived in Nashville, though, she'd carefully evaluated potential partners.

She had settled on Derek Jacobson, one of the young attorneys who worked for the entertainment law firm that represented Ava Grace. After several dates, she had told Derek she was a virgin and that she'd like for him to be her first lover. She'd made it clear her virginity was just a nuisance, and that he shouldn't read anything into the fact that he'd be her first.

Ava Grace had warned Amelia that her approach wouldn't work. She said guys were more than happy to use women, but they didn't like being used.

Her best friend loved being right, and in that instance, she'd been dead-on. Derek hadn't even driven Amelia home after her explanation. He'd left her at the restaurant.

When she had identified another prospective sexual partner, she hadn't said anything about her virginity or her lack of experience. That's why the encounter had been so painful and embarrassing, for her partner, not for her.

"I hope you don't think this means anything," he'd sputtered while she was still naked in his bed. Her ego had taken a bit of a beating at his obvious dismay.

Since her first sexual experience had only been so-so, and she hadn't even had an orgasm, she'd decided to give it one more go. Ava Grace had set her up on a blind date with a guitar player who had "long, capable fingers," according to her best friend, and she had found out just how long and capable those fingers really were.

The sound of the workshop door opening and closing interrupted her musings. The tall racks of swatches surrounding the table made it impossible to see her visitor.

"I'm over here," she called.

Hard, heavy footsteps headed her way, and her heart began to pound. Her palms dampened at the thought it might be Quinn.

She turned toward the footsteps just as Quinn's dark head poked around the closest rack. Her spirits lifted at the sight of his handsome face, and she realized she'd missed him.

How is that possible?

"Hey there," he said, stopping about three feet away from her.

His Rileys were so old and so worn they were nearly white with faint shadows of blue along the seams. The hem and pockets were frayed, and there were worn patches in some very interesting places. His brown cowboy boots looked just as worn as his jeans, conforming to the slope of his foot.

He'd topped his ancient Rileys with a sweater patterned in thin stripes of light gray, navy, and orange. It clung to his broad shoulders, outlining his muscular arms, and she recalled how easily he'd lifted her to the kitchen island.

She was desperate to shape those muscles with her hands and run her fingers over his chest. She hadn't had the opportunity that night in the penthouse, and she squeezed her hands into fists to keep from reaching out.

Pulling her gaze from his chest, she immediately noticed he'd gotten a haircut. The shiny, dark strands were cut close to his head in short layers around the back and sides and a little longer on top, and she wanted to run her fingers through the thickness. She didn't know if it was the haircut or the fact that she hadn't seen him in four days, but his eyes looked bluer, and his cheekbones seemed sharper.

As she stared at Quinn, he smiled slowly. "I'm glad you came back. I'm really happy to see you."

She was unable to look away from his mouth as those beautiful lips shaped his words. When she didn't reply, he cleared his throat.

"I wanted to talk to you about what happened in the penthouse. I wanted to talk about where we should go from here."

Realizing she had barely grasped a word he'd said, she jerked her eyes from his lips only to fall headlong into his deep blue gaze. He shot her an alert glance, stepping closer to her.

She could smell him, and his scent was no longer unfamiliar to her. She recognized it on a cellular level, and she knew she would be able to identify him in a room full of other men even if she was blindfolded.

Amelia could feel herself unraveling. She had to get herself under control. She'd promised Ava Grace she would stay away from Quinn. But here she was . . . alone with him in a room that offered plenty of privacy.

Ava Grace's voice echoed in her head, *Amelia Deanne Winger, you know better!*

Walk away! Just walk away from him.

QUINN LOOKED CLOSELY AT AMELIA'S FACE. HER CHEEKS WERE flushed, and her dark brown eyes were glazed. She hadn't said a single word to him since he'd entered the room, not even hello.

"Amelia." He touched her arm lightly. "Sweetheart, did you hear me?"

Shaking her head slightly, she took several steps away from him. "I'm sorry. I didn't hear what you said," she responded coolly, her face closed and lacking the animation and warmth he'd come to expect. "Can you repeat it?"

She looked at him, but it felt as if she looked through him. He realized she was sending a clear, albeit silent, message. She had no interest in getting involved with him, and she would barely tolerate him professionally.

"It wasn't important," he said, his voice sounding like he had swallowed gravel.

Disappointment swamped him, but he wasn't the kind of guy to pursue a woman who was clearly not interested. Hell, he'd never had to chase a woman in his life, and he wasn't going to start now.

Amelia nodded. "Okay. If you didn't need anything, I'm going to just . . . go," she said, stumbling over the last few words.

As she moved toward the door, he got a good look at her clothes. "What the hell are you wearing?" he barked.

She spun around to face him, and he pointed at her short denim skirt. It ended several inches above the enticing dimples of her knees, and she'd paired it with a gauzy, cream-colored top with a drawstring around the neck, a brown leather vest, and brown cowboy boots.

He didn't understand how she could look so cute and so sexy at the same time. There should be a law against that kind of thing.

She looked down in confusion. "What?"

"You're wearing a skirt with the name of my number one competitor stamped on your ass. Did you think I wouldn't notice?"

Her pink mouth dropped open, and she reached behind her as if she wanted to cover the logos. The movement pushed out her chest, outlining her breasts and the hard little points of her nipples against the cotton.

Aggression flooded his veins. He had the ridiculous thought that if Amelia wanted to brand herself with someone's name, it damn well better be *his* name. He felt like pulling her down across his lap, jerking up that damn skirt, and spanking her sweet round cheeks right where his competitor's logos were located.

Before his mind could even think about what to do next, his body moved toward her. When she saw him coming, she pivoted and darted toward the exit. He reached her just as she opened the door, slamming a palm against it and forcing it closed with a bang.

Her lush little body was sandwiched between him and the door, and he crowded even closer until she had to turn her head to the side to keep from smashing her nose. He put his mouth to her ear.

"Don't *ever* wear another piece of denim that doesn't have my name on it," he growled.

She gasped. "Riley skirts don't even exist."

"Say 'Quinn, I won't ever wear another piece of denim that doesn't have your name on it.' "

She pushed back against him, trying to break his hold, and all that wiggling made him hard. He ran one of his hands down her side to her behind until he reached the logo on the skirt.

He squeezed. "Say it."

She let out a tiny squeal. "Quinn O'Brien! What are you doing? Have you lost your mind?"

He was breathing hard, and his brain felt like mush, but her words finally penetrated. When they did, he dropped his forehead against the door next to her face and let his hands fall to his sides.

"I'm sorry," he said hoarsely.

He took a deep breath, the sweet smell of her hair flooding his lungs. "I'm sorry," he repeated. "You make me crazy. I don't know why, but you do. I do crazy things when I'm around you. I say crazy things that I . . ."

He let his sentence trail off, backing away from her so she could turn around. She looked up at him and licked her lips before pulling her bottom lip under her front teeth.

"I make you crazy," she said, somehow making it sound like both a question and a statement. The overhead lights in the workshop made her eyes sparkle and her skin glow.

He nodded. "Yeah. You really—"

He wasn't able to finish his sentence because Amelia launched herself at him, fisting a hand in his hair and pulling his mouth down to hers. She devoured his mouth, and he moaned against her lips.

God, she tastes so good.

He wanted this woman like he'd never wanted another, and he was going to take what she offered. Hooking his arm under Amelia's butt, he pulled her against him. The movement raised her tiny skirt, and she spread her legs and wrapped them around his waist.

With his mouth still sealed to hers, he stumbled toward the door until her back pressed against it. He shoved his hands under her skirt, gripping the smooth globes of her ass. Her panties had slipped into the crease between her cheeks, and he followed them until his fingers met in the damp crevice.

She gasped against his mouth and pulled his head back so she could look into his eyes. "I need to stay away from you."

"No. That's not what you need," he said roughly before giving her another deep kiss.

He couldn't get enough of her mouth, and he sipped at her lips until they were both breathless. Drawing back, he sucked in a lungful of air before nuzzling the corner of her mouth and moving toward her neck.

She turned her head, arching her neck to give him access. He licked the silky skin below her ear before trailing his tongue down her throat until he got to the top of her breasts.

Using his teeth, he undid the drawstring tie on her shirt. The edges of her shirt gaped open, revealing freckled breasts encased in a lacy, flesh-colored bra. He ran his tongue across the top edge of the bra, taking time to suck on her smooth skin.

"Oh, God, Quinn," she moaned.

Letting go of his head, she slipped her hands under his sweater. She ran her fingers across his back before delving under the waistband of his Rileys. They were cool against his hot skin, and he broke out in goose bumps. She dipped her fingers into his boxer briefs, tugging him closer, and he ground his denim-covered erection against her.

He moved his lips back to hers. "This is what you need," he whispered against her mouth before kissing her again.

Sliding his fingers under her panties, he parted her slick folds with the tips of two fingers, dragging them gently against her flesh until he reached her clit. He circled it tenderly, flicking his fingernails against it. She moaned loudly, the sound reverberating through his body.

"This is what you need," he repeated hoarsely.

She panted against his ear, hot little gusts of breath, and he squeezed his eyes shut. He was on the verge of coming just from the feel of her pussy against his fingers. She was so hot and silky, and he wanted to unbutton his fly and go into her so deeply he couldn't tell where he ended and she began.

He shifted his hand to plunge two fingers into her and pressed his thumb on her clit. She jerked against him, gasping softly.

"That feels so good," she breathed. "More."

He gave her what she wanted, thrusting his fingers into her again and again while circling and flicking her clit with his thumb. She began to ride his hand, and he knew she was close when she threw back her head and dug her nails into his back.

Pressing hard on her clit, he pushed deep inside her. With a raspy cry, she came apart. He fed her a deep kiss as her pussy squeezed and convulsed around his fingers.

Resting his face against the hollow of her throat, he waited until her pussy had stopped pulsating before removing his fingers and tugging her panties back into place. As she pulled her hands from his jeans, he leaned back to look into her face. Her eyes were slumberous, her lips plump and rosy.

She ran her hand through his hair. "You got your hair cut."

It was not what he'd expected her to say, and it took him a moment to formulate a reply. "I wanted to look good when you saw me again."

"You always look good to me."

He leaned in and kissed her softly, sucking gently on her lower lip before pulling back. "Obviously, you look good to me, too."

She laughed huskily, wiggling in a silent demand that he let her down. He complied, watching as she adjusted her skirt and retied her blouse. She kept her face averted and fiddled with her neckline for a moment.

Her body language warned him that he wasn't going to like what she'd say next. He tensed, knowing he was about to do battle.

"Quinn, we can't do this again."

Reaching under her fiery hair, he settled his hand on the back of her neck. He pulled her to him, forcing her head to tilt so he could see her face.

"Why not?"

"It's too risky. We're business partners, and we should keep things professional. If anyone found out, it could blemish our reputations, maybe even the reputation of Riley O'Brien & Co."

"I know the risks, Amelia. I've considered them, and I still want to see where this goes."

She swallowed deeply. "I can't."

"We can handle a personal relationship without jeopardizing our professional relationship," he replied, his voice cajoling. "Give it a chance."

"No."

Her voice was resolute, and he dropped his hand. She immediately stepped away from him, and he had to curl his hands into fists to keep from jerking her back to him.

"I don't understand. I'm damn sure you want me as much as I want you."

"Please." Misery filled her face, and his heart pinched a little. "Please just accept my decision."

"Are you saying you want to forget this ever happened? That you want to go back to the way things were before?"

She nodded. "Yes, exactly."

"Forget it," he said curtly. "My life moves forward, not backward."

She turned her face away without replying. After a moment, he forced his feet to move forward, taking him out of the workshop and away from her.

Chapter 19

AMELIA GRABBED HER TOWEL AND WIPED THE SWEAT OFF HER face. The barre exercise class was kicking her butt, and she knew she would feel some pain tomorrow.

Even though the instructor was a meanie, Amelia was glad she'd decided to come to the class. It had helped take her mind off what had happened with Quinn in the workshop yesterday.

She had discovered barre exercise shortly after moving to Nashville. The classes combined ballet, Pilates, and yoga and provided a low-impact, high-intensity workout.

After only a few minutes of her first class, Amelia had known she'd found the exercise that would work for her. She was convinced it was the only thing standing between her and a butt that would require its own zip code.

One of the first things she had done when she'd arrived in San Francisco was search for a barre studio. The instructor for her class at home wasn't nearly as demanding as the one who currently shouted out orders like she was in charge of an all-female army.

Amelia had the fanciful thought that the instructor was punishing her for the deplorable lack of self-control she'd shown with Quinn. She knew she deserved some form of castigation for her behavior.

She had been so close to escaping the workshop without making the situation between them any worse. But then he'd touched her, pressing his hard body against hers like he had in so many of her X-rated fantasies, and she'd just combusted.

Boom!

Her face burned when she thought about how she'd attacked Quinn, jumping into his arms, squeezing her legs around his lean waist, and grabbing his hair. When he had given her the best orgasm of her life, she'd rebuffed him and kicked him out of the workshop. She was such a horrible person, a liar and a user and an opportunist all rolled into one short, freckled body.

Mercifully, her thoughts were diverted when the tough instructor signaled an end to the class. Eager to get back to the penthouse and take a shower, she quickly gathered her bag, mat, and water bottle.

She was ready to leave when she saw a voicemail on her mobile phone from someone with a 323 area code. Recognizing the number as Los Angeles, she pressed the button to listen to the message, holding the phone to her ear as she left the studio.

"Amelia, it's Gary Garson. I need you to call me. Cherry won't need any of the pieces you designed for her. We should probably talk about compensation since you've already done some of the work. Call me."

Her stomach dropped to her toes, and she came to an abrupt stop in the middle of the sidewalk. Cherry had dumped her. No, she corrected herself, Cherry's manager had done the actual dumping. It didn't really matter, though, because the result was still the same.

One of the other pedestrians on the sidewalk bumped into her. "Get out of the way," he snarled before stepping around her.

Forcing her feet to move, she stumbled toward the edge of the sidewalk where she leaned against one of the glass storefronts. *Why didn't Cherry want her designs? Had they been that bad?*

Tears burned the backs of her eyes, and she blinked rapidly to suppress them. *All that work for nothing. What did I do wrong?*

She tried to pull in a deep breath, but it felt like something was crushing her chest. Probably disappointment.

She had been so excited to work with Cherry. She had wanted it too much, and she should have known it wouldn't work out. She wondered if the singer had found another designer, maybe someone she liked better or someone who had the training and experience Amelia lacked.

She looked down. She still clutched her phone, and she dropped it into her shoulder bag. Pushing away from the storefront, she started the trek back to Riley Plaza.

As she walked, she was swamped with doubt about her design abilities. Cherry had only wanted ten designs.

Ten simple little designs.

Amelia hadn't been able to deliver. Well . . . that wasn't entirely accurate. She had delivered. Cherry just hadn't liked what she'd done.

She shook her head in disgust. She couldn't even do a small project like Cherry's. How was she supposed to create an entirely new line of accessories for Riley O'Brien & Co., not to mention the redesign for the women's division?

She was an idiot for thinking she could do it. And the O'Briens were even bigger idiots for hiring her when they should have chosen someone far more qualified and established.

Her best course of action was to sit down with Teagan and bow out of the projects. She was not the right person for the job, and she didn't want to mess things up for the company. And most important, she didn't want to mess things up for Quinn, whose commitment and devotion to his family company could not be doubted.

She had conflicting emotions at the thought of not working with Riley O'Brien & Co. The overwhelming one was relief, even if that relief felt remarkably like despair.

Yes, she was relieved to let go of the pressure involved in such huge projects. And if she wasn't working on them anymore, she wouldn't be forced to deceive Quinn. She wasn't ready to think about how that could change things between them.

Amelia managed to make it back to the penthouse without running into anyone she didn't want to see, which was just about everyone. Once inside, she dumped her bag and exercise mat on the sofa and grabbed her phone to call Gary.

He picked up immediately, as if he'd been on the phone all morning.

"Amelia. Thanks for calling me back so quickly."

"I'm sorry I missed your call earlier."

"It's no problem. *I'm* sorry we won't be using your designs."

She clenched the phone in her hand. She needed to know what had gone wrong, but at the same time, she was afraid to hear it.

"What happened? Did Cherry not like them?" She hated that her voice sounded so pathetic and wimpy.

"No, she loved them. You wouldn't believe the noise she made when she received the FedEx with the sketches."

She was sure she hadn't heard him correctly. "I'm confused. If she loved them, why doesn't she want me to finish the pieces?"

Gary sighed gustily. "The little twit is pregnant, if you can believe that bullshit," he said, his voice full of disgust. "The news leaked last night. Someone in her gynecologist's office blasted it all over the web."

She gasped. She hadn't heard anything about it, but she could understand the gravity of the situation. Cherry wasn't a teenager anymore, but her pregnancy would certainly damage her squeaky-clean image. The media would probably brand her a slut, and she'd end up losing millions of fans.

When she didn't respond to his bombshell, Gary continued. "Cherry decided not to do the cover for *Allure* because she'll be showing by the time it comes out, and her label wants to postpone her tour. They're afraid ticket sales will be way down."

"For what it's worth, I think she made a smart decision about *Allure*. And I'm sure the label is just thinking about money, but being on tour has to be stressful. It can't be good for a pregnant woman."

"That's the only smart decision she's made lately because she wasn't smart enough to use birth control," he snarked, and she chose not to comment on that inflammatory statement. "How am I supposed to manage the situation when she won't tell me who the father is? Maybe she doesn't even know."

Gary's voice had thickened, almost like he was crying. He'd been Cherry's manager since she was thirteen years old, and he probably saw himself as both a protector and surrogate father figure since her father had died well before she'd become a celebrity.

"I'm sorry, Gary," Amelia said.

She felt bad for him and for Cherry. A baby might not wreck the singer's career, but it would definitely put a dent in it.

He cleared his throat. "You've been great to work with. Maybe you can do some new designs for Cherry once the baby's born and things are back to normal."

She could tell he had doubts things would ever return to "normal," but she assured him she'd love to work with him and Cherry anytime they wanted. They discussed how much Amelia should be paid for her work, and she named an amount she thought would be fair.

He let out a rough chuckle. "Cherry may be an unwed mother, but she's a rich one, Amelia. I think you deserve more than that." She heard him shuffling paper in the background. "Where should I send the check? I heard you're in San Francisco doing a big design project. Do you want me to send it there?"

She wasn't sure where Gary should send the check. Before she'd talked to him, she had been dead set on resigning the Riley O'Brien gig.

Maybe she had been too hasty in thinking she couldn't handle the accessories line and redesign for the women's division. Her shaky self-confidence had received a big boost when Gary had said Cherry had loved her designs. Not only was Cherry a known fashionista; she was also part of a younger demographic segment that Riley O'Brien & Co. wanted to target. Moreover, Gary had been sincere when he said she had been great to work with.

"Send the check to San Francisco," she directed Gary. "Let me give you the address."

QUINN STARED AT THE NUMBERS NEATLY PRESENTED IN SAM Sullivan's report. He'd stopped by the older man's office to continue their discussion about new real estate opportunities, and for what seemed like the first time in days, he was focused on business instead of Amelia.

After he'd left her in the workshop earlier in the week, he had made sure he wouldn't run into her. He'd worked from home that afternoon, and during the rest of the week, he hadn't ventured any higher than the second floor of Riley Plaza. For added security, he had come in late and left early so he wouldn't chance an accidental meeting in the elevator.

He knew his avoidance tactics were slightly ridiculous. But he still hadn't recovered from Amelia's crushing rejection.

He had replayed the scene in the workshop over and over, and he didn't know where he'd gone wrong. How had they gone from Amelia's orgasm, which he was pretty confident she'd enjoyed if her moans were anything to go by, to him raging out of the room, physically unsatisfied and emotionally raw?

He cringed inwardly at the memory. He had almost begged Amelia to be with him.

What the hell is wrong with me?

He'd never begged a woman for anything in his life. Well . . . that wasn't entirely true. He begged his mom to make his favorite meal of beef stroganoff and lemon meringue pie whenever he visited. But other than that . . . no begging.

He had no reason to beg, damn it! There were three and a half billion females on the planet. Surely he could find one who fired him up like Amelia Winger. He didn't want to think about the fact that he'd been with plenty of women, and not one of them had managed to make him feel the way she did.

Between his college girlfriend and Luna, he'd had a few short-term relationships, but nothing serious. When he had first come back to San Francisco, he had been focused on carving out a place for himself within the company, and when he returned to school to work on his MBA, his personal life suffered greatly. There was no way he could have juggled graduate school and a serious relationship. He didn't know how people with families handled it.

He had always put Riley O'Brien & Co. ahead of his personal life, even when he was with Luna. She hadn't been his priority, and she'd known it because he never pretended otherwise.

Lately, though, Quinn had started to think that spending every waking moment of his life worrying about the company was not healthy. Actually, it was kind of pathetic.

Cal had Saika and Valerie, for now at least, and Teagan had . . . well, he didn't know about Teagan. His sister was downright secretive about her private life. He used to joke with Teagan about her mysterious love life, but she had mastered the art of the deep freeze and employed it at will. She'd been employing it a lot lately. In fact, she had been frosty with him for a few months now.

Her teasing, always razor-edged, was even sharper and had an underlying anger that confused him. He'd asked Cal about it, and she treated his younger brother the same way.

Her attitude bothered him. *A lot.* There was no one he loved more than his little sister, and he didn't want her to be unhappy.

"What do you think?" Sam asked.

Quinn scowled when he realized he'd gotten distracted—again. Running his hand through his hair, he rubbed the top of his head in frustration. He gave the report a quick look, noting the list of expansion opportunities was pathetically short.

"Sully, this list isn't complete, is it? Please tell me it's not."

With a laugh, Sam leaned back in his chair, making the abused office furniture squeak in protest. He linked his hands behind his head, the movement forcing his blue dress shirt to stretch over his small Buddha-like belly.

"Sorry, son, but it is."

Quinn eyed Sam for a moment. He was not a body language expert, of course, but even he knew Sam's position indicated a high level of confidence and a feeling of power.

It made sense Sam might subconsciously feel authority over Quinn since the older man had known him all his life. In fact, he couldn't remember a time when Sam hadn't been around. Sam was one of his dad's oldest and closest friends, and for most of Quinn's life, he had called him Uncle Sully.

"So what are we looking at? A maximum of five new department stores for the entire U.S.?"

"That's right."

Riley O'Brien & Co. generated the majority of its revenue from jeans sold in department stores. The stores were almost always located in regional malls, although some department stores now had stand-alone locations.

The company had distribution agreements with the big department store operators, allowing them to sell Rileys and receive a percentage of the sale. In most instances, Rileys had their own sections, a space of the store dedicated exclusively to Rileys. The company leased the dedicated space, paying rent to the department stores.

"We've relied on department stores to provide expansion opportunities for years. I don't think that strategy is going to work anymore, Sully."

Although the average consumer would never know it, only a couple of new malls were under development in the entire country. Each mall usually housed three to four department stores, and Riley O'Brien & Co.'s expansion opportunities were limited by the number of new department stores.

In addition to department stores, the company had distribution agreements with select boutiques across the nation. Although it had an entire department dedicated to vetting boutiques for possible distribution deals, boutiques were secondary to department stores and did not generate a large portion of revenue for the company.

In general, Quinn was not a fan of selling Rileys in boutiques, and in this instance, he and his dad disagreed. He thought it was too hard to police all the boutiques to make sure they were the kinds of places that would enhance the brand rather than damage it. His dad was of the opinion that it didn't matter where Rileys were sold, as long as they sold.

Sam sighed loudly. "If you're talking about opening up more company-operated stores, you know your dad would be against that idea."

Along with department stores and boutiques, Riley O'Brien & Co. also leased space in malls, open-air centers, and urban retail locations for its own company-operated stores. Quinn's dad wasn't a fan of selling Rileys through this channel because of the expense and management supervision involved. As a result, there were fewer than seventy-five company-operated stores across the U.S.

Quinn rubbed the back of his neck, trying to get rid of the kinks. "I know, but we have to keep expanding. We can't continue to grow our revenues by relying only on our existing stores."

Removing his hands from his head, Sam grabbed the arms of his chair to push himself to a standing position. "Let's postpone any decisions until your dad comes back and things get back to normal," he suggested, moving around the desk to Quinn.

Normal? Quinn didn't even know what that meant anymore.

He hadn't felt "normal" in a long time, since before his dad had gotten sick. And he definitely didn't feel normal with Amelia around. She made him off-balance, like he was standing in an open room during an earthquake. He didn't know how to regain his equilibrium.

Sam patted him on the shoulder. "Get on out of here, boy. I need to make a phone call."

Quinn stood. Sam's jovial, familiar manner had started to grate on him, and he no longer found it comforting so much as condescending. He doubted the older man would ever adapt to answering to someone who'd played doctor with his daughters.

Something was going to have to change. But he didn't know what or when.

Chapter 20

QUINN CHECKED HIS PHONE AGAIN TO MAKE SURE HE HADN'T missed a text from Teagan. She was running late, which was understandable given the crowd of people who had come out this Saturday to enjoy the annual chocolate festival in Ghirardelli Square.

His sister had stopped by his office yesterday after his unsatisfying meeting with Sam Sullivan. Although he'd been in a bad mood, he had said yes when she asked him to attend the festival with her.

He moved closer to the stop sign so he wouldn't block the pedestrian traffic. Looking up and down the street, he tried to spot Teagan's dark head.

A black four-door sedan pulled up to the curb, catching his attention. The driver came around to open the door, and Quinn immediately recognized the red head that poked out of the car, along with the curvy body that followed.

He let out a low groan, although he couldn't say whether it was one of pleasure or dismay. Had Teagan invited Amelia to join them?

He watched intently for his sister to emerge from the car, but once Amelia was safely on the sidewalk, the driver closed the door and handed a business card to her.

Although Quinn and Amelia hadn't parted on good terms, he was happy to see her. A jolt shot through his body, almost as if he'd gulped a double espresso.

He couldn't help but smile at the sight she made as she stood on her tiptoes looking for someone. She was just so damn cute. She'd clearly dressed for comfort rather than style, and she looked like a tourist.

She had pulled her curly hair back into a messy ponytail, and she wore a pair of khaki cargo pants that hugged her round ass and red Converse tennis shoes. Her leather backpack pulled her navy blue T-shirt tight across her chest, emphasizing the curves of her breasts.

Amelia had yet to spot him. She continued her scan, and he tensed as her gaze brushed past him. He knew the exact moment her brain communicated with her eyes because her head jerked back to him, and her eyes widened.

He raised his hand in a casual wave, and she slowly walked toward him. Stopping right in front of him, she looked up. They stared at each other for a few moments before she spoke.

"Hi," Amelia finally said, her voice low.

"Juice," he acknowledged.

Her eyes narrowed. "I'm surprised to see you. I was supposed to meet Teagan here."

Her voice was faintly accusing, and it pissed him off. He didn't have to trick women into spending time with him.

"I'm surprised to see you, too," he replied in an unfriendly tone. "She asked me to meet her here, too."

His phone chimed to let him know he had a text message, and he heard Amelia's phone vibrate at the same time. His message was from Teagan. It read: "Change of plans. Not coming. Make sure Amelia has fun. You're welcome."

What a manipulator! He didn't know whether he wanted to hug his conniving little sister or shake her until her teeth rattled.

He looked at Amelia, who had pulled her phone out of her pocket to read her own message. As she reviewed it, her plump lips turned down in a frown. He was pretty sure he had an idea what her message said. They'd been duped by a master.

"Bad news?" he asked innocently.

She raised her eyes to his. "Teagan's not coming."

"I know. I just got the same message."

She immediately pulled out the card the driver had given her, clearly intending to ask him to come and get her. He placed his hand on her forearm to stop her.

"Wait a second."

She jerked away from him. "What?" she asked rudely.

"Stay. Spend the day with me."

Shaking her head, she opened her mouth. He rushed to speak before she could say no.

"I promise to keep my hands to myself."

Her russet eyebrows shot up. "What about your mouth?"

Her question shocked a laugh out of him. "That, too. You don't need to worry. My mouth will be too busy eating chocolate to bother you."

She harrumphed, the sound making him smile. After several seconds, she tucked her phone and the driver's card back into her pocket.

"Okay."

He gave an internal sigh of relief. She was his, for a few hours, at least.

"This way," he said, tilting his head toward Ghirardelli Square.

He put his hand on the small of her back to usher her forward only to jerk it away when she tensed. He tucked his hands in his pockets to keep them under control.

"Teagan told me Riley O'Brien & Co. sponsors the event," Amelia said.

"We're one of the sponsors. It's part of our philanthropic efforts since the proceeds from the festival go to a local nonprofit. We've been a sponsor for a long time."

"Do you have any other charitable programs?"

"Yes. We have quite a few. The most successful is our annual special-edition jeans. We donate the sales proceeds to a different charity every year. My mom came up with the idea when Teagan was a baby, and my dad signed off on it."

His dad was hard as nails when it came to business. But he was a marshmallow when it came to his wife and his kids.

And Teagan had taken advantage of it when she'd lobbied for the new line of accessories.

"How long have your parents been married?"

"They're going to celebrate their thirty-sixth anniversary this December. They got married on New Year's Eve. My dad said they chose that date because he never again wanted to kiss anyone else at the stroke of midnight."

Amelia sighed. "That's romantic," she said. "Are they still happy together?"

He considered her question before shaking his head. "Happy isn't a good description."

She glanced at him quizzically, and he tried to think of the best way to explain his parents' marriage. As a kid, he hadn't realized how unique their relationship was, but as an adult, he recognized how rare it was to find the kind of love they had.

"They're *absorbed* with each other. When they're in the same room together, it's like they breathe in concert."

A big group of people passed by, and Quinn moved to shield Amelia from any possible jostles. When they were alone on the sidewalk again, he resumed their conversation.

"My parents have a very intense, passionate relationship. My dad never has to wonder if he's done something wrong because my mom yells loudly enough that you can hear it in every room."

Amelia laughed. "Is she only like that with him, or is she that way with everyone?"

"Now that you mention it, she's only like that with him. She says he makes her crazy."

She sucked in a breath, and he realized he'd said the same thing to her when they had been in the workshop. He didn't want to consider the possibility there were any similarities between his parents' relationship and the way he felt about Amelia.

He cleared his throat. "Let me tell you about the festival."

He explained that attendees purchased tasting cards, which served as currency to purchase treats from the vendors. "One of the perks of being a sponsor is free cards, so we won't have to purchase any." He patted the front pockets of his Rileys. "I have a few right here. You can have anything and everything you want."

When she didn't reply, a disturbing thought crossed Quinn's mind. "*Shit.* Is chocolate one of your don'ts? Like coffee and alcohol?" His horror was evident in his voice.

"Are you kidding?" she asked, laughing incredulously. "In my world, chocolate is one of the major food groups."

He exhaled gustily. "I'm relieved. This festival would be a huge waste of time if you didn't eat chocolate."

She smiled. "I don't *eat* chocolate. I *devour* it."

Her emphasis on the word "devour" made his skin feel tight and hot. Forget chocolate. He wanted to devour *her.*

AMELIA TOOK A BIG BITE OF MOLTEN LAVA CAKE. GOOEY chocolate oozed over the spoon, and she had to catch it on her tongue to keep it from dripping down her chin and onto her shirt.

As the rich, dark flavor hit her taste buds, she closed her eyes and moaned, long and loud. She couldn't help it. The cake was orgasmically delicious.

She heard Quinn's muffled laughter, and she opened her eyes. He was enjoying his own mouthful of lava cake, his cheeks resembling a chipmunk's, and he already had another big bite loaded on his spoon.

"I'm glad we decided not to share this lava cake because we would have had a throw-down over who got the most bites," she joked.

He nodded vigorously in agreement and shoved another bite in his mouth. This time he was the one who closed his eyes and moaned. She was entranced by the expression on his face. Did he look like that when he climaxed?

She had a hard time looking away, and she was snared in his gaze when he opened his dark blue eyes and stared right at her. He licked his lips.

"What's next?"

She looked around. They'd visited several tents, and she was glad she had agreed to stay and spend the day with Quinn.

She enjoyed Quinn's company way too much. He was funny, smart, and surprisingly insightful. And despite his well-developed ego, he was also self-aware enough to laugh at himself. Perhaps more important, she sensed an innate goodness in him, and after her childhood, she was adept at identifying both ends of the spectrum.

"Do you still have room for more?"

He chuckled. "I always have room for more chocolate."

She nodded in agreement. Because each tasting was pretty small, she had yet to have her fill of treats.

"Cupcakes," she suggested, pointing to a tent that had a pink-and-white-striped awning. "Babycakes" was written in brown script across it.

His eyes lit up. "Babycakes has the best cupcakes in town."

They got rid of their empty containers and headed toward the tent. Apparently everyone at the festival agreed with Quinn because the line was long.

Quinn eyed the throng of people with a frown. "Do you want to wait?"

"You said they're the best in town. Are they worth waiting for?"

He jerked his head toward her, an arrested expression on his face. "There are only a few things I'm willing to wait for."

She felt like she was missing something. "Okay. But is Babycakes one of those things?"

He cleared his throat. "Sure, we can wait."

They took their place in line, and there were so many people crammed in the small space that she and Quinn touched from shoulder to hip. His heat radiated through her clothes, and she wanted to move away, but there was nowhere to go.

The line moved forward, and the person behind Amelia bumped into her. When she stumbled slightly, Quinn moved closer to her, sliding his arm around her waist and resting his hand on her hip.

Her chest tightened, and she started to sweat. She couldn't handle being this close to him without thinking about his mouth and hands on her body. She already thought about it too much.

The line was noisy, and he leaned down so she could hear him. His breath was hot on her ear, and she shivered.

"What kind of cupcake do you want? They have chocolate raspberry and chocolate peanut butter."

She didn't want a cupcake. She wanted Quinn.

"They both sound good. I don't know."

He caressed her hip. What happened to his promise to keep his hands to himself?!

"How about you get one flavor, and I'll get the other, and we'll share?"

She nodded. "That sounds fine," she said, lying through her teeth. She didn't want to share his cupcake, unless "cupcake" was a code word for "penis."

Finally, they reached the counter, and he placed their order. Mercifully, he had to remove his hand from her hip to grab the cupcakes, and she breathed a sigh of relief.

Passing one of the cupcakes to her, he returned his hand to the small of her back to move her in front of him. She wondered if he was this protective and possessive with all the women he dated.

She mentally slapped herself. *We aren't dating. This isn't a date.*

They found a quiet place between two tents to enjoy their treats. The small space was remarkably private despite the fact that it was in the middle of the festival, and the noise from the crowd was muted.

Amelia lifted her hand so she could appreciate the delectable sight of her cupcake. It covered her palm with a swirl of chocolate icing at least three inches on top. Quinn's was identical.

"Which one do I have?"

"I don't know." He smiled widely. "I guess it will be a surprise."

She peeled the wrapper from the side of the cupcake. "Please tell me you got some napkins."

He nodded before taking a bite of his cupcake, smearing icing all over his upper lip. She took a bite of her own cupcake and got a bit of icing on her nose.

She savored the flavors creating a symphony in her mouth. She definitely had the chocolate peanut butter cupcake, and the mix of nutty goodness and rich chocolate was delicious. Grabbing a napkin in his free hand, he swiped the icing off her nose.

"Thanks. Eating cupcakes is messy business."

He mumbled a reply around a mouthful of cupcake, and she pointed to his lips. "You have icing all over you."

He licked his lips before rubbing the napkin across his mouth. "Is it gone?"

She nodded and held out her hand for his cupcake. He frowned.

"What?"

"You said we were going to share, and I want to try the chocolate raspberry."

He eyed her suspiciously. "Is your cupcake not good? Is that why you want mine?"

"Of course it's good. I just want a bite. I'm not going to eat both of them."

He held out his cupcake but snatched it back when she reached for it. "No, I'm going to hold on to it."

She scowled. "Don't be so selfish."

He laughed. "I'm not being selfish, Juice. I'm being smart." He offered his cupcake. "Here, take a bite."

"You better not smash it in my face," she warned him.

"This isn't our wedding," he shot back, freezing when he realized what he'd said.

His eyes widened, but before he could say anything else, she grabbed his wrist and took a huge bite of his cupcake. "Oh, this is so much better than mine," she moaned, unconcerned with the fact that she was talking with her mouth full.

Quinn stared at her unblinkingly as she swallowed. She felt icing all over her lips, and she looked for the napkin that had been in his hand, but it was gone.

"You look like a clown with a big brown mouth and a curly red wig," he said, cocking his head to the side.

She was torn between mirth and indignation. "That's *so* rude."

"Yeah," he agreed, laughing softly. "But *so* true."

He reached out to wipe some icing from her upper lip and brought his thumb to his mouth to lick it off. She couldn't pull her eyes from his mouth, and her stomach turned warm and liquid.

Quinn repeated the movement, slower this time, dragging his thumb against her lower lip before sucking the icing off his finger. She jerked her attention from his mouth and met his eyes. The desire burning in his blue gaze made her knees tremble and her heart pound.

Dropping his cupcake to the ground, he shaped her face with his palms. "You taste better than anything we've had here today." He leaned forward. "Let me have another taste," he whispered against her mouth before stroking his tongue along the seam of her lips.

She opened to him, and he plunged his tongue inside her mouth. Letting go of her own cupcake, she fisted his shirt and sucked on his tongue. His chest was hard and hot, and she wanted to tear open his buttons and run her hands all over him.

"You're sweeter than sugar," he rasped.

He gave her several deep kisses, sucking and licking at her lips and tongue until she panted. He drew back, his chest heaving.

"You promised to keep your hands and your mouth to yourself," she murmured, uncertain if the reminder was for Quinn or herself.

He leaned his forehead against hers. "I know," he replied, but he didn't apologize.

As Quinn wrapped his arms around her, she dropped her head to his chest. He rubbed her back with his big hands, and the soothing motion relaxed them enough for their breathing to return to normal.

Nuzzling her hair, he kissed the top of her head. She stood within his embrace, feeling a bewildering mix of peace and arousal. Somehow she knew that she would never feel this way about anyone else. She had never known anyone like him.

One moment he embodied the classic bad boy, sexy and intense, and the next, he was the proverbial golden boy, easy-going and kindhearted. She found the contrast fascinating and addicting.

And irresistible.

She wanted to be with Quinn, and she finally gave herself permission to take what she wanted. She told herself it would be okay. She told herself *she* would be okay no matter what happened.

Maybe he would embrace the work she was doing for

Teagan. Maybe he wouldn't feel she'd gone behind his back. Maybe her heart wouldn't end up broken and in pieces under his booted feet.

Maybe. And in this moment, maybe was good enough.

She gave a gentle push to his chest so he'd loosen his hold. He was still close enough that she had to tilt her head back to look into his eyes.

"Do you live near here?"

His gaze sharpened, and he nodded slowly. "Pretty close. Just a few miles away."

"I'd like to see where you live."

Chapter 21

AMELIA STOOD IN QUINN'S LARGE LIVING AREA, TRYING NOT to look as awkward as she felt. She had a hard time dealing with spur-of-the-moment decisions, and even though she had fantasized about him, coming back to his house definitely had not been premeditated.

She turned in a slow circle to get a good look at Quinn's personal space. It wasn't anything like she had expected.

For one thing, he lived in a house, and she had been sure he was a high-rise condo kind of guy. Unsurprisingly, the fact that she'd been wrong about his living arrangements made her feel even less certain about getting naked with him.

His Victorian was gorgeously maintained, although very obviously lived in. Although he was a bachelor, his house lacked the single-guy vibe. Instead it felt comfortable and cozy, and under different circumstances, she would have found the space relaxing and inviting.

She tensed when Quinn moved to stand in front of her. He waited, still and silent, until she met his gaze. He extended his hand toward her face, and she flinched in nervousness. Halting mid-motion, he let his hand fall back to his side and gazed deeply into her eyes.

She was so annoyed with herself. She hadn't been this

anxious when she'd been a virgin or when she'd had sex with Neal, the guitar player with the talented fingers.

She knew she was being stupid. She wasn't afraid of Quinn, yet she acted as if he were a Viking who had gathered forces to raid her village. She laughed nervously when she realized the analogy wasn't too far off, although her "village" was between her legs.

A high-pitched giggle emerged from her mouth, and Quinn nodded as if he agreed with someone. Taking a deep breath, he ran his hand through his hair.

"Juice, I think we should go and grab some dinner. Do you like Chinese? There's a pretty good place just down the street. Their moo shu pork is really tasty."

Moo shu pork? He wants moo shu pork?

When she didn't answer, he sighed loudly and reached out to wrap a big hand around the back of her neck. It was so hot against her clammy skin that she shivered.

She let her head drop forward against his chest, and he kneaded the tight muscles of her neck for several moments before speaking. "Amelia . . . Sweetheart, you asked to see my house, and now you've seen it. We don't have to do anything else. There's nothing to worry about."

His voice was quiet, soothing. She could hear his heartbeat, a steady thump that proved he was much calmer than she was. She didn't know if that made her feel relieved or not. At the festival, she'd thought he was as turned on as she was.

Why am I the only one who's nervous?

She wrapped her arms around his waist, and he stiffened slightly, briefly halting the neck massage before resuming the gentle motion. He settled his other hand on her lower back just above her butt, a possessive and protective action that made the knots in her stomach loosen.

"If you don't like moo shu pork, we can get Mongolian beef or sweet-and-sour chicken."

Pulling back, she looked up into his face. His eyes were dark and serious, not even a tiny glint of humor.

"You want to go out to eat right now?" she asked incredulously.

He frowned. "No. There are a lot of things I want to do instead of eating Chinese food." He paused meaningfully, his voice deepening. "I want to strip you naked and put my hands and mouth all over your body. I want to be so deep inside you that you scream my name until your voice is gone."

His voice faded to a husky whisper. "I want to make you come so many times you forget who you are and where you are. I want to take you over and over until the pleasure feels like pain."

His raspy voice and raw words sent a flood of lava-like desire through her. She swallowed to ease the tightness in her throat so she could respond, but he stepped back, putting more space between them.

Holding out his hands, palms up, he shrugged his shoulders. "But I'm trying to be a decent guy here, Juice. I don't think you're ready for this. And I don't want you to regret it." He pointed to himself with his thumb. "Because *I* won't regret it. And I'll probably want to do it, and *you*, as often as possible."

When she didn't respond, he continued. "Do you understand what I'm saying?"

His honest words shocked her. She must have a poor opinion of men in general because she had expected him to be annoyed. She had been so sure he would try to persuade her to get naked, and she never imagined he, or any other guy, would be understanding.

Apparently, he was willing to wait until *she* was ready, despite the fact that he obviously was raring to go. How astonishing.

How *wonderful*.

His attitude made her want him even more. And interestingly, his restraint convinced her that she wasn't making a mistake.

"I understand," she finally said. "But you're wrong."

His dark eyebrows rose. "About what?"

"You said I've seen your house, and that's not entirely accurate, is it? I've only seen *part* of your house. I haven't seen your bedroom."

He gazed at her intently before his lips quirked in a slow, sexy smile. His eyes heated, and he closed the space between them until they touched. Reaching out, he gently rubbed her bottom lip with his thumb.

"That was clearly an oversight on my part."

"Clearly," she agreed. "Do you plan to address it?"

"Yes. Immediately, in fact."

Tilting his head toward the staircase, he extended his hand to her. She took it, allowing him to lead her up the hardwood stairs, which were slick and shiny from decades of foot traffic.

He brought her to the door at the end of the hallway and ushered her in. She let her gaze wander around his bedroom. Decorated in shades of gray, it was almost monochromatic except for the clean lines of licorice-colored wood furniture.

His king-sized bed was situated against the longest wall, its tall headboard inset with black leather panels. Two nightstands flanked the bed, each boasting a lamp with a clear glass base and gray shade. A seating area near the bay window on the far side of the room featured two tall-backed chairs upholstered in gray velvet, while a long dresser with an attached mirror occupied one wall.

All in all, the room was masculine without being oppressive. And it would have been gorgeous if not for the fact that it was so messy.

The bed was unmade, and the light gray sheets were tangled as if he hadn't slept well. Or maybe he'd been with someone the night before. She shot a censuring look toward Quinn, and he laughed at the mix of disapproval and dismay she didn't bother to hide.

"I didn't expect company," he admitted.

"If you've had *company* recently, then we need to change the sheets."

Her remark made him choke on his laughter. "What?" he sputtered.

"You heard me."

Staring at her in disbelief, he shook his head. "I told you that I don't have one-night stands. And I haven't had *company*, as you so delicately put it, in a while."

She eyed him skeptically. *How long was "a while"?* She wanted to ask, but couldn't bring herself to do so. She hadn't been with anyone since Neal, and that had been more than a year ago.

He frowned when she didn't respond, and after a moment,

he stalked back into the hallway. She heard a cabinet door open and slam shut before he returned to the room with a set of sheets identical to the ones on the bed.

"While I'm changing the sheets, I want you to take off every piece of clothing you're wearing," he ordered as he made his way toward the bed. "The moment I finish, I am going to throw you on this bed, and you're not going to get off of it for a good long while."

Pulling back the duvet-enclosed comforter with one hand, he tossed it over the footboard, his movements quick and economical. When he noticed she hadn't moved, he dropped the stack of clean sheets on the bed and pointed at her.

"Why are you still dressed?"

She recognized the look on his face. "I'm making you crazy again, aren't I?"

He propped his hands on his hips, an aggressively masculine stance. Tilting his head back, he closed his eyes.

"God, *yes*, you make me crazy."

Amelia joined Quinn by the bed. She unsnapped the first couple of buttons on his checked shirt before he gripped her hands.

"Uh-uh. You first," he demanded, grabbing the hem of her T-shirt and whipping it over her head. He didn't move for a moment, just stared down at her breasts in their midnight-blue bra.

After years of buying clothes in thrift shops and underwear in cheap discount stores, she now had the money to splurge, and she liked lacy, girly underwear. The set she wore was one of her favorites, a deep demi-cup and cheeky panties. She was so glad she'd worn them today because they made her girls look bigger and her butt look smaller.

Quinn ran the tips of his fingers across the lacy edge of her bra. The fleshy pads were slightly rough, and her breath caught in her throat as he moved them closer to her cleavage.

He abruptly jerked his hands away and turned to sit on the side of the bed. Widening his legs, he pulled her in between them. The new position put her breasts right in his face, and he murmured his appreciation.

"*This* is the best view in the city," he said reverently, making her smile.

She ran her hand over his hair, the strands silky and cool against her palm, and traced his hairline with the tip of her finger. His eyelids fell as she touched his face, and she noticed his long, spiky eyelashes.

He opened his eyes, and they stared at each other, their faces only inches apart. His dark blue gaze was hazy with desire.

For me.

She leaned forward to kiss him, and he wrapped his arms all the way around her, pulling her closer and deeper into the V of his legs. As their lips met, he palmed her butt cheeks and squeezed. The unexpected gesture made her gasp and pull back slightly.

"Sorry. Too hard?"

She shook her head, and he rubbed the spots where he had squeezed. "I love your ass," he breathed. "It's so round and delicious, and I can't wait to get you out of these pants so I can touch it skin-to-skin."

A strangled laugh escaped her. "I hate my butt. It's too big."

He shook his head. "No," he countered fiercely. "You can't hate something that makes me hard every time I see it."

Well, when you put it that way . . .

Leaning forward, he placed tiny kisses on the corners of her mouth. "I don't want to let go, so you're going to have to take off your bra. I need to put my mouth on you."

His words made her nipples harden. Quinn was a talker, and it made her *hot.* Her panties were already soaked, and he hadn't even touched her below the waist. And he was still fully clothed, something she needed to remedy immediately.

"Not yet," she said, shaking her head. "You need to give me something first."

A naughty smile crossed his face. "What do you have in mind, Juice?"

In response, she unsnapped the rest of the buttons on his shirt and spread it open, uncovering a strongly muscled chest and well-defined abs dusted with fine, dark hair. She pushed on his shoulders to get his attention.

"You need to let go so I can take off your shirt."

Releasing his grip on her butt, he shrugged off his shirt,

the muscles in his shoulders and arms flexing. After tossing it on the floor, he pulled her back to him.

Reaching into her cleavage, he unhooked the clasp of her bra and pulled the lacy cups away from her breasts. Once freed, they bounced into his face, and he moaned at the sight, a deep sound that made her break out in goose bumps.

"Bring one of those sweet nipples to my mouth."

She protested. "But I want to touch you."

"Later," he growled. "Now give me what I want."

Cupping one of her breasts, she fed him a plump nipple. He sucked it into his mouth, and she moaned at the exquisite feeling of his hot mouth. Blood rushed through her veins, and her skin flushed from the heat of it.

He licked and sucked until her nipple was pebbled, and she brought her other breast to his mouth. "Good girl," he murmured against her nipple, squeezing her butt cheeks again. She would have bruises there tomorrow, and perversely, the thought made her even wetter.

He tongued her nipple until it was so tight and hard it was almost painful. He bit down gently, sending a spark of pleasure from her nipple straight to her center. She didn't want to wait even one more second to feel him inside her.

"Quinn," she gasped. "You need to take off your pants. *Now.*"

Chapter 22

NOTHING INFLATED A MAN'S EGO—OR HIS COCK—MORE THAN a woman who wanted to tear off his clothes. Quinn laughed softly as Amelia fumbled to open the buttons on his fly, both amused and aroused by her eagerness.

"I want these off," she panted, tugging at his Rileys.

"I have a better idea," he countered. "Let's take off *your* pants."

Nodding eagerly, Amelia stepped back to toe off her shoes. He brought her back to him by the waistband of her cargo pants before flicking open the button. Staring into her eyes, he pulled down the zipper and slid his hands into her pants to cup her ass. It was both soft and supple, and he clenched his fingers in the round cheeks.

Her pants fell to her upper thighs, and she balanced herself by grabbing his shoulders as she stepped out of them. A couple of coppery curls tickled his face, and he tilted his head so he could feel the silky strands against his lips.

She leaned forward, licking and sucking the crook between his shoulder and his neck. Her teeth bit into him, and he gasped as his cock pulsed. He had the fleeting thought that he should have taken a few minutes alone to masturbate so he didn't feel like a rabid dog. He was afraid he'd barely get inside her snug body before he exploded.

"This is getting out of control," he said hoarsely, a warning to himself and the curvy redhead in front of him.

Clenching his arms under her butt, he stood and picked her up in one smooth movement. He twisted his upper body, tossing her on the bed. Her hair came loose from its ponytail, the fiery curls contrasting sharply with his gray bedding.

"I'm the only person who's slept on these sheets, so don't say a word," he growled before stepping back to remove his shoes.

As he unbuttoned his fly, he ran his gaze up and down her body. Pale pink areolas tipped her plump breasts, and her high-cut panties emphasized her creamy white skin and luscious hips.

He couldn't hold back his appreciation. "*Goddamn*, Amelia. You're gorgeous."

Her whole body flushed at his words, and as she shifted restlessly against the comforter, her panties edged up. He held his breath, eager to see if the curls between her legs were as bright as the ones on her head, but he was denied the erotic vision.

That didn't stop him from thinking about how wet she would be, and he fumbled a bit with the buttons on his jeans. When he finally got all of them open, he sighed in relief. It felt like he'd had an erection for hours, and his jeans had been strangling it.

Pushing his Rileys down his legs, he kicked them off. He hooked his thumbs into the waistband of his boxer briefs to remove them, too, but reconsidered. Maybe he should leave on his underwear since he was already so close to the edge.

Amelia rose up on her elbows, distracting him from his thoughts. Her big brown eyes focused on his crotch, and he grew even harder under her lustful gaze, although he didn't know how that was possible.

She bit her plump lower lip, and the sight of that tiny gap between her front teeth made him think about what his cock would look like sliding in and out of her mouth. He took several deep breaths, hoping the extra oxygen would allow him to muster some control over his unruly and too-long-deprived body.

"Take them off," she demanded, her voice low and raspy. When he didn't move, she cleared her throat. "Take them off."

He shook his head. "Not yet."

Her eyes shot sparks at him, and her lower lip pushed out in a tiny pout, making him want to suck on it. Crawling onto the bed, he covered her body with his, moaning when his chest rubbed against her breasts.

She shifted, opening her legs, and he gasped when his cock settled snugly between her legs. He leaned down to kiss her, and when her tongue touched his, things quickly went from hot to incendiary. Her heat already scalded him, and he wasn't even inside her yet.

Releasing her mouth, he rolled to the side and wiggled his fingers inside the waistband of her panties, pulling them down her legs. He could smell her arousal, and he was torn between wanting to taste it and plunging his cock into her.

He trailed his hand across her stomach and shifted slightly to eye her mound, smiling when he saw the hair covering her pussy was even redder than the curls on her head. Everything about Amelia was so vibrant, and he had the fanciful notion that his life before her had been as gray as his bedroom.

Quinn brushed his fingers across the springy hair, tracing the edge of her labia before sliding his finger down her wet, silky slit. When he reached the entrance to her body, he circled it tenderly until she panted. As he plunged two fingers inside her, she gasped and grabbed his shoulders.

"Does this feel good?" he asked, pumping his fingers slowly into her pussy. She nodded, and he dropped his head to whisper in her ear, "Tell me how much you like it."

Withdrawing his fingers, he gave some attention to her hard little clit. He pressed against it, and she jerked. Her nails dug into his shoulders, and he pressed against the bundle of nerves again, making her moan.

"Should I do that again?"

"Yes," she gasped. "Please."

He licked a trail down the side of her neck as he slipped

his fingers back into her body. He brushed his thumb lightly, so lightly against her clit, and she bucked against him.

"I need you to come for me." He pressed harder, flicking her clit and pumping his fingers inside her. "I want you to be all hot and wet around me when I slide into you."

She cried out his name, her pussy contracting around his fingers. She writhed against him as her internal muscles clenched rhythmically.

He waited as long as he could before pulling his fingers from her body. His head felt like it was about to pop off, and he couldn't think of anything but plunging balls-deep into her sweet little body.

Reaching over her, he grabbed a condom from the nightstand. She took it from him as she leaned over to give him a deep kiss.

"I'll do it."

He tugged down his boxer briefs, and she gave an appreciative sound that made his testicles tighten. She put the condom aside and grasped his cock in her hand, her fingers struggling to reach around it completely.

"Oh, yeah," she breathed. "You *are* bigger than average. And you definitely won't hear any complaints from me."

He laughed breathlessly when he recalled their conversation on the day they'd met. "I'm glad you're pleased." His voice was little more than a croak.

She swiped a finger across the head of his penis where a drop of fluid had oozed out, licking her lips. The sight of her wet tongue created a sharp twinge deep inside his lower body.

He lightly squeezed her hand so she'd stop touching him. He knew where this was heading, and he wasn't going to be satisfied with a hand job. He wanted to be deep inside her when he came.

Picking up the condom, he had it on in less than five seconds. He maneuvered Amelia under him, settling his cock against her pussy. Lust made his vision hazy, and her face was all he could see.

He stared into her dark eyes. "I can't wait any longer."

"Then don't."

He pulled one of her legs around his waist and over his

back to give him more room before palming her ass with both hands so he'd be able to control how deep he went. "Ready?"

She nodded, and he thrust inside her with one deep stroke. They both moaned as he bumped against her cervix, and she gripped his ass tightly, pressing him even deeper.

Resting his weight on his arms, he squeezed his eyes shut. He knew it had been a long time, but he couldn't remember anyone or anything feeling this good. Lights sparked behind his eyelids, and he tried to count backward from one hundred to keep from exploding.

Amelia lightly touched his face, and he opened his eyes to see a tiny smile on her lips. He bent forward to trace it with his tongue.

"You should move, just a little," she whispered against his mouth.

"You're bossy," he teased. "But you need to be more specific. Do you want it deeper?"

He nudged his hips, and she gasped. "Maybe faster?" He gave a series of hard, quick thrusts that had her moaning and his heart thundering in his chest.

"Both. Now."

"You're also greedy and demanding." And he *loved* it.

She slapped his ass lightly. "Watch it."

He grabbed her hand and shackled her wrist above her head. The position pushed out her chest, and he took the opportunity to tongue her nipple, swirling around it before sucking hard on the tip.

He was rooted deep inside her body, motionless, and she tightened her vaginal muscles around him. Those tiny internal squeezes forced him to move, and he set a fast pace, riding her lush body in deep strokes. Letting go of her wrist, he moved his hand between them, finding her clit and pressing against it counter to his thrusts.

They were panting, and he sensed the telltale tingle in his lower body. It radiated out from his spine to his testicles and finally spread to his cock. He gasped, trying to hold back until she was there with him.

"Close?" He was too far gone to even put together an entire sentence, but thankfully she understood him.

"Yes," she moaned. "I'm there."

Her pussy clenched around his cock, and he let go, erupting inside her in a huge gush that made his vision go dark for several heartbeats. She shifted her legs higher, the movement wringing several more deep pulses from him.

He lowered himself onto her body, just for a moment because he didn't want to crush her. He was drained, emotionally and physically, and he pressed his face into her hair.

After a few moments, he dragged himself from the bed and headed to the bathroom to dispose of the condom. Returning to his bedroom, he grabbed the top sheet from the foot of the bed and pulled it and the comforter over Amelia. She was lying on her side, her dark brown gaze locked on him.

Climbing back into bed, he faced her. She leaned forward and gave him an openmouthed kiss.

"Thank you," she said huskily.

"If you can still talk, I didn't do a very good job."

She laughed softly. "I disagree," she said before rolling over and tucking her back against his front.

She wiggled her butt against his spent penis, and he dropped his arm across her waist to pull her closer. "You can try to make me speechless later," she suggested. "If you're up for it."

Knotting his fist in her thick hair, he put his lips against her ear. "If you keep pressing your sweet ass against me, I'll be up for it *sooner* rather than later."

Chapter 23

AMELIA WOKE UP ALONE IN QUINN'S BIG BED, WRAPPED IN HIS luxurious bedding like a burrito. The alarm clock on his nightstand read 10:33, and she double-checked the big red numbers with surprise. She'd never slept this late in her whole life. Of course, she had never had so much sex in a twenty-four-hour period either.

Rolling onto her back, she stared at the ceiling. This was her first official "morning after." She'd been eager to leave her previous lovers, and she'd never spent the night with them.

Quinn had asked her to stay, though, and apparently she was unable to say no to the man since she'd agreed to that request and so many more. She blushed at the thought of all the ways she had said yes with her mouth and her body.

She had given him everything he said he wanted, calling out his name until she was hoarse. After her fifth or sixth orgasm, she'd lost her ability to think. He'd had her over and over, including some early morning sex that sent her into a coma.

Untangling herself from the sheets, she searched the room until she found the T-shirt Quinn had loaned her. She pulled it on and headed to the bathroom, where she slipped on the panties she'd washed out last night.

As she brushed her teeth with the extra toothbrush Quinn had offered, she realized a sexy sleepover was fun until you had to put on the same underwear you'd worn the day before.

After she rinsed her mouth, she looked in the mirror. A bleat of horror escaped her at the sight, and she clapped her hands over her mouth to silence the sound. Her hair was frizzy, and ringlets protruded from her head like tiny copper snakes.

I'm Medusa!

If Quinn saw her this way, he'd surely turn into stone. At the very least, he would run screaming from the house.

She looked around frantically for anything that could subdue the terrifying mess on her head, but all she could find was a measly plastic comb. She whimpered when she remembered she had left her backpack downstairs in the living area. It held the tools she needed to get her hair under control.

Opening the bedroom door as quietly as she could, she scampered down the stairs in her bare feet, trying to avoid any squeaky boards. She peeked around the wall to see if she could spot Quinn, and when it looked like the coast was clear, she tiptoed to her backpack.

"Why are you sneaking around like Inspector Clouseau in *The Pink Panther*?"

Quinn's deep voice startled her, and she let out a little scream of surprise. She spun around with her hands on her heart to find him leaning against the breakfast bar. Even though he wore a faded USC T-shirt and a pair of plaid flannel pajama bottoms, he looked gorgeous.

He smiled slowly, his dark blue eyes glinting with amusement. "Good morning."

Dropping her hands, she smiled weakly. "Hi."

He straightened and walked over to her. He smoothed a hand over her hair before putting his finger under her chin and tilting up her head. He placed a gentle kiss on her lips.

"How are you feeling, Juice?" he asked softly, staring into her eyes. "I worked you over pretty good last night."

She suddenly felt shy, and she dropped her gaze. Unfortunately, she now had a much better understanding of how awkward the morning after could be, and she had a hard time untangling her tongue.

"Fine," she finally mumbled.

He laughed softly before kissing her again, a deep caress that made her insides liquid. "I hope you're better than fine, sweetheart."

Clearing her throat, she managed to squeeze out another word. "Yes."

"Good. Because I thought we could play tourists today and visit Alcatraz. We can drop by the penthouse so you can change."

"Haven't you had enough of my company yet?"

"I haven't had enough of *you*." He tapped her on the tip of her nose. "Not even close."

SIGHING IN EXASPERATION, AMELIA LEANED HER ELBOWS ON the kitchen counter. "Just try it. It's not going to kill you."

Quinn eyed the juice she'd given him. "What's in it?"

"Stuff that's good for you."

Frowning, he picked up the glass and sniffed it. He looked longingly at the cup of coffee sitting on the bar nearby.

On the drive from his house to Riley Plaza, she had agreed to make a late breakfast at the penthouse. He had asked if she had any coffee, and when she'd said no, he'd cut off another car to dart into the Starbucks drive-thru.

She'd already mixed together the ingredients for an egg white and vegetable frittata, and while it cooked in the oven, she had made some juice for both of them. She didn't really expect him to drink it, but it was fun to tease him.

He shifted on the barstool. "I guess I should be relieved it's purple instead of green."

"The beets make it purple."

He looked up, disgust filling his handsome face. "Seriously?"

She laughed. He obviously hadn't been paying attention when she made the juice.

"No. It's just blueberries, you big baby."

She turned to pull the frittata from the oven, and when she glanced back, his glass of juice was empty. Her glass, however, nearly overflowed. He was sneaky, no doubt about it.

"Did you just pour your juice into my glass?"

"Why would you think that?"

"Because my glass was nearly empty and now it's full."

He widened his eyes in an effort to look innocent. "I don't know what you're talking about."

She gave him a look of mock outrage, and he winked at her. She pushed down a smile, knowing it would only encourage him, and turned her attention to their brunch. She sprinkled a mix of white and yellow cheddar on top of the frittata, pleased with the way it had turned out. The spinach, red peppers, and mushrooms were a colorful, tasty combination.

Plating the frittata, she added a couple of orange slices and strawberries before delivering the plates to the dining room table. He grabbed his coffee and her juice and followed her.

He pulled out a chair for her, and when she sat down, he kissed the top of her head. He was so affectionate, and she wasn't used to being touched.

She hadn't been with her other lovers long enough to experience the casual affection most couples shared. She hadn't wanted it from them, but she was afraid she could become addicted to Quinn's attention.

Amelia had grown up with little or no affection. Her mother certainly hadn't paid any attention to her, so she hadn't exactly been showered with hugs and kisses.

Ava Grace's grandmother had been the only other person in her young life, and she had been more of the "spare the rod and spoil the child" mentality. In fact, Amelia couldn't remember receiving a hug of comfort from anyone other than Ava Grace.

Amelia was physically and emotionally reserved with everyone except her best friend. She had no doubt Ava Grace would rather die than hurt her so she didn't need to protect herself.

Somehow Quinn had slipped through her protective outer shell, though. Sometimes she forgot to be careful and cautious with him, and she'd relax enough to laugh and tease . . . to be herself. She was more vulnerable with him than she wanted to be, and it scared her.

She and Quinn didn't have a chance at a real relationship until she stopped lying to him, and once she told him the truth, she doubted he'd want anything to do with her. Her chest ached at the thought of how he would respond when he knew about her project with Teagan.

His low moan distracted her from her depressing thoughts. The man really loved his food.

"Whatever this is, it's delicious," he said, pointing to his plate before taking another bite. "Thank you for cooking for me."

His praise gave her a warm glow. She didn't like to fail, and she didn't like to do things if she couldn't do them well. That was why she'd been willing to give up the gig with Riley O'Brien when she thought Cherry hated her designs.

"You're welcome. But you have to do the dishes."

"That seems fair."

While they enjoyed the frittata, she and Quinn talked about Ava Grace's recent nomination for two awards from the American Association of Country Music. It was a big deal to win one of the awards, which were called Aces. This was the first year Ava Grace had been nominated, and she also had been asked to perform at the awards show, which was scheduled for early November.

"Have you heard Ava Grace's newest song?"

Quinn nodded. "Yes. I like it a lot."

"So you're a fan?"

He shrugged. "I'm a fan of all music. I can find something to like about every song and every singer."

"So you're not one of those guys who constantly changes stations?"

He laughed. "No. I'm good with anything you want to listen to."

She studied him across the dining room table. He was a lot more complicated than he seemed. He masked his intensity with banter and laughter, but she wasn't fooled. She had witnessed it up close and personal. She'd felt it against her skin and inside her body.

They finished their meals, and she decided to help him with the dishes. They worked side by side without speaking until he abruptly broke the silence.

"You don't have to worry, Juice."

His words came out of the blue, and she eyed him intently. "What are you talking about?"

"Whatever we do in private won't affect our professional

relationship." His voice was quiet, but the sincerity was evident. "I promise you it won't."

She looked down, staring at the damp dishcloth in her hands. If she were concerned solely about her lack of professionalism, his words would have gone a long way toward soothing her.

"Do you really think that's possible?"

"Yes, I do."

"I don't."

She had been very stupid to think she could have sex with Quinn without it impacting every other part of her life.

"Amelia, we can keep things just between us. No one has to know if you don't want them to. Not Teagan. Not Cal. No one."

His efforts to reassure her spoke volumes about the innate decency she had recognized in him, and she felt even worse about her deception. Squeezing her eyes shut, she tried to ignore the voice in her head. It reminded her that she didn't have to lie to Quinn if she was willing to give up the redesign and turn down Teagan's offer to fund her boutiques.

"I know you believe what you're saying. I just hope you're right." She tossed the dishtowel on the counter. "I'm going to take a shower and change."

As she turned to walk out of the kitchen, Quinn hooked his fingers in her waistband to stop her. "How would you feel about some company?"

She shivered at the thought of some sudsy sex with him. It was a fantasy she'd had for a few weeks now, and she just didn't have the willpower to turn him down.

"What about Alcatraz?" she asked.

"Alcatraz has been standing for more than one hundred years, and I'm pretty sure it will still be standing no matter what time we get there."

Moving behind her, he pulled her to him. She could feel his erection, and her knees trembled a little.

"I hope you've got plenty of soap," he said, pressing his hard length against her, "because I'm feeling really dirty."

Chapter 24

QUINN SAT DOWN ON A STOOL NEXT TO DEDA AND BRACED HIS elbows on the restaurant's long bar. He'd asked the other man to join him for a drink after work because he wanted to talk with someone who knew Riley O'Brien & Co. inside and out but wasn't part of the family.

As soon as he finished up with Deda, he planned to head back to Riley Plaza to see Amelia. When he'd dropped her off at the penthouse after their outing to Alcatraz two days ago, he had reiterated his promise that their personal activities wouldn't interfere with their professional relationship.

He was doing his best to keep that promise, too, even though he wanted to call her to his office, throw her on the sofa, and shove his face between her legs. When he'd stopped by her workshop yesterday, he hadn't talked about anything other than business. And today when he'd swung by to say hello, he'd managed to keep his hands to himself despite her figure-hugging dress.

Forcing himself to stop thinking about Amelia, he turned his attention back to Deda. "Thanks for meeting me."

Deda gave him an assessing glance, and he quickly picked up on Quinn's mood. "What's going on, Quinn?"

He had a moment to collect his thoughts when the

bartender approached and asked for his order. He ordered a Fat Tire for himself, and Deda requested a vodka tonic.

"You think you're going to need hard liquor for this conversation?" he asked, not entirely in jest.

Deda chuckled. "Maybe."

Quinn trusted Deda implicitly because the older man always had the company's best interests at heart. And right now, he needed to talk with someone unbiased. He knew Deda would tell him the truth, even if it wasn't pretty.

"My dad's not coming back to work."

Deda silently absorbed Quinn's bombshell for a few moments. "I had doubts he would."

"He plans to make the official announcement in December. He's going to name me as his successor at the same time."

Deda nodded. "He's making the right decision."

Deda's loyalty made Quinn smile. "I've done my best to run the company as he would have if he hadn't been sick. I've been careful not to make any big changes."

"I know you've been dancing to your dad's beat."

In James's mind, Rileys were practical and comfortable, not a fashion statement. He was more concerned about quality than style, and for most of his life, he had focused on making Rileys better. He had improved the quality and craftsmanship of the jeans.

And he had led the charge in the apparel industry to embrace sustainable manufacturing and farming. In fact, Riley O'Brien & Co. had been the first company to introduce jeans made from organic cotton.

His dad was innovative in his own way, but he wasn't going to suddenly change the way he thought about the fashion industry. He'd never wanted to be part of it. But once his dad turned the company over to him, Quinn would be able to implement any changes he wanted.

"Deda, once Dad hands over the company to me, I'm not going to hold back any longer."

The bartender delivered their drinks, and Deda took a big swallow before speaking. "What do you have in mind?"

Quinn shook his head. "I'm not sure yet. But I need you to give me some information."

"I will if I can."

"Have you noticed there are fewer retailers interested in partnering with us? Are you seeing fewer requests from boutiques interested in carrying our jeans?"

"Yes." Deda's answer was pithy but powerful.

Quinn exhaled roughly. "Explain."

"Boutiques that sell apparel exclusively for women are choosing other designers and manufacturers." Deda swirled his vodka tonic around in its glass. "The ones that target men are more interested in upscale clothing: suits, business casual attire, and apparel of that nature."

"And what about the regional retailers?"

"They want to stock what sells, and women aren't buying Rileys. The retailers don't want to manage too many vendor relationships, and they prefer brands that appeal to both men and women." Deda swiveled on his stool toward Quinn. "Am I telling you anything that you didn't already know?"

"Not really," he answered, shaking his head. "If we don't have products that sell, smart retailers aren't going to waste space on them."

"That's right."

"Do you think we can change their minds? Get them on our side again?"

Deda shrugged. "Maybe. Maybe not. Definitely not if things stay the same." He paused. "Amelia has a good handle on what needs to change."

He cocked his head. "Amelia?"

"Yes. She's not some empty-headed fashionista, you know."

Deda was fierce in his defense of Amelia, and Quinn was secretly pleased the other man liked her so much. God knew, Quinn liked her.

A lot.

He held up his hands, palms out. "Whoa, man. I never said she was."

Deda gave him a long look. "She has some really good ideas, Quinn."

"Like what?"

Deda tapped his fingers against the bar without answering, and Quinn resisted the urge to slam his hand down on top of them. "What ideas, Deda?"

Draining the remainder of his vodka tonic in one big swallow, Deda returned the glass to the bar. "You should ask her," he suggested before standing. "I need to get home."

Deda pulled a twenty-dollar bill from his wallet, but Quinn stopped him by holding up a hand. "I've got it. Thanks again for meeting me."

"Quinn, you know the company needs to make some big changes. But just in case you didn't know this: I am behind you one hundred percent." Deda patted him on the back. "See you tomorrow, boss."

ON HIS WALK BACK TO RILEY PLAZA, QUINN MULLED OVER THE conversation with Deda. Riley O'Brien & Co. had to maintain a strong network of retailers. *Period.* If Rileys weren't available in the stores where people shopped, they'd just buy something else.

He wondered if Amelia's designs would attract any new retail partners given their interest in designers that appealed to both men and women. Deda's mysterious comments about Amelia and her ideas had made him curious about her plans for the new accessories.

She had promised to have the first set of designs available for review in mid-November. He made a mental note to check in with her to see if she felt good about her progress so far.

He also needed to talk with her about their upcoming trip to the manufacturing facility that would be retrofitted to produce her accessories. The visit was important because he wanted her to understand the investment Riley O'Brien & Co. had to make to take her designs from concept to reality.

They were scheduled to fly to Georgia this Thursday to tour the facility, and she was supposed to head back to Nashville afterward. But he was going to suggest they postpone the trip until next week. He wanted her to meet his parents before she returned home. And yeah, maybe he was looking for a reason to keep her in San Francisco for a little longer.

Turning right at the corner, he increased his pace. He was eager to see Amelia. He wanted to hear about her day and tell her about his. And he wanted to kiss her pink lips, touch her soft skin, and sink into her snug body.

His cock twitched, and he shoved his hands into his front pockets to ease the pressure behind his fly. He had been sure that once he'd ended his dry spell with Amelia, his desire for her would decrease to more manageable levels . . . that he wouldn't be so crazy. But he was worried he wanted her even more than before. And he'd been pretty desperate before he had spent hours inside her.

It had been impossible to keep his hands off her at the chocolate festival, and when she'd suggested that he take her home, he'd employed every bit of self-control he possessed to prevent himself from pouncing on her in his car.

Once they'd gotten to his place, though, her obvious nervousness had made him hesitate. Although he wanted Amelia, he also wanted her to feel good about being with him. When she had said she wanted to see his bedroom, he'd almost fallen to his knees in thanks.

He hadn't been able to get enough of her luscious body, and he'd been more than a little greedy. After he had pinned her to the wall in the penthouse shower and kept her there until the hot water ran out, he'd promised himself that he would give her some time to recover.

The visit to Alcatraz had been fun, but his hyperawareness of Amelia had increased rather than decreased. He'd wanted to touch her constantly, even if it was only his hand on her lower back or his arm around her shoulders.

Quinn reached Riley Plaza, and he used his keycard to let himself into the skyscraper. As he rode the escalator to the company's reception area, his heart began to thud heavily. By the time he arrived on the penthouse floor, his palms were sweating and his heart was racing. He shook his head in irritation.

Why am I so nervous?

Chapter 25

AMELIA WAS WORKING ON TEAGAN'S REDESIGN PROJECT when she heard a knock on the penthouse door. She wasn't expecting company, but she expected to find Quinn or Teagan on the other side of the door.

She closed the sketchpad. She'd been drawing for a little over two hours now, and she had several great ideas for some new jeans. She hoped Teagan would be happy.

She'd focused on the accessories line all day, and she had made a lot of progress. A few of the designs had sparked some ideas for Teagan's project, so she'd left the workshop to come up to the penthouse a little early.

Peering through the peephole, she saw Quinn's tall form magnified within it. She was happy to see him and was about to fling open the door when she remembered that she'd left her sketchpad on the cocktail table.

"Give me just a second," she shouted through the door.

She didn't hear Quinn's response because she'd already darted back to the living room to grab her sketchpad. She turned in a circle, trying to figure out the best place to hide it.

She didn't want him to find it and discover her designs for the new Rileys. She thought about her bedroom but discarded that idea. Given her appalling lack of control when it came to Quinn, they might end up there.

She zeroed in on the hall closet and placed the sketchpad on the shelf above the clothes rod. Closing the closet door, she pushed down the guilt that blossomed because of her sneakiness.

Rushing back to the front door, she jerked it open. They stared at each other for a moment without speaking. Every time she saw him, he looked even better than the last time. And now that she knew what was under his button-down shirt and Rileys, she had a difficult time thinking about anything else.

"May I come in?"

She smiled, thinking he wasn't nearly so polite in bed. "Sure," she said, opening the door wider.

He walked in, and she closed the door behind him. She had barely turned around before he backed her against it. He slammed his mouth down on hers, thrusting his tongue into her mouth when she opened to him.

He tasted delicious, a mix of his own unique spiciness and the yeasty bitterness of beer, and she moaned against his mouth. He fed her several deep kisses before releasing her mouth with a gentle lick across her bottom lip.

"Sorry. I couldn't resist your lips."

"You think my lips are irresistible," she tried to tease, but her voice was raspy.

He nodded, his eyes smoky in the dim lighting. "The rest of you is pretty damn irresistible, too. Especially those red curls between your legs."

Blood rushed into her cheeks, and she placed her palms against them to cool her skin. Quinn wasn't hiding his attraction to her any longer, and the full force of his sexy attention overwhelmed her.

His gaze roamed over her face, and a slow smile turned up the corners of his lips. "Are you embarrassed, Juice?"

She made a sound of disgust, pushing past him into the living room. With a deep chuckle, he followed.

She sat down on the sofa and tucked her bare feet under her, making sure her wrap dress didn't fall open. She didn't want to flash him, even though he'd probably love it.

He dropped down next to her and propped his booted feet on the cocktail table. He crossed his legs at the ankle, the movement drawing her attention to the bulge between his thighs.

As arousal bloomed at her center, she decided that he wasn't going to leave the penthouse until both of them enjoyed a couple of orgasms. She was evaluating whether the sofa met her needs when he spoke.

"I want to talk to you about our trip to Georgia. We're scheduled to leave day after tomorrow, but I'd like to postpone it until next week."

"Okay." She shrugged. "It's not a big deal for me to stay here for a few more days."

He smiled. "Great. We can fly out next Thursday and tour the facility on Friday. I'll drop you off in Nashville on the way back to San Francisco."

She nodded. "That sounds good."

Glancing down, he pulled at a loose thread on the cuff of his shirt. A long piece unraveled, and she grabbed his fingers.

"Stop that," she ordered. "You're going to make the whole seam come undone."

He brought his gaze to her, his eyes hot. "I want you to meet my parents."

Jerking away from him, she jumped off the sofa. *"What?"*

He dropped his feet to the floor and leaned forward, resting his elbows on his knees. He shot her an alert glance.

"There's no reason to freak out, Juice. I thought you'd want to get to know my dad since he's been running the company for the past thirty years, and I thought you'd enjoy meeting my mom since she's the one who came up with the idea for our special-edition jeans."

Amelia immediately felt foolish. Of course, he didn't want her to *meet* his parents, like she was his girlfriend or something. He was thinking about business.

"Oh," she said weakly. "That's fine then."

She tried to ignore the little pang of disappointment deep inside her, but she couldn't help but wonder what it would be like to have a real place in Quinn's life. She feared she was little more than a convenient sex partner for him, when he was starting to mean a lot more to her.

He smiled at her acceptance. "The 49ers are playing your home team here this Sunday. We have a big suite in the new stadium, and I thought it would be a good place for you to spend some time with my parents. The game should be pretty good."

Like most Texans, Amelia loved football, and she knew the 49ers were playing the Tennessee Titans. She lived in Nashville, but her home team was definitely *not* the Titans.

"My home team is the Dallas Cowboys." Her tone made it clear she thought he was an idiot.

He grinned. "Do you like football?"

She propped her hands on her hips. "I grew up in Texas, Quinn. What do you think?"

"I think you're even sexier now than you were thirty seconds ago." He leaned back and patted the cushion next to him. "Come and sit down."

QUINN EYED AMELIA, TRYING TO ASCERTAIN WHETHER SHE would do what he'd asked or if he would have to drag her onto his lap. Thinking about her balanced on top of him made his cock thicken.

She still stood with her hands on her hips, and the stance accentuated her curves. It also pulled the bodice of her plum-colored dress tight against her breasts. Saliva pooled in his mouth as he stared at the white skin exposed by the deep V neck of her dress. Her skin was so pale it was almost translucent, and he now knew she had freckles almost everywhere except her round ass.

He let his gaze roam over her, noting the way her dress wrapped across her body and knotted on the side. He wondered what would happen if he pulled on that tie.

He lunged forward, tangling his fingers in the tie and pulling it loose. The side of her dress fell open a little bit, but it didn't loosen completely.

With a loud gasp, she grabbed her dress. While her hands were busy, he pulled her toward him. They fell backward onto the sofa with her sprawled on top of him.

The fall had hiked up her dress, and he pushed it higher so he could grip her ass in his hands. Pulling her against him, he groaned when he felt her mound against his cock, scalding even through his jeans.

He realized he was acting a little bit like an animal, but he couldn't stop. For some reason, he was more out of control right now than he had been the first time they'd had sex, even though he hadn't been with anyone for a long time before that. Amelia had stoked a fire in him, and he was throwing gasoline on it.

Grabbing his shoulders, she struggled to regain her balance. Her long, curly hair fell across his face, tickling his nose and lips, and she threw back her head to get it out of their faces. He surged up to lick her cleavage.

"Quinn," she moaned. "Let me catch my breath."

"No. I want you to be breathless," he said but leaned back against the sofa and let go of her ass.

She wiggled a bit against his crotch, and his vision blurred. Finally, she got settled and sat up, perching on his lap just like he'd imagined a few minutes ago. He gazed into her face. Her cheeks were the color of cherries, and her eyes were so dark they were almost black.

"Take off your dress."

Without any hesitation, she opened the front of her dress, slipping it from her shoulders and letting it slither to the floor. He moaned when he saw her breasts. A sheer black bra with hot pink piping around the edges covered the plump mounds, and tiny hot pink bows decorated her cleavage.

"I like your underwear, Juice."

He sucked her nipple through the fabric of her bra before he noticed her matching panties. They had a tiny pink bow on the waistband just below her belly button.

Oh, yeah, I'm going to unwrap her just like a birthday present.

Leaning forward, he slid his hands inside her panties to fondle her bare ass. He couldn't get enough of it, and he squeezed gently before trailing his fingers down the crease between her cheeks until he reached the springy hairs covering her pussy.

He swirled his fingers through the abundant wetness of her body, and she let out a breathy sound that made all the hair on his body stand on end. He brought his knees up so he could support her back.

"Unbutton my jeans."

His voice was barely a growl, and he could feel his control fraying. If he didn't get inside her soon, he was going to make a mess on this expensive leather sofa.

Shifting on his lap, she reached between them. Her fingers grazed his cock, and the light touch made him hiss. She froze, staring into his eyes.

"Do you have a condom? Please say you do because I don't have any."

Shit.

He leaned his head back against the sofa cushion and squeezed his eyes shut. He didn't have a condom. He'd brought a couple with him after they had left his house on Sunday, but they'd used them already.

Opening his eyes, he raised his head. "No. I'm sorry. I don't."

She pulled her bottom lip between her teeth. "Where can we get one? Is there someplace nearby?" she asked hopefully.

It would take him at least twenty minutes to run to the corner store and get back. Plus, he wanted to spend the entire night with her, and he wouldn't be able to stay overnight in the penthouse. Someone from Riley O'Brien & Co. might get to work early and see him come down from the penthouse wearing the same clothes he'd had on the day before.

"Let's just go back to my place. You can spend the night."

She shook her head, her coppery ringlets spilling across her shoulders and over her left eye. She swiped the curls away, and the action pushed her breasts into his face.

Leaning forward, he pulled down one of her bra cups and caught a hard nipple in his mouth. She sank her hands into his hair as he sucked and licked the tip.

"How would I get to work tomorrow morning?" she gasped.

He released her nipple with a soft pop. "I'll drive you."

"But someone could see us," she protested. "They'd wonder why we were together so early in the morning."

He groaned in frustration. He didn't want to hide his

relationship with Amelia. He wasn't ashamed of it. They were both adults, and they weren't doing anything wrong.

At the same time, however, he knew she worried about her professional reputation. He could understand her concerns. Some people might think the partnership between Riley O'Brien and Amelia had more to do with sex than her design talent. And he never wanted to do anything that could possibly tarnish Amelia in the eyes of her existing and future clients.

She shifted again, the movement sending a twinge deep into his testicles. He didn't want to stop, and there was only one way they could continue.

He sighed. "I'm clean."

"What?" she asked, blinking owlishly.

"I don't have any STDs or STIs, or whatever they're called now. I had a checkup a few months ago, and all the tests came back fine."

She considered his words for several moments. "A few months ago? What about your . . . activities since then?"

"I told you I haven't been with anyone in a while."

She tilted her head. "Quinn, you're going to have to be a lot more specific before I'm willing to have unprotected sex with you."

He sat up, and she wobbled on his lap. Wrapping his arms around her waist, he brought her face close to his.

"Okay, Juice, I'll be specific. Before we had sex, the last person I was with was my ex-girlfriend and that was more than a year ago. Actually it's closer to two years."

Her eyes widened in disbelief. "Why?"

He shrugged uncomfortably. He didn't want to explain why. He wasn't even sure he knew.

"I just . . . wasn't interested. I was dealing with a lot of stuff."

She didn't respond, and he lifted her off his lap and onto her feet. "Never mind," he said, scooting forward on the sofa.

At that point, he didn't know if he was leaving to buy condoms or just leaving. Either way, he was done with the conversation.

She pushed him back with the heel of her hand, stepping

between his knees. Reaching down, she began to unbutton his shirt, her fingers fast and nimble. She leaned forward and kissed him, swiping her tongue across his lips.

"I'm clean, too. I had my well woman exam last month, and all the tests were clear." Her words came out in a rush. "I haven't been with anyone in more than a year. And I'm also on the Pill, so there are no worries there."

She swallowed, her white throat moving sinuously. "I've never had sex without a condom," she admitted. "This is going to be new for me."

He instinctively understood what she meant. She was *trusting* him, and that was new for her.

A mix of desire and tenderness flooded him, and he pulled her closer so he could kiss her belly button. "I haven't either, even when I was young and really stupid," he admitted, tracing his finger over the bow on her panties. "I've always been scared shitless of catching a disease or getting a girl pregnant."

She laughed softly. "Me, too. I was afraid of getting pregnant and ending up a poor single mother with no hope of making my life better."

He rubbed her back, enjoying the feel of her silky skin. Every word she said gave him a much clearer idea of how she'd grown up and how far she'd come.

As she finished with his buttons, she pushed open his shirt and ran her small hands across his chest and over his stomach. He quivered a little when her nails scraped through the hair trailing toward his jeans.

"Take off your shirt."

He rushed to comply with her request, almost tearing it off in his haste before falling back against the cushions. If she wanted to be in charge right now, he was fine with that.

Moving her hands past his waistband, she cupped him through his Rileys. He let out a strangled moan.

"Don't torture me."

She licked her lips. "No, that's not what I have in mind."

She dropped her hands to his button fly, and one by one, she popped open the buttons. Pushing the edges of his fly apart, she slipped her hand inside his jeans and boxer briefs. She wrapped her hand around his cock and squeezed.

"If we do this . . . if we have sex without a condom, we're exclusive," she said quietly. "No sex with anyone else while we're together."

He struggled to catch his breath. He had no problem with her demand. He didn't want to be with anyone else. He couldn't even think about anyone else but Amelia. She filled his thoughts, constantly and completely.

And he sure as hell didn't want any other man to put his hands on her. Fury coursed through him at the thought of her sharing her luscious body with anyone but him. He wanted her to be his and his alone.

"I agree."

Chapter 26

AMELIA SAT BACK ON HER HEELS TO APPRECIATE THE SIGHT OF Quinn lounging on the sofa. She pressed her thighs together, trying to give herself a little relief from the arousal flooding through her.

She sent a quick prayer of thanks to the heavens that Quinn was half-naked in her apartment. Ready, willing, and able to give her toe-curling pleasure. His blue eyes were dark with desire, his color heightened.

She trusted that Quinn had told the truth about his lack of a sex life, and she was surprised by herself. She didn't trust anyone but Ava Grace.

In fact, she actively *distrusted* people. Why was Quinn the exception? Why was she different with him? She wasn't ready to do the soul-searching required to answer that question.

When he had told her that he hadn't been with a woman in nearly two years, she'd been dumbstruck. First of all, she couldn't believe women hadn't made fools of themselves to get him into their beds. The man was a walking advertisement for sex, and unlike a lot of good-looking guys, he had no trouble delivering.

In addition to his physical appeal, he was obscenely rich.

She imagined gold diggers around the world would love to get their hands on his big bank account, among other *big* things.

She wondered what he'd meant when he had said he had been dealing with "stuff." She knew about his dad's illness, of course, but she was intensely curious about his ex-girlfriend. Who had dumped whom?

Had it been a bad breakup? Was that why he hadn't been interested in sex? She hadn't asked because she knew it wasn't the time or the place since she was nearly naked, and he'd been ready to leave.

Did it mean anything that he'd chosen to get back in the saddle with her? She wanted it to mean something. To be more accurate, *she* wanted to mean something to Quinn.

She placed her hands on his thighs. They were rock hard under the worn denim of his jeans, and she squeezed the muscles lightly. She wanted his pants off. *Now.*

When she realized he still wore his boots, she giggled like a preteen girl. Shaking her head, she rolled her eyes at how easily he made her abandon her serious, reserved nature.

"What's so funny?"

"You still have your boots on."

His delectable lips curled up at the corners in a devilish smile. "Why don't you help me take them off?"

She stood and turned to grab his boot before remembering she only wore a few scraps of lace. Looking behind her, she realized his eyes were glued to her butt.

"*Oh, yeah,*" he breathed. "Bend over just a little more so I can get a better look at your ass."

She dropped his foot like it was on fire and spun around. He jerked his eyes to her face.

"Why did you stop?" he asked fiercely.

She groaned, torn between extreme mortification and mind-numbing lust.

"Turn around right now," he demanded.

He obviously liked to be in charge in the bedroom . . . or in the living room, as the case may be. Her sexual experience was limited, but her other lovers had not been nearly so dominating.

She was surprised to find that she delighted in his aggression. But right now, she had her own agenda. He'd made her scream his name, and she wanted to return the favor.

"I'll turn around and take off your boots if you promise not to touch me while I'm doing it."

"*Hell, no.* There's no way I'm going to make that promise."

She shrugged as if his answer didn't matter to her. "Then you can take off your own boots."

He gave her an assessing glance. "So I can look but not touch? Is that it?"

She nodded. "Exactly."

"What about talking?"

She was confused. "What do you mean?"

"Can I talk while you take off my boots?"

"Sure."

He nodded. "I accept your terms." He twirled his finger in a motion that indicated he wanted her to turn around. "Get busy."

She glared at his bossiness but followed his direction, straddling his leg and tugging on his boot. He didn't move a muscle to help her.

She could feel his gaze burning against her backside for several moments before he spoke. "Your skin is so creamy. I can see bruises on your ass where I gripped it when I was deep inside you."

She sucked in an embarrassed breath but continued to pull on his boot. So that was what he'd meant when he had asked if he could "talk." She should have known.

"I love the way your panties are trapped between your round cheeks. I want to shove my face right there."

Her whole body flushed with heat. She was so wet she could feel her arousal on her inner thighs, and she silently vowed to do everything she could to make him beg . . . once she got his boots off.

"Shut up."

"What's wrong?" he asked, his tone deceptively innocent. "You told me it was okay to talk."

With a growl, she gave his boot another tug. Finally, it slipped off, and she turned her attention to the other boot. He braced his sock-covered foot against her butt, pushing a little to help her.

"We weren't very adventurous over the weekend," he continued. "Except for the shower. That was fun." He paused. "I'm going to love fucking you from behind, holding your sweet ass in my hands and pushing my cock into your tight pussy over and over."

Her breath got stuck in her chest at the image he had painted with his words, and blood roared in her ears. He had absolutely *no* inhibitions, nothing to censor the dirtiest thoughts from spilling out of his mouth.

"I can't believe you!" she sputtered. "I could *never* say the things you just said. I don't even think them."

He chuckled. "I'm just getting started, Juice."

Lyndon Baines Johnson!

Clenching her hands around his boot, she gave a firm tug. She stumbled a bit as it came off, but caught herself by grabbing the edge of the table.

She stepped back, and he pushed off his jeans and underwear. His erect penis rose from a tuft of dark hair, a thick stalk marked with an intricate tracing of veins. It curved upward toward his stomach, a drop of shiny fluid oozing from the plump tip.

Saliva pooled in her mouth. She wanted him between her lips and against her tongue. She had never given a blow job, but she didn't really care if her inexperience showed.

Dropping to her knees in front of him, she bent forward and gave the tip of his penis a long lick. His taste filled her mouth, earthy and salty, and she wrapped her lips around the purplish head to suck deeply. The skin of his penis was smooth against her tongue, and she laved it gently.

With a loud gasp, he fisted his hands in her hair. She pulled back and looked into his gorgeous face.

"Is this okay?" she asked.

His eyes widened. "*Holy shit.* Of course it's okay. It's better than okay."

He smoothed her hair away from her face, and she took in as much of his length as she could. She did her best to create suction with her lips and mouth, using her tongue to circle the head of his penis.

She hoped she was doing it right. She hoped he liked it because she sure did, a lot more than she had thought she would.

Quinn trembled under her hands, breathing heavily as he began to thrust into her mouth. Cupping his testicles in her hand, she squeezed gently, trying a move she'd read about in a magazine but had never had a chance to use.

"*Goddamn*," he moaned as he abruptly pulled out of her mouth.

She looked up at him, licking her lips, and he groaned. "Amelia, I'm going to embarrass myself. If you take me in your mouth again, I'm going to shoot off in seconds. Or I'm going to explode the moment I get inside your body. I'm too close, and your hot pussy will be the first one I've ever felt without a rubber." He rubbed his hands over his face. "Let me get you off first so I won't feel so selfish."

"No," she countered, shaking her head. "I want to finish."

She didn't wait for him to reply, sucking his penis into her mouth and sliding her lips up and down his thick length. Within seconds, he fisted his hands in her hair and held her head still.

He moaned her name, barely audible, as his hips arched off the sofa. Hot pulses of semen splashed into her mouth, surprising her with the volume and velocity. She swallowed greedily, loving the taste of him.

After a moment, he loosened his fingers from her hair, and his penis slipped from her mouth. She swept her hand across her lips to catch any excess fluid before wiping it on her panties. Glancing up, she fell into his deep blue gaze.

"You're going to destroy me," he said hoarsely, his eyes dark and serious.

She crawled onto his lap, careful to position herself sideways so she didn't crush any important parts. She snuggled against his chest, and he looped his arms around her to pull her close.

He stroked her side and hip in a long caress, up and down, over and over, and her nipples hardened as his fingertips rasped over her skin. He nuzzled her hair, and when he found her ear, he sucked gently on the lobe.

"Thank you," he whispered.

Something loosened in her chest. Tears stung her eyes, and she tucked her face against her shoulder.

What's happening to me?

He took advantage of the new position to run his tongue down the side of her neck, biting the skin lightly before pulling it into his mouth. He licked and sucked her throat, paying special attention to the place where her pulse beat rapidly.

Palming her cheek, he turned her face back to his. "Kiss me," he demanded, his eyes focused on her lips.

She placed her mouth against his and sank into a kiss so deep it felt like her soul was pulled from her body. He sucked her tongue into his mouth, and when she retreated, he followed with his, aggressively stroking the interior of her mouth.

He nipped at her lips before following with several light darts of his tongue. She savored his taste, realizing that Quinn was quickly becoming her favorite flavor.

Moving his hand from her face, he cupped her breast, kneading it gently through the fabric of her bra. Suddenly, the flimsy material felt too heavy.

"Take it off," she requested.

He reached around her and unhooked the clasp on her bra. The undergarment fell forward, and she untangled it from her arms and pulled it from her breasts.

He rubbed his thumb across her nipple, rolling and pinching lightly. He scraped his fingernail gently across the tip, and a tingle shot through her entire body, radiating out from her center.

Shifting her on his lap, he pulled her nipple into his mouth. He created a strong suction, and she felt it deep inside. She squirmed against him, surprised to find him fully erect. Hugely erect, in fact.

Ooh, I'm a lucky girl.

She wiggled again, desperate to feel him inside her, and he laughed softly. Reaching down, he tugged off her panties in one smooth movement. He was like a magician. They were there one second and gone the next.

He grasped her arms, drawing her over him until she straddled his lap with her inner thighs clamped around his hips. Her knees dug into the sofa cushions, and he steadied her with one hand cupped around her butt cheek.

He brought her closer, his penis brushing against her curls, and her vision blurred around the edges. He sucked in a breath, and suddenly his other hand was between her legs, his fingers stroking deeply inside her.

"Amelia." Her name was a guttural groan, almost inhuman. "*Fuck.* You're so goddamn wet you're drenching my hand."

His words made her quiver. Wetness spilled from her body, and she tucked her face against his shoulder, beyond embarrassed.

Removing his hand from her body, he placed his fingers under her chin to raise her mouth to his. She could smell her scent on his fingers, and at the same time, she could still taste him.

He slanted his lips over hers, plunging his tongue into her mouth the same way she wanted him to plunge his thick penis into her body. She moaned against his lips, and he released her mouth.

He leaned his forehead against hers. Pressed against him, she could feel his heart thundering in his chest.

Placing both hands on her hips, he curved his fingers to clench her butt cheeks. He kissed her forehead before shifting backward to gaze into her eyes.

"Are you ready for this?" he rasped. "Because I'm not sure I can survive much more pleasure."

She laughed softly in agreement. Even though she hadn't had an orgasm, going down on him had been rather pleasurable for her.

She rose up on her knees to take his hard length into her body. He groaned as his penis entered her, and she shivered when she felt how hard and hot he was.

The friction was incredible, and she tried to take more of him. She wasn't sure if it was the position or something else, but he felt huge inside her, and she stopped when a pinch of pain intruded on the haze of pleasure.

"*Quinn,*" she gasped, curling her hands around his shoulders. "Help me."

"Shh," he crooned. "It's okay. Just relax."

He settled his hands flat against the upper swells of her butt and pressed upward slowly until he filled her completely. The pressure inside her was so delicious she whimpered.

He stilled. "Are you okay, sweetheart? Am I hurting you?"

She was on the edge, ready to climax, and she wanted to hold off as long as she could. She moaned.

"Yes."

"Yes, what? You're okay, or I'm hurting you?" His voice sounded tight, like he could barely breathe.

She was so focused on her own pleasure she couldn't speak, and when she didn't answer, he pulled out of her slightly. The drag of his penis inside her set off a series of internal trembles—not a full orgasm, more like the small shakes before a massive earthquake.

"Amelia." His voice was fierce against her ear. "Talk to me."

"I'm okay," she gasped. "I'm okay. Just don't move."

He froze, and after a moment, she relaxed against him. The movement forced him back into her body, and they both moaned. He nudged deeper, so deep she could feel his heartbeat in her core. She gave a tiny shimmy to pull him even deeper, and he sucked in a breath.

"I'm coming," he groaned. "Right now."

As he pressed her down on him, his penis jerked inside her, deep explosions that set off her own orgasm. Her internal muscles clenched tightly around his length.

He shouted out his release while she moaned, grinding against him. Her orgasm seemed to go on and on, and when it was finally over, she collapsed on top of him. She'd never been so mindless with pleasure.

"I think you might be my Kryptonite," he muttered weakly.

She smiled at the idea that Quinn was Superman, and she was the material that weakened him. "Well, you definitely felt like the Man of Steel just a few seconds ago," she replied and then giggled . . . *yes, giggled* . . . as his shoulders shook with mirth.

Chapter 27

THE HALLWAY LEADING TO THE LUXURY SUITES IN THE 49ERS stadium was remarkably silent, especially since there were nearly seventy thousand football fans cheering inside the sports venue. Quinn's footsteps echoed on the hard tile floor, along with Teagan's lighter tread. He had run into her as he'd exited the bathroom. It was well into the first quarter, and he'd wondered if she would show up.

As they reached the suite, Amelia's laughter filtered through the door. It was such a light, happy sound he couldn't help but smile. He'd been smiling a lot lately, and it wasn't just because he finally had Amelia in his bed . . . although she had spent quite a bit of time there.

After he had visited her in the penthouse and she'd given him the best hummer of his life, he'd taken her out for dinner the next night and back to his place where they'd had each other for dessert. She had come home with him Friday evening, and he had suggested that she bring an overnight bag with her so she could stay the weekend.

He'd quickly become accustomed to falling asleep with her curly hair stuck in his stubble and her luscious ass pressed against him. He dreaded the day he had to leave her in Nashville, and he was suddenly anxious to see her again, even though he had been gone less than ten minutes.

Opening the door to the suite, he held it for Teagan. Once they were inside, he immediately looked for Amelia's bright head. His smile slid from his face when he saw her talking with Nick Priest.

Teagan gasped, and he shot a quick look in her direction. She was unnaturally pale, her lipstick garishly bright in the fluorescent lighting.

"What's wrong?" he asked sharply, following Teagan's gaze, which was focused on Amelia and Priest. He brought his eyes back to his sister, and she flashed a smile that looked more like a grimace.

"Nothing," she answered before hurrying to join their parents in the stadium chairs near the windows.

He frowned at Teagan's odd behavior but forgot all about it when Amelia laughed again as she visited with the man she had previously described as eye candy. He didn't want to admit it, but he was jealous. The thought of Amelia preferring another man made him want to throw his head back and howl.

He clenched his fists. *Fucking Nick Priest.* Why wasn't he on the field with his team?

Priest smiled when he saw Quinn, and Amelia looked over her shoulder to see what had caught his attention. When she saw him, she smiled, too, revealing the little gap between her teeth that drove him nuts.

He had to remind himself that he couldn't go caveman and drag Amelia away from Priest since their relationship was supposed to be a secret. Instead, he held out his hand toward the other man. Priest grabbed it in a modified shake, giving him the classic half hug, half backslap.

"Priest. It's good to see you, chief. But I have to ask . . . What are you doing here?"

"Suspension."

As usual, Priest's response was quiet and monosyllabic, and he didn't bother to expand on his answer.

"Nick got suspended for helmet-to-helmet contact during last week's game, and he can't be around the team while he's suspended," Amelia chimed in, her understanding of NFL rules further proof she was the hottest woman on the planet.

Rocking back on his heels, he shoved his hands in his pockets to stop himself from snaking his arm around her waist and pulling her closer. He brought his attention back to Priest.

"I remember now. That was a bad hit. I was worried for a second that you wouldn't walk away from it."

Priest nodded. "It hurt."

"Since you're suspended, I'm surprised you didn't stay in Nashville and catch up on your beauty sleep," Quinn joked.

Priest looked down, rubbing his thumb over his eyebrow. "Too long since I'd seen my favorite family," he mumbled.

Quinn narrowed his eyes, noticing for the first time Priest looked a little rough around the edges. His blond hair was shaggy, his eyes had dark circles under them, and stubble covered his face.

"Have you seen Mom and Dad yet?"

Priest nodded.

"Where's everyone else?" Amelia asked.

"Cal and Saika are at Valerie's dance recital, but they'll be here later," Quinn explained. "Teagan just got here. She's sitting with my parents."

Priest sucked in a breath like he'd been punched in the gut before rubbing his chest with the palm of his hand. Amelia gave him a concerned glance.

"Nick, are you okay?" she asked, placing her hand on his forearm.

"Heartburn."

She made sympathetic noises as she stroked Priest's arm, and Quinn wanted to grab her hand and tuck it into his. He was extremely annoyed by the attention she was giving Priest. *Bastard.*

"You should see if Tums needs a new spokesperson," he suggested sarcastically, trying to figure out how he could get Amelia away from the man he used to consider his best friend.

Priest laughed, but it sounded forced to Quinn, and his aggression transformed into concern. Something was going on with Priest, but Quinn knew it would take an act of God to pry it from the man's lips.

"Let's sit down," he suggested, snagging two beers from the catering cart for himself and Priest along with a bottle of water for Amelia. He nodded toward the empty seats near his parents and Teagan. There were only three seats left, two on the back row and one on the first row next to his sister.

As Priest glanced toward the seats, Quinn felt his friend stiffen. "There's plenty of room," he added, trying to make sure Priest knew he was welcome. "You can have the seat next to Teagan."

Priest didn't bother to reply. He just headed toward the empty seat.

Quinn shifted closer to Amelia. "You're sitting next to me, not Eye Candy."

She let out a breathy laugh that made his skin tingle. "If you insist."

"I do insist. And I might insist that we leave the game early."

She shot him a quizzical glance. "Why? Aren't you having a good time?" She smiled wryly. "I am." He detected a bit of surprise in her voice.

He leaned down. "I'm having a good time, Juice, but I don't think I can wait another three hours before I get you naked again," he whispered into her ear. "What would you think about sneaking off to the janitor's closet down the hall?"

Her brown eyes widened, and she looked around before replying. "Seriously? We had sex right before we left."

His cock twitched at the reminder. The sex they'd enjoyed in his Audi had been fast and rough, and it had barely taken the edge off his hunger for her. He imagined he was just like a junkie who needed more and more heroin to achieve the mind-numbing rush.

He was a little worried his hunger for Amelia might never be sated. His feelings for her were more intense than simple affection and basic desire.

He had told Amelia that meeting his parents wasn't a big deal—that it was just business. But when he'd introduced her to them, he realized he'd been lying to himself and to her.

It *was* a big deal.

Quinn had wanted to claim her. He had wanted to let his parents know she meant something to him beyond their professional relationship—that she was important to him not only as the future president and CEO of Riley O'Brien & Co. but also as a man.

He had studied Amelia as she'd talked with his parents. She was engaged but reserved. Friendly but not warm. Her brown eyes had been wary, like she had expected rejection or something worse, and he'd fought the urge to wrap her in his arms and reassure her.

He knew his parents were no threat to Amelia, but he'd stayed close in case she had needed him. She'd unearthed his protective instincts—instincts that usually lay dormant unless the situation involved someone he loved.

"SO TELL ME, AMELIA, HAS MY SON BEEN HELPFUL? HAS HE given you what you need?"

Oh, yeah, he's given me what I need. Several times, in fact.

Praying her cheeks weren't red, she met Kate O'Brien's dark blue gaze. Even the most innocent question made her think naughty thoughts, and she couldn't believe she was thinking about sex when Quinn's mother stood right next to her.

Kate arched a blond brow at Amelia, reminding her that she'd not answered Kate's question. "He's been very helpful," she replied.

"I'm glad to hear it. Has he been hands-on?"

An image of Quinn's hands on her breasts flashed through her mind, and Amelia knew there was no hope of avoiding a blush this time. Heat raced across her face like wildfire.

Ronald Wilson Reagan!

"No, he hasn't been hands-on," Amelia averred. "He told me that he didn't want to be too involved with the project."

Kate sighed. "I had hoped Quinn would be more interested in the women's division than James." She shook her head. "But O'Brien men are so stubborn, and my sons are the rules not the exceptions."

Amelia laughed. Quinn caught her eye from across the room and winked at her. She smiled, and Kate turned to see what had caught her attention.

It was halftime, and the suite was full of people, but Kate

realized the recipient of her smile. The older woman returned her gaze to Amelia, giving her an appraising glance that made her smile fade.

"Your relationship with Quinn is not strictly business," Kate said baldy, a statement rather than a question.

She didn't know how to respond. Even if she'd had an idea of what to say, her tongue was stuck to the roof of her mouth. Kate stared into her eyes, and whatever she saw there made her frown. She opened her mouth, but the arrival of James and Cal silenced her.

"What are you lovely ladies discussing?" Cal asked, his voice light and teasing.

Saika's daughter, Valerie, was perched on his shoulders, still dressed in the pink tutu from her dance recital. It was obvious he loved spending time with her, and the little girl clearly felt the same way about him.

Kate looked toward Amelia before answering her youngest son. "We were chatting about Amelia's progress on the new accessories."

"Are you going to have something to show us soon?" Cal asked.

Amelia nodded. "Soon," she promised.

James hadn't said anything, and Amelia took the opportunity to study him. It was obvious he'd been ill. His skin carried the strange yellowish-gray pallor common with cancer patients. Even though it was apparent he wasn't well, it also was obvious he had been an extremely handsome man. He was still handsome, but illness overshadowed his good looks.

James's gaze fell on Amelia, and she was embarrassed she'd been caught staring. His lips curled up, a duplicate of Quinn's enticing smile.

"And how do you think Riley O'Brien & Co. customers will respond to your accessories, Amelia?" James asked.

"At the very least, I hope they're going to like them," she answered. "But I really want them to love them."

She knew James had little or no interest in the women's division, but she didn't know why. Was he sexist?

Given the way he treated his wife and daughter, she couldn't imagine he was. It was obvious Kate and Teagan were strong women who wouldn't put up with any kind of sexist behavior.

So what was behind James's indifferent attitude toward the women's division? And more important, did Quinn feel the same way? She had tried to bring up the subject several times with him, but she'd clearly been too subtle with her questioning because she still was in the dark.

Was it simply about tradition? Was James unwilling to embrace change? Perhaps he'd passed along his way of thinking to his oldest son along with his smile.

Either way, she needed to tell Quinn the truth about her project with Teagan. She'd become very adept at silencing her conscience, but she hadn't been able to silence Ava Grace's warning. It rang in her ears constantly, reminding her that it didn't matter how she felt about Quinn as long as she continued to lie to him.

James's derisive snort interrupted Amelia's internal musings. "The fashion world is fickle," he noted with a frown. "They might love you today and hate you tomorrow."

Unfortunately, he was right. That's why she was so determined to become a brand that extended beyond a pair of boots or a stylish bag. Her boutiques would play a huge role in the creation of that brand, cementing her as more than a trend.

She nodded. "I know. It can be ugly."

Suddenly, Cal yelped, and Amelia glanced up to see Valerie's tiny fingers twisted in his dark hair. The little girl giggled.

"Sorry, Cal," she said.

He patted Valerie's leg. "It's okay, ballerina. Do you want down? The game's starting again."

Valerie's high-pitched squeal made everyone laugh, and Cal carefully plucked her off his shoulders and placed her on the ground. She did a quick pirouette before running to the glass to look down onto the field.

Amelia took advantage of the break in conversation to excuse herself. She had planned to run to the bathroom during halftime, but Kate had distracted her.

She swiftly made her way toward the ladies' room. It was quite a walk from the Riley O'Brien & Co. suite. She followed a sign directing her down a long hallway, feeling like a rat in a maze.

The hallway dead-ended, and Amelia realized she was lost. She turned toward the right but came to an abrupt stop when she saw who was there.

Teagan and Nick Priest were wrapped in each other's arms, totally oblivious to the rest of the world. He had her backed up against the wall, his hands clenched in her dark hair, and his mouth devouring hers. She was kissing him back, her hands tightly gripping his lean waist.

Blood rushed into Amelia's face. She had never seen such a passionate embrace except on television, specifically daytime TV. She felt like a voyeur, and she tried to back up as quietly as her boots would let her.

She hesitated when she heard Teagan's voice. It was thick with a bitter mix of tears and anger.

"Stop, Nick!" Teagan exclaimed.

Amelia was suddenly unsure about what she had interrupted, and she decided to stay put in case things got ugly. She didn't think Nick was dangerous, but there were some men who took what they wanted regardless of what their partners were willing to give.

"I told you to leave me alone," Teagan continued, her voice climbing in volume and intensity. "No! Don't touch me!"

Amelia stomped her foot, making a loud cracking noise on the tile floor. Nick jerked back from Teagan, dropping his hands from her head, and they turned to seek out the source of the noise.

She swallowed when she saw their faces. Obviously, something had gone terribly wrong between the two of them. Teagan's eyes were bright with tears, and Nick's visage was etched with such misery she had to avert her gaze.

In her peripheral vision, she saw Teagan push Nick away and rush toward Amelia. Tears had escaped Teagan's eyes, and they rolled down her cheeks, leaving shiny tracks on her smooth skin.

"Please, please, don't tell anyone about this," she begged, grabbing Amelia's hand.

Amelia had no idea what "this" was, exactly, but she made a soothing noise to calm the other woman. "I won't, Teagan. I promise."

Swiping her fingers under her eyes, Teagan tossed one

last glance toward Nick before hurrying away, leaving him and Amelia alone in the secluded hallway. He leaned back against the wall and tilted his head to look up at the ceiling. Sighing loudly, he ran his hands over his face before turning his head to look at her.

She debated what to do. Should she just walk away? Offer him a shoulder to cry on?

"What's going on, Nick?"

Shaking his head, he straightened to his full height and walked toward her. He stopped when he reached her side, looming over her.

He patted her shoulder awkwardly. "Not your problem," he said gruffly.

"But it is a problem?" she persisted.

He stared at her, his light green eyes glowing against his tan skin and his wheat-colored hair gleaming under the overhead lights. All that gorgeousness took a backseat to his obvious emotional distress.

He nodded curtly before he strode away, leaving Amelia in the hallway, lost in more ways than one.

Chapter 28

"DO YOU OWN THIS PLANE?"

Quinn leaned back in the aircraft's leather seat and propped his foot on his knee. Amelia sat across from him, belted in and ready for takeoff.

"Me personally? Just how rich do you think I am?" he teased, enjoying the color that surged into her face.

He loved to make Amelia blush, and he'd already figured out the easiest path to cherry-red cheeks. All he had to do was tell her exactly what he planned to do with his body and hers the next time they were naked. It worked every time.

Shifting in his seat, he gave his overstimulated body a mental directive to calm down. If he wasn't inside Amelia's lush body, he was thinking about how soon he could get there. It was ridiculous how much he wanted her.

"I doubt your bank balance could be any bigger than your sense of self-importance," she responded. Her tone was mild, but her eyes shot sparks at him.

He laughed but decided to answer her question before she kicked him with her pointy-toed boots. "I don't own the plane, and neither does Riley O'Brien & Co. It's kind of complicated. We lease the jet for a defined number of flying hours and share it with other people and companies that do the same thing."

She nodded. "Like a timeshare in Florida."

"Yes, but we're guaranteed access to the plane anytime we need it."

"That explains why you don't fly coach."

"Hell, I'd rather walk than fly coach," he said, not entirely joking.

In his opinion, "coach" was another word for "torture." He didn't even like to fly first class on a commercial flight.

Amelia blew a coppery curl away from her mouth. "You are so *spoiled*. You know that, right?"

He shrugged. She was right, but he wasn't going to apologize for who he was.

He knew he had been blessed in so many ways, and he was grateful. He also was smart enough to take advantage of the things that made life easier, and a private jet was one of them.

He arched an eyebrow. "If you want, you can get off this plane and fly coach to Georgia. I'll just meet you there."

She rolled her lips inward, and he could tell she was trying not to laugh. She waved her hand around the cabin.

"Since I'm already here, and you have plenty of room, I'll keep you company during the long, boring flight. I'm sure we can find something to occupy us."

He glanced at her alertly. That sounded like a sexual innuendo to him, and his cock twitched with eagerness. His thoughts must have been obvious on his face because she snickered.

"We can talk," she clarified.

He gave an exaggerated groan as if talking with her for five hours would be painful. But privately, he was happy to have her to himself with no interruptions.

In fact, talking with Amelia now ranked as his favorite thing to do, even more than getting her naked. Every conversation with her started out with her being reserved and standoffish. But after a while, she stopped holding back.

He had realized she was a lot like his mom's convection oven. She took some time to heat up, but once she did, it was worth it because she warmed from the inside out. He loved the moment when she finally gave him what he wanted: the real Amelia.

The one who was both sweet and tart and just a little bit quirky.

He used to roll his eyes when other couples claimed that they never ran out of things to talk about, but now he knew what they meant. He and Amelia always found something to discuss, and whether the conversation was silly or serious, he liked her more with every word that came out of her mouth.

She stimulated his brain as much as she stimulated his body. The two of them came from very different backgrounds, and her way of looking at things intrigued him so much that he found himself wanting to ask her opinion on a variety of subjects.

His thoughts were interrupted when the flight attendant delivered their drinks and told them the plane would take off in a couple of minutes. Nodding his thanks, he returned his attention to Amelia.

"What do you want to talk about, Juice?" he asked as the plane jerked and started to move forward.

"Once we're in the air, I want to show you the designs I've worked up for the new accessories."

He nodded his agreement as the plane sped down the runway and lifted into the sunny sky. Once they achieved cruising altitude, Amelia unbuckled her seat belt and leaned down to grab her big leather bag, which she had placed under her seat.

The position gave him a great view of her breasts. They were accentuated by her blue V-neck sweater, and he couldn't pull his eyes away from her creamy cleavage. He thought about sucking her sweet pink nipples, and his lips tingled.

Amelia cleared her throat, and he jerked his gaze back to her face. Her expression indicated that she knew exactly what he'd been thinking. He flushed when she gave his crotch a pointed look.

"Feeling a little overheated?" she asked archly.

He smiled slowly. "Are you sure you want to go down this path? Because I have no trouble telling you exactly what I'm feeling."

She shook her head in exasperation. "You're a terrible influence on me, Quinn O'Brien."

"That's the best thing I've heard all day. Except for when you screamed my name this morning when you came."

He had expected that statement to get him a kick in the shin. Instead, Amelia's plump lips tilted up, and her eyes turned dark and liquid.

"Which time?"

Her response shocked a laugh out of him. Maybe he *was* a terrible influence on her.

She stood and pulled a leather-covered folio out of her bag. Crossing the narrow aisle, she sat down next to him. She started to flip open the folio, but he placed his hand on hers.

"Seat belt, Juice."

"There's no turbulence," she pointed out with a frown.

He wasn't a nervous flyer, but something unexpected could happen while they were thirty-five thousand feet above the ground, and he didn't want to take a chance with her safety. She was too important.

"I know. But just in case."

With a shrug, she handed him the folio. While she buckled her seat belt, he opened the leather cover, flipped past the cover page, and examined the colorful sketch covering the next page.

His first thought was, *Wow*. The second was that Amelia was obviously very organized because she had included fabric and leather samples with the sketch so he could get an idea of texture and color.

"What do you call this kind of bag?"

She leaned closer to him, and her hair brushed his shoulder. He got a whiff of the almond oil she used, and he barely controlled the desire to bury his nose in her curls.

"It's a tote bag," she explained. "I've used light-colored cotton twill for the body of the bag, and the polka dots are leather. The straps are also leather."

He took a closer look at the sketch. The tote was embellished with four large, randomly placed polka dots, and each dot was a different color.

"I'm guessing all these colors have fancy, girly names."

She laughed softly, making him break out in goose bumps. "Not so fancy. Turquoise, tangerine, tomato red, and tan."

"I like this," he said, pointing to the way the straps affixed to the tote's exterior with large metal studs.

"It provides some visual interest in addition to the colors." She indicated the adjacent page. "I've also designed a matching wallet. You could sell them as a set or separately."

He ran his fingers over the swatches. "How expensive are the materials?"

"Rachelle and I worked together to make sure the materials would be cost-effective but still decent quality. The profit margin for every piece should be high double digits."

"What kind of price point are we looking at?" he asked.

"I have a spreadsheet with my recommendations for prices. It also outlines material costs for each piece. I went ahead and chose substitute materials that would be less expensive if you think the material costs are too high with my original choices."

He nodded and turned to look into her eyes. They were just inches from his, glinting with intelligence and warmth.

"Are you always so detail-oriented?"

She tilted her head in consideration. "Hmm . . . I do tend to prefer order over chaos."

"The mess in my bedroom must really bother you."

She pulled her bottom lip between her teeth and quickly released it, leaving her lips shiny and wet. Reaching up, he put his thumb in the middle of her lower lip.

"Stop doing that," he ordered.

Amelia stilled. "Doing what?"

"I'm having a hard time concentrating with you sitting right next to me, and you're making it worse by biting and licking your lips."

Her eyes widened. "I'm anxious! I want you to like my designs." Her voice rose. "I've worked really hard on them, and my lips are all you can think about?"

He knew he was in deep shit when she jerked the folio from his hands and reached for her seat belt. They'd spent a lot of time together, and he had seen her irritated and annoyed, but never truly angry.

And, oh, man, she was angry now. She was almost breathing fire.

"Amelia . . ." he began in a placating voice, but she cut him off.

"I knew it would be a mistake to sleep with you," she said fiercely. "*I knew it.* It's impossible to keep things professional." She sucked in a deep breath. "You don't even respect my work. You only care about . . . about what's between my legs."

Anger and alarm rushed through him. "That's *bullshit*! I'm excited to see your designs, and I'm impressed you've already done all the work to cost out the materials and suggest alternatives."

He grabbed the folio, and for a few moments, they fought over it like kids playing tug-of-war. She abruptly let go, and it ricocheted into his face, slapping against his nose and lips with force.

"Oww," he mumbled, rubbing his nose.

Jumping out of her seat, Amelia knelt in front of him. "*Quinn!* I'm so sorry. I didn't mean for it to hit you."

She put her hand on his cheek, turning his face sideways to inspect it for damage. Even though he was fine, he let her do it, enjoying the feel of her palm against his skin.

Once she was satisfied the folio hadn't harmed him, she dropped her hands and sat back on her heels. He moved the folio to the side and bent forward to look into her eyes.

"I know this partnership is important to you, Amelia, and I know you want to do a good job for us." Wrapping his hand around her neck, he pulled her closer. "I promise I will devote one hundred percent of my attention to every single page in that folio."

He gave her a quick peck on her freckled cheek. "*We* are not a mistake," he added emphatically, holding out his hand to help her to her feet. "Now sit back down so we can review the rest of your designs."

She stood, but she didn't immediately take a seat. He couldn't tell if his apology had soothed her anger, but he hoped it had. He had meant every word.

Regardless of how much he had pissed her off, he didn't think she would walk away from her commitment to Riley O'Brien & Co. And if she did . . . well, there were other designers out there. They might not be as talented or have as much name recognition, but someone else could design accessories for the women's division.

When it came right down to it, Amelia was replaceable . . . to the company. But she wasn't replaceable to him.

Panic built in his chest. He didn't want to lose her. Had he messed up so badly she was going to break things off?

He swallowed, trying to get rid of the tightness in his throat. What could he say to neutralize the situation?

Before he could build a reasonable argument in his head, she reclaimed the seat next to him. He fell back against the leather cushion, relief making him a little breathless. She shot him a quizzical glance, and he hastily picked up the folio and settled it across his lap. He was determined to be all business even if it killed him.

Flipping through the pages, he found the sketch following the tote bag. "Tell me about this one," he said.

She didn't answer for several moments, but then she sighed loudly. "Okay." She ran her nail across the page, tracing the bag. "The shape is a modified tote called a shopper bag. See how it's wider at the top and narrower at the bottom?"

He nodded, and she continued her explanation. "I chose coated cotton canvas for this one. It's durable, and the coating makes it less vulnerable to stains."

"I know my fashion sense is questionable, but I like these prints together," he said, tracing his fingers over the swatches that showed a bright combination of hot pink, white, turquoise, and navy.

She smiled. "They're fun, aren't they? I thought the hand-drawn floral pattern worked well for the body of the bag, and I mixed in the gingham print for a nice contrast on the sides."

He nodded his agreement. "I could see this appealing to teenagers and younger women."

Her eyes lit up. "Exactly. That demographic group wears jeans more often, so I designed most of these pieces with them in mind."

He flipped to the next page, and they repeated the process. It took them nearly three hours to review the rest of her designs. She had included a mix of bags, wallets, and belts, about forty pieces in total.

When they were finished, she took a deep breath. "So what do you think?"

He paused to gather his thoughts before shifting in the

seat to meet her eyes. He wanted to make sure she knew he was being completely honest.

"I think they're great," he answered sincerely. "And I mean for this to be a compliment when I say it. I'm surprised by how talented you are. Some of the designs were better than great. They were awesome."

A huge smile blossomed on Amelia's face. "Really?" she asked, her voice a little higher-pitched than normal.

He nodded. "I would be proud to put the Riley O'Brien logo on every single one of the designs I saw here today. I'd be proud to put *my* name on them."

Chapter 29

THERE HAD BEEN VERY FEW INSTANCES IN AMELIA'S LIFE WHEN the reality had been better than anything her imagination had conjured up. But Quinn's response to her designs had far exceeded her wildest fantasies, and she was surfing a wave of euphoria.

She had hoped he would like her sketches, but she had prepared herself for a lukewarm response. Disappointment was her old friend, and even though she hadn't hung out with him in a while, he was always around and often dropped by unannounced.

Amelia had no doubt Quinn truly liked her designs. He didn't pull punches when it came to business, and even though they were sleeping together, she knew he wouldn't lie to her about something so important.

He took his responsibilities seriously, and his comment that he would be proud to put the Riley O'Brien logo on her designs had sent a rush of pleasure through her. His obvious appreciation for her work meant a lot to her because she knew he was protective of his family name and the jeans that bore it.

In some of her more fanciful moments, she thought Quinn was like a pair of Rileys. At first glance, the comparison might seem unflattering, but the same attributes that made Rileys so special were also the same elements that made him such an amazing man.

The jeans were marketed as "genuine" Rileys, and she thought "genuine" was a great word to describe Quinn. Rileys also were known for their quality, and again, that word fit Quinn perfectly. With the exception of Ava Grace, he was the best person she knew.

Ava Grace had a word for men like Quinn: "solid."

In her best friend's mind, solid wasn't a physical attribute; it was a personality trait. Men who were solid did what they said they were going to do and took care of the people they loved.

Solid guys were few and far between. And before Quinn, Amelia had never really known one.

While she held herself back, he was open. He expected the best from people and was disappointed when he didn't get it. She, on the other hand, expected the worst and felt validated when she got it.

And, having witnessed Quinn with his parents and siblings, she knew their differences were even more fundamental. He wasn't afraid to love. He gave it expansively and generously.

For Amelia, love wasn't so simple. She hadn't had an abundance of it in her life, and she hoarded it like a miser. Loving someone was even more difficult because she always worried the recipient would take more from her than she could give.

"Where did you get your inspiration for these designs?" Quinn asked.

"All kinds of places."

He cocked his head. "Like where?"

"Pick a sketch, and I'll tell you how I came up with the idea."

He flipped back to the first page, the one with the sketch of the polka-dot tote. "This is my favorite."

She smiled. "There's a reason why it's on the first page."

He returned her smile. "So it's your favorite, too?"

She nodded. "I got the idea from Teagan's dress. The one she wore last week. Do you remember it?"

Quinn frowned. “How could I remember? She wears a dress *every* day, damn it.”

Amelia laughed at his chagrin. “The top was red with black polka dots, and the bottom was black with red polka dots.”

He nodded. “Okay, yeah, I remember it.”

“I thought it was gorgeous, and I was jealous that I could never wear anything like it. My consolation was designing a purse with polka dots. That’s where I got the original idea.”

Quinn glanced at her quizzically. “Why couldn’t you wear anything like it?”

Teagan’s dress had been vintage, and it had featured a corset bodice, tight waist, and wide, full skirt. It would have overwhelmed Amelia’s short, pear-shaped frame, making her look stocky.

“I’m too short to wear that kind of dress,” she explained.

His eyes darkened to a smoky blue, and he tugged on a curl that had fallen into her face. “I don’t think you’re too short, Juice. You’re the perfect height for some of my favorite activities.”

Her nipples hardened. It just so happened that his favorite activities were also her favorite activities.

He smiled slowly. “Can I stop being professional now and kiss you?”

She stared at him. No wonder she had given into temptation. A nun would raise her habit for Quinn O’Brien and his sexy smile.

“Yes.”

Leaning forward, he caught her mouth with his, a somewhat chaste kiss given the look he’d had in his eyes. He pulled back and stroked her bottom lip with the tip of his finger.

“I’m sorry about earlier,” he said.

His apology flooded Amelia with guilt. She was the one doing something wrong.

“It’s okay,” she choked out, hating herself for continuing to keep Teagan’s project a secret. Hating herself for being too much of a coward to tell the truth.

At first she had stayed quiet because she hadn’t wanted to risk the accessories partnership. Of course, she hadn’t wanted to ruin her chance to finally open her boutiques, either.

Now she was more concerned about how Quinn would react to the knowledge that she had been working behind his back *while* they were together. Her deception was a personal betrayal, not just professional.

Earlier in the week, she had stopped by Teagan's office. She had wanted to talk to her about what happened with Nick Priest at the football game. But Teagan had deflected her questions, and somehow Amelia ended up in the hot seat.

Teagan had wanted to know exactly what was going on between Amelia and Quinn. Despite the other woman's skillful interrogation, she had managed to remain silent. But that hadn't stopped Teagan from making sure Amelia realized how beneficial the relationship could be for the redesign.

"If you're sleeping with him, he's more likely to listen to you," Teagan had said. "He's like every other guy who thinks with his penis. He'll go along with whatever you want to do."

Amelia had been horrified by Teagan's comment. What kind of sister thought it was okay that someone used her brother to get ahead?

Would Quinn think she had slept with him because she was trying to curry favor for the redesign? Would he feel she had manipulated him with her body, just like Amelia's mother had done with so many random men?

It had never occurred to her that Quinn might think she was using him to further her career. She tried to work through the mess she had created. Was there anything she could do now to stop the train that already chugged down the tracks?

Quinn's deep voice interrupted her internal debate. "Why didn't you design any footwear?"

The change of subject threw her for a moment, and she struggled to focus on his question. "I'm not sure it's a good idea."

He frowned. "Why not?"

"If you want to produce boots and shoes that won't fall apart, they're going to be fairly expensive. More expensive than a pair of Rileys."

"But you think there's a market for them?"

She thought about how to answer his question. This conversation was turning into a minefield.

"Yes, there's a market. But you heard Shelby's presentation,

Quinn. Rileys are known for being casual. They're not an upscale brand, and the footwear I would design would require upscale branding. We're talking about price points well above three hundred dollars for boots, maybe closer to five hundred."

Closing the folio, he tapped his fingers against the leather cover. "So you don't think women would associate Rileys with high-end footwear?"

She hesitated before answering, and Quinn turned toward her. He leveled a probing look at her.

"No." She took a deep breath. "But they might if Rileys produced a line of designer denim. Or jeans that were more stylish and flattering."

With a loud sigh, he leaned his head back against the leather seat. "So, you feel the same way Teagan does. You don't like Rileys. That's why I've never seen you wear a pair."

His voice wasn't angry. It was strangely flat, almost unemotional.

She saw his lack of anger as a good sign so she pushed forward. "Have you thought about getting rid of your existing styles and starting over? Producing several different designs and sizes, along with different price points?" She paused. "Maybe even expanding your product line to include shirts and skirts?"

He rubbed his hands over his face but didn't answer. She decided she'd come too far to turn back now.

"Do you remember that day in the workshop?" she asked.

He dropped his hands to his thighs and glanced at her alertly. He obviously didn't need her to explain which day she referred to because his eyes darkened.

"Yes," he answered warily. "What about it?"

"I was wearing a denim skirt, and you got upset because your name wasn't on it."

His face flushed. "Yeah, I was a little upset," he admitted.

She nodded. "More than a little."

His face tightened. "What's your point, Amelia?" he asked harshly. "Why are we rehashing my crazy behavior?"

Reaching over, she stroked the top of his hand. "I explained that Riley skirts didn't even exist. Did that sink in?"

He stared at her. "No."

"Is it sinking in now?"

He frowned. "So you think we're losing customers for two reasons: they don't like our jeans, and we're not giving them other kinds of apparel."

"Exactly," she answered with a nod. "If I want to wear a denim skirt, it's not going to be Rileys."

He pulled his hand from hers before unbuckling his seat belt. He sprang from his seat and began to pace the small cabin area.

"You have no idea how difficult it would be to implement the changes you described, or how expensive it would be." He made a deep sound in his throat, turning to spear her with his dark blue gaze. "We're talking about tens of millions of dollars, maybe hundreds of millions. It's a huge risk. No, it's more than a risk."

He thrust his hands through his hair, making the dark strands stick up in several places. He looked away from her.

"It would be suicide if it failed."

She studied Quinn. His shoulders were stiff, and his hands were clenched into fists. It was obviously a bad time to tell him about Teagan's project, and she turned a deaf ear to her conscience.

She'd tell him later. She *would.*

Chapter 30

A RUSTIC SIGN MADE OF WOOD SHINGLES MARKED THE ENtrance to the resort's driveway, and Quinn turned the rental car to follow the winding path. He and Amelia had landed in Georgia about an hour ago and had been on the road ever since. The long flight, coupled with the time change, meant it was early evening already.

He eyed Amelia. She had been quiet for most of the ride, and he couldn't tell if she was just tired or if something was wrong. Their conversation during the latter part of the flight had not been lighthearted, and although he had apologized for acting like an ass, he didn't know if that had smoothed things over.

Maybe she had picked up on his tension. He was worried she might not go along with his plans for the weekend. He rolled his shoulders, trying to ease his tight muscles. They were getting stiffer by the second.

He had asked his assistant to book two rooms at Reynolds Plantation, a luxury resort on Lake Oconee. He normally favored a hotel that catered to business travelers, but the resort was about the same distance to the manufacturing facility, so it was just as convenient. The big difference was its lakeside locale.

He'd never stayed at the resort, but he had heard a lot of good things about it, most notably that it was perfect for couples. He really wanted to have a romantic getaway with Amelia before he had to say good-bye to her in Nashville.

He sighed loudly at the thought, and she looked at him sharply. He tried to smile, but the idea of not being able to see her every day and sleep with her at night made him feel like shit.

"Everything okay?" she asked.

Hell, no. Everything was *not* okay. He grunted and let her draw her own conclusion from the sound.

Large magnolia trees shaded the path, along with a few weeping willows. Their long, thin leaves gracefully swept the ground.

As they rounded the turn, the resort came into view. It was an impressive sight, even for Quinn, who had stayed in some of the most luxurious hotels in the world. The architect obviously had drawn inspiration from the grand plantation houses of the Old South, although the resort was designed on a much larger scale.

Amelia gasped in admiration. "Wow." She slanted a look toward him. "Is this where you normally stay?"

"No," he replied but didn't elaborate because that would require him to share his plans.

They rode in silence until they reached the resort's entrance, identifiable by its white porte cochere. He brought the car to a stop, and the valet attendants rushed to help them.

In a matter of moments, the bellman had taken care of their luggage, and they made their way inside the resort. He suggested that Amelia take a seat on one of the plump sofas scattered around while he took care of the rooms.

She nodded her acceptance, and he headed to the check-in desk, where an older woman waited to help. He felt a little guilty about his sneakiness, but hopefully it would be worth it.

He made sure to keep his voice down as he confirmed his reservation extended until Sunday and that the hotel staff had taken care of his special request. He also checked into the room his assistant had booked for Amelia.

Quinn wanted her to stay with him, but he didn't want her to feel any pressure. If she preferred to stay in her own room, he'd just have to accept it. More important, he didn't want anyone in the company to wonder why only one room showed up on the expense report.

With both hotel keys in hand, he beckoned Amelia to the bank of elevators. He pressed the button for the fourth floor, where her room was located. His suite was on the top floor of the six-story resort.

They didn't talk during the short ride, and once they had exited the elevator, they headed to her room. Using the electronic key card, he unlocked the door and held it open so she could enter first.

He followed, closing the door behind him, and she turned in a slow circle to take in the room. It was beyond luxurious. If this was a regular room, he couldn't wait to see what his suite looked like. He hoped he'd be able to enjoy it with her.

"This is your room," he said, shoving his hands into the front pockets of his Rileys.

She nodded slowly. "Okay."

He took a deep breath. "I don't want you to stay here."

"What?" She cocked her head to the side. "You want to stay somewhere else?"

He shook his head, frustrated that he wasn't explaining things well. "Sorry. What I mean is that I want you to stay with me, in my suite on the sixth floor." He paused. "I booked it through Sunday. I hoped we could spend the weekend together."

She gazed at him, her brown eyes so dark he almost forgot what he wanted to accomplish. When she didn't answer immediately, he began formulating his argument to get her to say yes.

Moving closer to him, Amelia placed her hands on his chest, her palms heating him through his sweater. He pulled his hands from his pockets and wrapped his arms around her curvy body.

"You've been plotting," she said, her voice softly accusing.

He stared down into her face. He didn't think he'd ever get tired of seeing her brown-sugar freckles.

"Yes," he admitted.

She glanced at him quizzically. "Why did you get two rooms if you wanted me to stay with you?"

"Because you want to keep our relationship private, and sharing a room would make it pretty obvious we're more than business partners." He squeezed her against him. "Come on, Juice. Say yes."

She smiled, and that was all the "yes" he needed for relief to flood through him. Three more days with her.

And three more nights.

"What else have you been plotting?" she asked with a teasing lilt to her voice.

He rubbed his face against her hair, loving the way the springy curls felt. Most of his plans involved her naked with him deep inside her warm, welcoming body, but he didn't share that information with her.

"I've made reservations for dinner tonight. The restaurant here in the resort is supposed to be really good."

She nodded. "What time?"

He looked at his watch. "In a little over an hour."

She gave him a naughty look that sent blood rushing to his cock. Reaching between their bodies, she deftly unbuckled his belt.

"I'm not sure that's enough time for what I have in mind," she said huskily before unbuttoning his jeans. She slid her hand into his boxer briefs, palming his cock.

His heart surged into a pounding rhythm. She rarely instigated sex. He was the one who usually attacked her like a starving man at an all-you-can-eat buffet. Her obvious interest was a huge turn-on, and a tingle ran up and down his spine before settling in his groin.

She gave his cock a little squeeze, brushing her thumb over the tip and forcing a moan from his throat. Gripping her upper arms, he tried to gain a little control over himself and her busy hands.

She stretched up to kiss his chin, the closest she could get to his lips without him bending down. "Quinn, would you be very disappointed if we missed our reservation?"

AMELIA COULD HEAR THE DEEP RUMBLE OF QUINN'S VOICE through the bathroom door. He'd been on the phone with Deda for nearly an hour discussing some kind of problem with a new denim supplier. They'd missed their dinner reservation, but not for the reason she had anticipated.

Stretching her leg toward the faucet, she used her toes to turn on the one marked with a big H. Her bathwater had cooled, and she needed to warm it up since she wasn't ready to get out yet.

She and Quinn had been in the elevator headed to his suite when he had received the call from Deda. He rarely ignored the other man's calls, so it hadn't been a surprise when he'd given her an apologetic glance before answering the phone.

She had been disappointed, and if the erection pressing against his fly was any indication, he'd felt the same way. But she understood he had a lot of responsibility resting on his broad shoulders, and she also realized she wasn't the most important thing in his life.

They should have stayed in her room and indulged in a quickie, but he had been insistent they go to his suite before they got naked. When he had unlocked the door, she'd understood why.

He obviously had asked the resort to set the scene for seduction. A huge bouquet of white orchids occupied a place of honor on the entryway table, votive candles were scattered around the room, and a bottle of sparkling apple juice had been chilling instead of the typical champagne. He always made sure she had something nonalcoholic to drink.

When she had shot him a surprised glance, he had smiled and cupped his hand over the phone. "So much for my grand plans," he'd said wryly. "I'm sorry. This is going to take a while. I'll make it up to you later."

Then he'd given her a hard kiss and patted her butt. "Why don't you check out the spa tub," he had suggested before turning his attention back to Deda and the denim drama.

She had taken his advice, and now she had firsthand knowledge that the tub was quite comfortable. In fact, the whole suite was downright sumptuous. She was thrilled he had booked it for the weekend. She looked forward to spending time with him, all alone.

They had only a handful of days together before he returned to San Francisco while she stayed in Nashville. She tried not to think about the thousands of miles that would separate them.

This romantic weekend would likely be the last time she would experience his lovemaking. She had little doubt what would happen once she finished with Teagan's project and Quinn found out about her involvement.

In an effort to distract herself, she grabbed the bubble bath provided by the resort and poured it into the running water. Almost immediately, citrus-scented steam enveloped the room, and she swore her hair kinked into tighter curls.

She probably looked like little orphan Annie. It didn't matter, though, because Quinn never seemed to notice the things she disliked most about her appearance: her big booty, her crazy hair, and the wide gap between her front teeth.

He obviously had questionable taste because he seemed to like all her imperfections.

A draft of cool air washed over her as the bathroom door opened. Quinn poked his head around the door and met her eyes.

He smiled slowly, and she looked down to see how much of her body was exposed to his gaze. Unsurprisingly, the bubbles weren't doing a very good job covering all the important parts.

"Enjoying yourself?"

She nodded. "I don't usually take baths. This is a nice treat."

He entered the bathroom, shutting the door behind him. "I was thinking we could order room service and just hang out here in the suite."

She smiled. "I'm all for eating dinner in my pajamas."

"Me, too," he replied, laughing softly. "It's been a long day."

Grabbing the stool from under the vanity, he sat down on it gingerly as if he were afraid it would collapse under his weight. It was way too small for him, and he should have looked ridiculous, perched on it like an elephant balanced on a beach ball. Instead, he somehow looked more masculine.

He leaned forward to settle his elbows on his thighs, dangling his hands between his knees. The position drew her attention to his broad shoulders and muscular arms, which were outlined by his red sweater. The bright color made his hair look darker and his eyes more intense.

Quinn was so gorgeous. And he was all hers.

Until the weekend is over.

She didn't know what would happen once he dropped her off in Nashville. He hadn't mentioned anything about continuing their relationship long-distance, and she hadn't either.

Redirecting her mind from that depressing thought, she asked, "Everything all settled with Deda?"

"Hopefully."

With a loud sigh, he ran his hand through his hair. He looked tired, and she had an overwhelming urge to comfort him. To do something that would remove the burdens weighing so heavily on him.

"Is there anything I can do?" She laughed a little self-consciously at the idea she could accomplish something he couldn't. "I mean, I'm sure there's not, but I'm here if you need me."

Quinn straightened from his half slouch and ran his gaze over her face before meeting her eyes. He pulled in a deep breath.

"I do need you," he replied finally. "I'm . . ."

They stared at each other, the air in the bathroom suddenly charged with emotion. She froze, anxious to hear what he had to say. Clearing his throat, he dropped his eyes. He stood and rushed to the door.

"I'll bring the room service menu in here so you don't have to get out until the food comes," he said, reaching for the doorknob. "I'm sure they can make anything, though. Do you have an idea of what you might want?"

She swallowed, trying to ease the tightness in her throat. She knew exactly what she wanted.

But she was never going to get it.

Chapter 31

QUINN LEANED HIS SHOULDER AGAINST THE DOORJAMB AND gazed at the early morning sky. From his position on the suite's balcony, he could see the stars twinkling over the dark shape of Lake Oconee and smell the distinct odor of marshy water. It was four in the morning, and the landscape was still and quiet except for the intermittent chirp of insects.

He should be dead to the world since it was the middle of the night in San Francisco, but he hadn't been able to sleep, even with Amelia's warm body snuggled up against him. She, meanwhile, had passed out within minutes of finishing dinner, exhausted by the flight and her anxiety about showing her sketches to him.

In fact, he'd never seen a sober person fall asleep so quickly. One minute, she had been sitting on the sofa talking to him, and the next minute, she'd been asleep with her head in his lap.

Fortunately, she had already been in her pajamas, a set printed with eggs and bacon, of all the random things that could be on sleepwear. He'd helped her to bed, and when he had joined her several hours later, she'd wrapped herself around him like a climbing vine and let out a series of tiny snores.

He'd had a hard time falling asleep, and once he had drifted off, he hadn't stayed in the land of nod very long. There were just too many things going on in his head for him to rest.

He would officially take over a multibillion-dollar company in roughly six weeks. The transition probably wouldn't go smoothly, despite the fact that he'd been running it in his dad's absence for the past three years. He expected a certain level of skepticism from the board, along with some pushback from a number of employees, especially those who had been there for a while.

The denim shortage had become a bigger problem, the women's division was a mess, and retailers weren't as eager to sell Rileys as they used to be. On top of that, his dad had not fully recovered from his cancer, Teagan was behaving bizarrely, even for her, and Cal's problems with Saika were still unresolved, making his usually easygoing brother a short-tempered asshole.

But those things didn't fill his thoughts. Amelia did. There was almost no room in his head for anything but her. Even when he was working, she was there on the periphery.

He had never resented Riley O'Brien & Co. and the time he had to devote to it. But when he'd received the call from Deda last night, he had felt like throwing his phone to the floor and grinding his boot heel into it.

He hadn't wanted to talk about how much they could afford to pay a new denim supplier. He'd wanted to be with Amelia. The whole time he had been on the phone, part of his mind had fantasized about her in the tub.

He had imagined how pink and glistening her skin would be from the warm bubble bath, and he'd wondered if she had pinned her hair up or left it down to float in the water. He'd thought about joining her, pulling her onto his lap, and sucking on her pink nipples while she rode him.

He'd had to undo his fly because the buttons had pressed painfully into his hard-on, making it even more difficult to focus on the conversation. His lack of attention hadn't gone unnoticed by Deda, and he wondered if everyone else could sense his distraction.

Frowning, he scrubbed his hands over his face. He doubted he would regain his focus once he and Amelia were in different states. It was more likely he'd be angry at the world if he couldn't see and touch her.

Now that Quinn was trying to balance a relationship and work, he had far more respect for his dad. His father clearly could juggle better than a circus performer because somehow he'd managed to keep all the balls—Riley O'Brien & Co., a demanding, albeit loving, wife, and three rascally kids—in the air.

James had been a great father. He'd never missed a football game or a dance recital, and he had been home every night for dinner with the exception of the rare business event or out-of-town travel. He'd helped with homework, coached Little League, and participated in a million other things Quinn had forgotten.

He wondered what kind of dad he would be. He had always expected to have kids. Preserving the Riley O'Brien legacy for his children and grandchildren was the primary reason he worked so hard to make sure the company was successful. But he'd never really thought about how hard it would be to manage a family and the company. And he purposely had avoided thinking about the unknown woman who would bear his children.

He heard a noise, and seconds later, Amelia wrapped her arms around him from behind. She gave him a squeeze before coming to stand next to him, and he hugged her to his side.

It was too dark to see her clearly, her face just a pale smudge against the night sky. She leaned against him, her head tucked under his arm.

"Couldn't sleep?" she asked.

Her voice was husky, and it raised the fine hairs on his body. Sometimes he felt like she was lightning, and he was a lightning rod.

"No."

She sighed softly, clearly dissatisfied with his pithy answer. "Do you want to tell me what's bothering you?"

It wouldn't be the first time he'd shared his worries with her. In fact, she had become his confidante, his best friend, and he wished he could talk things over with her. There was one big problem, though. *She* was the cause of his insomnia.

To be more accurate, her feelings about him, or lack thereof, were keeping him awake.

Quinn rubbed his palm up and down her arm, the flannel of her pajamas soft against his fingertips. He was in love with Amelia. Hell, maybe he'd fallen in love with her the first moment he had looked into her chocolate-brown eyes.

He didn't know when it had happened, and he didn't know why it had taken him so long to figure it out. Maybe he was just stupid.

He'd realized how he felt last night when she had been in the tub, and they'd been talking about work. He had looked at her, all pink-cheeked, wild-haired, and surrounded by bubbles, and his heart had given a big thump, almost like it had restarted.

She's mine, his heart had claimed, *mine, mine,* mine.

Suddenly he had understood his future happiness was wholly dependent on her. She had become the most important part of his life, far more important than Riley O'Brien & Co. and even more important than his parents or his siblings, whom he loved beyond measure.

He would do anything to keep her with him.

He'd almost blurted out his feelings, but his sense of self-preservation had kicked in at the last second. For the first time in his life, he'd been terrified of his feelings for a woman, especially since he had no idea how she felt about him.

Oh, he knew she liked having sex with him. And she seemed to enjoy spending time with him when their clothes were on. But sometimes he caught her looking at him when she didn't know he watched, and the expression on her face was dark and unhappy.

He had a strong suspicion he wanted more from Amelia than she was willing to give. The thought of her holding out on him, of not giving him what he wanted, made him crazy.

Her voice cut into his thoughts. "If you won't tell me what's wrong, will you at least come back to bed?"

Suddenly, he was starved for her, and in response to her question, he faced her and bent down to cover her mouth with his. Placing his hands on either side of her face, he plundered her sweetness. He was too hungry to be gentle, too eager to go slowly.

He stroked the seam of her lips with his tongue until they fell open. Plunging his tongue into her mouth, he traced her depths until he had to pull back for air.

Once he'd satisfied his need for oxygen, he headed back for more, sucking on her tongue and giving her deep, wet kisses. He licked the corner of her mouth and trailed his lips across her cheek so he could whisper into her ear.

"I've never wanted anyone the way I want you," he told her, his voice little more than a growl. But what he really meant was, *I've never loved anyone the way I love you.*

Drawing her earlobe into his mouth, he nipped it sharply. She gasped, and he soothed the sting with his tongue before moving toward the smooth, soft skin of her neck. He caressed her throat with his thumbs as his tongue danced along the sensuous curve.

"Do you want me as much as I want you?" he asked. *Do you love me as much as I love you?*

She drew in a shaky breath. "Yes."

Palming her ass, he pulled her up against him, groaning when he felt the heat between her legs against his cock. He kissed her again, creating a delicious suction that had her whimpering in moments.

She slid her hands under his shirt and traced the muscles around his spine, kneading gently when he moaned. "You're so tense," she said, her lips rubbing against his as she spoke.

Yeah, she'd completely tied him in knots, and he hoped he'd done the same thing to her. He pulled away from her lips.

"Tell me how much you want me," he demanded, but she didn't reply. Instead, she stepped back and held out her hand.

"Come to bed, Quinn."

Chapter 32

A HEDONIST HAD DESIGNED THE SUITE'S BEDROOM. A MAHOGany four-poster bed dominated the room, the king-sized mattress covered by expensive linens and a fluffy, white down comforter. Several plump pillows were pushed against the tall headboard, providing the perfect setting for what Quinn had in mind.

He stripped off his T-shirt and pajama pants before unbuttoning Amelia's top. He pulled the edges apart, baring her pink-tipped breasts to his gaze. Cupping the creamy mounds in his hands, he kneaded gently. He rubbed his thumbs over her nipples, fascinated by the way they pebbled at his touch.

She shrugged out of her top and pushed her pajama bottoms to the floor. She stepped out of them before wrapping her arms around him. His erection pressed into her stomach, and he groaned. He was so hard it was painful.

"Touch me," he said, a demand and a plea all wrapped into two simple words.

She stroked his torso, her fingertips gliding over his chest. He shivered when she raked her nails lightly through the hair on his stomach. Leaning forward, she licked his nipple before biting it gently.

He pushed one of her hands to his cock and wrapped her fingers around him. His vision blurred when she squeezed softly. She started to kneel, but he stopped her.

"On the bed."

She tossed him a teasing smile and turned to crawl onto the bed, giving him an up-close view of her round ass. He saw a flash of red curls between her legs, and he couldn't pull his gaze away. He licked his lips, wanting a taste of that sweet pussy . . . wanting to make her writhe and come against his mouth.

Rounding the bed, he settled himself against the headboard, inclining slightly against the pillows. He beckoned her toward him, and she scooted up the bed. She started to lie down beside him, but he put his hand on her arm to stop her.

She tilted her head questioningly. "What?"

He stared into her brown eyes. "Closer."

She frowned in confusion, and he reached over and moved her until she straddled his upper chest and held on to the headboard. The red curls of her pussy were just inches from his face.

He looked up past her stomach to her full breasts before finally resting his gaze on her face. Her cheeks were on fire with a fierce blush.

Keeping his eyes locked on hers, he stroked the springy curls covering her mound. "Have you ever said the word 'pussy' out loud?" He traced her labia with the tip of his finger. "Is that one of your don'ts?"

She swallowed, her white throat rippling with the movement. She shook her head.

"No? To which question?"

He found her clit and rubbed it lightly between his fingers, a whisper of a touch that made her breath break. "It's one of my don'ts," she gasped. "I've never said it out loud."

He slid his fingers through her wet folds until he reached the entrance to her body. He slowly eased two fingers inside her, and she let out a long moan.

"What about 'fuck'? It's one of my favorite words." He pressed his thumb against her clit, and she jerked. "Have you ever said 'fuck'?"

"Quinn."

He withdrew his fingers and removed his thumb. "Tell me."

She groaned softly. "No. I've never said it."

He nodded. "Because you think only bad girls say those words."

He could tell she was surprised by his comment, but he knew he was right. He *knew* her, and by the time the sun rose, she would understand that fact.

He had to bite his tongue to keep from telling her that he loved her. She wasn't ready to hear it, or maybe he was too afraid he wouldn't get the same words back from her.

"You can be anything you want with me," he said instead. "You can be an angel, you can be a slut. I don't care. I just want you."

Her knees trembled, and he squeezed his hands around her waist to help steady her. "Spread your legs," he commanded, smiling when she widened her stance without protest.

As he caressed her curvy hips, he pulled her closer to his face. Leaning forward to nuzzle the curls between her legs, he sucked in a deep breath. The smell of her arousal was tangy and sharp, and he loved it.

He loved the taste of her even more than her scent, and he slipped his tongue between her folds, lapping the silky wetness from her body. She quivered, clenching her fingers in his hair.

He slid down against the pillows so he could get a better angle, and she gasped his name. He plunged his tongue into her again and again before sucking lightly on her clit.

He alternated with strong pulls and lighter licks, building a rhythm that had her rocking against his mouth. She'd started to make those delicious little noises that told him her climax was near, and he clenched his hands on her hips to still her movements.

He drew back to look at her. Her eyes were glazed, her lips open in a rosy pout.

"Please don't stop," she begged.

Cupping his hands around the smooth globes of her ass, he circled the entrance of her body with the tip of his finger. "Tell me what you want."

She blinked and pulled her bottom lip between her teeth.

He slipped the tip of his finger inside her body, sliding in and out with teasing strokes.

"Come on," he cajoled. "Tell me."

With a tortured moan, she tried to pull his face back to her curls, but he resisted. He pulled his fingers from her body, gently scraping his fingernail against her sensitive nub.

She shuddered. "*Please, Quinn.*"

"Where do you want my tongue?"

She closed her eyes and turned her head away, her fiery hair shielding her face from his gaze.

"Amelia, look at me."

She slowly brought her gaze back to his.

"I'll give you what you want," he promised. "You just have to ask for it."

"I can't," she whispered, smoothing her hand over his hair.

"Yes, you can," he coaxed.

He'd almost given up hope when she took a deep breath and spoke. "I want you to lick my pussy," she said, her voice barely audible despite the cocooning silence in the room.

He stared into her eyes. "Louder."

She fisted her hands in his hair. "I want you to lick my pussy," she repeated, and this time her voice was loud and clear. "I want to come with your fingers inside me and your tongue against my clit."

Her surrender gave him hope he wasn't the only person in the room who was crazy in love. "Hold on tight to the headboard, sweetheart," he ordered, and then he made good on his promise and gave her what she asked for.

YOU CAN BE AN ANGEL, YOU CAN BE A SLUT. I DON'T CARE. I JUST want you.

Quinn's words echoed in Amelia's head, while her body still pulsed with the pleasure he had given her. She rolled to her side, and he wrapped an arm around her waist to pull her back against him.

How had he known her deepest fear, her greatest worry? She lived her life by a certain set of rules so she wouldn't end up like her mother, and she had broken one of the promises she'd made to herself decades ago simply because he had asked her to. He had stripped her bare, physically and emotionally, and she knew there was no hope of walking away from him in one piece.

She shivered when he sucked her earlobe into his mouth. He rubbed his big hand over her hip.

"Are you ready for more?" he asked, his penis hot and hard against her backside.

He wasn't done with her yet, and a part of her wanted to jump up, run into the bathroom, and lock the door until she could rebuild her emotional armor. The other part of her wanted to welcome him into her body and her heart.

Brushing her hair back, he placed a string of kisses along her shoulder. He bit the tender skin where her neck and shoulder met, and the pleasure-pain of it shot straight through her.

He licked a trail up the side of her neck, stopping to suck gently on the skin below her ear. He knew exactly where and how to touch her to make her insane. He obviously was in a take-no-prisoners mood.

He moved his arm under her head, and the shift brought them even closer together. He groaned when his penis slid into the crevice between her butt cheeks.

"I need to be inside you," he murmured against her ear. "I can't hold off any longer."

He reached down and canted her leg over his hip. He positioned himself at the entrance to her body and slipped the tip of his length inside her.

Placing his hand low on her belly to anchor her, he pressed into her with tiny nudges. The little teases of movement stretched her deliciously, and after several long moments, he was finally wedged deeply inside her.

She was so full she couldn't keep quiet. She moaned, and he laughed softly, the sound brushing against her ear and making goose bumps break out all over her body.

"Does that feel good, sweetheart?"

She nodded, unable to speak. Her earlier orgasm had left her flesh sensitive and swollen, and another one was already building.

"You feel so good around me," he rasped. "I swear nothing has ever felt so good."

She turned her head, and he placed a kiss on the corner of her mouth. "You're so tight. So hot. I can tell how much you want me because you're soaking wet."

She wiggled against him, trying to entice him to move, but he pressed his hand against her to keep her immobile. "No," he crooned. "We're going to stay just like this for a little while."

She whimpered. She needed him to move. She wanted to come. She dug her nails into his forearm, and he grunted. He pulled completely out of her body and plunged back inside but stopped after one delicious thrust.

She moaned in protest. "More."

"No," he bit out. "Not yet."

She was completely under his control, unable to move. Surrounded by his strong body and filled with his hardness. Her internal muscles gripped him tightly, almost vibrating with tension.

"Please move," she begged, no longer caring she had been stripped of her pride along with her clothes.

"I'm fine where I am," he said, but his voice sounded strangled. "Maybe you should touch yourself. Just reach down and give your clit a quick rub."

Sweat beaded on her upper lip. She and Quinn had made love so many times she couldn't even count, but she'd never been so turned on.

Curving her hand over his arm, she slid her fingers between the folds of her sex. As she touched the small knot of nerves, a jolt went through her whole body. It felt so good she did it again, and her internal muscles clenched.

He moaned. "*Goddamn.*" He pulled back and thrust into her but then remained motionless just like before.

She closed her eyes to focus on the pressure of him inside her and the texture of her clit against her fingers. She pinched it gently, and lights exploded behind her eyelids.

Oh, I'm so close. If only he'd move.

She knew what he was doing. She knew what he wanted from her. She could barely form a coherent sentence, but she managed to squeeze out two very important words.

"Fuck me," she said, hoping he could hear her over the pounding of their hearts.

He stiffened, whether from surprise or excitement, she wasn't sure. He gave a short, shallow thrust, nothing like the deep plunge she needed.

"No." She squeezed his forearm. "*Fuck me*. Fast and deep."

With a gasp, he pulled out of her body completely. In a flurry of movement, he removed his arm from under her head and knelt on the bed. She looked behind her in surprise. His eyes were so hot, hotter than she'd ever seen them.

"Get on your knees and bend over," he ordered, his voice guttural.

She hurried to comply, pushing her behind toward him. Gripping her hips, he jerked her back against him, his thick cock sliding deep.

"Oh, my God, Quinn. Deeper."

He laughed breathlessly. "*Amelia*." He sucked in a lungful of air. "Stop talking, or I'm going to come before you get what you need."

In response, she ground herself against him, and he surged into her. The force of his thrust sent her sliding across the bed several inches. He pulled her back roughly, thrusting into her at the same time.

Reaching beneath her, he pressed her clit between his fingers. Just like that she came apart, calling his name as he jerked and pulsed inside her. She splintered into millions of tiny fragments that would never again fit together as they had before Quinn had come into her life.

Chapter 33

"WHY AM I THE ONLY ONE WHO'S PADDLING?" QUINN ASKED.

He and Amelia sat in a big blue canoe on Lake Oconee, the second-largest lake in Georgia. It was a perfect Saturday afternoon. The sun shined brightly, creating a glare off the water, and the light breeze carried the tang of pine trees.

Reaching down into the lake, he flicked some water on Amelia, who perched in front of him. She wore the floppy straw hat he'd bought for her in the resort's gift shop because he had been worried her fair skin would burn.

She tossed a flirtatious look over her shoulder, fluttering her eyelashes. "Because you're *so* strong, and you have such *big* muscles," she replied, her voice breathy and high like an ingénue. "And because I'm a lady. Ladies don't paddle." She gave an exaggerated shudder. "Paddling makes you all hot and sweaty. Ladies don't get hot and sweaty."

He smiled. "Is that right? I seem to recall you got pretty hot and sweaty this morning."

Her eyes widened, and color flooded her cheeks almost immediately. He chuckled as she looked away, facing forward so he couldn't see her expression.

So far, their trip to Georgia had been all he had wanted it to be, if not more. The visit to the manufacturing facility had gone well. On the drive to the plant, Amelia had been full of questions about the machinery and the manufacturing process, as well as the facility.

She'd been impressed when he had explained the facility was one of the first in the nation to incorporate sustainable design to reduce its impact on the environment and to use energy more efficiently. Solar panels covered the building's roof, generating electricity for operations.

Amelia had toured the facility while he'd sat down with the plant manager. He had been a little unsure about letting her go without him. What if something happened and she got hurt?

But then he'd realized he was being ridiculously overprotective. His feelings were so new to him that he didn't want to let her out of his sight.

With the exception of the visit to the manufacturing plant, he had put Riley O'Brien & Co. on the back burner and focused his attention on Amelia. It had been a little weird to tell his assistant that he wasn't going to be available and that he was turning off his phone. He hadn't turned it back on, and he had no intention of doing so until he returned home.

They'd spent the majority of their free time walking the nature trails, talking, and making love. Amelia had woken up this morning determined to explore the lake.

Pulling his paddles into the canoe, Quinn scooted forward on his seat so he could slip his hands under her T-shirt on either side of her waist. He smoothed them across her belly and continued his path until he reached her lush breasts. He cupped them in his palms, rubbing his thumbs across her lace-covered nipples.

She sucked in a breath. "Are you seriously copping a feel while we're in the middle of the lake?"

Ducking his face under her hat, he kissed her hot cheek. "I'd do a lot more than that if I wasn't afraid I'd tip over this ancient canoe."

"Hmm, it sounds like you need some cooling off. Maybe you should take a dip in the lake."

"That's a good plan, Juice. Let's go skinny-dipping."

She giggled, and the happy sound made him feel as if his

heart expanded in his chest. "Quinn O'Brien! I am not going to skinny-dip in broad daylight."

He gently squeezed her breasts. "Does that mean you'll go skinny-dipping with me tonight?"

She shook her head, and her curly hair teased his nose. "No way."

Sliding his hands from her breasts to the waistband of her pants, he flicked open the button.

"Give me a kiss." She turned her head, just enough for him to kiss the corner of her mouth.

He found the tab of her zipper and pulled it down. Before he could get his hand inside her pants, she placed her hand on top of his.

"What do you think you're doing?" she asked.

"You said you wanted to spend the day exploring, and right now, I want to explore the landscape between your legs."

With a gasp, she gripped his hand. "I don't think that's a good idea."

"Why not? I think it's a great idea."

She didn't respond, and he shook off her hand before sliding the tips of his fingers inside her panties. "Lean back," he commanded.

She stiffened slightly but then relaxed against him. "I'm warning you now, if you get us all wet, I'm going to be *so* mad at you."

Chuckling softly, he eased two fingers between her folds. He circled her clit with light strokes before sinking his fingers into her body.

"Sweetheart, you're already all wet," he said, withdrawing his fingers and thrusting into her again.

"I guess I left myself open to that one."

Her comment put such an X-rated image in his mind he groaned. Maybe this wasn't such a good idea. He always thought he could control himself with her, but inevitably he devolved into a mindless beast concerned only with one thing—getting inside her. Right now he was so turned on he was afraid he was going to embarrass himself by coming in his jeans.

Even so, he couldn't force himself to remove his fingers

from her creamy pussy. He pressed his thumb against her clit, and she shivered.

"I think we need to do a little creative problem solving," he rasped.

She made a noise, somewhere between a gasp and a laugh. "What's the problem?"

"Logistics," he answered as pulled his fingers from her body and pumped them back in.

She moaned. "What logistics?"

"The logistics of us being in a canoe and me wanting to be inside you when you come," he answered, swirling his fingers inside her and giving her clit a couple of light flicks with his thumb.

"Too late," she gasped, "I'm coming now."

Her pussy clenched around his fingers. He pushed deeper, and she gave a low cry of pleasure.

"Oh, God, that feels so good."

He waited until she had ridden the last waves of her orgasm before withdrawing his fingers. She straightened and twisted her body so she could swing her legs over the seat and face him.

She leaned toward him, hitting him in the chin with the brim of her hat. He pushed it back so he could see her face.

"I'm sorry," she said, her brown eyes huge and apologetic. "It just happened so fast."

"Yeah, that was pretty fast." He winked. "I must be even better than I thought."

Growling, she slapped his upper arm lightly. He laughed, enjoying her embarrassment.

"You hit like a girl," he jeered before reaching down to pull up her zipper and button her pants.

He grabbed his paddles, dipped them in the water, and began to row, mostly to keep his hands busy and to take his mind off his hard-on. After several minutes of companionable silence, he spoke.

"What are you going to do after you've finished with our project?"

She pulled her lower lip between her teeth, biting down slightly. He made several pulls with the paddles before she answered.

"I don't know for sure. I'd like to . . ."

He tilted his head. "You'd like to what?"

Sighing loudly, she looked up at the cloudless sky. "I'd like to open my own chain of boutiques."

He whistled. "That would take a huge amount of work, not to mention a shitload of money."

The businessman in him cringed at the risk she would take on. More than fifty percent of all new companies failed within four years, and the number was even higher for retail stores. Frankly, he thought it was a miracle anyone had the guts to start a new business.

She brought her gaze back to his. "I know exactly what it's going to take," she replied, and he thought her voice sounded strange.

"What did you do before Ava Grace won *American Star*?"

"After I graduated from high school, I worked two jobs. During the day, I worked as an assistant manager at a women's clothing store, and at night, I worked for a company that made custom boots." She smiled, but there was little humor in it. "That's how I know one pair of your boots would cost more than most people's house payments."

Quinn frowned, sensing that her mood had taken a turn but unsure what had caused the shift. He tried to lighten it.

"Maybe you can make a pair just for me, and every time I wear them, I'll think of you," he suggested.

She smiled, and this time it was real. "Ava Grace says she feels happier when she's wearing something I made for her."

He nodded. "Because you made it with love."

She jerked her gaze to his, and he felt his face flush. Could his comment have been any sappier?

They stared at each other for several seconds without speaking. Finally, she cleared her throat.

"Yes, I love Ava Grace. She's more than my best friend. She's the only family I've ever had."

"What do you mean?" he asked, cocking his head. "What about your parents?"

Amelia sighed. "Quinn, I've got mommy and daddy issues," she stated flatly. "My mother had me when she was fourteen, and she didn't even know who my father was. She hooked up with a group of guys after a football game in a nearby town, and my father could have been any one of them." She took a deep breath. "She told me on a regular basis she would have had an abortion but she didn't have the money. She was a terrible mother and an even worse human being who only cared about getting drunk, getting high, and getting laid. I was lucky the strange men she brought home usually passed out before they could get to know me."

She had used her fingers to make air quotes around the words "get to know me," and a mix of emotions roiled inside him. He was overwhelmed with rage toward her mother for not giving her daughter the love and attention she had needed and deserved.

And he was flooded with tenderness for Amelia, who was even more remarkable than he'd realized. He had guessed she'd had a less-than-ideal childhood, but he'd had no idea how bad it really had been.

"I got away from her as soon as I could. I moved in with Ava Grace when I was fifteen. Her grandmother had just died, and her father was MIA. We only had each other."

She fell silent, and he stopped rowing and pulled the paddles back inside the boat. "When did your mother die?"

She clenched her hands into fists atop her knees. "Five years ago."

"What happened?"

She swallowed. "She was killed by a guy she picked up at a truck stop. She went back to his motel room, and he caught her trying to steal money from his wallet. He beat her to death with one of the legs from the coffee table."

Holy shit!

Leaning forward, he placed his hands on top of hers. He didn't know how else to comfort her.

"I've shocked you," she said finally, and he nodded.

What had happened to her mother was horrifying, and he couldn't imagine how much it had fucked up Amelia. He struggled to find the right words.

He wanted to tell her that he would make up for all the love she hadn't had growing up and all the pain she'd experienced. He wanted to promise that he would give her all the love she needed now. He wanted to assure her that he would be her family.

But he didn't know if she wanted those things from him. And he worried that if he offered them to her, he might mess things up between them. He'd never been in this position before, and he suddenly felt a weird kinship with all the pathetic losers who called radio talk shows to solicit advice about their love lives.

She waited for him to speak, and when he didn't say anything, she raised her eyebrows. "Quinn, you must realize the relationship you have with your parents, and with Cal and Teagan, is not the norm. Most people don't even like their families."

"I know how lucky I am. And I can't even find the words to tell you how sorry I am about your mom and your shitty childhood. But I'm glad you had Ava Grace. When I finally meet her, I'm going to thank her for being there for you."

Her mouth dropped open. "You're going to thank Ava Grace?"

He wondered why his statement had shocked her so much. "Yes, I'm going to thank Ava Grace," he repeated. "She has a lot to do with the person you are today, and I'm grateful to her."

Ava Grace had done a great job of loving Amelia. She'd taken care of her and kept her safe when Amelia's mother had fallen down on the job. But he was in Amelia's life now, and he was gunning for Ava Grace's job.

Chapter 34

THE LIMO'S HEADLIGHTS CUT A SWATH OF LIGHT ACROSS THE front of the farmhouse, illuminating the empty driveway. Amelia exhaled in relief. It was pure luck that Ava Grace wasn't home since she usually spent Sunday evenings catching up on her favorite television shows she'd recorded during the week.

Amelia had known Quinn would want to escort her home after they landed at the corporate airstrip outside Nashville. She'd been resigned to introducing him to Ava Grace and then suffering her best friend's interrogation after he left.

She hadn't been eager for him to meet her, though. Men tended to turn into slobbering idiots in the tall blonde's presence, and she didn't want to see his eyes bug out and his tongue roll out of his mouth like a cartoon character.

More important, she didn't want Ava Grace to witness them together. Her best friend was perceptive, way too perceptive for Amelia's peace of mind.

It would take Ava Grace less than sixty seconds to figure out Amelia and Quinn had breached the boundaries of their professional relationship. Within ninety seconds, she'd have a good idea they were getting busy. By the two-minute mark, Ava Grace would know Amelia was racing toward heartbreak.

During the entire flight from Georgia and the drive to the farmhouse, she'd tried to work up the courage to tell Quinn about the redesign. She cared more about protecting Quinn's feelings than she feared angering Teagan. Her conscience—her heart—wouldn't allow her to lie to him anymore.

Unfortunately, every time she had opened her mouth to tell the truth, something else had come out. She had babbled the whole time, and he had given her strange looks for the past three hours.

This was her last chance to tell him before he returned to San Francisco, and she turned toward him with the intention of coming clean. But he no longer lounged beside her in the limo's leather seats. He'd already opened the door and exited the car.

Quinn held out his hand to help her from the car, courteous and attentive as always. She grasped it, a tingle traveling up her arm. She closed her eyes briefly to savor the feel of his skin against hers before joining him outside the limo.

The lights from the car's interior cast his face in shadow, and she couldn't see his expression. She could feel him, though, and she shivered a little when he brushed her hair away from her face.

"Are you going to invite me in?" he asked quietly.

Yes, she was going to invite him in. And then she would get some gumption and tell him the truth about the redesign. In doing so, she would implode whatever this thing was between them.

"Come in."

She headed up the walkway. Ava Grace had left on the porch light, and she fished her keys from her purse and entered the house. She flicked on the foyer light, and Quinn and the limo driver followed with her luggage. She directed them to leave the bags in the foyer, and Quinn cocked his head toward the limo driver.

"I'm not sure how long I'll be," he said.

The driver nodded, assuring him that he'd be waiting. She knew Quinn wouldn't stay for long after she came clean with her secret project.

The foyer opened up into the living room, and she switched on the lamps situated around the room. His gaze swept the space, his face openly curious.

"This isn't what I expected when you said you lived in an old farmhouse," he admitted.

She looked around the room, trying to see it from his perspective. Before she and Ava Grace had moved in, they had done some minor renovations, including refinishing the wood plank flooring, painting all the rooms, and installing new light fixtures.

They'd chosen a fresh, buttery yellow for the living area, which provided a lovely contrast to the shiny oak floors. The far end of the room featured an entire wall of windows, and a huge stone fireplace occupied one wall.

An oversized sofa upholstered in a floral pattern and two coordinating plaid chairs filled the homey room. Reclaimed barn doors that had been whitewashed were repurposed as end tables and a coffee table.

All in all, it was obvious two women lived there. It was decidedly feminine.

"What did you expect?" she asked.

"I don't know. But I like this room a lot. Is the rest of the house this nice?"

She nodded. "We went a little overboard when we moved in."

They lapsed into an awkward silence. The tension in the room was palpable, and nausea churned in her stomach. He crossed his arms over his chest, and they stared at each other, several feet separating them.

"Quinn—"

"Amelia—"

They spoke at the same time, and she swallowed the rest of what she'd planned to say. He did the same. She cleared her throat loudly, and he frowned as he dropped his arms.

"What were you going to say?" he asked, his eyes intent on her face.

"I need to tell you something."

Looking down, she realized her hands trembled. She immediately clasped them together to hide her nervousness.

She had rehearsed what she wanted to say over and over, hoping that if she used the right words to describe her deal with Teagan, she could minimize the fallout. But now that she was here, she couldn't remember what she'd practiced.

Quinn closed the space between them, wrapping his big

hand around the back of her neck. "I need to tell you something, too."

She let her head drop forward. Tears burned the backs of her eyes, and she pressed her tongue against the top of her mouth to keep them from trickling out.

Placing his fingers under her chin, he lifted her face. He smoothed his thumb across her bottom lip before leaning forward and kissing her. She gripped his waist with both hands, wishing his kiss would never end.

Wishing they would never end.

He pulled back abruptly. "I think Ava Grace is home," he said, stepping away from her.

She heard footsteps in the foyer, and she growled. She was going to *strangle* Ava Grace for her rotten timing!

He shot her a quizzical glance. "Are you okay?" he asked just as Ava Grace entered the room.

Ava Grace's gaze landed on her, and a huge smile lit up her face. "Millie!" she squealed. "You're home!"

Amelia smiled, even though just moments before, she'd imagined wrapping her fingers around Ava Grace's slender neck. The tall blonde rushed toward her but stopped when she noticed Quinn.

"Oh!" she exclaimed, her eyebrows climbing up her forehead. "I didn't know anyone else was here."

Ava Grace and Quinn stared at each other for several heartbeats without speaking. Amelia looked back and forth between them, noting that her best friend wore a tight red sweater and a matching short suede skirt she'd made for her.

She glanced toward Quinn to see if he'd noticed Ava Grace's perky breasts, narrow waist, and long, tan legs. Surprisingly, he wasn't drooling, and a frown marred Ava Grace's pretty face.

Stepping forward, Amelia made introductions. "Ava Grace, this is Quinn O'Brien. Quinn, this is my best friend, Ava Grace Landy."

Neither Quinn nor Ava Grace looked in her direction. They continued to stare at one another, both of them still and silent. Amelia was bewildered by the undercurrents in the room. Was it sexual attraction?

Please, God, no. Not that.

Finally Quinn spoke. "Amelia says you've been inseparable since you were five years old. She told me that you're more than her best friend. She says you're her only family." He held out his hand to Ava Grace. "Thank you for being there for her."

Ava Grace's hazel eyes narrowed. "I'll always be there for her. *Always.*"

He nodded, and Ava Grace cocked her head. After a moment, she clasped his hand.

"You're not what I expected."

He smiled, reminding Amelia how gorgeous he was.

"Neither are you," he replied.

Amelia cleared her throat, more than a little annoyed they were gazing into each other's eyes like lovers. Ava Grace immediately dropped his hand.

"It was a pleasure to meet you, Quinn," she said before turning to Amelia. "We'll catch up later."

Ava Grace headed toward her bedroom with a long-legged stride, but Amelia knew the opportunity for her and Quinn to speak privately was gone. She sat down in her favorite chair and tucked her feet under her.

He opened his mouth to speak, but she stopped him. "Ava Grace is an unrepentant eavesdropper," she warned him. "So if you don't want her to hear what you're going to say, you better not say it."

Closing his mouth with a snap, he scrubbed his hands over his face. "Fuck me," he mumbled.

She felt like echoing his sentiment. She had no desire to tell him the truth about Teagan's project while Ava Grace listened. She wasn't happy with the alternative, either, which was waiting until she returned to San Francisco in early December.

Of course she'd probably have several samples finished by then, and she could show him what she'd done. Maybe Teagan was right. Maybe Quinn would react more favorably to the redesign if he could see and touch the new styles.

Throwing himself onto the sofa, Quinn looked up at the ceiling. "Listen, Juice. I want to keep our . . ." He paused. "Would you be willing to . . . to . . ." He stuttered a bit. "*Shit.*"

He sat up and speared her with his dark blue gaze. "I

know we live in different cities, but I don't have any interest in being with anyone but you. And I don't want you to go out with any other guys or . . ." He made a low sound in his throat. "Or let anyone else touch you."

His words surprised her so much she couldn't formulate a response. She had never imagined he wanted to discuss *this*.

He frowned at her silence. "Can we at least give it a try?" he asked, leaning forward to prop his elbows on his knees. "Just see how it goes?"

Even though she knew things would end badly, she wanted more time with him. She nodded.

"Okay."

His eyes widened. "Okay?"

"Yes."

He frowned. "Just to be clear, no dates and no sex with anyone else."

"Yes, I'm agreeing. Isn't that what you wanted?"

He rubbed his hand across his chin, the stubble making a slight rasping noise against his fingers. "It's a start," he answered before standing up and pulling his phone from the front pocket of his Rileys.

Looking at the screen, he pressed a button. "Damn. I need to get going, Juice. Walk me out?"

She rose and walked him to the door. He backed her up against the wall of the foyer before sliding his hands into her hair and tilting her head back until he could look into her eyes.

"I'm going to miss you," he said.

He gave her a deep kiss that made her knees tremble and her mind go blank. Before she could recover, he'd already opened the door and jogged to the limo. He didn't look back, and she closed the front door because she didn't want to see him drive away.

Slowly returning to the living room, she grabbed a quilt from the wicker basket beside the sofa and climbed back into her chair. She wrapped the comfy softness around her, pulling up her knees and resting her head on them. He had taken all the warmth with him, and she was freezing.

Amelia heard Ava Grace come back into the room. Her

best friend knelt beside the chair, smoothing her hand over Amelia's hair before resting her head against Amelia's.

"Did I hear that right? Quinn calls you Juice?"

Amelia laughed at the confirmation that Ava Grace had indeed eavesdropped. But then her laughter stuttered to a stop, and she burst into tears.

Chapter 35

QUINN DRAGGED HIMSELF UP THE STEPS OF HIS VICTORIAN, THE muscles in his legs limp like spaghetti. He had been wide awake at four a.m., and he'd figured he might as well go for a run.

The insomnia he had experienced during the trip to Georgia had intensified now that he was home. He hadn't been able to fall asleep until he'd indulged in a little self-pleasure, recalling the maple syrup he had poured on Amelia after they had finished Sunday brunch in the suite.

It was Wednesday morning, and he'd been away from her for a little less than seventy-two hours. Apparently, the actual number of hours didn't matter because he felt as if he was about to crawl out of his skin. He was a little ashamed at how pathetic he felt and more than a little worried that Amelia had so much influence over his emotional well-being.

He let himself into his house, and as he made his way to the staircase, he saw Cal asleep in the leather club chair in the living room, his feet propped on the ottoman in front of him.

Cal's tablet computer was balanced precariously on his lap, and Quinn removed it as quietly as he could. He placed it on the coffee table before grabbing the cashmere throw from the sofa and draping it over him.

His brother looked worn out, his face shadowed with stubble and his eyes ringed with dark circles. Things had to be bad with Saika if Cal sat in Quinn's living room when it was barely five thirty in the morning.

He made his way upstairs and took his time in the shower, letting the hot water pour over his tight muscles. He'd done a lot of thinking since he had left Amelia in Nashville, not only about his feelings for her but also about the women's division.

He'd made some big decisions, and he didn't want to have those conversations with her via Skype or phone. He was considering a trip to Nashville early next week.

Grabbing the shampoo, he lathered his hair. Amelia planned to attend the American Association of Country Music awards on Tuesday. Maybe he could surprise her and attend the show with her. He made a mental note to ask Teagan for Ava Grace's phone number to see if his idea was feasible.

He finished with his shower and dressed quickly before heading downstairs. Cal was still asleep, and he made his way to the kitchen where he found a box of pastries and a couple of to-go coffees. He was lucky to have a brother who still managed to be thoughtful even when he was going through some serious personal shit.

He grabbed the coffee and a cream cheese Danish and settled himself on the barstool before powering up his laptop. He was still behind on the work he had ignored while he'd been in Georgia, and he made a serious dent in some of his backlogged emails by the time Cal woke up and ambled into the kitchen with his tablet in hand.

"Hey," Quinn said.

Cal grunted before depositing the tablet on the island. He scratched his chest through his long-sleeve T-shirt and dug in the box of pastries until he found one he liked. He bit into the pastry, almost halving it in one bite.

Pushing aside his laptop, Quinn leaned his elbows on the bar. He caught Cal's eyes.

"I know guys aren't supposed to talk about their feelings, Cal, but you need to tell me what's going on with Saika. You're miserable, and maybe we can figure out how to fix things if we tackle the problem together."

Cal choked on his pastry. He grabbed his coffee, taking a big gulp of it. He swallowed noisily.

"Who are you and what have you done with my brother?" Cal asked, depositing the pastry and coffee back on the island.

"Very funny, asshole. Now out with it."

Sighing loudly, Cal massaged his forehead with the tips of his fingers. "Saika's ex-husband has decided to move here. He says he wants to be closer to Valerie, but I know what the fucker really wants. He wants his family back."

Quinn tried to recall what little he knew about Saika's ex-husband. He didn't know much more than the fact that they had divorced when Valerie had been a baby.

"What's his name? You told me once, but the only thing I remember is that it was something weird."

Cal rolled his eyes. "Noble. His name is Noble, like he's some kind of fucking prince charming or something."

The name jarred loose another fact, and Quinn snapped his fingers. "And he's in the military, right?"

Cal nodded. "Yeah, I guess he's some big-shot Navy SEAL. The dickhead." He snorted. "She said she was going to talk to him when she visited her sister in Southern California, and I didn't handle it well."

Quinn gave him a minute before prodding him. "And?"

"And when she got back, I asked her what happened, and she kept changing the subject. Finally, she told me it was none of my business."

He winced, but Cal wasn't done. "Then a few days later, she told me that he had resigned his commission and found a job at one of the corporate security firms here in San Francisco. His job was the main reason why they split up." He swallowed. "She's still in love with the bastard. She denies it, but I can tell that she is."

Cal looked down. "I'm going to lose her. Her and Valerie."

Quinn sighed. Now that he had fallen in love with Amelia, he had a lot more empathy for his brother. He couldn't imagine how crazed he would be if he had to compete with another guy for her affection. He didn't have any competition, and he still questioned her feelings for him.

"Are you in love with Saika, Cal?"

Cal's whole body tensed. "Yeah."

"Have you told her that you love her?"

"Of course. I tell her all the time."

Quinn was bewildered. "Why would you do that if you don't think she loves you back?"

"Because I love Saika regardless of whether she loves me, and not saying it doesn't mean I don't feel it. Before her fucking ex-husband came back into the picture, I'd planned to ask her to marry me."

He sucked in a surprised breath. He'd had no idea Cal had considered marriage.

"What are you going to do?"

"There's nothing I can do," Cal answered flatly. "I can't make her love me. I can't make her stay with me."

Quinn was overwhelmed with sadness for his brother. "No, you can't," he agreed. "But what if you . . ."

Cal held up his hands. "Quinn, I appreciate that you're trying to be a good brother, but I'm done talking about this."

He nodded. "Okay."

Cal pointed at him. "And you . . . you've got your own relationship problems to work through, don't you?"

"What makes you say that?"

Cal laughed softly. "Come on, Quinn. Sometimes I think I know you better than I know myself."

He eyed his brother. "Maybe you're right. So what do you think I should do?"

"First of all, you should man up and tell Amelia that you're in love with her," Cal suggested with a smile. "And then you should go buy a ring, brother, because you're not going to rest easy until you've tied her to you in every way you can think of. Getting her pregnant is the next step."

His whole body jerked at Cal's statement, and he knocked over his coffee. Dark liquid spilled across the bar, but he just sat there as it dribbled down the sides of soapstone.

Cal grabbed a handful of paper towels and mopped up the mess. He threw the sopping paper into the trash can before turning toward him.

He chuckled when he saw the look on Quinn's face. "I guess you hadn't progressed that far yet."

Quinn shook his head. "No. But I was close," he admitted.

Soon after he had realized he was in love with Amelia,

he'd thought about what that meant for the long term. He wasn't an impulsive guy. He liked to consider all the pros and cons, mulling over different strategies until he felt comfortable with his decision. In fact, he was more risk-averse than most people, probably because he felt responsible for all the men and women who worked for Riley O'Brien & Co., along with their families.

When it came to Amelia, though, his logical, problem-solving side shut down, and his emotions ruled. Letting them take the lead wasn't easy, but when it came right down to it, he wasn't afraid of commitment.

His parents had shown him how great marriage could be with the right person, and he had no doubt Amelia was the one for him. He just didn't know if she thought *he* was the one for *her.*

Cal speared him with his icy blue gaze. "I know you're scared shitless right now, but you need to tell Amelia. You're fucked up because you don't know how she feels. Just think of how happy you'll be when she tells you that she loves you, too."

He tapped his fingers on the bar. Cal was right about at least one thing: he *was* fucked up. But he'd be even worse off if Amelia didn't love him back.

He broke out in a cold sweat as he imagined baring his soul to her. She might give him a look of pity before saying she was sorry because she just didn't feel the same way.

It would destroy him.

Chapter 36

QUINN SCOWLED AND THREW DOWN HIS PHONE ON THE kitchen island when he got Teagan's voicemail for the fifth time. He hadn't talked to his sister since he'd asked for Ava Grace's phone number earlier in the week. Surprisingly, she'd handed it over without a single question.

He tunneled his hands through his hair. He needed to talk with Teagan and Cal before he left for Nashville, and he had hoped they would come over for takeout tonight.

His phone dinged, and he saw a voicemail from Teagan. They must have called each other at the same time.

Her voice came over the line, her message succinct. "Quinn, I'm taking some time off. I'll be back around Thanksgiving. My team has everything under control. I'm not going to be available via email or phone. Bye."

He stared at his phone. *What the fuck?* It was only the first week of November, and Thanksgiving fell during the last week of the month.

This wasn't like Teagan at all. She never took vacation for more than a few days at a time. And she never was out of touch.

He placed a call to his mother. "Mom, have you talked to Teagan?"

"Hi, honey. I was just thinking about you. I tried a new recipe for lemon meringue pie and—"

"Mom," he interrupted, "have you talked to Teagan?"

Kate was obviously taken aback by his rudeness because she didn't answer for several seconds. "Not since yesterday. We got our nails done. We had a lovely time. But you'll never guess who we ran into. Nick."

"Did she tell you that she was taking a trip?" he asked and then frowned in confusion. "Nick who?"

His mom laughed. "Priest," she replied. When he didn't respond, she added, "You know, your best friend."

His frown deepened. "You ran into Priest in a nail salon?"

His mom laughed again. "No, honey. He was outside. I'm pretty sure he was waiting for somebody."

He shook his head. "I don't care about Priest right now. Teagan left me a voicemail that she's taking the next three weeks off. Did you know about this?"

His mom made a *tsk*ing noise. "She should have asked for your permission. You're her boss."

"Mom," he groaned. "Focus! I don't care about that. She never takes off for more than a couple of days, and she didn't say where she was going. I'm worried."

"Quinn, honey, you need to stop worrying about everyone." Kate sighed. "She talked to your dad this morning and gave him all the details. She asked him not to tell anyone so she could be off the griddle."

Quinn rubbed his forehead, the anxiety draining out of him. "You mean off the grid. She's not a pancake."

Kate laughed, and he imagined her waving her hand at her mistake. "Do you want to come over for dinner? Cal's coming."

"With Saika and Valerie?"

"No, sweetie. It's just him."

Her answer made his heart sink. He wanted his brother to be happy, and it wasn't good news that Saika and Valerie weren't accompanying Cal.

"What's for dinner?"

THE SPICY AROMA OF LASAGNA TEASED QUINN'S NOSE AS HE let himself into his childhood home. His stomach rumbled loudly. His mom wasn't Italian, but you'd never guess it from her cooking.

Following the delicious smell into the kitchen, he found his mom chopping vegetables for a salad. She smiled when she saw him, her blue eyes lighting up.

"Hiya, handsome."

He returned her smile. "Hi, Mom," he said, leaning down to kiss her cheek. "Where are Dad and Cal?"

"Dad's upstairs resting, and Cal's out on the deck," she answered, gesturing toward the French doors with her knife.

"Whoa! Easy with the knife!" he exclaimed, moving several feet away from her. "You almost sliced off my ear." He cocked his head. "Is Dad doing okay today?"

She nodded. "Yes, he's fine. You know he loves to take naps on Sunday afternoon."

He shrugged off his leather jacket and hung it on the back of one of the chairs grouped around the farmhouse table. A bright blue vase filled with daisies sat in the middle of the table.

He smiled. He'd bet his last dollar his dad had given them to his mom.

Kate loved flowers, and for as long as Quinn could remember, James had brought her a bouquet every Wednesday. He never had them delivered. He believed flowers should be presented in person. When he had been weakened from his cancer treatment, he'd asked his kids to buy the bouquets so he could continue to surprise his wife with flowers.

"Do you need any help with the salad?"

She laughed. "Sweetie, the last time you helped me, you almost cut off your finger."

He scowled. "That was because Teagan ran into me, Mom."

He let his gaze wander the kitchen. It was different from the one he'd grown up in because his mom had renovated it right before his dad had gotten sick. It reminded him a lot of his own kitchen with its shiny, commercial-grade appliances.

The big difference was the light green cabinets. When his mom had first shown him the color sample for them, he'd wondered if her good taste had deserted her. But once the cabinets were installed, they had looked great.

The most interesting thing about the kitchen was the light

fixture. Made from at least twenty mason jars of different sizes, it hung over the butcher-block island like pendant lights.

A bakery box on the granite counter caught his attention, the pink and white stripes and brown script lettering instantly recognizable. Crossing the kitchen, he opened the box to find a variety of Babycakes treats including their famous red velvet cupcakes.

He stared down at the gastronomic delights, smiling when he thought about Amelia's mouth covered in icing at the chocolate festival. But the smile slipped from his face as a huge wave of loneliness crashed over him.

He missed Amelia. He missed her Texas twang, her sweet smile, and her brown-sugar freckles. He missed the peace she gave him when he was with her, the sense he was exactly where he was supposed to be. It was easier for him to breathe when she was with him, easier for him to face the day and all the problems he had to solve.

"Don't you dare!" his mom exclaimed fiercely from her place by the island. "Those cupcakes are for dessert." She pointed toward him with the knife. "You'll ruin your dinner."

Rolling his eyes, he closed the bakery box. "I think I just regressed to a ten-year-old boy."

In response, she gestured toward the stainless steel fridge. "Grab a beer and go keep your brother company. He's moping."

He nodded. "I think it's going to get ugly."

She gave him an assessing glance. "I think so, too. All three of my children are in love, and apparently it's not all wine and roses." She tilted her head toward the French doors. "Now get out of my kitchen."

He frowned. "What? Teagan's in love?" he asked incredulously. "Since when? And do we know him? Or her?"

Kate snickered. "Why don't you worry about your own love life? By the way, how is Amelia?"

He cleared his throat. "How did you know?"

This time it was his mom who rolled her eyes. "Please."

When it was obvious she wasn't going to elaborate, he grabbed two bottles of Anchor Steam, popped them open, and joined Cal on the redwood deck. He set the beers down on the weathered patio table before dropping into the seat next to his brother.

Cal's USC baseball cap shadowed his face, and when he looked up, Quinn noticed his eyes were bloodshot. He felt a rush of anger toward Saika that she was making his brother so miserable. He wanted to tell her that she'd never find a better man than Cal, but he had a feeling she already knew that.

Propping his leg on his knee, Quinn took a swig of his beer. "Are you aware our sister has gone MIA?"

Cal shot him a quizzical look. "What are you talking about?"

"She left me a voicemail that she's taking some time off and she won't be back until Thanksgiving."

Cal pushed back the brim of his cap. "No shit?"

"Yeah. And then she told me that she wouldn't have access to phone or email."

His brother's eyes widened. "Where did she go?"

"I have no idea. She told Dad, but she asked him not to tell anyone."

"Bebe probably knows where she is," Cal said, his mouth turned down in a frown.

Cal and Teagan's best friend, Bebe, didn't like each other much, although no one could figure out why. Most women loved his younger brother, but Bebe was nice to everyone *except* Cal. He, meanwhile, insulted her with every word that came out of his mouth.

"I don't want to track Teagan down and ruin her vacation. I just think it's weird. Don't you?"

Cal nodded before taking a pull on his beer.

"Mom says Teagan's in love," Quinn said.

Cal choked, falling into a coughing fit. Finally, he caught his breath and wiped his mouth with the back of his hand.

"Did you have to wait to tell me that until I had beer in my mouth?"

Quinn smiled. "They say timing is everything," he said, laughing when Cal glared at him.

"So who is she supposedly in love with?"

"I have no idea," he answered with a shrug.

"Too bad she's not here. You could hold her down while I tickled the truth out of her. And then we could beat up the guy."

Quinn chuckled. Teagan was incredibly ticklish, and he and Cal had shown her no mercy when they'd been younger. They sat in companionable silence, enjoying their beers until his gaze fell on Cal's tablet. It was face down on the table.

"What were you looking at?" he asked.

"A report on the social media buzz generated from Priest's ad campaign."

"How's it going?"

"Much better than I ever could have imagined."

"What do you mean? Didn't you think the campaign was going to be successful?"

"We knew Priest was popular with guys, and since we were looking to increase awareness with men and improve sales for the men's line, he was a great fit. But women love Priest. Apparently he has universal appeal, and we're getting buzz from female consumers."

Quinn recalled Amelia's comments about the pro football player. Universal appeal was one way of putting it.

"So you expect a bump for the women's division, too?"

"No. The buzz is for our men's jeans, which makes sense when you think about Shelby's point that women buy clothes for their men. Hell, a lot of wives pick out their husbands' entire wardrobe. The guys never even step inside a store."

Quinn considered what Cal had said. He had chosen his own clothes since he was a teenager, and no one he'd dated had ever commented on his clothes, nor had they tried to change his style. Luna had been his longest relationship, and the most personal gift she had given him was a hardback novel by his favorite mystery author.

He figured Amelia would definitely have an opinion about his clothing. Strangely, the idea of her telling him what to wear didn't bother him at all. He was glad Cal didn't know what he was thinking, though, because his brother would say something like "You're so whipped, your girlfriend dresses you."

"Speaking of female consumers, Amelia showed me her sketches for the accessories line on our way to Georgia."

"Were they any good?"

"They were really good. Unfortunately, I don't think they're enough to save the women's division."

Cal opened his mouth, but then closed it without speaking. He rolled his lips inward until they were nothing but a flat line.

"Nothing to say?" Quinn asked.

"Maybe later," Cal muttered, "after I've had a few more beers."

Quinn shrugged. He wasn't going to push the issue. Cal would talk when he was good and ready. Badgering his younger brother had never achieved anything.

Changing the subject, Quinn announced, "I'm flying to Nashville on Tuesday morning."

"Business or pleasure?" Cal asked innocently, his blue eyes sparkling with devilry.

"Pleasure. I'm going to surprise Amelia and attend the awards show with her. She was going to be in the audience by herself because Ava Grace is performing and presenting."

"What does one wear to a country music awards show?" Cal asked, pulling his baseball cap down over his eyes. "A tuxedo with rhinestones on the lapels?"

Quinn laughed. "I'm not sure. I wish I could ask Amelia but that would spoil the surprise."

Cal rose from his chair and headed toward the sliding glass door. Pausing with his hand on the doorknob, he slanted an amused glance over his shoulder.

"Brother, you are so whipped you *want* your girlfriend to dress you."

Chapter 37

AMELIA TRIPPED OVER THE RUG IN THE FOYER IN HER RUSH TO get to the front door. "Rutherford Birchard Hayes," she muttered as she balanced on her tiptoes to peer out the peephole.

When she saw who stood on the porch, she stumbled back from the door and then reared up again to look into the round hole. She couldn't believe her eyes.

Quinn!

Her heart stuttered, and she sucked in a surprised breath. Grabbing the doorknob, she yanked open the door at the same time he pulled open the screen door.

Her face cracked with a huge smile, and they stared at each other for a heartbeat before she threw herself at him. He dropped the garment bag he held over his shoulder and caught her, stumbling backward and grunting as her body barreled into his.

Hugging her to him, he buried his face in her hair. He laughed softly. "Well, I guess that answers my question if you're happy to see me," he said, rubbing his big hands up and down her back.

She nodded, nuzzling her face against his chest and pulling in a deep breath. Oh, she had missed his scent and the feel of his hard body against hers.

He wove his hands into her hair and tipped her head back. Leaning down, he kissed the corner of her mouth.

"Damn, I missed you," he said before placing his lips against hers in a gentle kiss.

She wanted to tell him eight days wasn't that long to go without seeing each other. Military spouses went months without seeing their loved ones. But she couldn't force the words from her throat because every one of those eight days and nights had dragged by even though she'd been busy with work.

Pulling back from his kiss, she bent down and picked up his garment bag from the ground. "Let's go inside. It's kind of cold out here."

He smiled, the skin around his eyes crinkling. "That's because you're barefoot and wearing a robe, Juice."

Amelia looked down in surprise. In her excitement to see Quinn, she'd forgotten she wasn't dressed. The glint in his dark blue eyes told her that he hadn't overlooked that fact.

Taking the bag from her, he ushered her into the house. He threw it on the mission-style bench in the foyer and grabbed her around the waist, lifting her a little bit.

"Are you naked under that robe, sweetheart?" he asked huskily.

She clutched his shoulders and nodded slowly, feeling a little bit shy. He let her drop to the floor and reached for the tie at her waist. She placed her hands on top of his to still his agile fingers.

"I'm so happy to see you." She bit her lip. "But what are you doing here? I have to get ready for Ava Grace's awards show. The hair and makeup girls are going to be here soon."

"I know. I'm going with you."

"You are?" she asked, her voice high and breathless.

He nodded. "Yes, ma'am."

"But how?"

"I called Ava Grace last week and asked if she would help me surprise you. She arranged a ticket to the show for me, and here I am."

With a loud squeal, she threw her arms around him,

squeezing tightly. She was thrilled, and not just because she got to enjoy his company. She couldn't wait to see his face once she was all dressed up.

She had no illusions about her looks, but a fabulous dress could do a lot for a short girl with a big butt. Plus, she'd seen the way women looked at Quinn. He drew the eyes of every female from nine years old to ninety, and she'd like to feel equal to his good looks for one night, at least.

He laughed at her exuberance, scooping her against him with his arms under her behind. She wrapped her legs around his waist and her arms around his neck.

"How long can you stay?"

"How long do you want me?"

Before she could answer, Quinn bunched her robe in his hands and palmed her bare behind. His hands were warm, and suddenly, all she could think about was how hot and hard the rest of him was.

He turned toward the wall and backed her up against it, pressing his jean-covered erection into her. "Where's your bedroom?" he rumbled against her ear.

Just then, the doorbell rang. He dropped his forehead against hers with a heartfelt groan. "I seriously regret stopping for that Starbucks coffee because I could have been here ten minutes earlier," he muttered. "And trust me when I say that I would have used that time wisely."

She snickered as he loosened his arms and let her slide down his body. "You think you would have lasted ten minutes?" she asked. "I wouldn't have."

He grinned. "I know."

She lightly slapped his chest in mock offense before turning toward the front door. "Wait," he directed, hooking a finger in the belt of her robe. "I need a place to hang out while you primp. And I need a shower."

"You can use the guest room. It has a TV and an attached bath. Down the hall, first door on the right."

He patted her rear before grabbing his garment bag and striding away. Opening the door, she greeted the hair and makeup girls and then ushered them into the house.

She was lucky Jasmine and Selena had been available this

evening. They were fast and fabulous, and they knew how to make the most of Amelia's curly red hair and fair skin.

"By the time we're finished with you, you're going to feel like a completely different woman," Selena promised as they traipsed up the stairs to Amelia's bedroom.

Three hours later, Amelia definitely *looked* like a completely different woman.

Her sapphire-colored dress floated around her feet. The vertical ruching at the waist minimized her midsection, while the contrasting diagonal ruching on the bodice elongated her torso and emphasized her breasts before draping over one shoulder and leaving the other bare.

It was a beautiful dress. The color drew attention to her hair without turning it orange and made her skin look creamy instead of pasty. The strappy silver sandals with their stiletto heels and crystal buckles were the perfect complement.

Jasmine and Selena had left right after they helped Amelia into her gown. She had stayed in her room, though, hoping she could regain some of her earlier excitement.

A strange mood had swept over her while Jasmine had piled her curls into an elaborate updo adorned with crystal pins. She'd looked into the mirror above her dresser and had seen someone she hadn't recognized. Someone with flawless makeup and artfully arranged hair.

Minutes later, she had slipped into a nine-thousand-dollar dress and twelve-hundred-dollar shoes. When she had glimpsed herself in the full-length mirror on the back of her bedroom door, she'd felt like a princess in a fairy tale. The air had seemed to sparkle and shimmer around her body.

She'd stared at herself, and her strange mood had intensified. Everything seemed so unreal. The dress, the awards show, Quinn. The word "unreal" had echoed in her head, and she'd started to dissect what it meant.

Unreal meant imaginary, dreamlike, fantasy. It was the *opposite* of real.

"Juice, the limo's here," Quinn called from downstairs. "You need to get a move on."

Amelia stared down at her freshly manicured hands, the nails painted with shiny scarlet polish. No matter how different she looked, she was still the same woman. She wasn't a princess, Quinn wasn't her prince, and her life wasn't a fairy tale.

Even she knew princesses were honest and brave. Most of all, they always got their happily ever after.

Amelia wasn't honest, and she wasn't brave. If she were, she would have told Quinn about Teagan's project. She would have admitted her involvement in a scheme that could end up costing him the CEO job.

And no matter how much she wanted happily ever after with Quinn, she knew that wasn't reality. When he found out she had been working behind his back, he would end things between them—she was absolutely sure of it.

"Amelia, are you ready yet?" Quinn asked through the door. "We really need to go."

She clenched her hands into fists, her nails digging into her palms. She didn't want to see him. She didn't want to go to the show. She wanted to crawl into bed, pull the covers over her head, and fall into a dream where she had never deceived Quinn.

But she couldn't—*wouldn't*—disappoint Ava Grace by not showing up on her big night.

Grabbing the jeweled clutch that matched her dress, she opened the door. "I'm ready. Do you have . . ."

She lost her train of thought when she got her first look at Quinn in his suit. Except for the launch party when he'd worn a blazer, she'd never seen him in anything but Rileys and a casual shirt.

The finely woven black wool suit coat outlined his broad shoulders and emphasized his lean waist, while the matching pants were just tight enough to show some definition in the crotch and thigh area. The bright white of his dress shirt set off his dark hair and made his blue eyes glimmer.

She looked down at his feet. Cowboy boots, of course. She would estimate this particular pair cost several thousand dollars, more evidence he lived in a different world than most people, her included.

While she'd checked him out, he had done the same to her. "Amelia," he said hoarsely before clearing his throat.

Raising her head, she looked into his face. Her strange mood had morphed into something that felt remarkably like grief, and a horrible pressure filled her chest.

He stepped toward her, touching a loose curl that rested on her bare shoulder. "There are so many things I want to say to you," he murmured, rubbing the strands between his thumb and forefinger. "But I'm going to start with this: we're late."

Chapter 38

QUINN OPENED THE FOURTH CABINET DOOR AND FINALLY found the drinking glasses. He grabbed one and pressed it against the water dispenser in the fridge's door, filling it to the brim.

Leaning against the granite island, he took a big gulp. Champagne always made him thirsty, and he'd had more than his fair share of the bubbly tonight, even though Ava Grace hadn't won the award for Best Female Artist.

Amelia had already made her way upstairs, and as he took another drink, he let his gaze wander over the farmhouse's kitchen. He smiled when he saw a shiny juicer on the counter next to the sink and several pots of herbs on the windowsill above it.

Her personality was stamped all over this house, and he wondered how he was going to convince her to move to San Francisco. She loved living in Nashville, and more important, Ava Grace was here.

He might have to think about splitting his time between the West Coast and Tennessee. It wouldn't be ideal, but if it was the only way he could be with Amelia, he would make it work.

Placing the glass on the island, he rubbed the back of his

neck with both hands. Amelia had been subdued all evening. Although she'd seemed fine when she had gone upstairs to get ready, her mood had been as dark as her dress when they'd left.

At first he'd attributed her silence to nervous excitement. He had expected her to relax after Ava Grace had performed and the winner had been announced, even though she had been disappointed her best friend had lost.

But after the show had ended and they'd done the after-party rounds, she had remained quiet and withdrawn. He couldn't figure out what had happened.

Maybe she was upset he hadn't complimented her when he'd first seen her all dressed up. There were a lot of words he could have used to tell her how beautiful she had looked, but the first thing that had popped into his head was *mine*, followed quickly by *I love you.*

Prior to Amelia, he hadn't realized how possessive he was. In fact, he'd always considered those guys kind of pathetic and insecure. At worst, he had wondered if they knocked around their women at home.

But Amelia brought out all kinds of new emotions in him. Some of them, like the possessiveness, were surprising. His overwhelming desire for her was another surprise. It didn't matter how often he got her naked; it wasn't enough.

She seemed to want him just as much. Her obvious delight when he'd arrived had given him hope that she felt more for him than just lust and casual affection. Her admission that she'd thought about him while they'd been apart had given him a boost of confidence to tell her that he loved her.

But now . . . well, now he wasn't so sure. He knew she was a lot more reserved than he was, so he didn't expect her to be effusive or clingy. But all evening, he'd had the impression she would rather be anywhere else but with him at the awards show.

He was worried. And there was also a part of him that was a little resentful, a tiny bit angry. He felt powerless, out of control, and he wasn't used to feeling that way.

He didn't like it.

Flipping off the kitchen light, he headed upstairs to Amelia's bedroom, his sock-covered feet silent on the wood surface. He hadn't had the opportunity to see her bedroom earlier, and he was more than a little curious about where she slept in her bacon-and-egg-printed pajamas.

As he pushed open the door, his breath seized. Amelia was hanging up her dress in her closet, and she stood with her back to him wearing nothing but a cream-colored bustier, matching thong panties, and her heels.

Blood rushed from his head to his cock so quickly he felt dizzy. He shook his head, more than a little annoyed by his unruly body.

He should be exhausted from the long flight and the excitement of the awards show. But his body said otherwise. In fact, it told him it wanted her. *Several times.*

She turned her head, the sparkly pins in her hair catching the light. When she caught sight of him, her eyes widened. He wondered what she saw in his expression.

Hunger? Possession? Love? Probably all three.

As he walked toward her, he pulled the tails of his dress shirt from his suit pants and removed his cufflinks, placing them in his pocket before beginning to unbutton his shirt. He wanted his skin against hers.

She turned to face him, and he barely managed to hold back a groan. The bustier pushed up her breasts, and because it was almost sheer in the front, he could see her nipples through it. The tiny triangle of material masquerading as panties barely covered her pussy, and he could see the shadow of her red curls.

He shrugged off his shirt and grabbed the hem of his undershirt to pull it over his head. Throwing it to the floor, he placed his hands on her hips and drew her toward him.

She braced her palms against his chest, and he shivered a little at how cool they were against his hot skin. She caressed him, running her fingers lightly across his nipples.

"I'm sorry for not telling you how beautiful you looked tonight. You took my breath away. I was speechless."

The corners of her lips tipped up. "I don't believe it. You always have something to say."

"That's true. Do you like what I have to say?"

He laughed softly when she blushed and leaned down to whisper in her ear. "I hope you're not too tired because I want to spend the rest of the night inside you. Loving you."

She shuddered against him, and he pulled back to stare down into her face. Her eyes were dark and shiny, like she was on the verge of tears.

With a frown, he cupped his hands around her face, his fingers edging into her thick hair. "What's wrong, sweetheart?"

Shaking her head, she pushed his hands away from her face. He let them drop to his sides, and she stepped away from him.

"We need to talk," she said.

The expression on her face and the tone of her voice warned him that he wasn't going to like what she had to say. His heart began to pound, and he broke out in a cold sweat. His knees were a little shaky, and he searched the room for a place to sit. The bed was the obvious choice, but he didn't want to sit there.

An overstuffed chair occupied the corner, and he sank into it, propping his leg on his knee and settling his hands on his thighs. She hadn't moved, and he nodded, a silent demand for her to talk.

She swallowed and looked down. "Quinn, I . . ."

She looked up again and drew in a deep breath before exhaling slowly. It seemed unlikely she planned to profess her undying love, and he waited, praying she wouldn't end things.

He shifted and something poked his upper thigh, just below his right butt cheek. He squirmed, and whatever it was jabbed into him. He grunted, and she looked at him quizzically.

Leaning over to reach beneath him, he found what poked him, a hard piece of metal. As he felt around it, he realized it was an article of clothing—jeans from the feel of the material.

Gripping the denim, he pulled until it came loose. He placed the jeans in his lap and leaned back before looking down at them.

They were a dark indigo wash with white contrast stitching along the seams, and he turned them over to see what had stabbed him. Several small metal studs decorated the pockets, and he ran his finger over them and then across the pocket flap where the Rileys logo was sewn into the material.

Looking up from the jeans, he caught Amelia's eyes. "What are these?"

QUINN HELD A PAIR OF JEANS IN HIS BIG HANDS, BUT THEY weren't just any pair of jeans. They were one of the new pairs she had designed for Teagan.

The secret was out . . . just when she'd finally mustered the courage to tell him about it.

Quinn tilted his head. "Amelia?"

She opened her mouth, but nothing came out except a tortured gasp. She shot him a pleading glance, and he stared back at her with narrowed eyes.

"What are these?" he repeated.

She massaged the tense muscles of her throat with the tips of her fingers, and finally she was able to squeeze out a single raspy word. "Jeans."

"I can see that. But we don't manufacture any Rileys that look like the pair I'm holding. Where did they come from?"

His question made her tremble, and she wrapped her arms around her waist. "I made them in my workshop . . . I designed them."

Late last night, she'd brought them back to the house so she could try them on. She had wanted to check the fit and see how they looked on a real woman instead of a tailor's pants form.

His eyebrows shot up. "You did?"

"Yes."

He seemed intrigued rather than incensed, and the tight knot of panic inside her started to unravel. Maybe Teagan had been right when she predicted that Quinn would react more favorably to the redesign if he could see the goods.

"Are these the kind of jeans you think female consumers want?"

"Yes. They're stylish and upscale enough to be considered designer denim. They could be dressed up with a jacket and heels. Or they could be casual with a sweater and flats." Her anxiety made her babble. "They probably wouldn't look that great with tennis shoes, but a nice pair of sandals would be okay. And boots, of course. Everything looks good with boots. Well, not an evening gown."

He brought the jeans close to his face as he inspected them, paying close attention to the seams. She had incorporated elements from traditional Rileys including the rivets and black pocket tag.

"They fit differently, too," she added, gesturing toward her hips. "They're made for a woman's body . . . one with hips and a booty and even a little bit of a belly. Part of the problem with the old design is that you have to be shapeless to look good in them."

He traced the shape of the hip and outer-thigh area with the tip of his finger before bringing his attention back to her. "I really like these," he murmured. "I thought your accessories were impressive, but these are awesome."

Amelia shook her head in disbelief. His reaction was the exact opposite of what she had expected. Had Teagan somehow misconstrued Quinn's feelings about the women's division? Had their deception been unnecessary?

Had she agonized for weeks over *nothing*?

"Did you design anything else?"

She nodded. "About twenty different styles of jeans. And I also designed some skirts, dresses, shirts, and jackets."

She had worked hard to come up with some really unique designs including a suede jacket with leather pockets and a denim minidress. She also had made a few pairs of jeans from colored denim. Her favorite was a pair of coral-colored skinny jeans with a low-rise waistband and triangular back pockets.

His eyes widened. "When did you have time to do all that work? It must have taken hundreds of hours."

Since she had returned home, she'd spent nearly every waking moment working on the redesign. She'd sketched and sewn until her eyes were blurry and her fingers were stiff and sore.

He carefully folded the jeans before placing them on the arm of the chair. "I'm sure Teagan told you that I didn't support her idea to partner with you for the accessories. I doubted your design talent. I thought you were only popular because of your connection to Ava Grace."

A little dart of pain pierced her, but she tried to ignore it. "Yes, she told me."

"I was wrong about you, and I knew it the moment I saw your boots. You're exceptionally talented. We're damn lucky to have you, and I'm impressed you took the initiative to expand your work beyond the scope of accessories."

"You're not mad?"

His eyebrows shot up. "*Hell, no,* I'm not mad. I'm excited to see your other designs. Maybe you can model them for me . . . show me how good those jeans look on a woman with a sweet round ass." He tilted his head. "Why would you think that I'd be mad, Juice?"

"Because you made it clear during our first meeting that you thought the women's division was a lost cause. You said it was a short, skinny branch on the Riley O'Brien & Co. tree."

"It is a short, skinny branch. But I've been doing a lot of thinking, and I think it's time for it to grow into a big branch . . . maybe the biggest branch on the tree."

She gasped. "You do?"

He met her in the middle of the room and wrapped his arms loosely around her waist. "Yes. And I've been thinking a lot about you and me, too." Tightening his hold, he drew her closer to him. "I think we make a good team."

"A good team?" she echoed dumbly.

"Yes. Don't you?" He didn't wait for her to answer, which was good because she was speechless.

"Together, I think we can make women fall in love with Rileys again," he continued. "If you're willing, I want you to head up the women's division. Your work to redesign the jeans proves how much you care about Riley O'Brien & Co. and how much you care about me." He dropped his head to kiss her, his lips warm against hers. "You're perfect for the company, and you're perfect for me."

As Amelia stared into Quinn's eyes, she realized that everything she had ever wanted was within her reach. She could have her chain of boutiques. She could have a high-profile design job with one of the most iconic apparel brands in the world. She could have an extraordinary man in her life and in her bed.

She could have it all as long as she kept her mouth shut about her deal with Teagan. She could have it all as long as she continued to lie to the only man she had ever loved.

Chapter 39

QUINN IMPATIENTLY WAITED FOR AMELIA TO RESPOND TO HIS job offer to run the women's division. If she accepted it, maybe she would accept another offer . . . one that involved a ring and his last name.

He couldn't believe he'd been lucky enough to find a woman who understood how important Riley O'Brien & Co. was to him. It would be much more difficult to lead the company if his wife wasn't supportive.

She stared at him for several moments before a resigned expression came over her face. "I didn't redesign the jeans because I care about Riley O'Brien & Co.," she stated flatly. "And I didn't do it because I care about you, either."

He frowned. "Then why did you do it?"

"Because Teagan hired me to redesign Rileys for women and to expand the product line."

"I don't understand."

She stared into his face, her eyes dark and solemn. "Yes, you do."

He dropped his hands from her waist. Her face was nearly colorless in the overhead lighting, the remnants of her makeup looking like heavy brushstrokes.

"No," he countered, "I'm not sure I do understand. Are

you saying that you and Teagan have been working behind my back?"

She nodded. "Teagan thought you needed to see the potential for the women's division so she hired me to give it a makeover. She didn't want you to know what we were doing because she thought you would put a stop to it. She wanted to keep it a secret until I was finished with the new designs, and then she wanted to present them to you as a done deal."

For years, Teagan had talked about giving the women's division a makeover. His dad had always put her off, not ignoring her, exactly, but not listening to her, either.

When Quinn had stepped in as the interim president and CEO, she'd become even more insistent. He'd tried to explain that what she had in mind needed a lot of planning and money. He had done his best to make her understand how risky her idea was, but she'd been undeterred.

He backed away from her. "A done deal? She can't force me to accept your designs. I'm the one who makes the final decisions."

When she didn't reply, he thought about what he'd said. He *wasn't* the one who made the final decisions, not yet. His dad hadn't officially stepped down, and even when Quinn took control of the company, he'd still have to answer to investors and financiers.

"What were her plans if I didn't like your new designs?" She looked away, but he placed his fingers under her chin and forced her eyes back to him. "Tell me."

"She planned to go to the board."

He digested her answer. "And you were okay with that? You didn't care that I could lose my job, my birthright . . . everything I care about?"

She didn't reply, and an ugly wave of rage and despair washed over him. "I guess it didn't matter since you would get paid regardless of what happened," he said bitterly.

She swallowed. "No, that's not the deal."

"Then what is the deal?" he asked harshly.

She stared up at him, and he swore he could hear their hearts beating in the silence of the room.

"Teagan agreed to invest in my chain of boutiques . . . to provide the start-up financing."

"How much?"

"Thirty-five million."

He couldn't believe Teagan would be so reckless with her inheritance. *Would she?*

"Thirty-five million," he repeated. "For a few sketches that might be shoved in a drawer and forgotten?" He shook his head in disbelief. "That's insane. There has to be something more."

"The financing is contingent on whether you put my designs into production. If you don't, I get nothing."

He tried to wrap his mind around what Amelia had said. She wouldn't get the money for her boutiques unless he signed off on her designs. She needed his approval—his goddamn *blessing*—before Teagan would open her checkbook.

The truth hit him squarely in the chest. "*Jesus.* I'm such an idiot. I actually thought everything was falling into place . . . that everything was going to work out." He laughed mirthlessly. "You were just playing me. You were fucking me to get the money for your boutiques."

QUINN'S JAW WAS CLENCHED, AND AMELIA COULD TELL HE was struggling to control his anger. He took several deep breaths, his bare chest moving like bellows.

"I wasn't playing you."

His eyes narrowed into slits, and she knew her denial had made him even angrier. A chill chased over her, reminding her that she wore only a bustier, thong, and high heels. She shivered, not just from the cold but also because her near nakedness made her feel even more vulnerable.

She hastily scanned the room, desperate to find her robe. She shivered again, the movement drawing Quinn's gaze to her chest. His eyes zeroed in on her nipples. They were pebbled from the cold and, if she were honest, his nearness. He was close enough she could feel the heat from his muscular chest.

He made a sound deep in his throat, one of disgust rather than lust or pleasure. "Would you put on some fucking clothes?"

His harsh tone made her flinch. She lunged toward her dresser, pulling open the bottom drawer and jerking out the first piece of clothing she touched, a faded Dallas Cowboys T-shirt she sometimes used as a nightgown.

As she dragged it over her head, her hair came loose from its pins. Ignoring the tangled strands, she pulled down the T-shirt to cover her body, feeling ridiculous because she still wore her heels.

Quinn's gaze swept over her wild hair before he focused on her face. "When did you and Teagan cook up your little plan? Before or after we started sleeping together?"

She met his eyes, and the icy anger in them made it hard for her to pull in a deep breath. "Before," she admitted. "I agreed to Teagan's deal before I even met you. I didn't expect this . . . this attraction between us."

"You didn't expect it, but you definitely took advantage of it," he snarled.

"Took advantage of it?" she repeated incredulously, her voice shrill. "I tried to keep things professional!"

"Were you trying to keep things professional when you sucked my dick in the penthouse? Or when you fucked me in the front seat of my Audi? Or when you sat on the kitchen counter with my face between your legs?"

She sucked in an agonized breath. "Don't. Please don't do that. Please don't turn something wonderful into something ugly."

He grimaced. "I need to leave or I'm going to say things I will regret later."

She met him in the middle of the room and placed her palms on his chest. His pectoral muscles jumped under her fingers.

"Don't go. We need to talk about this."

"I don't want to talk about it," he replied, shoving her hands away. "I just want to forget. I want to forget that you were lying every time you were with me."

His voice was a pained whisper, and Amelia's chest ached with sorrow that she had hurt him so badly.

"I wasn't lying," she countered. "I didn't have sex with you to get the financing for my boutiques."

Reaching for the hem of the T-shirt she'd just put on, she pulled it over her head. His eyes widened as she threw it on the bed.

"I had sex with you because I wanted to be with you," she added.

She trailed her hands down her bustier, and his eyes followed them intently. She began to undo the hooks, starting with the one at the very bottom. His eyes grew darker as the hooks opened, baring her stomach first and then the valley between her breasts.

The bustier fell open, and he sucked in a breath as it slid to the floor. She reached for the waistband of the thong resting low on her pelvis and hooked her fingers in it. His hand shot out and gripped her wrist before she could pull it down.

"What are you doing?" he asked hoarsely.

"Showing you the truth."

As she stepped closer, her breasts brushed against his chest, the fine dark hair on it tickling her nipples. The front of his pants was tented with his erection, and she danced her fingers across the hard length.

Closing his eyes, he released his grip on her wrist. She immediately pushed her thong over her legs and somehow managed to step out of it without falling. He was breathing heavily now, his eyes still closed. She unbuttoned his pants and released his zipper just enough to delve inside his boxer briefs.

As she wrapped her hand around his penis, he groaned and dropped his head back. She rubbed her thumb against the plump head where fluid had seeped out, and then suddenly he moved, pulling her hand from his underwear.

She met his gaze for one burning moment before he pushed her backward and down onto the bed. He fell on top of her in a light pounce, forcing her legs open and settling between them.

In one frantic movement, he shoved his pants and underwear down just enough to free his thick penis before pinning her to the bed with his weight. He threaded his fingers through her hair and brought her face close to his.

"This isn't going to get you what you want," he warned, the expression on his face one she didn't recognize.

She ran her hands up his sides. "You don't know what I want," she replied, clenching her fingers into his back.

He dropped his forehead against hers, and she raised her

legs, hooking her feet over his back. She purposefully dug her sharp heels into his butt cheeks, and he hissed when his erection brushed against her folds.

"*Fuck*," he said before thrusting roughly into her.

She held him tightly, allowing him to use her. Hoping he would spill his anger and disillusionment in her body. Praying he would forgive her.

After only a few deep strokes, he stiffened and groaned, his penis pulsing inside her. Turning his face away, he released a shuddering breath. Seconds later, he pulled out. He reared back on his heels and pulled up his underwear and pants, fastening them quickly.

He moved to the side of the bed and sat there, his head drooped forward and his broad shoulders slumped. She touched his back where her fingernails had made deep crescents in his skin, and he flinched before vaulting to his feet.

As he began to gather his clothes from the floor, Amelia grabbed her Cowboys T-shirt and quickly pulled it on. She knelt motionless on the bed, her throat tight with the knowledge that she had just made things so much worse.

"I'm sorry."

She was sorry for so many things she didn't even know where to start. He snatched up his dress shirt, ignoring her apology.

"I know you're angry with me."

He barked out a laugh. "I'm not angry with you. I'm angry with myself for fucking you when I know you don't give a damn about me. If you did, you would have told me about what you and Teagan were doing. But you didn't tell me, not even after we started sleeping together. You cared more about your boutiques than you did about me."

She was tempted to defend herself by telling him that she'd wanted to be honest with him, but Teagan had demanded her silence. But she swallowed the words, knowing that information would only fuel his anger.

Plus, when it came right down to it, she had kept the project a secret for her own benefit, first so she could get the financing, and then because she'd wanted to have Quinn for as long as she could.

He shrugged on his dress shirt and clumsily fastened the

buttons. Scanning her bedroom, he found his undershirt and scooped it up from the floor. He shook it at her, the opposite of a surrender flag.

"There's only one reason you didn't tell me and that's because you were taking advantage of my feelings to get what you wanted—the financing for your boutiques."

"I wanted to tell you the truth, but I was afraid . . ."

He glanced at her alertly. "Afraid of what?"

She looked down, the floral print on the duvet blurring a little from her tears. She'd been afraid of losing the money for her boutiques, of course, but she didn't even care about that anymore. She'd been afraid of losing him, and right now that seemed inevitable.

But mostly she had been afraid to let herself love him. She had been afraid to give herself to him . . . to give him the power to hurt her.

He waited several seconds, offering her the opportunity to explain. When it became clear that she had nothing to say, he sighed tiredly.

"I'm leaving." He balled his undershirt in his hands. "Lock the door behind me."

"Lock the door?"

He frowned. "Yes, lock the door. It's not safe for you to be here alone in the middle of the night with the door unlocked."

Her heart cracked open. Even though she had hurt him, and even though he thought she had used him, he still wanted to keep her safe. Only an idiot would let that kind of man walk out of her life. Amelia was a lot of things, but she wasn't an idiot.

Quinn will take care of my heart. It's safe with him.

He stalked toward the door.

"Wait!"

He ignored her. When he reached for the doorknob, she jumped off the bed.

"Please don't go. I love you."

He froze, and for several seconds, he didn't move. Finally, he turned to face her. His cheeks were flushed with color, his eyes intensely blue.

"What did you say?"

"I love you," she repeated.

It was the first time she'd said it to anyone other than Ava Grace, and it came out much easier than she had thought it would. In fact, she felt lighter now that she no longer denied her love for him.

He stared at her, his face unreadable. "Since when?"

Since when? What kind of question was that? She didn't know when she had fallen in love with him, not exactly. And why was that fact important?

"I don't know," she answered, shrugging uncomfortably.

He cocked his head. "Did you just realize it?"

"No."

"No?" he repeated. "Then why didn't you tell me before?"

She blew out a breath. "Ugh! I don't know! I just didn't."

He nodded. "So . . . you love me," he said, an edge in his voice.

She hesitated. His questions were unexpected, and her stomach started to cramp with anxiety.

"Yes, I love you."

He narrowed his eyes. "I don't believe you," he replied flatly.

"I know my timing seems a little suspicious. I'm sure you think this is about my deal with Teagan . . ."

He raised his eyebrows. "Why don't you believe me?" she asked, her voice wobbly.

As he stared at her, tears formed in the corners of her eyes. He turned and opened the door, and she frantically tried to think of what else she could say to stop him from leaving.

Quinn paused at the threshold, and hope bubbled in her chest. But it dissolved when he shifted to face her, his face devoid of any emotion.

"Because you told me that you don't lie to people you love," he answered before walking out.

Chapter 40

QUINN TOOK ANOTHER SWING AT THE PUNCHING BAG HANGING from the ceiling of his garage. His boxing gloves smacked against the leather, pushing the bag forward. As it swung back he heard the squeak of the interior door.

Glancing toward the noise, he saw Cal out of the corner of his eye. After closing the door, his brother jogged down the stairs and stepped behind the bag to hold it steady.

"I drove by and saw the light on," Cal explained, peering around the bag. "I decided to check it out since you're supposed to be in Nashville until Sunday and it's only Thursday. I figured someone broke in and suffered cardiac arrest when they saw the mess in your bedroom."

Quinn grunted and slammed his fist into the bag. The impact reverberated up his arm, and he followed up with several more satisfying punches. The silence was broken only by the sound of his gloves making contact with the bag until Cal sighed loudly.

"Why don't you stop beating the shit out of this bag and tell me why you came home early."

"I don't want to talk about it."

"Yeah, well, I didn't want to talk about Saika either, but I did. Now open your fucking mouth and start talking."

All the hurt and anger he'd tried to stifle flooded him, starting out as little pinpricks under his skin. Within seconds, every inch of his body seemed to pulse with agony. He loved Amelia so much he ached with it. But the whole time he'd been losing his heart and planning a future with her, she had been scheming with his sister and putting his job in jeopardy.

He clutched the bag with both gloves and dropped his sweaty forehead against it. "I thought it was meant to be, Cal," he said, his voice barely audible in the hollow silence of the garage.

"What was meant to be?"

"Me and Amelia. I had it all planned out. She'd take over the women's division and give it an extreme makeover. With her help, Riley O'Brien & Co. would crush the competition and regain the market share it lost. We'd get married, have a few kids with curly red hair, and when they grew up, they would have a heritage they could be proud of."

Cal pushed against the bag, forcing Quinn to raise his head. He straightened and met Cal's eyes.

"That sounds like a damn good plan," Cal said. "But when did you decide to make over the women's division? You've shot down Teagan's ideas over and over again."

"I've been thinking about the women's division for a while now, even before Teagan started pushing her ideas. But I didn't want to step on Dad's toes, and I didn't want to do something that would harm Riley O'Brien & Co. There's no guarantee the women's division will ever be successful, no matter how much money we pour into it. A lot of businesses that try to remake themselves fail."

Cal nodded. "That's true. But I still think we have to try."

"I agree. Shelby's presentation was an eye-opener. Female consumers have too much buying power, and we're hurting the entire business by ignoring them. Hell, I think we've done more than ignore them. I think we've alienated them."

In addition to Shelby's presentation, his conversations with Amelia had profoundly impacted him. Her faith in him had given him the confidence he needed to move the company forward. He could accomplish anything as long as she was with him.

But she's not with me.

"Did you tell Amelia about your plan?"

"Yes, the part about the women's division. But she has her own plan."

Cal's dark eyebrows arched. "What kind of plan?"

"She wants to open her own chain of boutiques."

"Maybe she can do both," Cal suggested. "Maybe you can provide the financing so she doesn't have to bring in other investors."

Quinn laughed, the sound shaded with bitterness. "She already has an investor lined up. She and Teagan worked out a deal. Teagan hired Amelia to revamp the women's division behind my back and promised to fund Amelia's boutiques if she could get my buy-in for the new designs."

"Holy shit," Cal breathed. "Our sister is a modern-day Machiavelli. She's ruthless."

Just the thought of Teagan's duplicity filled Quinn with fury. He could barely wrap his head around what she had done.

"She thinks it's easy to run a multibillion-dollar company . . . to make decisions that affect thousands of people. But it's not easy. It's fucking terrifying. Four generations of our family dedicated their lives to Riley O'Brien & Co., and every day I wake up thinking this is the day I'm going to make a decision that will destroy it all. My ass is on the line when things go sideways, not Teagan's."

Cal eyed him sympathetically. "I know it's not easy, brother." He suddenly gasped, horror filling his face. "*Jesus Christ on a pogo stick!* Was Amelia fucking you to get the financing for her boutiques?"

"I don't know." Quinn squeezed his eyes shut. "She said she wasn't. She said she loves me."

"Do you believe her?"

"No."

Learning about Amelia's scheming and then hearing her say she loved him had felt like a one-two punch. He'd already been stunned, and then she had delivered a knockout blow. He was still down for the count, and he wondered if he would ever find his feet again.

Amelia had made him off balance from the moment he'd

met her. He'd spent hours thinking about her, agonizing over how she felt about him. He had lounged on his blue-jean sofa and daydreamed about telling her how he felt. He had imagined how amazing it would be to hear "I love you" float from her luscious mouth.

Every night before he had fallen asleep beside her, he had prayed that she loved him as much as he loved her. He had prayed that she would want to spend her life with him—that she would wear his ring and bear his children. He had prayed that they would have a long and happy life together.

He had prayed for things he had never prayed for before. And when Amelia had finally said, "I love you," it seemed as if his prayers had been answered. For a brief, wonderful moment, he had forgotten what she and Teagan had done. Pure joy had radiated throughout his body, filling him from the soles of his feet to the top of his head.

But then he'd remembered that she had lied to him—that she had used him. Her deceit and the suspicious timing of her profession of love had tainted those three little words, casting doubt on her true feelings.

Although his joy had dimmed, even then a splinter of hope had remained inside him, trying to work its way to the surface. But as she had knelt on her bed in that oversized T-shirt with her gorgeous hair tangled around her face, her voice had echoed in his head: *I don't lie to people I love, either.*

He knew her—her difficult past, her dreams, her fears. He knew her, and he knew she wouldn't violate such an important don't.

If she loved me, she wouldn't have lied.

"I'm sorry, Quinn," Cal said, rubbing the top of his head. "What are you going to do?"

"I don't know. Amelia is the perfect person to head up the women's division. Her designs for the accessories were great, and I'm sure the designs she did for Teagan are just as great."

"You still want to work with her?" Cal asked incredulously.

"No. I want to make a big bonfire out of her designs and then I want to shutter the women's division." He sighed. "But

I can't do that to Riley O'Brien & Co. The company needs Amelia *and* her designs."

His heart chimed in, *You need her*, but he did his best to ignore it.

"It would be a fucking disaster to work with Amelia after this," Cal warned. "You would want her every time you saw her, but you would never have her. It would be torture."

Quinn studied Cal. His brother was staring at the wall, his eyes slightly unfocused.

"Are you talking about Saika?"

Cal met Quinn's gaze. "No."

"Another woman?"

"I wasn't talking about me," Cal replied, but Quinn could tell he was lying. "I was talking about you and Amelia. We need to find someone else to lead the women's division."

Quinn shook his head. "Before we do that, I think we need to ask Shelby to expand on her research. We know how women view Rileys, where and how they spend their money. But we didn't ask them what they want. We need to know what women want so we can give it to them."

"I think that's one of the smartest things I've ever heard you say," Cal said sincerely.

"This is going to be a big project. It's a huge risk."

Cal pushed on the punching bag until it rammed Quinn in the gut. "There's a reason why you're the one who's going to run this company when Dad steps down. If anyone can make the women's division a success, it's you."

Chapter 41

AMELIA PRESSED THE TIPS OF HER SHOES AGAINST THE WOOD slats of the porch and pushed off, making the hanging swing glide back and forth. A cold wind swept across her, and she pulled her thick sweater closer to her body.

She heard the farmhouse's front door open, followed by the squeak of the screen door. Turning her head, she saw Ava Grace standing a few feet away with two steaming mugs in her hands.

"I made hot chocolate."

"With marshmallows?"

"Of course," Ava Grace replied as she handed over one of the ceramic mugs. She sat down in the porch swing next to her and snuggled up.

"It's cold out here. Do you want me to get a quilt from inside?"

Amelia shook her head. It didn't matter how many quilts she piled on or how many layers she wore; she was always cold. She'd been frozen inside since Quinn had gone back to San Francisco more than two weeks ago.

Ava Grace sighed. "I can't believe Thanksgiving is next week." She blew on the hot chocolate before taking a small sip. "A few people have invited us to dinner. Do you want it to be just us or do you want to take someone up on their invitation?"

Amelia shrugged. "I don't care. Whatever you want to do is fine."

She leaned her head against Ava Grace's shoulder, comforted by her best friend's presence. Together, they moved the porch swing back and forth while sipping their creamy drinks.

"Why aren't we spending Thanksgiving with the O'Briens?" Ava Grace asked quietly.

Amelia stiffened. It was the first question Ava Grace had asked about Quinn since she had come home from a long night of celebration to find Amelia curled up on the sofa in her Cowboys T-shirt, red-eyed and alone. Somehow Ava Grace had known Amelia hadn't been ready to talk about what had happened before now.

"Because we weren't invited. I'm pretty sure they limit holiday guests to family and friends."

In fact, she hadn't talked to Quinn or anyone else in the O'Brien family since he'd walked out of her bedroom. She had called Teagan to let her know that he was aware of their project, but she hadn't been able to reach her. She'd left a voicemail, and she'd also texted but received no answer.

"Hmm. I thought you and Quinn were *close* friends. Bosom buddies," Ava Grace said archly.

"You know we were more than friends. We were sleeping together."

"I can see why you couldn't resist."

She laughed sadly. "Oh, Ava Grace, you have no idea how hard I *tried* to resist him."

"Why don't you tell me?"

Several minutes passed, the silence broken only by the sharp creak of the porch swing and the occasional sounds of nature. Amelia finished her hot chocolate and leaned down to place the mug on the ground.

"I tried to keep things professional. I knew getting involved with him—having sex with him—would be a huge mistake." She sought out Ava Grace's gaze. "You told me to stay away from him, and I tried to do that. I really did." She exhaled a shaky breath. "But I wanted him so much. I've never wanted anything, or anyone, so much. And finally I just gave in because I couldn't stand *not* being with him."

"Well, he definitely deserves his own category of tall, dark, and handsome."

She smiled. "I've never known anyone like him. He's so bossy. And a know-it-all. And, oh, my God, he's so spoiled. And messy. You should see his bedroom. It's horrible. He doesn't take care of his things because he has plenty of money to replace them. . . ."

Ava Grace leaned closer to her. "Have you figured out yet that you're in love with Quinn? Because if you haven't, I'll have to slap you silly."

"What makes you so sure I'm in love with him?"

Ava Grace snorted. "I probably knew before you did. By the way, it was the produce that sealed the deal. Who wouldn't fall in love with a man who buys *three* bags of organic fruit and vegetables? If he'd just bought one bag, you probably would have only had a crush on him."

She laughed. "Maybe you're right."

"A better question is how did it happen? You're so closed off . . . with everyone except for me, that is."

She had wondered the same thing. "I know! I'm emotionally unavailable, according to all the self-help books I've read. I don't know what happened."

But she should have suspected her feelings for Quinn were more than lust. Her unreasonable anger toward the employees who didn't support him and her desire to comfort him at the launch party should have been her first clues.

Amelia groaned. "I never thought I would feel this way. I daydream about marrying Quinn, what our children would look like, organizing his bedroom . . ."

Ava Grace laughed. "You seem a little preoccupied by how disorganized his bedroom is. Weren't you too busy doing other things to notice the mess?"

Amelia smiled, but the reminder of making love with Quinn made her chest tight . . . especially the last time. She had tried to show him how much she loved him without saying the words. Unfortunately, her efforts had backfired.

She wished she could go back in time and warn herself that getting involved with Quinn would change her . . . that it would make her vulnerable to the kind of pain she had felt as a child and never wanted to feel again: the pain of rejection, the pain of loving someone who didn't love you in return, and the pain of being alone.

Ava Grace sensed the shift in her mood. "What went wrong?" she asked, settling her arm around Amelia's shoulders.

"I admitted that I was working behind his back, and it didn't take him long to come to the conclusion that I had used him to get ahead."

Ava Grace groaned. "Oh, Millie."

"I had decided to tell Quinn about the redesign. I thought that was better than him finding out on his own. We were in my room, and the jeans I'd made were on my chair, and he sat on them. It was . . ." She shook her head in disbelief. "It was like watching a bad movie in slow motion."

She told Ava Grace what had happened, and the other woman listened attentively. She gasped when she heard how Quinn had responded to Amelia's "I love you."

"He didn't believe you?" Ava Grace asked incredulously.

"Why are you so surprised? You warned me this would happen. I think your exact words were that I couldn't expect anything but heartbreak since I was lying to him about something so important." She nudged her shoulder against her best friend. "This is where you say, 'I told you so.' "

"Okay. I told you so."

Despite her despair, Amelia laughed. "There's the Ava Grace I know and love."

Her laughter died as she remembered the look on Quinn's face when he'd reminded her that she didn't lie to people she loved. His face had been blank, wiped free of all the warmth and affection she'd soaked in during their time together.

Before Quinn, she had never loved anyone but Ava Grace, and being honest with her best friend wasn't difficult, although it occasionally resulted in shouting. With the exception of the redesign, she hadn't found it a challenge to be honest with him, either. The biggest problem was being honest with herself.

"Now I'm going to tell you something else, and you need to pay attention this time," Ava Grace said seriously. "You did something bad, and Quinn has a right to be angry. I would say he's a fool for walking away from you, but you don't give love easily, so he must not be a fool. In fact, I have no doubt he's an amazing man."

Tears welled in Amelia's eyes. "He is amazing," she agreed thickly. "And I did something to him that he never would have done to anyone, let alone someone he loves. He's a better person than I am."

She gulped back her tears. "Quinn is everything I'm not, and in all the best ways. He's so open with his emotions, and he doesn't expect the worst of people." She sniffled loudly. "He deserves better than me."

"*Amelia*. Listen to me. Every day I thank God you're my best friend. Your love is a gift. It is a *privilege* to be loved by you. You need to make sure Quinn understands exactly what he's giving up."

She brushed away the tears dribbling down her cheeks and off her chin. "I don't think I'm strong enough to face him again," she admitted, her voice barely audible. "I know it sounds dramatic, but when he left, it felt like he shredded my heart *and* my soul. I can't take any more rejection."

A sob escaped her, and Ava Grace pulled her closer. "Your fear of rejection is a by-product of our shitty childhood, you know. You're messed up because of your mom. Hell, I'm messed up, too. But you need to believe you are worthy of love. You deserve to be happy, and I think Quinn made you happy. Am I right?"

Amelia nodded. "When I was with him, I didn't think about all the things I'd never had because he filled those empty places inside me. For the first time in my life, I didn't feel like everyone else got what they wanted while I got nothing."

Amelia could tell she had surprised her best friend.

"I think I'm jealous. That's way better than happiness." Ava Grace lightly patted her shoulder. "How do you think Quinn feels about you?"

"I don't know. There were times when I thought he might feel the same way. But he's really affectionate so maybe I confused that as something more."

"For what it's worth, I think Quinn is in love with you, too. I noticed he's very protective of you, and I don't think a guy acts like that unless his emotions are engaged. And he can't take his eyes off you. He looks at you like you're cocaine, and he's a drug addict."

She frowned. "That's a horrible analogy. Couldn't you have come up with something more pleasant?"

Ava Grace waved her hand. "Whatever. The point I'm trying to make is that I think his heart is involved. But he was blindsided by all the shit you dumped on him. Now that he's had time to calm down, he's probably ready to listen to you."

"I'm not convinced he feels the same way. Quinn's a talker, and I don't think he could have kept quiet about his feelings if he loved me."

"A talker? What do you mean?"

She wanted to slap herself for disclosing something so personal. A fiery blush raced across her cheeks.

"Oh, it's not important," she said, striving for nonchalance.

Ava Grace snickered. "I think I get it." She flipped her long hair over her shoulder. "I've never been with a talker. What's it like?"

Amelia shifted on the swing. "I'm not going to discuss it."

"Oh, come on, Millie. Have mercy on me. I'm not getting any right now."

She laughed. Even before Ava Grace had become a celebrity, men had drooled over her. She certainly never lacked for male attention.

"You could if you wanted to."

Ava Grace's husky laugh joined Amelia's lighter one. "If you're not going to share Quinn's best lines, at least tell me what I can do to make you feel better."

She considered Ava Grace's question. "I can't think of anything that would make me feel better."

"Oh, I'm sure that's not true. There must be something," Ava Grace teased gently. "What do you want more than anything?"

Her heart thudded heavily. Just a few months ago she would have said she wanted success more than anything, and that meant the respect of the design industry and her own chain of boutiques. Now she wanted something else.

"I want Quinn."

"I know." Ava Grace dropped her arm and squeezed Amelia's cold fingers. "But you're going to have to convince him."

"And how do I do that?"

"I have no idea. I don't *know it all*, I'm just a know-it-all."

Amelia laughed soggily. "Oh, Ava Grace, I love you."

"I love you, too, Millie."

Amelia turned her head to look into her best friend's eyes, and an entire conversation took place in that one glance.

"I think you're really going to love living in San Francisco," Ava Grace said as she rocked the swing sideways. "I don't know about you, but I'm a big fan of fog, clam chowder, and trolleys. Plus, there's so much to see. The Golden Gate Bridge. Alcatraz. Fisherman's Wharf. Chinatown. I can't imagine that you'd ever run out of things to do. But if you get bored, you can always organize Quinn's bedroom."

Chapter 42

AS QUINN DROVE UP TO HIS VICTORIAN, HE NOTICED CAL'S OLD Caddy parked on the street in front of his house. He and his brother were living proof of the old adage that misery loves company.

Shortly after Quinn had returned from Nashville, Cal and Saika had broken up. His brother had refused to discuss it, but he had the feeling Cal was responsible for the split rather than Saika. Given their previous conversation, he was baffled by his brother's actions.

For the past three weeks, they'd spent almost every evening together, eating takeout, drinking beer, and watching sports. No doubt about it, the two of them were serious sad sacks, another of his dad's favorite sayings.

He parked his Audi in the garage. Leaning his head back against the headrest, he sat in the SUV for several minutes, recalling the day of the football game when he had pulled Amelia onto his lap and fucked her senseless.

He sighed, pressing his fingers against his forehead where a headache had settled. He couldn't go on like this. He was useless at work, unable to focus because he thought about Amelia constantly.

He rubbed a hand across his chest. He knew it had to be

his imagination, but an ache had settled near his heart, and any thought of Amelia made it worse. It was probably just a serious case of acid reflux from all the beer and pizza he'd consumed with Cal.

He'd had plenty of time to think about what Amelia and his sister had done. He understood why Amelia had agreed to the project, but he still didn't understand how Teagan could have gone behind his back. In his mind, there were just some things you didn't do to people you loved, and lying was one of them.

With every day that had passed, his anger toward his sister had burned brighter and more intense until suddenly it had faded like a supernova. Now there was a black hole where the anger had been, a hole filled with grief and disappointment.

Quinn shook off his melancholy, grabbed his bag from the passenger seat, and exited the SUV. He let himself into his house and found Teagan and Cal sitting in the living room.

Dumping his bag on an empty chair, he faced them. Amelia had obviously given Teagan a heads-up that he knew about their secret project because his sister was perched tensely on the edge of the sofa. Her eyes were dark behind her glasses, her face stamped with guilt.

Cal, meanwhile, slouched in the club chair, looking as if he might fall asleep at any moment. His long legs were propped on the ottoman, his long feet covered in a pair of burnt-orange socks patterned with turkeys. They must have been a gift from Saika's daughter.

Quinn turned his attention back to Teagan. "I wondered when you'd show up."

Her shoulders stiffened under her cream-colored sweater. "I said I would be back before Thanksgiving, and I am. Thanksgiving is the day after tomorrow."

"And how was your trip?" he asked casually.

She swallowed. "Fine. I needed a little time to work through some things."

He tilted his head. "What things?"

"It had nothing to do with you or Riley O'Brien."

"So I'm not allowed to interfere in your life, but you can stick your nose into mine? That doesn't seem fair," he said, his mild tone hiding the anger that swirled through him.

Her eyes narrowed. "If you're talking about the women's division, I have a right to *stick my nose in*."

"Does that include lying to me and stabbing me in the back?" he shot back. "Does it include manipulating my feelings for Amelia to get your way?"

"Your *feelings*? You wanted to get in her pants, and you did. You should be happy."

Cal groaned, muttering something under his breath. They both ignored him.

"Well, I'm not happy. In fact, I'm pretty damn miserable."

She sprang to her feet. "Miserable? Aren't you being a little dramatic?"

Cal dropped his feet to the floor and sat up. "You should probably know that Quinn is in love with Amelia," he said, directing his gaze toward Teagan.

She snorted. "Yeah, right."

When neither Quinn nor Cal responded to her sarcastic comment, her mouth dropped open. "Are you serious?" she asked, looking back and forth between them. "I knew you liked her, but I never expected you would . . ."

"Fall in love," Cal chimed in.

Quinn eyed his sister. "What did you expect? Actually, I think I know the answer to that question. You expected me to lead with my dick and go along with everything Amelia suggested. Am I right?"

She flushed guiltily but didn't answer his question. Rage stung his veins, but he managed to control it.

"You knew she was lying to me the whole time she was fucking me . . . that she was using *me* to get *your* money. Do you know how stupid I feel? I was going to ask her to marry me."

She gasped. "Oh, Quinn, I'm so sorry."

Her sympathy shattered his control. "Shut up!" he roared.

She flinched. As they stared at each other, Cal stood and left the room.

After several moments of tense silence, Teagan said, "I *am* sorry about what happened with Amelia. I was only concerned with what I wanted, and I didn't think about whether it would hurt you or her. You were right. I thought it would be easier to get your buy-in on the redesign if the two of you were involved."

Turning away from Teagan, he paced around the room. She watched him with wary eyes, obviously worried she had pushed him too far.

"Did she . . ." He swallowed to ease the dryness in his throat. "Was that Amelia's plan, too?"

She shook her head. "No, I don't think so."

He let out the breath he'd held. Amelia might not love him, but at least their time together hadn't been a complete farce. That made him feel slightly better.

"In fact, I don't think she had any intention of getting involved with you, although I could tell she was attracted to you. She tried to hide it, but it was pretty obvious, and I . . ."

He raised his eyebrows. "What?"

"I made sure you spent some time together."

"You're not very subtle if the chocolate festival was an example of your matchmaking skills."

Her lips twitched. "Yes, I am. You're just not very perceptive."

He cocked his head. "What do you mean?"

"Your first meeting. Lunch on her first day of work. The launch party."

He digested what she'd said and then snorted in disgust. "You are the most conniving woman I've ever met."

"I know. It's a bad habit," she said unapologetically, and he couldn't help but laugh.

"Quinn, you need to know that Amelia wanted to tell you about the redesign, but I told her that I'd find someone else to work on the accessories and the redesign if she breathed a word of it to you."

He sucked in a breath, struggling to control his temper. "In other words, you bullied her into keeping quiet."

She nodded, not an ounce of guilt on her face.

"When did that happen?" he asked.

"At the launch party. You were upset, and she thought telling you about the redesign might make you feel better. But I had no doubt you would have shut her down."

He frowned. He didn't know how he would have reacted.

His thoughts about the women's division had changed a lot since that night.

"Amelia said you planned to go to the board if I didn't put her designs into production. Would you really have done that?"

Teagan didn't answer for a long time. Finally, she said, "I don't know. I was so tired of you ignoring me, and one day I'd just had enough. Enough of you ignoring my ideas and my opinions. So I decided to do something about it."

He eyed her. "That doesn't sound like an apology."

"Why should I apologize for doing something that would help Riley O'Brien?"

"How do you know a redesign would help the company instead of hurt it?"

She blinked, obviously surprised by his question. "Well, things can't get much worse for the women's division."

"Probably not," he agreed. "But they can get a lot worse for the company overall. Bigger companies, stronger companies, have been brought down by one bad decision."

"Revamping the women's division isn't a bad decision," she shot back.

"Why are you so sure you're right? Why do you think you know better than everyone else, especially me? Do you really think I've done such a bad job running the company in Dad's absence?"

She frowned. "You're just too stubborn to see what's right in front of you."

"And you're not stubborn?" he asked dryly, shaking his head in frustration.

She flipped her long ponytail over her shoulder. "I did this to help Riley O'Brien. It was the right thing to do."

He took a deep breath to defuse his anger. "It wasn't the right thing to do, Teagan. This isn't just about the company. You did something that hurt *me*."

Tears suddenly filled her blue eyes—the same eyes he saw when he looked in the mirror. "Quinn . . ." She swallowed audibly. "I'm sorry. I didn't mean to hurt you. I love you."

And that was exactly what he needed to hear.

"I love you, too. But I want you to understand something: if anyone else had gone behind my back like you did"—he clapped his hands together and then held them up like a blackjack dealer clearing the table—"it would be over."

Her shoulders slumped and all the bravado and defiance left her. She looked like a flower deprived of water and sunlight—wilted and lifeless.

"I know," she replied, her voice barely above a whisper. "I really am sorry for hurting you."

He dropped into the chair Cal had vacated. "I'm responsible for everything that happens at Riley O'Brien & Co.—good or bad. I just want to make sure I'm doing the smart thing for the company. Haven't you ever been afraid of making the wrong decision? Afraid to take a chance because the risk seems greater than the reward?"

She stared at him, an arrested expression on her face. "Is that how you feel, Quinn?"

"That's how I felt for a long time, but not anymore."

She sat down on the sofa and kicked off her boots. "What changed?" she asked, pulling up her legs and resting her head on her knees.

"I met Amelia."

Teagan cocked her head. "And?"

"When I'm with her, I feel stronger . . . like I'm capable of handling whatever life throws at me." He met her gaze, aware that he had surprised her. "Have you ever felt that way about anyone, T?"

Pain shadowed her eyes. "Yes." She shook her head a little. "I mean, no, I haven't."

Damn. His mom was right. Teagan was in love, and she was hurting.

"Does Amelia know how you feel about her?" Teagan asked, putting the focus back on him.

Before Quinn could answer, he heard the clink of crystal nearby. Turning toward the noise, he saw Cal holding three crystal flutes in one hand and a bottle of champagne in the other.

He raised his eyebrows. "What's this?"

Cal smiled and handed him a flute. "Now that Teagan's back, we need to celebrate the next phase of Riley O'Brien & Co."

Teagan frowned. "What are you talking about?"

"Didn't Quinn tell you?" Cal asked as he passed a glass to her.

"Tell me what?" she asked, dropping her feet to the floor.

After placing his flute on the end table, Cal began to untwist the wire around the cork. "He wants to expand the women's division. We've engaged Shelby's research firm to help us figure out the best strategy for product development and distribution."

She gasped, her eyes darting to Quinn's face. "Really?"

Quinn watched as Cal popped the cork. Champagne bubbled over his brother's fingers, and he held out his glass so Cal could fill it. He took a sip before answering her.

"Really."

Chapter 43

"DO YOU HAVE A MINUTE?" QUINN ASKED SAM SULLIVAN, standing in the doorway of the older man's office.

Sam looked up from his computer monitor with a smile. He gestured for Quinn to come in.

"How are you, son?"

"Fine," Quinn replied, struggling to keep his face impassive.

He didn't expect this meeting to go well, which explained why he was here in Sam's office bright and early. He didn't want to put off this conversation any longer than he already had, and the office was closing at noon today in advance of the Thanksgiving holiday.

Closing the door behind him, he took a seat in one of the chairs in front of Sam's desk. He got a strong sense of déjà vu when the older man leaned back in his chair and put his hands behind his head.

"What can I do for you?"

"I've been thinking about the situation with the department stores, and it's time for us to move forward with other expansion opportunities."

Sam sighed. "Quinn, we've already had this conversation. James doesn't like company-operated stores."

"I hear you, Sully. But I think company-operated stores

are our best bet. I'd like for you to get in touch with our outside real estate firm to investigate potential locations for company-operated stores."

Sam's dark eyes narrowed. "That's a waste of my time, and it's a waste of the company's resources," he said flatly.

Quinn took a deep breath. "I disagree," he replied, pleased to hear that his voice was even, betraying no anger even though he seethed inside. "And it's not a request, Sully. By year-end I want to see recommendations for at least one hundred new stores."

Sam dropped his arms to his desk and leaned forward as Quinn continued to talk. "We need to evaluate whether we should expand in markets where we already have stores or if we want to go into new areas. You'll also need to work with the logistics group to determine if we would have to add distribution warehouses if we go into new markets."

Sam's nostrils flared. He opened his mouth to speak, and Quinn held up his hand.

"It's not a request," he repeated, holding Sam's gaze until the other man looked away. "I also want to evaluate an entirely new channel." He paused to make sure that Sam paid attention. "Outlet centers."

"Outlet centers," Sam repeated.

"Yes."

"That's *ridiculous*! What are we going to sell in outlet stores?"

"Amelia Winger's accessories will be sold at different price points, some of which will be suitable for outlet stores. Also, once we expand the women's division, we'll have more products to stock the outlet stores."

Sam's eyes widened. "What are you talking about?"

"The women's division is getting a makeover."

"What does James have to say about this?"

"He trusts me to do what's best for the company."

Sam laughed incredulously. "None of your ideas will be implemented once he comes back."

"Dad has decided to retire, and I'm officially going to take over the company next month."

Sam rolled his lips inward, clearly upset by the news. Quinn stood up.

"Let me know if you run into any problems," he said as he made his way to the door. "Thanks for your time."

"Are you ready to take the blame when your bad decisions damage this company?"

He tensed with his hand on the doorknob, but he didn't turn around. "Yes," he answered as he opened the door. "But I think it's more likely I'll be given the credit when my good decisions make it stronger."

Quinn left Sam's office, surprised to find he was energized by the conversation. He'd expected to be wiped out, but he felt more alive than he had since he'd abruptly left Nashville.

The fear that had paralyzed him over the past several months had vanished. He still recognized the challenges, but they no longer seemed insurmountable. He was excited by the opportunity to change things for the better.

He knew Amelia was responsible for his changed attitude. He was a different man today than he had been before he met her.

On the way back to his office, he stopped by the executive lounge to grab some coffee. As he filled a mug with the dark brew, he admitted to himself that he didn't want things to be over with Amelia.

He just didn't know how to fix things. He wondered if there was anything he *could* do.

Last night after Teagan and Cal had left his house, he'd realized one very important fact—something he had overlooked in his anger and disappointment: Amelia could have continued to lie, but she hadn't. When he had discovered the jeans and told her that he wanted her to head up the women's division, he'd given her the perfect excuse to maintain her deception, but she had come clean.

She'd had no reason to tell him that she loved him—no reason except that it was the truth, and she was done lying. And, at this point, he really didn't care that she had lied about everything else as long as she'd told the truth about loving him. He loved her enough to forgive her.

Making the trek back to his office, Quinn mulled over possible solutions to his relationship woes. He stopped to pick up a stack of mail from his assistant's desk on the way, and with his hands full of envelopes and his coffee, he kicked the door to his office shut.

As he did so, he bobbled the mug, splashing hot liquid over his hand and onto the cuff of his shirt. "Shit!" he exclaimed, lunging toward his desk, where he quickly dumped his mug and the mail.

He shook the excess coffee from his fingers before wiping them on his Rileys. He hissed a little as the rough denim rubbed over his scalded flesh. Holding out his hand, he assessed the damage.

"Did you burn yourself?"

He jerked his head up to see Amelia standing next to his denim sofa. He blinked, wondering if his subconscious had conjured her.

No, she's really here.

They stared at each other without speaking, and his heart gave a contented sigh as it soaked in her presence. Her dark eyes, her brown-sugar freckles, her rosy lips . . . He could look at her face for the rest of his life and never grow tired of it.

He ran his gaze down her short, curvy body. Her brown sweater was so dark it matched her eyes, and her dark-washed jeans hugged her luscious hips.

His eyes lingered on her jeans, and she turned, showing him her backside. The Rileys logo was prominently displayed on one pocket, along with the telltale black tag. The jeans cupped her ass beautifully, the seam between her cheeks perfectly straight.

As she walked across the room, he tracked the movement of her round ass, her curly hair swinging above it. She looked over her shoulder, russet eyebrows raised.

"You told me to never again wear a piece of denim that didn't have your name on it." She licked her lips nervously. "So what do you think?"

I think I'm a lucky man.

He cleared his throat, hoping his voice would work. "They look good. Did you make them?"

"I did. I call them Plain Jane because they don't have any embellishment."

He smiled a little. The jeans might not be all tricked out,

but there was nothing plain about the way she looked in them. They were tight in all the right places.

Amelia walked toward him, stopping just a few inches in front of him. He could smell the sweet scent of her hair, and he pulled in a deep breath, the first one he'd taken in several weeks. She looked up at him, meeting his eyes.

"Quinn, I'm sorry for so many things. I'm sorry I went behind your back. I'm sorry I didn't have the guts to tell you the truth even when I wanted to. And I'm sorry you thought I used you."

He didn't know what to say because he wished those things hadn't happened, too. When he didn't respond, she sighed and stepped closer, her chest brushing the front of his shirt.

"If someone had asked me a few months ago what I wanted most, I would have said success. My answer would be different now." She swallowed. "Please ask me what I want most."

He stared down into her eyes. They were shiny and wet with tears. She might think she lacked guts, but the fact that she was here, standing in his office, proved otherwise.

"What do you want most, Amelia?"

Holding his breath, he waited for her answer. He hoped she wanted the same thing he did.

"You," she answered. "I want you."

AMELIA GAZED INTO QUINN'S DARK BLUE EYES. IT WAS ALL SHE could do to keep from throwing herself at him.

She'd missed him so much, a physical ache that had never seemed to go away. Now that she was here, close enough to touch him, that ache had vanished.

He looked so good . . . the best thing she'd seen in her entire life, even though his hair was a little too long and there were dark circles under his eyes. She was selfish enough to hope he'd been as miserable and lonely as she had.

He cupped his hands around her face, smoothing his warm fingers against her cheeks before edging them into her hair. She closed her eyes, her whole body sighing in relief at his touch. As he leaned down, his breath fluttered against her lips. Opening her eyes, she met his gaze.

"I want you, too."

She exhaled in relief. She'd been so scared he wouldn't give her another chance . . . that he wouldn't want her anymore.

"I'm *so* sorry," she repeated because she thought he had let her off too easily. "I understand why you didn't believe me when I said that I loved you."

He smoothed his thumb across her bottom lip. "Tell me again. I promise my response will be different this time."

She gulped, trying to hold back her tears but failing. They began to trickle from her eyes.

"I love you, Quinn. I love you more than I've ever loved anyone."

He smiled slowly. "I believe you." He brushed away the tears that trailed down her cheeks. "And I love you, too."

"You do?" she asked, her voice shaded with wonder.

He laughed softly. "Why are you so surprised, sweetheart?"

"Because I wanted it too much. I wanted you too much. I wanted everything."

"That's an interesting statement," he said, cocking his head. "What's everything? Me and your boutiques?"

She frowned, worried her answer might freak him out. He smoothed the lines between her eyes with the tip of his finger.

"What's everything?" he repeated, dropping his hands to her waist and squeezing lightly.

She bit her lip, trying to figure out what to say. She'd been too afraid to be honest with him in the past, and that was a mistake she wouldn't make again.

"I'm not talking about my career."

His eyes darkened before he pressed his lips against hers. She let her lips fall open, inviting him in, but he pulled back.

"Okay," he said, his lips tilting up at the corners. "Then what's everything?"

She took a deep breath. "Everything is marriage, children, 'til death do us part."

His eyes widened, and his mouth fell open. She'd obviously shocked him, and she felt compelled to backpedal a little bit.

"That's just my definition. It's okay if it means something different to you."

She fell silent. Several seconds passed before he spoke.

"It does mean something different to me."

Some of her happiness drained away. But then she reminded herself that she should be ecstatic he was even talking to her after what she'd done.

"In fact, I think my definition of 'everything' is a lot more expansive than yours, Juice." He smiled, his eyes so intensely blue they looked like the inside of a flame. "It means marriage, children, 'til death do us part . . . but it also means I'm going to give you so much love you're going to feel like you're drowning in it. It means I'll find a way to give you whatever you want, no matter what it takes. And it means you'll have a family, our family, and you'll never have to wonder where you belong because you'll belong with me."

She was sure all the blood in her body had turned into bubbly champagne. She was effervescent, almost weightless. She grinned, and he cupped his hands around her hips, pulling her closer. A lock of dark hair had fallen over his forehead, and she brushed it back.

"What do you think about my definition?" he asked.

"I like it a lot better than mine."

"I'm glad to hear that," he said before leaning down to kiss her lightly.

She gasped as heat zinged through her. "Now that we've clarified the definition of 'everything,' I think I should add another don't to my list."

His hands roamed lower. "Am I going to like this don't, Juice?" he asked as he gently squeezed her butt cheeks.

"I think so," she answered with a nod. "I don't live in Nashville."

"That's a good one," he said, his lips quirking in a sexy smile. "And since you're modifying the list, I'd like to add a couple."

She drew back. "What do you have in mind?" she asked warily.

"Let's start with this: I don't wear bacon-and-egg-printed pajamas to bed, or anywhere else, for that matter."

She'd had no idea he didn't like her pajamas. That was really too bad because they were very cozy.

"You know, those are my favorite pajamas. Ava Grace bought them for me."

His eyes widened. "She has *really* bad taste in sleepwear." After a moment of consideration, he shrugged. "We'll have to negotiate that don't. And in the meantime, I'll just strip you out of them whenever you put them on."

He kissed her again, this time a little longer and a little deeper. When he finally raised his head, his erection pressed into her stomach and her knees trembled.

"I have one more don't for you," he said as he backed her toward his blue-jean sofa. "And it's definitely nonnegotiable . . ."

"What is it?" she asked, more than a little breathless.

"I don't argue with my future husband about the length of our engagement."

Epilogue

Ten years later

QUINN GRABBED HIS OLDEST SON BY THE WAISTBAND OF HIS jeans as he ran by, pulling him to an abrupt halt. He turned him so he could look into his brown eyes.

"Stop kicking your brothers."

Jamie scowled, the action distorting his little face and making the freckles on it dance. "They're annoying," he complained, pushing a sweaty red curl off his forehead.

Quinn laughed. "Yeah, I know."

He pulled Jamie down beside him on the bench, which was situated near one of the larger playgrounds in Golden Gate Park. "Why don't you sit here with me until Mommy gets back from the bathroom?"

He glanced toward his other children, who were edging toward the merry-go-round. Killian was old enough to play on it, but Liam was too little to enjoy it without an adult. Since Liam had a meltdown if he couldn't do everything Killian did, Quinn knew he needed to distract them, fast.

"Boys! Come here," he called.

Surprisingly they obeyed, trotting toward the bench. They stopped in front of him and Jamie, and he smiled down at them. With their dark hair and blue eyes, they were little replicas of him.

He tapped both of them on their noses, making them giggle. Killian climbed up on the bench beside Jamie, and Quinn situated Liam on his lap.

"Daddy, let's play Who's Wearing Rileys?" Killian suggested.

It was the same game Quinn had played with his dad, and now he played it with his own children. Killian's suggestion made Jamie bounce on the bench and Liam squeal, the sound nearly splitting Quinn's eardrums.

He winced, and they began to chant. "Rileys, Rileys, who's wearing Rileys?"

Despite the ringing in his ears, he laughed. Liam still had trouble pronouncing words, and his sounded more like "Wileys."

"Okay! Okay!" he said over their childish voices. "Who can spot a lady wearing Rileys?"

His sons immediately eyed all the women around them, staring at their butts. Even Liam got in on the action.

Jamie pointed. "There, there's one," he said, indicating a teenage girl who had just walked by with her boyfriend.

"Me, too," Killian chimed in, pointing his dirt-crusted finger at one of the moms on the playground.

And so the game went for several minutes until his boys caught sight of their mommy on the walking path. Jamie and Killian jumped off the bench, and Quinn dropped Liam to the ground so he could join them.

"Mommy!" they called as they ran to her. "Mommy! Guess what we were doing."

When they reached her, they gathered around her, hugging her legs and waist. Even though Jamie was only seven, the top of his head already reached Amelia's shoulders.

Their ginger-haired son obviously took after the original Riley O'Brien. He was taller than all the other boys in his class and most of the ones in the grade above him, too. Quinn suspected there would be a lot of basketball games in their future.

Amelia's laughter floated to where he sat, followed by the low murmur of her voice. Like always, his heart gave a big thump when he saw his wife and his children together.

All mine.

His family headed toward him, the boys skipping and running around Amelia as she slowly made her way to the bench. He would never tell her, but she was waddling, just a little.

As the boys ran off to the playground, she dropped down onto the bench beside him, exhaling loudly. With one eye on the kids, he reached over and rubbed her belly. "How's Baby Girl O'Brien doing?"

"She's fine, but my back hurts. I'm ready for her to come out."

He made a sympathetic noise, and she leaned her head against his shoulder. "My maternity jeans barely fit," she groused.

He stifled a smile. He'd heard that complaint before.

He vividly recalled the day Amelia had told him she was pregnant with their first child. He'd gone to visit her in the Riley Plaza workshop, and he had noticed a pair of Rileys with a big stretchy waistband on her worktable.

"Are you thinking we should expand into maternity wear?" he'd asked.

Their efforts to transform the women's division had been going well and they had stolen some market share from their fiercest competitors. He'd thought Amelia was onto something . . . that maternity wear could be a good way to expand their product offerings.

She had slanted an amused look toward him. "They're for me."

"Why would you wear them?" he'd asked.

Her eyebrows had lifted mockingly. "Why do you think?"

Eight years later, Quinn was still embarrassed by how clueless he'd been.

A strong breeze blew one of Amelia's curls against his face, pulling him out of the past and into the present. He brushed the strands from his stubble and settled his arm around her shoulders.

"Jake forwarded the preliminary third-quarter numbers to me last night," he said. "Riley O'Brien & Co. officially had its best quarter ever."

"Congratulations." She kissed his cheek, her lips warm and soft against his skin. "Apparently, you're not just a pretty face."

He squeezed her shoulder. "Neither are you. The women's division also had its best quarter ever. It now accounts for seventy-five percent of all revenue."

"The biggest branch on the tree," she murmured as she rubbed her belly.

"The biggest and the strongest."

As he placed his hand on top of hers, he felt the baby shift under his palm. They had planned to name their daughter Keira Grace, a moniker they both liked a lot. But then Ava Grace had begged them not to curse their child with two first names, so now they were rethinking the decision.

Regardless of what they named her, Quinn was excited for her to arrive. He had waited a long time to finally have a little girl, and he couldn't wait to see if she would have her mother's beautiful red hair and chocolaty eyes. He really hoped she would.

"Are you sad that you missed your grand opening?" he asked.

Amelia had opened her first boutique nearly eight years ago when she'd been pregnant with Jamie. That store, located in San Francisco's Fillmore Street shopping district, had been a huge success. It had given Amelia the confidence to roll out an entire chain of Millie boutiques. Her twenty-fifth store had celebrated its grand opening today in Austin, Texas, but with the baby due at any time, it hadn't been safe for her to make the trip.

She shook her head. "It's not a big deal. There will be more grand openings." She gave him a sideways glance. "But there will *not* be any more children."

He chuckled. "If I remember correctly, that's exactly what you said after Killian kept us up all night for seven weeks straight. And look where we are today—three little O'Briens and another one on the way."

He scanned the playground to make sure their little boys were safe and sound. "By the way, Teagan's going to pick up the boys later today so we can have some alone time before we have four children demanding our attention."

She groaned softly. "I have no idea how we're going to do it." She shook her head. "I don't know why I let you convince me to try one more time for a girl. I'm an idiot."

He nuzzled her hair. "You didn't require a lot of convincing, Juice."

She giggled, tilting her head so he could nibble on her earlobe. "You're a terrible influence on me, Quinn O'Brien." She lightly jabbed him in the ribs. "And you're a terrible influence on our children. The boys said y'all were playing Who's Wearing Rileys? I thought we agreed that staring at behinds was not the polite thing to do."

Pulling her closer, he rubbed her arm. "Do you know your ass was the first thing I noticed about you?"

She jerked away from him. "The first thing?" she asked incredulously. "We were facing each other when Teagan introduced us."

"That wasn't the first time I saw you. I was behind you on the escalator that morning." He chuckled, shaking his head. "How could I *not* notice your ass? It was right in front of my face, so round and perfect."

She snorted. "After four pregnancies, it's not so perfect anymore." She darted a quick glance toward the playground to make sure their kids were still alive and kicking. "It's definitely rounder though."

He grinned but continued to share one of his fondest memories. "I wanted to reach out and squeeze it . . . until I realized you weren't wearing Rileys."

"You should be ashamed," she admonished. "You're obsessed with butts."

"Yeah, they were my favorite part of the body."

She shot him a quizzical glance. "Butts aren't your favorite part of the body anymore?"

"No." He kissed the corner of her mouth. "I'm more of a heart man nowadays."

Her rosy lips turned up in a small smile. "I'll make sure to remind you of that fact the next time you grab my butt."

Turn the page for a sneak peek at
the next Riley O'Brien & Co. novel,

Coming Apart at the Seams

Coming soon from Berkley Sensation!

San Francisco—Present Day

BLUNDER. GAFFE. MISSTEP. ERROR. SNAFU. ALTHOUGH PLENTY of words described the huge, life-altering mistake Nick Priest had made, none of them quite conveyed his stupidity. He'd had a chance with Teagan O'Brien, but he'd blown it. That was his biggest regret, and he had a lot of them.

As he stared at her across the ballroom, he had to remind himself to breathe. Her long red dress clung to her curvy body, just tight enough to make every man in the room wish his pants were a little looser behind the zipper.

She reminded him of a starlet from the 1950s with her abundant breasts, narrow waist, and round hips. He'd had the pleasure of shaping those hips with his hands, tonguing her rosy nipples, and sinking into her luscious body, although pleasure didn't really describe what he'd felt when he had been with her.

She laughed, her deep blue eyes glinting in the light from the chandeliers, and her date leaned closer, licking his lips as he got an eyeful of her tits. Nick clenched his hands into fists, barely controlling the urge to ram the fucker's head into the wall.

For more than a year and a half, he had been trying to persuade Teagan to give him another chance. But she hated him with all the passion she'd given him during their one and only night together.

He thought about approaching her but discarded the idea. She had become a master at avoiding him, and she would find a reason to excuse herself immediately.

Forcing himself to relax, he settled more comfortably against the wood-paneled wall. He wasn't trying to blend in. He knew that was impossible.

His face and form were highly recognizable from years of playing pro football, and most recently, appearing in commercials for Riley O'Brien & Co., the nation's oldest designer and manufacturer of blue jeans. Since he'd thrown his lot in with the company, he had figured he ought to attend the annual holiday party. Plus, he had known Teagan would be here.

This wasn't the first O'Brien celebration he had attended. He'd known the family for about fifteen years. He had played football with Quinn O'Brien at the University of Southern California, and he had formed friendships with both Quinn and his younger brother, Cal.

The O'Brien brothers were Nick's best friends, two of his favorite people. But his absolute favorite person was their little sister, Teagan. He'd known her almost as long as he had known Quinn and Cal, and before he'd messed things up, they had been friends. Best friends, in fact.

He let his gaze wander the ballroom of the Westin St. Francis in downtown San Francisco. With its lavish holiday decorations, it could have been any company party. But the huge photo banners hanging from the ceiling made this one unique.

Every black-and-white image showed a different view of Riley O'Brien & Co.'s signature blue jeans. He was pretty sure the jean-clad ass in the photos was his own.

He chuckled wryly. The banners proved what he'd always known: he was nothing but a giant ass. He had no doubt Teagan would wholeheartedly agree with that assessment.

Teagan's date touched a curl that had fallen to her shoulder, and Nick growled under his breath when the fucker stroked the smooth skin of her upper chest. He would rather take a direct hit from a three-hundred-and-fifty-pound linebacker than watch that loser put his hands on her. Hell, he'd rather be buried under the entire defensive line than suffer the torture of watching another man paw the woman he wanted for himself.

Moving his gaze from her body, he focused on her face. Her full lips were painted a deep scarlet that matched her dress, and he took a moment to remember the taste of her mouth, addictive in its sweetness.

Her wavy, dark hair was pulled into an elaborate updo, emphasizing her graceful neck and smooth shoulders, which were bared by her strapless dress. Years ago, he'd had his mouth on that supple skin before he had trailed his tongue down into her creamy cleavage.

"Priest."

Jerking his head toward the voice, he was surprised to find Quinn standing next to him. Nick mustered a smile for his old friend, clasping the hand he offered and slapping him on the back.

"It's good to see you," Quinn said. "I'm glad you could make it."

Nick hadn't been sure if he would be able to attend the party. His schedule had depended on whether his team made the playoffs. But they'd lost their last three games, dashing those hopes.

Although it didn't reflect well on him, he hadn't cared much that his team wasn't heading to the playoffs. He was ready to move on, and although he had yet to announce it publicly, he'd decided to retire. He had given enough of his life to the game, and it had given him what he had needed in return. Now, he needed something else.

He needed Teagan.

A waiter passed with champagne, and Nick plucked a crystal flute from the tray. "Congrats. Times two," he said, tapping his glass against Quinn's highball.

Only days ago, Quinn had officially taken over as president and CEO of Riley O'Brien & Co. More important, he'd become engaged to Amelia Winger, a sweet little thing with a real talent for fashion design.

"Thanks," Quinn said, a big grin on his face. "I'm a lucky man. A *very* lucky man."

His happiness was almost tangible, and Nick experienced

a stab of envy, not because the other man didn't deserve to be happy, but because he wasn't. Far from it.

The two of them slouched side by side with their backs against the wall. The party was in full swing, the band wailing away and the dance floor packed. Hundreds of people milled around the ballroom, the men dressed in dark suits and the women garbed in cocktail dresses. It was one of the few times Riley O'Brien & Co. employees had to dress up. Usually, they all wore Rileys and T-shirts.

Quinn scanned the crowd, visibly relaxing when he spotted his redheaded fiancée. The look on his face was a mix of pride, possession, and adoration. The guy was obviously head over heels in love with his future bride.

Pulling his attention from Amelia, Quinn looked toward Nick. "Listen, Priest, I need to talk with you about something important."

He tensed. As far as he knew, the O'Brien brothers were still unaware that he and Teagan had hooked up. He really had no idea how they would react if they discovered the truth.

He nodded, silently directing Quinn to continue. He preferred to say as little as possible so he could hide the severe stutter that had plagued him since childhood.

Quinn was one of the few people who knew about his speech impediment. They'd spent too much time together over the years for the other man not to notice, but he'd never said anything about it. He wondered if they were drawn to each other by the simple fact that Quinn talked too much and Nick didn't talk enough.

"I've persuaded Amelia to have a short engagement, and we're in a hurry to nail down the wedding plans."

Nick stifled a grin. He had little doubt how Quinn had persuaded Amelia.

"Cal is my best man, and I'd like you to be my one and only groomsman."

He studied the groom-to-be. He knew it wasn't manly to admit it, but he loved Quinn like a brother. It would be an honor to stand beside him as he made his wedding vows.

Of course he didn't tell Quinn any of this because it required too many words. It was too much effort to get his brain and his mouth to work together. They were enemies.

"Okay." He focused on shaping the sound that caused him the most problems. "W-w-w-when is the w-w-w-wedding?"

"The first Saturday in March." Quinn sighed. "Ten long weeks away."

Nick chuckled. Compared to the time he'd spent chasing Teagan, ten weeks was nothing. A hit from the kicker instead of a thumping from a linebacker.

"When are you heading back home?" Quinn asked.

Nick shrugged. He had played for the Tennessee Titans for the past two years, and he currently lived in an upscale suburb outside of Nashville. But now that the season was over, nothing prevented him from staying in San Francisco as long as he wanted. As long as it took.

Quinn narrowed his eyes. "Where are you spending Christmas?"

"Not sure."

"With your dad?"

He laughed, the sound shaded with bitterness he didn't bother to hide. "No."

"Why don't you stay and celebrate Christmas with us? You know Mom and Dad would love to have you." When he didn't reply, Quinn punched him on the shoulder. "And Amelia and I are having a New Year's Eve–slash-engagement party. You can't miss that."

Quinn had unknowingly given Nick the perfect opportunity to spend more time with Teagan. It was more than he could ever have hoped for.

TEAGAN'S FEET HURT, HER HEAD POUNDED, AND HER FACE ached from the fake smile she'd pasted on hours ago. She grabbed another glass of champagne from a passing waiter and downed it in one swallow, hoping the alcohol would dull the pain.

It had been a huge mistake to bring Evan to the company's holiday party. In the span of three hours, he'd transformed from a man into an octopus. What else could explain the sliminess she felt when he touched her?

Evan had seemed like a decent guy when she'd met him at an ugly Christmas sweater party. He and his sweater, a truly hideous garment that illustrated the twelve days of Christmas, had caught her eye.

When he'd asked for her number, she'd given it to him without a thought, and she had forgotten about him until he had called a few days ago. He'd asked her out, and she'd suggested they attend the party together.

She hadn't wanted his company, not really. But she had been afraid Nick would be here, and she'd thought a date would be a good buffer.

Teagan didn't trust herself to be within one hundred miles of Nick. No matter how hard she tried to force her body and mind to work together, they just didn't agree. Her mind knew best. It wanted to stay far away from him. But her body . . . Oh, it wanted him so badly.

His hard kisses, his hot caresses, his deep thrusts.

It had been years since they'd been together, but she remembered it like it was yesterday. She remembered everything—his taste, his scent, his size.

Warmth trickled between her legs, and she scowled. She *hated* Nick Priest. She hated him for breaking her heart. She hated him for not being there when she had needed him most.

She hated the way her body came alive when he was near. She hated the way her mind always found its way to him when it was left to wander. And most of all, she hated herself for letting him get to her after all this time.

She shifted on her heels, using the pain to force her thoughts from Nick. She looked around the room. Where was Evan?

She wanted to leave, and she needed to let him know she intended to take a cab back to her place. She planned to go home and enjoy a long soak in the tub, and she wasn't up to fending off octopus man.

Teagan rubbed her forehead with the tips of her fingers but stilled when someone came up behind her. She knew without looking it was Nick. She instinctively recognized his scent and the heat of his body.

Stiffening slightly, she tried to move away from him. But he moved closer, placing his hand on her waist to stop her. He leaned down close to her ear, and his breath made her shiver.

"Stay," he ordered quietly.

"I'm not a dog," she snapped.

He chuckled softly. "Stay," he repeated, dropping his hand to her hip and squeezing lightly to emphasize his command.

A flash of energy traveled from his fingers to all the nerve-rich places on her body—her nipples, her clit, her lips. Desperate to get away from him, she jerked sharply and stumbled into Amelia.

"Whoa!" Quinn exclaimed as he caught his fiancée against him.

Teagan blinked in surprise. She hadn't even noticed her older brother was nearby. He glared at her, his protective instincts on high alert.

"Be careful, T. You almost knocked Amelia over."

She managed to squeeze out an apology, and Nick, damn him, resumed his place behind her. He loomed over her by several inches even though she wore five-inch heels. His height made him one of the best wide receivers in the NFL.

Amelia stared over Teagan's head, her brown eyes speculative. "Nick, I thought I'd see you here," she said, a faint Texas twang in her voice. "How have you been?"

"Fine," he said, drawing out the word, his baritone rumbling through Teagan's body.

"I was sorry to see you guys didn't make the playoffs," Amelia said. "But there's always next year."

Teagan felt Nick shrug. "Not for me."

At his announcement, Teagan, Amelia, and Quinn all chorused "What?" in varying volumes. Teagan's definitely had been the loudest.

She jerked away from Nick, and this time, he let her go. She spun to face him, and even though she struggled to digest the bomb he'd dropped on them, she noticed how his expensive black suit outlined his broad shoulders. The dark color made his blond hair look even lighter, and his blue French dress shirt showed off his tan.

"What are you talking about?" she asked, staring into the face she dreamed about almost every night.

He was gorgeous—beyond gorgeous.

He knew it; of course he did. But unlike a lot of extraordinarily handsome men, he didn't seem to care much about his looks.

"I've decided to . . . um . . . retire," he said.

She gasped. "Why?"

"It's time."

"What are you going to do?" Quinn asked.

"Not sure," Nick replied, running a hand through his short hair.

Her hands itched to touch the silky strands. He'd cut his hair since she had seen him a few weeks ago, and the color seemed to change depending on the length. Right now, his hair was a mix of honey and caramel, and as it grew out, it would turn lighter, almost the shade of morning sunshine.

Quinn cocked his head, staring at Nick with a calculating look. He turned toward Amelia.

"Juice," he said, using his nickname for his bride-to-be, "did you know Priest has a degree in American history from USC?"

Amelia smiled, showing the sizable gap between her front teeth. "No, I didn't know that."

"Priest, you didn't know my grandma Violet, but she was an interesting woman. Kind of eccentric. She was ten times richer than my grandpa Patrick, maybe even a hundred times richer. The O'Briens made their money as clothing prospectors, but her family actually found gold."

Teagan stared at Quinn. Why was he talking about Grandma Vi? Was he drunk?

Nick narrowed his eyes. "And?"

"Well, you see, Grandma Violet set up an endowment to create a museum that celebrates the history of Riley O'Brien & Co. and the role it played during the California Gold Rush. And that endowment money has to be used by 2017."

Teagan sucked in an appalled breath. *He wouldn't! Would he?*

"What would you think about heading up that project? Laying the ground work for the museum?" Quinn asked Nick. "It would be part of the company's charitable foundation, which falls under Teagan's purview. She'd be your boss."

Nick slanted a cunning look toward Teagan, his light green eyes glowing like peridots. He smiled slowly.

"I'm in."